Flesh & Blood

John Harvey is the author of the [...] sed sequence of ten Charlie Resnick [...] of which, *Lonely Hearts*, was [...] one of the '100 Best C[...]. In 2004 William He[...] *h and Blood*, the first nove[...] Detective Inspector Frank Elder, w[...] he CWA Silver Dagger Award.

He is also a poet, dramatist and occasional broad-caster.

Praise for *Flesh and Blood*

'John Harvey writes with enviable elegance and economy and a flawless grasp of both character and narrative. *Flesh and Blood* is a gripping and powerfully atmospheric thriller from a writer at the very top of his game. It's quite simply the best thing Harvey's written yet and from a writer as good as he is, that's really saying something.' **Mark Billingham**

'*Flesh and Blood* is one more vindication for those of us who have long known we've been riding with a master of the craft. John Harvey is lights out one of the best and with this book the word is going to spread far and wide.' **Michael Connelly**

'There is a power and a dignity in Harvey's storytelling, and his finely drawn characters propel the story to a conclusion which is both surprising and satisfying' **Susanna Yager, _Sunday Telegraph_**

'Harvey quietly orchestrates a sinister thriller with economy and empathy and proves once again that he is one of Britain's leading masters of atmosphere'
Maxim Jakubowski, _Guardian_

'If anyone could make you feel sorry for a serial killer, it's John Harvey, who always writes with tender feeling about commonplace people – killers among them – damaged by criminal violence'
New York Times Review of Books

'. . . a terrific comeback, restoring John Harvey to the very top echelons of British crime writing . . . what takes _Flesh and Blood_ into the highest league are Harvey's exquisite writing and utterly convincing characters' **Marcel Berlins, _The Times_**

'A book with a depth few works of crime fiction attain' **Jane Jakeman, _Independent_**

'A major novel: thrilling, urgent, important'
Literary Review

Flesh and Blood

John Harvey

arrow books

Published by Arrow Books in 2005

3 5 7 9 10 8 6 4 2

First published in the United Kingdom in 2004 by William Heinemann

Arrow Books
The Random House Group Limited
20 Vauxhall Bridge Road, London, SW1V 2SA

Random House Australia (Pty) Limited
20 Alfred Street, Milsons Point, Sydney,
New South Wales 2061, Australia

Random House New Zealand Limited
18 Poland Road, Glenfield
Auckland 10, New Zealand

Random House (Pty) Limited
Endulini, 5a Jubilee Road, Parktown 2193, South Africa

The Random House Group Limited Reg. No. 954009

www.randomhouse.co.uk

A CIP catalogue record for this book is available from the British Library

Papers used by Random House are natural, recyclable products made from
wood grown in sustainable forests. The manufacturing processes conform to
the environmental regulations of the country of origin

ISBN 9 78 0 09 951362 9

Typeset by SX Composing DTP, Rayleigh, Essex
Printed and bound in Australia by
Griffin Press

Flesh and Blood

John Harvey

arrow books

Published by Arrow Books in 2005

3 5 7 9 10 8 6 4 2

Copyright © John Harvey 2004

John Harvey has asserted the right under the Copyright, Designs and Patents
Act, 1988 to be identified as the author of this work

First published in the United Kingdom in 2004 by William Heinemann

Arrow Books
The Random House Group Limited
20 Vauxhall Bridge Road, London, SW1V 2SA

Random House Australia (Pty) Limited
20 Alfred Street, Milsons Point, Sydney,
New South Wales 2061, Australia

Random House New Zealand Limited
18 Poland Road, Glenfield
Auckland 10, New Zealand

Random House (Pty) Limited
Endulini, 5a Jubilee Road, Parktown 2193, South Africa

The Random House Group Limited Reg. No. 954009

www.randomhouse.co.uk

A CIP catalogue record for this book is available from the British Library

Papers used by Random House are natural, recyclable products made from
wood grown in sustainable forests. The manufacturing processes conform to
the environmental regulations of the country of origin

ISBN 9 78 0 09 951362 9

Typeset by SX Composing DTP, Rayleigh, Essex
Printed and bound in Australia by
Griffin Press

For Patrick:
Geezer *Extraordinaire*

It is done. Nothing can undo it; nothing can make it otherwise than as it was.

Charles Dickens: *David Copperfield*

But yet thou art my flesh, my blood, my daughter,
Or rather a disease that's in my flesh,
which I must needs call mine.

William Shakespeare: *King Lear*

1

Soft and insinuating, the cat brushed against his face and Elder, still three-parts asleep, used his arm to push it away. Moments later, it was there again, nudging itself against him, its purr loud inside his head. Sharp, the cat's claws kneaded the soft flesh at the top of his shoulder, the back of his neck. Beneath him, the pillow was rank with sweat. With an effort he turned and lifted the animal clear, its thick coat matted and damp, skin flaccid and loose across its meagre ribs. The bright slits of its eyes yellow in the almost dark.

As Elder struggled himself upright, the cat twisted inside his grasp and bit deep into the base of his thumb. With a curse, he dropped it down on to the bed and it jumped, hissing, to the floor. When he brought his hand to his mouth, the taste of blood was sour and bright.

And now there were other cats, close in groups of two or three, emerging from the shadow round the edges of the room. Elder could hear the faint rasp of their feral breathing, ragged and low. Throwing back the sheet, he began to pull on his clothes, the cats close about him now, rubbing against his ankles, running over his bare feet.

When he held the door open and tried to urge them out,

they slithered back between his legs and moved in a softly undulating mass towards the stairs.

In the room above, eyes stared back at him, unblinking, and, as he stepped forward, something pliant and smooth gave beneath the bones of his foot. Hairless, a swathe of newborn kittens writhed, mewling and blind, along bare boards. Vomit caught in his throat. From somewhere close above his head, a full-grown cat launched itself towards him, claws unsheathed. A ribbon of blood fell from his upper arm, another laced across his cheek. The door he had come through stood closed.

Shaking, Elder crossed towards a further set of stairs. At the top, the tread gave way beneath his weight and he had to brace himself against the walls before jumping clear.

Through gaps in the roof, light spilled, weak, across the floor.

Nothing moved.

On the far side of the room was a narrow bed. Not empty. Quite. Beneath a blanket, grey and threadbare, something lay curled. The skin on Elder's legs and arms seized with cold. His body cramped. He knew, or felt he knew, what lay beyond his sight. The cats, almost silent now, had followed him into the room and massed about him, quiescent, waiting. The space between the bed and where he stood was vast, a pace or so away; the blanket rough and cold between finger and thumb. When he pulled it back, it shredded in his grasp.

The girl's legs were pulled up tight towards her chest, her breasts small and empty, bone of her buttocks breaking through blotched skin. The stench fouled his mouth and filled his nose. One side of her face, the face of a girl, a young woman of sixteen or maybe seventeen, had all but disappeared. There were bite marks, small and deep, around the socket of the eye.

As Elder bent forward, one of her arms reached suddenly towards him, hand outstretched and feeling for his own. Seized him and would not let him go.

2

From his position atop the rough stone wall, Elder tracked the progress of the bus as it trailed around the road's high curve, the rough-hewn moor above, the fertile bottom land below. Today the sky was shade on shade of blue, and palest where it curved to meet the sea, the horizon a havering trick of light on which the outline of a large boat, a tanker, seemed to have been stuck like an illustration from a child's book. Elder knew there would be lobster boats, two or three, checking their catch close in against the cliff and out of sight from where he stood.

He watched as the bus stopped and Katherine got down, standing for a moment till the bus had pulled away, a solitary figure by the road's edge and, at that distance, barely recognisable to the naked eye. Even so, he knew it was her: the turn of the head, the way she stood.

With a quick movement, Katherine hoisted her rucksack on to one shoulder, hitched it into position and crossed the road towards the top of the lane that would bring her, eventually, down to the cottage where Elder lived.

Dropping from the wall, he hurried across the field.

◆

The cottages were three in a line, built for the families of labourers who, in earlier days, had worked the land. Beyond these stood a single house and studio belonging to a local artist, a pleasant enough woman who kept herself largely to herself, merely nodding at Elder when they passed on the path that led down towards the sea, rarely bothering to speak.

'You're not a writer?' the owner had asked when Elder paid over his deposit, the first month's rent.

'No. Why d'you ask?'

She had smiled. 'Oh, we get 'em sometimes, hoping something'll rub off. D. H. Lawrence, you know, he lived there with Frieda, his wife. One of the cottages. Katherine Mansfield, too, for a while.'

'Yes?' Elder had said. 'Right, right.'

Well, he had heard of Lawrence, at least.

That had been something over two years ago, early spring and little enough in bud. One day Elder had been an officer in the Nottinghamshire force, a detective inspector with thirty years in, a marriage that had endured more than half that time, a daughter of fourteen – and the next, or so it seemed, he had resigned, retired, walked out on them all.

He had gone almost as far as it is possible to go in England without running out of land, seen this place by chance and here he had stayed. Two up, two down, and little more; flagged floors, stone walls; light that when it struck right seared through the house from front to back. The occasional postcard aside, he did not write; and, after a while, not even that. He read. Tried Lawrence, but soon cast him aside. He found a small cache of dampening paperbacks beneath the stairs: Priestley, du Maurier,

Dornford Yates. When they ran out he picked up cast-offs at church sales and the like. Sea stories, he found he liked those, Forester, Reeman and Alexander Kent. More recently, he'd taken a shine to H. E. Bates.

It fascinated him, he who'd scarce picked up a book in two score years or more, the way the tale would draw you out of yourself, pull you in.

Evenings, some evenings, he played the radio loud, anxious for the sound of voices. Knowing there was no need to answer back.

◆

From just beyond the last cottage, he watched now as Katherine stepped into view around the last curve in the lane.

She was wearing light walking boots, socks folded back over pale green tights, a cord skirt in a darker shade, knee-length, a borrowed anorak, several sizes too large, unzipped. When she saw Elder and ran the last dozen yards towards him, her hair, brown and slightly curled, streamed out behind much as her mother's would once have done.

'Dad!'

'Kate.'

He had wondered about this, some awkwardness or hesitation after what, six months? More. The previous summer, it had been, back in Nottinghamshire, and brief. But no, she hugged him and he felt, beneath the layers that she wore, the relative smallness of her bones. Her face, below his, pushed high against his chest, and slowly, with closed eyes, he pressed his own face down against the top of her head, remembering the smell of her hair when she had been two or three or four.

'Come on,' he said, releasing her and stepping back. 'Let's go inside.'

◆

Katherine hadn't known what to expect: a jumble of unwashed clothes and strewn socks, empty beer cans and unwashed pots? The house of the Seven Dwarfs before Snow White? A single man who'd gone to seed? But no, everything was folded and in place; her father's morning cup and saucer, bowl and plate rested on the drainer, waiting to be put away. Of course, he would have made an effort against her coming: hoovered, straightened, dusted.

'Tea or coffee? Not instant, beans, the proper stuff.'

Katherine shrugged off her anorak and draped it over the back of an easy chair. 'You don't drink coffee. You never even used to like the smell of it in the house.'

'I can change, can't I?'

She looked at him through lowered lashes. 'Tea will be fine.'

'PG Tips.'

'Whatever.'

While her father busied himself in the kitchen, Katherine prowled. The furniture had come with the house, she supposed, the kind you saw piled high beneath signs advertising houses cleared. Curtains with a floral print, rush matting on the floor. A book case crammed with paperbacks. The heavy dining table ringed here and there and scored along one side. On the narrow mantelpiece a photograph in a plain black frame, herself at fourteen, not long before it had all come apart; in the grate below, a fire had been set ready, paper, wood and coal. No stereo, no TV. Upstairs, the door to her father's room stood open: the quilt thrown back evenly across the bed, pillows bunched; on a small table stood a radio alarm, a lamp, an empty glass, a book.

'Katherine. Tea's ready.'

Dumping her rucksack on the single bed in the adjacent room, she went back down.

◆

It was just warm enough to sit in the small garden at the back, the breeze off the sea fresh but not biting. The late April sun still high but weak in the sky. At the garden edge a low stone wall led into a field where, heads down, black and white cattle mooched. Two magpies chattered raucously from the branches of a nearby tree.

'So? How was your journey?'

'Fine.'

'Coach or train in the end?'

'Neither.'

'How come?'

'I hitched.'

'You what?'

Katherine sighed. 'I hitched as far as Penzance and caught the bus from there.'

'I sent you the fare.'

'Here.' Half out of her seat. 'I'll let you have it back.'

'That's not what I mean.'

'What then?'

8

'Hitching like that. It's not safe. It's unnecessary. It's . . .'

'Look. I'm safe. I'm here. See. All in one piece.'

'You're catching the train back. If I have to put you on it myself.'

'All right.'

'I mean it, Katherine.'

'And I said, all right.'

But she was smiling, not sullen the way she might once have been.

'How's the tea?' Elder asked.

Katherine shrugged. 'Like tea?'

◆

They walked along the narrow track between the fields, past the farm buildings, to where the cliff jutted out over the sea.

'So what on earth d'you do with yourself all day?' She gestured widely with both arms. 'Fish?'

'Not exactly.' Sometimes he drove across to Newlyn and watched the catch being landed, bought mackerel or sole and brought it home.

'I'd go crazy. In a week.'

Elder smiled. 'We'll see.'

'Dad, I'm not staying that long.'

'I know.' He had hoped she might stay longer.

'There's a party, Saturday. I want to get back.'

Elder indicated the direction the path took between two stands of rock. 'If we head down there we can circle round, come back across the far field.'

'Okay.' For just a short way she took his hand.

◆

That evening they went for dinner to a pub between Trewellard and St Just. A dozen tables in the dining room off the main bar and most of them filled. Katherine had changed into a long denim skirt, and a T-shirt that fitted her more snugly than Elder felt comfortable with. He was wearing his usual blue jeans and faded cotton shirt, navy blue sweater folded now over the back of his chair. Elder ordered rack of lamb and watched, amused, as Katherine devoured a fillet steak without seeming to draw breath.

'Not vegetarian this week, then?'

Grinning, she poked out her tongue.

Plates cleared away, they sat comfortably, talking of this and that, the hum of other conversations sealing them in.

'How's the running?'

'Okay.'

'Spring training?'

'Something like that.'

Katherine had begun running seriously when she was around ten and it had been Elder who had first encouraged her, run with her, been her coach. The first time she had represented her club at two hundred metres she had finished third, the youngest in her event.

'First meeting must be soon?'

'County Championships, middle of the month.'

'And you're doing what? The two hundred and the three?'

Katherine shook her head. 'Just the three.'

'How come?'

'I can win that.'

Elder laughed.

'What?'

'Nothing.'

'You think I'm big-headed, don't you? Conceited.'

'No.'

'Yes, you do.'

'No,' Elder said again. 'Self-confident, that's what I'd call you. Self-assured.'

She looked at him then. 'Maybe I've had to be.'

Catching the waiter's eye, Elder signalled for the bill. Katherine was twisting a silver ring around the little finger of her left hand.

'How's your mother?'

'Ask her.'

'I'm asking you.'

Slipping her mobile from her bag, she set it on the table before him. 'Ask her yourself.'

He scarcely glanced at the bill when it came, passed across his credit card, lifted his sweater from the chair. Katherine dropped the phone, unused, back from sight.

◆

Small stones crunched and turned beneath the car wheels as he drove slowly down the track. The upstairs light in the cottage had been left burning.

'I'm pretty tired,' Katherine said once they were inside. 'I think I might go straight to bed.'

'Okay, sure. Do you want anything? Some tea or . . .'

'No, thanks. I'll be fine.'

Reaching up, her lips brushed his cheek. 'Good-night, Dad.'

'Good-night.'

He poured Jameson's into a glass and carried it outside. The shapes of cattle nudged each other across the dark and, as he moved, something scuttled close along the wall's base. Here and there, pinpricks of light blinked back from the black mass of sea. Perhaps tonight, with Katherine in the house, the dream would let him rest in peace.

3

From her room across the landing, Katherine heard her father's scream.

When she pushed open his door, he was half-sitting, half-leaning, slick in his own sweat.

'It's all right,' he said. 'Nothing. Just a dream.'

◆

Wrapped in silence, they sat across from one another in the downstairs room. Katherine had made tea and they drank it sweet and strong and, in Elder's case, laced with whiskey. The hour hand of the clock meandered towards four. In not so very long it would be light or something close. When she'd asked him about the dream, all he had done was shake his head.

Katherine set down her tea and went back upstairs, returning with a disposable lighter and a pack of cigarettes. Elder hadn't even known she smoked.

'Don't worry,' she said, 'I'm giving it up.' And when Elder didn't respond, 'It's not the first time, is it?'

He shook his head.

'How long?'

13

'Long enough.'

Six months after he had moved here the dreams had started, sporadically at first, once or twice a week, no more; always variations on a theme, the cats, the stairs. Usually he would wake before the final stage, the final steps, the shape upon the bed. And then, as winter bit, they came thick and fast until he was loath to go to bed and sat up instead, listening to the radio, the image of his own face, tired and drained, staring back at him from the window glass. He went to the doctor, took pills, visited a therapist and in the cloistered comfort of her upstairs room uncovered an early incident with half-wild cats when he was still a child. He didn't go back.

'Do you want to talk about it?' Katherine asked.

Another shake of the head.

'It might help.'

'I don't think so.'

'But Dad, you can't . . .'

'Can't what?'

She didn't know, or if she did she didn't say.

He could smell the perspiration where it had dried on him and dreaded that she could smell it too, that and the residue of fear.

Katherine stubbed out her cigarette and rose to her feet. 'Come on, let's take a walk.'

'No, I don't think . . .' Elder started, and then, 'Yes, sure. All right.'

Where the sky braced the sea, a narrow ring of orange showed beneath black and purple cloud. Violet light. The slow beat of waves against the foot of the cliffs, their rise and fall. Dampness on the fields and in the air. The first bird call of the day.

'Being on your own,' Katherine said. 'I don't suppose that helps.'

'I wasn't on my own last night. You were just across the landing.'

'That wasn't what I meant.'

There had been a woman – in her thirties, bustling, attractive, a waitress in a café at Sennen Cove. Elder had talked to her at intervals for months before finally asking her out: the cinema in Penzance, dinner in a restaurant where the food was mediocre and the music over-loud. In the end she could no longer take his silences, the parts of his life from which he kept her closed out. 'If I'm going to be by myself,' she said, 'I'd just as well be on my own.'

He had seen her once or twice since, laughing on the arm of a fisherman with white hair and weathered cheeks. Happy, or so it had seemed.

'You could always advertise, you know.' A smile played on Katherine's face. 'Fiftyish ex-policeman seeks female companion. Photo appreciated. Handcuffs a speciality.'

Elder laughed. 'Thanks very much. Think it's come to that, do you?'

Stopping in her tracks, she studied him, the lines of his face, the fading blue of his eyes. 'Probably not.'

Back at the cottage, he stripped off his clothes, slid back into his bed and slept until a little after nine, waking then to the sound of the radio playing, the smell of coffee and hot buttered toast.

◆

For the rest of Katherine's visit the dream was not mentioned, nor did it return. Together they visited the Tate

Gallery at St Ives, Elder more impressed by the building itself, the way its largely glass front followed the curve of the bay, than by the works of art it housed. At Cape Cornwall they clambered to the highest point and watched the seals, sleek amid the waves. Three hours being tossed in a small fishing boat yielded one skinny mackerel and a pair of crabs. They tramped the fields to Zennor, the coast path west and east; ate pasties, cod and chips, cream teas. In Barbara Hepworth's Sculpture Garden, they sat on white chairs, eyes shaded against the brightness of the sun, and when a small cat, grey and white, jumped on to Elder's lap, instead of pushing it away he let it settle, tail curled, one paw shielding its eyes.

On Katherine's last night, Elder took her to the Porthminster Beach Café and after dinner they walked on the sand.

'What's it like at home?' Elder asked. Aside from a man walking his dog, and a youth in a wet suit desperate to catch that last wave, they had the beach to themselves.

'All right, I suppose.'

'Martyn,' Elder said, 'he's all right with you?'

'He's fine.'

Martyn Miles owned a clothes shop on London's King's Road, another in Kensington, and a chain of hair salons named Cut and Dried with branches in London and Bath, Cheltenham, Derby and Nottingham. When Elder and Joanne, seven years married, had moved from Lincolnshire to London, Joanne had worked as a stylist in one of Martyn Miles's salons. After a year, with Elder having difficulty finding his feet in the Met and the relationship going through a bad patch, Joanne and Martyn had a brief affair. When it was out in the open, Elder and Joanne took stock,

16

faced a few home truths, dug in. Elder suggested she change jobs, find a new boss, but Joanne disagreed. 'I need to see him every day and know I don't want him any more. Not turn my back and never know for sure.'

Eight years down the line, Katherine on the point of starting secondary school, Joanne was offered the chance to manage a new salon Miles was opening in Nottingham. They moved again. Settled in. Katherine was happy in her new school. Elder had slipped into the Major Crime Unit with relative ease. Sometimes you never saw it coming until it was too late.

'I've been seeing him again. Martyn. I'm sorry, Frank, I . . .'

'Seeing him?'

'Yes, I . . .'

'Sleeping with him?'

'Yes. Frank, I'm sorry, I . . .'

'How long?'

'Frank . . .'

'How long have you been seeing him?'

'Frank, please . . .'

Elder's whiskey spilled across the back of his hand, the tops of his thighs. 'How fucking long?'

'Oh, Frank . . . Frank . . .' Joanne in tears now, her breath uneven, her face wiped clear of colour. 'We never really stopped.'

◆

He and Katherine had the beach to themselves now, the soft sound of the tide slowly starting to turn.

'Another coffee before we head back?' Elder asked.

17

'I'd better not. I've got an early start.'

By the time they arrived back at the cottage, the sky was grey shading into black. For some minutes they stood outside, silent, looking up at the stars. Katherine's rucksack was already packed and leaning against the foot of the stairs.

'Good-night, Dad.'

Holding her close, he kissed her hair, her cheek. 'It's been good.'

'Yes. Yes, it has.'

In the small kitchen, moths jousting with the lamp, he stood, glass of Jameson's in hand, listening to her moving around above. Then silence. When he and Joanne had separated, he had been anxious to reassure his daughter, not wanting her to imagine the break-up was in any way her fault. 'I love you, Kate,' he had said. 'You know that, don't you?'

She had looked back at him with a sad little smile. Fourteen. 'I know, but that doesn't matter, does it?'

'What do you mean? Of course it does.'

'No. It's Mum. You should have loved her more.'

Elder swallowed down the rest of his drink and rinsed out the glass; that night he spent downstairs in the chair, blanket across his legs. A quick breakfast before seven and then the drive across the granite spine of the peninsula to the station at Penzance. The train stood waiting, doors open. A quick hug and then a turn away.

'You'll come and see me run?'

'Of course.'

A wave, the guard's last shout, Katherine's face at the window a blur of white. And Elder, at the platform end, hand raised, the twist and tug at his insides sharp and real as the train disappeared from sight.

4

The landlord of Elder's nearest pub was not best known, perhaps, for his good grace, but Elder had shown his face often enough to earn more than a sneer.

'Was a call for you,' the landlord said. 'Some woman. After you for unpaid maintenance, I'd not be surprised.' His roosterish laugh rose high above the bar. 'Got to be some reason, you hidin' out in that place the way you are. Said she'd ring back round nine.'

Katherine, Elder wondered? Joanne?

It was neither. Though he'd last heard it two years before, Elder had no trouble identifying the low lift and turn of Maureen Prior's voice. Previously Elder's sergeant, she was now a detective inspector in the Nottinghamshire Major Crime Unit, the same rank Elder had once held himself.

'Maureen. What's up?'

'Shane Donald.'

'What about him?'

'He's about to be released. On licence. I thought you'd like to know.'

'Thanks, Maureen.'

Seventeen and convicted of murder, Donald had been

sentenced to be detained at Her Majesty's pleasure. His co-defendant, Alan McKeirnan, older, the acknowledged leader, had been given life. That had been in 1989. By now Donald would be passing thirty.

'There's been a bit of a hoo-ha in the local press.'

'How did they latch on to it?'

'The victim's parents, they'd have been informed.'

'Of course.'

The victim, Elder thought: Lucy Padmore, at sixteen a year younger than Donald himself.

'If you're interested, I'll cut the pieces out, stick them in the post.'

'Yes, okay, Maureen, thanks. Do that.'

'All right, Frank. Take care.' And the connection was broken.

Despite working closely with Maureen Prior for almost three years, Elder knew little about her; where her private life was concerned, she hoarded details like a miser. Single as far as the evidence allowed, straight if he'd had to hazard a guess, she never shirked a task, no matter how tedious or repugnant, always stood her fair share in the pub after hours. He had never seen her drunk, rarely heard her swear. Compared to Maureen, Elder wore his heart on his sleeve, his backside, as the singer put it, out to the world.

He stood a moment longer before returning the receiver to its cradle and turning back towards the bar. Shane Donald. He remembered a scrawny youth with watery eyes, impressionable, easily held in thrall. He wondered who Donald had latched on to in prison, which way he had been led. Now he would be relocated to another part of the country, away from the scene of his

20

crime; he would spend, in all probability, the first six months in a probation hostel; be supervised closely to ensure that his readiness to re-enter the community had been well judged.

Elder bought a large Jameson's and carried it to the far corner of the low-ceilinged room. In his experience you felt many things about those you arrested, especially for murder, and pity was rarely amongst them.

◆

Donald was the last child of older parents, a mistake as he was often called, an afterthought, a wee sickly thing at birth who had only just survived and, as his mother was wont to point out, more the sodding pity for that. The family lived in the north-east, a run-down sump estate on the edges of Sunderland, three generations stumbling over one another in a house where half the windows were like as not boarded up and the back door swung off its hinges in the wind. His father did odd jobs, scrounged scrap metal and sold it where he could, lost money on the horses, drew the dole; his mother worked as a cleaner in the local school. Before they were in their teens, his three brothers had been in trouble with the police. One of his sisters fell pregnant at thirteen, the same year Shane was born.

It was a life sure to get worse and so it did. His father would beat him as a matter of course, the back of his hand around the boy's face, a thick belt laid hard across his arse. His grandfather abused him when he was drunk; when they were sober two of his brothers took it in turns to bugger him till he bled. Each time he ran away, the police or some well-meaning social worker would bring him back. Only his middle sister, Irene, showed him affection, would wipe away his tears and cuddle him on her lap. But when she left home, married to a gas fitter from Huddersfield some hundred or so miles away, one child already and another on the way, there was no one he could talk to, no one he could trust. More and more, he lived in that small dark space inside his head.

Around the time of his fifteenth birthday, not long after Irene left, something snapped. He lashed out at the wood-work teacher with a piece of two-by-four, smashed half a dozen windows along one side of the school, broke into his own house and took fresh wages from his mother's purse, bundled some clothes and anything worth stealing into an old holdall and began hitching south-west.

It wasn't easy. Most drivers, even if they slowed down, shot a glance in Donald's direction, then sped past. He spent one night huddled up against his belongings in a bus station in Darlington, another sleeping under a hedge near a lay-by just off the A61. By the time he arrived on his sister's doorstep he was hollow-eyed and filthy and his clothes reeked of damp and worse.

Irene hugged him and bundled him inside. Upstairs in the bathroom, she undressed him as if he were still a child and ran a warm flannel across his skin.

'He needn't think as he's stayin' here, cause he's bloody not,' were her husband Neville's words.

Ignoring him, Irene spread margarine across sliced bread, then jam, made tea. She was seven months' pregnant and it showed; the baby presenting itself the wrong way round though there was time enough for it to turn.

'Shane, pet, what've you done?' she asked, watching him devour the bread. 'You're not in trouble, are you?'

22

'Left 'em, that's what.'

'Not before time.'

'An' I'm never goin' back neither, no matter what.'

'I've told you,' Neville said from the doorway, 'you're not stopping here.'

'You keep out of this,' Irene said. 'It's my business, not yours.'

'Is it, hell as like!' He took a step towards her, fist clenched, but she stared him down.

'Time, isn't it, you were getting off to work?'

Neville turned and went without a further word.

'Don't you fret,' she said to Shane. 'It'll be all right. He'll come around.' She could make up a bed for him downstairs, she was thinking, a mattress on the floor. At least until the baby came.

But before that happened, Shane had met Alan McKeirnan and the chain of events that led to murder had begun.

◆

Elder tipped the last of the Jameson's into his mouth and savoured it for a moment on his tongue. He remembered one of his fellow officer's words when they finally had Donald handcuffed in the station, brown hair cropped close to his head, wisps of a moustache vying with cold sores around his bloodless mouth. 'Someone should have drowned him at birth, pathetic bastard. Either that or left him on the blanket where he belonged.'

◆

The envelope bearing Maureen Prior's precise writing arrived three days later. The postwoman left her van at the top of the lane and walked down, the first time she'd had occasion to call since early spring.

'Beautiful, isn't it?' she said with a quick glance skywards as Elder stepped out to meet her. 'Day like this, good news, got to be.'

'Let's hope, eh?' He doubted that it was.

There were pages from the *Mansfield Chad*, the *Nottingham Evening Post*. Photographs of both Donald and McKeirnan at the time of their trial, the one of Donald unfocused and ill-framed, snatched by a press photographer through the window of a moving van. *GIRL'S KILLER TO GO FREE* proclaimed one headline. Free, Elder thought, after serving thirteen years.

News that Shane Donald, one of two men found guilty in 1989 of the murder of 16-year-old Lucy Padmore, would soon be released from prison, was greeted with anger and disbelief by the dead girl's parents, David and Dawn Padmore of Station Road, Ollerton. 'What right has he got to be walking round scot-free,' asked a tearful Mrs Padmore, 'when my Lucy can never walk anywhere again?'

It is expected that Donald, who will be released on licence, will be relocated and possibly given a new identity. 'It doesn't matter what they do,' David Padmore said later in an emotional outburst, 'I'll find him and when I do he'll wish he'd stayed behind bars.'

There were two pictures of Lucy, one a regulation shot of her in school uniform, smiling blandly at the camera, the other a candid snap of a pretty, fair-haired girl in sweatshirt and jeans, laughing at something that had just been said.

Elder supposed she had looked much like that when she had met them, McKeirnan and Donald, on the sea front at Mablethorpe, where she was holidaying with her family. Alan McKeirnan, twenty-six, black hair greased into a retro fifties quiff, fairground tattoos on his arms, leather jacket studded and open, jeans buckled tight. He would have spoken to her first, a certain cocky charm. Donald she would scarcely have noticed, an ill-fitting shadow in the older man's wake. An older man – Lucy might have liked that, part of the appeal; that and the offer of a ride on his motor bike. A Norton 750, polished chrome. 'Hey, Shane. Give her your helmet. You can walk.' Elder could see McKeirnan in his mind's eye, leading Lucy off with a wink and a grin. Twenty minutes to the small caravan site where he and Donald were staying, inland from the coast.

They had kept her there for five days, a prisoner, subjecting her to a series of assaults which had escalated to the point of her eventual death. Her body had been found, torn and bruised, buried in a shallow grave amongst scrub and couch grass near the coast path across the dunes.

Similarities were found with a number of assaults that had taken place across the county border in Nottinghamshire, going back several years. In the most recent of these, one year before, a young woman named Michelle Guest had been kept prisoner for forty-eight hours and forced to take part in a variety of sexual acts, including penetration with a blunt implement, before being released, dumped out of a car on a nothing road between Retford and Gainsborough at dead of night. She was seventeen, not overly bright, and had worked as a prostitute in a casual sort of a way since leaving school. When a farmer found her, huddled against a hay bale early the next morning, and contacted the police, she was disorientated, terrified, scarcely able to speak.

An inter-force team was set up, with Elder and a detective inspector from Nottinghamshire, Terry Foster, leading inquiries in the field. Another DI ran the incident room where different elements of the investigation were logged and local records were checked, officers and civilians accessing the national HOLMES computer, sifting and categorising before a decision was made as to which names could be discarded, which should be considered potential suspects and a trace initiated.

Alan McKeirnan was one of the latter. In his late teens he had been convicted of indecent assault and served eighteen months inside; in the intervening years he had been suspected of involvement in several similar offences, including one of attempted rape, brought in for questioning but never charged.

Of no fixed address, he worked occasionally as a mechanic; more frequently he was on the road with one or other of the small travelling fairs which criss-crossed the country, coming together for major annual events such as Nottingham Goose Fair. When Elder finally caught up with him, McKeirnan was repairing an errant bumper car in an amusement park in Skegness, Gene Vincent blaring distortedly through the overhead speakers, 'Be-Bop-A-Lula' and 'Bluejean Bop'.

'Can't beat it,' McKeirnan said, wiping greasy palms down the front of his overalls. 'Gene Vincent, Eddie

Cochran, Charlie Feathers.'

Elder remembered them vaguely as names from his childhood and wondered what someone roughly half his age was doing listening to them now.

'Can you turn it down?' Elder shouted above the sound.

McKeirnan signalled towards the control booth and, after a few moments, the volume diminished to normal levels.

'Who's that?' Elder asked, indicating the youth who had waved back at McKeirnan before obeying his instruction.

'That?' McKeirnan said. 'That's nobody.'

Elder would discover later that it was Shane Donald.

'You, though,' Elder said, 'you're Alan McKeirnan?'

'Nobody else.' Already the smile in place, self-assured.

'And you'll not mind answering a few questions?'

'Depends.'

'On what?'

'If there's a prize.'

'How about staying out of jail?'

'Sounds good.' McKeirnan took a packet of cigarettes from the top pocket of his overalls and held it out towards Elder and the officer with him, both of whom declined. McKeirnan tapped one out, set it between his lips and produced an imitation Zippo lighter. He liked the quick click of the lighter head, up and back with the side of his hand.

Elder asked him where he had been on the date that Lucy Padmore had gone missing, on the date that her body had been found.

'Hull,' McKeirnan answered without hesitation.

'What doing?'

27

McKeirnan shrugged and glanced around. 'This.'

'And there are witnesses, people you worked for?'

'I dare say.'

'When you were up in Hull,' the officer asked, 'where did you stay?'

'Caravan.'

'Yours?'

'Yes.'

'Where is it now?'

McKeirnan allowed himself a smile. 'Burned out, didn't it? On the journey down. Someone not too careful with a can of paraffin.' He shook his head. 'Lucky to get out in one piece.'

They found the caravan where McKeirnan had claimed it was, a charred wreckage with a twisted frame. Scene of Crime lavished attention on it for the best part of three days; labelled what remained of the interior and had it carried away for further scrutiny. Bloodstains belonged to the most common group, McKeirnan's own. Lucy Padmore's, too. 'Cut myself shaving. Too much of a hurry, yeah?' Apart from McKeirnan's, the fingerprints of one other person showed up several times. 'One of the lads from the fair, I was giving him a lift down, okay?' There was no clear evidence that Lucy had ever set foot inside.

At an identity parade, whether through fear or some traumatic loss of memory, Michelle Guest failed to pick him out.

McKeirnan dropped from sight.

And a week later another girl went missing, a hundred or so miles north, another county, but the similarities were striking. Susan Blacklock was a little over average height, slim and fair-haired, sixteen years old; the last time anyone had seen her was on the coast path between Robin Hood's Bay and Whitby at close to three in the afternoon.

Elder drove up the A1 and across the moors, where he liaised with Don Guiseley from the local force; he talked to the girl's parents, Trevor and Helen, to the staff of the caravan site where they had been staying, to the retired teacher who had been walking the Cleveland Way and passed Susan close by Saltwick Nab, acknowledging her with a greeting that had been faintly returned.

Five days missing and Elder dreaded the sixth.

5

Then they got a break. Two stray threads recovered from beneath the blackened frame of the folding bed were found, under a microscope, to match those from the sweater Lucy had been wearing when she disappeared.

Further examination of the blood samples taken from the caravan discovered DNA which matched Lucy Padmore's, not McKeirnan's at all.

An appeal for information as to McKeirnan's whereabouts led to another of his victims coming forward, a young-looking nineteen-year-old, Vicky Rawls, who, until then, had kept her own counsel about the terrifying day and night she had spent in the close company of Alan McKeirnan and his friend, Shane Donald. A fast flirtation that had gone horribly wrong.

It was not so long before McKeirnan was retraced, working at a garage north of Rotherham on the Rawmarsh road, bodywork mostly, beating out and welding, clocking on each day at seven, off at five. A youth answering Shane Donald's description spent a large part of his days hanging round the garage, running errands, doing odd jobs, handing McKeirnan his tools.

The two of them were living in a basement bedsit close to the town centre, bathroom on the first-floor landing, nearest toilet in the yard outside.

Along with three other officers, Elder met up with his opposite number from the Notts. force at motorway services. 'I'll toss you for it,' Terry Foster had said, and when the coin came up heads, 'Right. McKeirnan's mine.' Foster grinning, savouring the thought.

Foster's team were five strong. South Yorks. were providing backup, half a dozen uniforms and as many plain-clothes, an armed response unit standing by. Both garage and bedsit were staked out, officers well out of sight, no chance of tipping their hand too soon. At twenty to seven the message came through, McKeirnan had left for work alone.

Shane Donald, wearing grubby jeans and a grey T-shirt, trainers on his feet, had wandered, bleary-eyed, to the corner shop. Twenty Embassy, the *Sun* and a carton of milk. He was on his way back, glancing at the sports page, when Elder fell into step beside him.

'Bit of a fan, then?'

'Eh?'

'Soccer? Bit of a fan? United? Liverpool?'

'Who the fuck are you?'

But then Donald saw the two men outside the house, no more than fifty yards away, and he knew. Instinctively, he turned to run, milk and paper spilling from his hands, one corner of the carton splitting as it landed, leaking semi-skimmed on to the pavement.

Elder grasped Donald's arm between elbow and wrist.

'Don't. Don't be stupid. You'll only get hurt. No need for that.'

They took them to separate stations, McKeirnan with abrasions to his face and hands, a swelling over his left eye, the impression of a metal toecap faint alongside his groin. Whistling 'Summertime Blues' through splintered teeth.

'My client's already been waiting forty-five minutes to see a doctor,' the duty solicitor blustered, pink-faced.

'My old man waited eighteen months for a hip replacement,' the custody sergeant replied. 'The way it is these days.'

'This isn't funny . . .'

'What my dad said. Especially when the bastard thing kept slipping out of joint. But keep your shirt on. The police surgeon's on his way.'

Three-quarters of a mile away, in the bowels of another station, the custody sergeant asked Donald to confirm his age.

'Seventeen.'

'The truth, son.'

'Seventeen next birthday.'

'Is there anyone you'd like informed that you're here?'

Donald shook his head.

'Your parents?'

'What the hell for?'

Elder leaned across the desk. 'Let's get on to social services sharpish, explain the situation. Someone to attend the interview. When they show up, make sure he's cautioned again. Meantime, let's see if we can fix him up with a cup of tea and something to eat. Bacon sandwich, something of the sort.'

'Thought you were going to tuck him in,' the custody

sergeant said, nodding towards Donald's cell, the forma-
lities over. 'Read him a bedtime story.'

'Kiss him good-night, if I thought it'd help,' Elder
said. 'And whichever solicitor's assigned, let's try and
make sure it's not someone fresh out of law school, out to
make a name for themselves.'

◆

It took till mid-morning to get it sorted: a senior social
worker in a black skirt and crisp white blouse, rings of
tiredness around her eyes; the solicitor late fifties, genial,
semi-retired, doing his bit for legal aid. Elder had asked
Maddy Birch, a bright DS with soft eyes, to run the
interview with him. The room was windowless, low-
ceilinged and bare-walled – table, chairs, twin-deck
recorder, overhead light. Elder identified himself for the
tape and invited the others in the room to do the same,
Donald's voice so faint that Elder had to ask him to say
his name again.

For the first fifteen minutes Elder led Donald through
basic background information about himself, nothing
challenging, encouraging him to relax a little, lose some
of the tightness across his shoulders, the defensiveness in
his voice. When Maddy Birch asked him to tell them
about his first meeting with McKeirnan, Donald wriggled
in his chair and ran his tongue around his mouth and
answered haltingly. Maddy smiled and drew him on. A
good laugh. All the fun of the fair.

'Lucy Padmore, Shane,' Elder said, slipping in the
name without warning. 'What was she like?'

'She was nice.'

33

'Nice?'

'Yeah.'

'Nice to you?'

'Yes, why not?'

'Is that why you did those things to her?'

'I . . .'

'Pay her back for being nice to you.'

'I dunno what you mean.'

'Why you killed her?'

'No!' The chair skewed beneath him as Donald pushed himself to his feet, the social worker reaching out a hand, whether to save him or ward him off unclear.

'Shane . . .'

'No. Don't say that.'

'About killing her?'

'Don't say that.'

'She died, Shane. No bringing her back.'

Donald was breathing unevenly, open-mouthed, a rasp of air sucked in and then expelled; eyes wild, one hand to his mouth, the other rubbing at his crotch.

'Shane,' Maddy Birch said gently, 'why don't you sit back down?'

'She is dead, Shane, you know that, don't you?'

Not looking at Elder, at anyone, Donald slowly nodded his head.

'And if you didn't kill her, somebody else did.'

It was quiet in the room, quiet enough to hear the running of the tapes, the slightly asthmatic wheeze of the solicitor's breath. Elder thought he could smell pepper-mint, peppermint and sweat.

'Tell us about it, Shane,' Elder said. 'Tell us how she died.'

34

Donald jerked back his head, chewed on the remnants of a nail.

'Shane,' said Maddy Birch. 'You don't need to be afraid.'

Tears welled up in Donald's eyes.

'Shall I tell you what I think?' Elder said. 'I think you were fooling around, the three of you. You, Lucy and Alan. Drinking, having a laugh. A spliff or two maybe, I don't know. You were excited, all of you, and then – I don't know, Shane, and this is where you've got to help us – somehow it all got out of hand. Somebody got hurt. Lucy got hurt.'

Donald closed his eyes.

'And you liked her, didn't you? Lucy. You said so. You didn't want that to happen.'

Donald's eyes flickered open, focused on Elder for a moment, then away.

'You see, Shane, I think you got yourself mixed up in something you weren't happy with. Something you thought was wrong, but you were afraid to say. Alan was older, you looked up to him. He liked you, too. But what happened with Lucy . . . what he did . . . Shane, I don't think it's right if you take all the blame, do you? Murder, Shane, that's what it was, what it became. Murder.'

Elder reached out and, for a moment, took hold of one of Donald's hands.

'Help us, Shane. Help yourself. Tell us the truth.'

When it was over, twenty or so minutes later, they had a version – broken, repetitive, littered with gaps – of what had happened inside the caravan. McKeirnan having sex with Lucy, then persuading her to do the same with Donald before joining in. Then, later, after a few pills, some smoke, McKeirnan again, the music turned up loud to drown his laughter, her screams. His fist. A bottle. The handle of a broom. McKeirnan looking over his shoulder at Donald's face. Lucy's fingers scratching at his eyes, trying to escape. McKeirnan's anger. Rage. Then blood. The knife. McKeirnan cursing her for what he'd done.

In the interrogation room the silence held.

Elder knew they would get nothing more, not then. He got up, stretched, walked around the table, placed both hands on Donald's shoulders and squeezed. 'Good. You've done well. Now we'll try to help you. If we can.'

A sob broke from Donald's throat.

Elder's eyes, looking back across the table towards Maddy Birch, clear and hard as polished stone.

'See he gets something to drink,' Elder said, stepping away. 'To eat. A rest before we talk to him again.'

◆

'You know he's talking his way out of it, don't you?' Maddy Birch said. They were standing at the rear of the building, Birch smoking, Elder with a mug of dishwater coffee barely touched.

'You think so?'

'You've read Vicky Rawls's statement, heard the tape. He hit her with – what was it? – a piece of rubber hose.'

'Because McKeirnan told him to. Threatened him.'

'He did it just the same. That and more.'

'I know.'

Birch stubbed out her cigarette beneath the sole of her shoe. 'They killed her, Frank. Between them. That's what I think.'

'I expect you're right. In law, if nothing else. But if we need Donald to give us McKeirnan . . .'

'We have to go along with his lies?'

'We may have to buy his version of events for now, at least.' Not a man who noticed these things as much as, perhaps, he might, Elder was aware of the green of Maddy Birch's eyes.

'Are you going to finish that?' she asked, nodding towards the coffee in his hand.

Elder shook his head and tipped it out over the ground.

'You didn't ask Donald about Susan Blacklock,' she said once they were back inside.

'All in good time.'

In the Gents, Elder scrubbed his hands with almost exaggerated care.

◆

He pushed it all he could. The path between Whitby and Robin Hood's Bay. The end of August. You were up there, that way. The North York coast. That time. Susan, remember? He showed Donald photographs, watching him closely for some tell-tale sign of recognition, realising the possibility that he had never known her name. Sometimes he would begin the session with it, at others wait and slip back to it amongst other things. And never succeeded in shaking him once. Shane Donald who was so shaky on so many things.

Even then, Elder couldn't shift it from his mind. The coincidence. The chance. The almost certainty gnawing at his insides. He had never been able to let it go.

When he showed McKeirnan the photograph, all McKeirnan did was leer.

'You know her, Alan?'

'Like to.' With a wink.

'Where is she, Alan? What happened to her?'

McKeirnan's eyes glazed over and, just beneath his breath, he went back to Johnny Kidd and the Pirates, 'Shakin' All Over'.

Elder bit his lip and moved on.

Be thankful for what you've got.

Unless, like Helen and Trevor Blacklock, you had nothing. No daughter: empty rooms.

6

He set out from Cornwall early, bag on the back seat,
Thermos of coffee alongside him; unable to shake Susan
Blacklock's disappearance from his mind.

At the first service station he filled up with petrol,
checked the oil, pumped air into the tyres. It was a while
since the car, an anonymous-looking Ford, had made
such a run. In the garage shop he bought two bars of
chocolate, orange juice, a roll of extra-strong mints. Calls
of nature aside, he wasn't planning too many stops.

What he would do when he arrived he still wasn't sure
– poke around a bit, he supposed, maybe ask a few
questions, jog a few minds, walk the ground.

Outside Exeter the traffic picked up in volume. Elder
flicked the radio through the usual permutations: Radios
2, 3 and 4, Classic FM. Mostly he preferred silence.
Motorways and then narrow roads across the Yorkshire
Wolds before the circumlocution of the A171, twisting
between forest and moorland, the sea visible at intervals
to the right-hand side. By the time the ruined outline of
Whitby Abbey was in sight, the small of Elder's back was
aching, his legs felt cramped, his throat was dry. Slow
past the inner harbour, then he parked the car, hefted his

bag, and walked the short distance to the White Horse and Griffin, some fifty metres along the cobbles of Church Street.

The room he'd booked ahead was in the eaves: clean sheets, a comfortable bed, an easy chair. Three nights or four, he wasn't sure. A long slow bath and a change of clothes and, hungrier than he'd supposed, he ate an early meal downstairs, washing it down with a pint of beer. Almost as soon as his face touched the pillow, he was asleep. The sound of gulls, high-pitched and unyielding, woke him before five.

◆

Susan Blacklock had been on holiday from Chesterfield with her parents, two weeks in a caravan at the Haven Holiday Park, high on the cliffs above Whitby, overlooking Saltwick Bay. An only child, at primary school she had seemed happy enough, well-behaved and conscientious; she had her fair share of party invitations, fairy cakes and special dresses, pass the parcel and musical chairs, magicians who made things disappear before your eyes. In the first few years at the comprehensive, however, she had been submerged, so anonymous that at parents' evenings teachers had to be reminded who she was. But then, at fourteen, she had developed an interest in drama, a talent for acting previously unsuspected; as if when she stepped inside another character, took on a role, she found her voice. In palest blue with a large white bow, she was Alice following the White Rabbit into Wonderland; brave against all odds, as the deaf girl surrounded by war in *Mother Courage*, she moved more than her parents to tears.

40

All this brought her notice, gave her at least a surface confidence, earned her friends, the attention of boys. At fifteen she was sure she was in love – a seventeen-year-old with tattoos on his back and along his arms; who drank vodka from the bottle and occasionally sniffed glue. Susan's parents read the riot act, laid down the law. She broke her curfew, threatened, pleaded, cried, stayed out till two. You don't understand, she screamed, you just don't understand. But her mother understood all too well.

Then one day when Susan bunked off school to meet him, her beloved, he wasn't there. On the street, he turned away. When she plucked up the courage to go up to him in the pub, where he was sitting with all of his mates, he laughed in her face.

For six weeks her heart stayed broken, till one morning she woke up, got dressed, got on with whatever it was she had to do and realised, finally, she hadn't thought of him at all. That night, to her dad's annoyance, she and her mother giggled like sisters, talked in low voices for hours, held each other and cried.

This holiday marked a new stage in her life: she would start sixth-form college in September, courses in English and drama, media studies, art and design. And then on the third Tuesday in August she disappeared: August, fourteen years ago.

◆

Wearing two sweaters against the early morning chill, Elder walked the length of both piers sheltering the outer harbour. Dressed in all-weather gear, fishermen stood at intervals, rods propped against the rail, cigarettes a small glow inside cupped hands. Along by the fish market, one boat was unloading its night catch, another making its way in. He knew that in Britain almost ten thousand people went missing each year and that of that number roughly a third were never traced, never found.

But he had promised her parents that he would find her, sworn it and been rewarded with trust, bright and anxious on their faces; and, in his gut, he feared she was long dead, her body undiscovered, still waiting to be claimed after all these years.

◆

After breakfast, Elder climbed the hundred and ninety or so steps up to St Mary's church and the abbey, turning back for a moment to gaze back over the town, the whale's jawbone arched high on the west cliff on the far harbour side, the statue of Captain Cook close by. Beyond the town and the trees which marked the valley of the River Esk rose the moors, sullen and imposing beneath a patched grey sky.

He walked a short distance inland, crossing through the ridged mud of a farm before meeting the coast path further along. From there it was half a mile or so to the point where Susan had last been seen, a sharp promontory that jutted out over the sea, tufted grass leading to an almost sheer drop down the ridged cliff on to the rocks below. It could be a wild spot but not wholly remote, the path well used by hikers in most weathers; yet it was here, at somewhere between three thirty and four in the afternoon, that Susan Blacklock had last been observed, here that she had, effectively, disappeared.

Elder continued on, past the twin humps of reddish rock that broke the surface of the sea at Saltwick Nab, to the holiday park, a collection of white caravans clustered around a central site, a few brave tents pegged down on higher ground.

Little seemed to have changed: the same small convenience store, albeit with a fresh sign above the door, the same launderette, the office, pool tables and bar food available in the family entertainment club. On a patch of open ground, six or seven small boys stormed around the makeshift goalmouth of a beleaguered dad. A young woman in a neat uniform looked up at him expectantly and Elder nodded and carried on. At the far side, where a white flagpole flying the Union Jack announced the vehicle entrance, he turned about and set off back the way he'd come.

As the path made its slow turn past Saltwick Nab, curving with the contours of the land, Elder saw a woman in a green coat standing close against the spot where Susan Blacklock had last been seen; as he watched, she swung her legs over the low wire fence and stepped towards the edge. Elder began to run. Just for an instant her head turned at the sound of his shout. Then she withdrew a small bouquet of flowers from inside her coat, irises and roses intertwined, and laid it carefully on the ground.

◆

Helen Blacklock stood quite still, hands loosely clasped before her, outlined against the grey-blue of the sea. Her hair had darkened and was flecked here and there with grey. The coat she wore was loose and three-quarter-length, grey trousers, boots. Sensibly dressed. The face she presented to Elder was without make-up, lined about the eyes and mouth, thin-lipped, unsmiling. She was forty-five, Elder thought, forty-six, and could have passed for more.

Now that they stood face to face, he was uncertain what to say. 'I'm . . .'

'I know who you are.' Her voice quick and sharp as flint.

'Shouting like that, I didn't mean to startle you.'

'You thought I was going to jump.'

'Yes.'

'If I'd been going to do that, I'd have done it years ago.'

He looked beyond her to where the flowers were already being buffeted a little by the wind, and she angled her head round, following his gaze.

'I used to try and keep a garden here, a sort of memorial, I suppose. But it was difficult, being so exposed, and when anything did grow the kids from the camp would pull up the blooms and take them home to their mums. So now I just leave a few flowers, if I'm passing.' She paused. 'Sometimes the wind's so strong it almost snatches them from my hands. Here and gone. Suitable, don't you think?'

He held the wire down for her while she climbed back across the fence.

'What are you doing here?' Helen Blacklock asked.

Elder shook his head. 'I'm not sure.'

'But not an accident.'

'No.'

44

Gulls wheeled above their heads, roistering on the air.

'Are you going back into the town?' Helen asked, and when he nodded, she set off down the path, Elder alongside.

◆

At the foot of the steps, having walked more or less in silence, Helen asked if Elder would like a coffee. The place she chose was unprepossessing from the outside, one of several along a tourist street cramped with shops selling home-made fudge and Whitby jet, seafood and antiques.

They sat at a formica-topped table near the window, the waitress, school-aged, slow to take their order, sullen-eyed. The only other customer, an elderly man in a beige windcheater, sat near the side wall with a pot of tea and the *Sun*.

Helen brought a packet of cigarettes out from the side pocket of her coat. 'The guilt, that what it is?'

'Is that what you think?'

'I don't know, do I?'

'What you think I should be feeling?'

'I don't know.' She took a cigarette from the pack and tapped the filter down against the table edge; pushed it back from sight, unlit. 'Except I doubt you've been back here, all this time.'

Elder shook his head.

'Fourteen years. Thirty, that's what she'd be now. Susan. Thirty this March just gone.'

'Yes.'

'You think she died, don't you? That pair – McKeirnan

45

and the other one – you think they killed her. Like that other poor girl. Lucy.'

'There's no proof.'

'No.'

The waitress brought them cups of coffee on a tray, sugar in paper tubes, the teacake Helen had ordered but no longer wanted, Elder's toast.

'Have you heard something? Is that what it is?' As she spoke, Helen leaned forward, the tone of her voice changed, anticipation like a bruise behind her eyes.

'Not really.'

'What do you mean? Either you have or you haven't. Don't play games.'

Elder set down his cup, even in its saucer. 'Shane Donald, McKeirnan's accomplice, he's about to be released.'

'When?'

'I don't know. Not for sure.'

Helen leaned back, pushed the tea cake aside and reached for the ashtray, lighting the cigarette after all. 'That's why you're here then, sniffing round. You want to prove you were right this time, have him put back away.'

Elder kept his own counsel; with an automatic gesture, he wafted smoke away from his eyes.

'What'll it be this time? More fields dug up, farm buildings searched? The sewage pit by the caravans, you fancied that last time. The beck out by Hawsker Bottoms. The old railway line. Divers going down in the bay again in case they tossed her out to sea?' Bitterness and anger in her voice, the sharp curve of her chin. 'No need of that, she'd have washed up long since.'

46

Tears running freely down her face now, she turned away. When Elder reached out for her hand, she pulled it back as if from a sudden spark.

'Don't tell me. Don't say anything. I don't, I just don't want to know.'

He stubbed out her smouldering cigarette and waited for the sobbing to subside. Behind them the old man rattled the pages of his paper and poured more warm water into his tea. The waitress continued to gossip on her mobile phone about the ifs and maybes of the previous night.

After several minutes Helen pulled out some wadded tissues and wiped at her cheeks and eyes. 'I'm sorry.'

'No. It's okay.'

'I haven't done that in a long time.'

'Really, it's all right.'

She sipped her coffee, lukewarm.

'You want a fresh cup?'

'No. No, this is fine.'

◆

'I never imagined I'd bump into you the way I did,' Elder said. 'I'm sorry it's caused you as much upset as it has.'

He left money on the table for the bill. Outside, each hesitated while a straggle of small children crocodiled round them on the narrow street.

'When are you heading back?' Elder asked.

'Back?'

'Yes, I thought . . .'

But she was shaking her head. 'I moved up here a while ago. Trevor and I, we . . . well, we split up. Years back now. I bought a little place across the other side of the harbour. Susan, you see, I thought at least I could be near her, where she was when I saw her last.' She stepped a pace away. 'If you do find out anything . . .'

'Of course, I'll let you know.'

She told him her address and he committed it to memory, then stood there as she walked to the corner and on out of sight, a middle-aged woman, indistinguishable from many another, save for the way she had lost her almost grown-up child, here this minute, gone the next.

Elder wondered, since she'd been alone, what Helen did with her life; how often she climbed those worn stone steps, all hundred and ninety-nine, flowers held against her chest before relinquishing them to the wind; how she filled the spaces in between.

7

When Shane Donald had first met Alan McKeirnan – a patch of waste ground outside Newark-on-Trent, rain pitching down, and McKeirnan, dark hair flattened against his head, clothes soaked through, struggling with the wheel of a fairground trailer – McKeirnan had cast one eye on him, quick against the wind. 'You gonna stand there like a fuckin' statue or lend a hand?'

A short while later, inside McKeirnan's caravan, Donald had stood shivering while McKeirnan pulled off his clothing – denim jacket, T-shirt, trousers – until he stood in nothing but a pair of briefs and then not even those, Donald trying not to stare at the tattoos that snaked here and there across his body, the blue vein that ran up into the hood of his cock.

'Get your things off,' McKeirnan said, 'you'll catch your death.' And when Donald hesitated, adding with a wink, 'Don't worry, I'm not after your arse. At least, not yet.'

Laughing, he began to towel himself down, as Donald slowly pulled his sodden sweat-shirt over his head and then, embarrassed, back half-turned, peeled off the rest.

'Jesus!' McKeirnan exclaimed, Donald's ribs all too

49

visible through pallid skin. 'When did you last eat a fuckin' meal?'

At a burger bar off the market square, McKeirnan drank Coke and smoked several cigarettes, while Donald crammed first one, then two greasy quarter-pounders into his mouth, devouring several helpings of matchstick fries, coleslaw, ketchup, apple pie and a banana milk shake before rushing to the toilet where he brought most of it back up.

'You,' McKeirnan said later, 'have got to start eating regular. Treat your body like a fuckin' temple, know what I mean?'

They had hung out on the square with four or five others from the fairground, all of them older than Donald, around McKeirnan's age, mid-twenties, smoking roll-ups, a little dope, a couple of spliffs making the rounds, strong cider in cans. Calling out and laughing at the girls who ventured near, less than confident on high heels, tops pulled close across their tight little tits, at school still all of them while pretending otherwise. One of the blokes, tall and lean with peroxide hair, finally persuading a fourteen-year-old in sprayed-on scarlet pants into a shop doorway where he kissed her open-mouthed, one hand feeling her up inside her blouse, while with the other he stroked himself through his jeans.

Smile on his face, McKeirnan watching, watching every move, and Donald watching McKeirnan watching them.

Back in the caravan, a bottle of vodka passed between them, Donald not wanting it, not really, but not wanting to say no, the walls and the ceiling patchworked with old vinyl record covers and pages torn from magazines, rock-

and-rollers that Donald failed to recognise and women with full breasts, legs splayed.

More than a little drunk, fearful lest he might be about to throw up again, Donald rose gingerly to his feet.

'Where the fuck d'you reckon you're goin'?'

Reaching down, McKeirnan pulled out a mattress and a couple of army blankets from beneath the narrow bed. 'You can kip down here. A couple of days. We'll go round in the morning, see if we can't get you some work with the fair.'

Donald lay awake a long time, listening to the rich fall of McKeirnan's breathing, the sounds of traffic, sporadic on the nearby road. Not since his sister, Irene, had anyone looked out for him, spared him anything other than a contemptuous word.

He got taken on next day, collecting money on the dodgems, helping out on the coconut shy. McKeirnan lent him a black cord shirt, several sizes too large, a pair of Levi's, cinched tight with a leather belt and rolled up twice at the ankles. Donald painstakingly wrote his name, Shane, down the backs of both hands in biro, breaking the skin.

On the third night, McKeirnan, cock slick with Vaseline, slid down on to the mattress and buggered him, no more than Donald had expected, no more, he thought, than he deserved.

◆

Spring became summer, Donald stayed. Newark became Retford, Grantham, Boston, Skegness. When Donald pushed his way back into the caravan one afternoon, blinds closed, McKeirnan had a girl bent back over one end of the extended folding bed, bare-chested, skirt high above her waist; McKeirnan still wearing his leather jacket, the one with studs, naked from the waist down as he thrust into her, anger for a moment darkening his face as Donald entered and then grinning, shouting, 'Shut the fuckin' door.' The girl staring, frightened, at Donald and calling, 'No! Get him out of here.' And McKeirnan, with a ferocity that stopped Donald's breath in his mouth, striking her with an upwards-rising back-handed slap that knocked her face sideways and back, the edge of his ring cutting the top of her lip, the corner of her eye.

'Stay!' McKeirnan yelled. 'Now you're here, fuckin' stay and fuckin' watch.'

Donald transfixed, not needing McKeirnan's urging to watch the way the girl flinched, eyes squeezed shut, the slow run of blood below her ear, around her neck, the thickness of McKeirnan's cock as it drew back, then disappeared from sight. His own cock hard and straight against his leg.

McKeirnan every now and then glancing over his shoulder at his audience, spellbound.

The beginning but not the end.

◆

A few nights later they were drinking vodka, Donald developing a taste, downing a few pills, one of McKeirnan's tapes near full volume from the dodgy old cassette player, that singer he was forever on about, the one who had polio, or was it a road accident buggered up his leg, Donald could never remember. Anyway, him,

McKeirnan singing along and suddenly he stopped and pulled out his wallet from the back pocket of his jeans, opened it and lifted out a creased and tattered Polaroid which he glanced at with a grin before spinning it round.

'Here. What d'you reckon to that?'

Face blurred, the image of a woman leaning back against a chair, naked, a piece of rope dangling from one wrist, what could be blood staining the insides of her thighs. On the floor, close by one foot, an old-fashioned poker, or was it some kind of tool?

'Well? What d'you think?'

Unable, quite, to take his eyes from the photograph, Donald didn't know what he was supposed to say.

'Michelle,' McKeirnan said. 'Nice girl. You'd've liked her. Quiet.' He was smiling. 'Stayed with me for a bit last year.'

Fingering the lighter from his pocket he flicked it to life.

'No call to hang on to this now. Not when we can do better, eh? You and me.'

Holding one corner of the Polaroid, he watched it curl and burn, finally dropping it and watching till there were ashes and nothing more.

'You and me, Shane.' Laughing, he lifted the bottle in a toast, then brought it to his mouth and drank. 'You and fuckin' me.'

8

Unlike Elder who, for a variety of reasons, some of which he had never perhaps quite understood, had turned his back on the job almost as soon as his thirty years were in, Don Guiseley had laboured on for ten years more, falling finally on his sword when not so short of sixty, and opting for the quiet of the country-side, a village just west of the Cleveland Hills and the North York Moors National Park, where he and his wife, Esme, ran a small sub-post office and general store.

It was a surprisingly humid day, April turning into May, and Elder's shirt stuck damply to his back.

'Sweatin' a bit, lad,' Guiseley observed, shaking Elder's hand.

Wearing a loose check shirt and dark shapeless trousers, grey, almost white hair falling across his eyes, Guiseley had been sorting through what remained of a sack of onions, throwing out any that were too soft or otherwise showing signs of decay.

'Come on through here. Any luck Esme'll reward us with some tea.' The last of this with his voice raised in the direction of his wife, who was behind the small post office counter at the far corner of the shop, talking hysterectomies with one of her regulars.

In the small conservatory that had been added out back, two cushioned wicker chairs faced the open door, beyond which a broad garden sloped unevenly down towards a narrow stream. The far end was given over to vegetables, cucumbers under a cold frame; the rest, where not set to lawn, burgeoned with roses, dahlias and sweet peas.

'It's grand,' Elder said. 'The view, the garden, everything.'

'Fancy it then, do you? This sort of life.'

Elder grinned. 'Maybe not.'

'Aye. Up at five, sorting out papers. To say nothing of deliverin' bloody things when the lass as is supposed to do it overlays. And as for this garden, I'll tell you what, it gives my back bloody gyp.'

Guiseley took a pipe from one pocket of his coat, a pouch of tobacco from another. 'Cornwall, isn't it now? How come you fetched up down there?'

'As good a place as any.'

'Long way from kith and kin.'

'I think at first that was the point.'

'And now?'

Elder hesitated. 'I don't know.'

'You're still married?'

'Not so's you'd notice.'

'But you never, like, divorced?'

'There didn't seem to be a lot of point.'

'Clean break, some as'd see a virtue in that. Unless you think it's not done with, that is.'

Elder shuffled his feet.

'You've got kids?' Guiseley asked.

'Just the one. A daughter, Katherine. Sixteen.'

Guiseley tamped tobacco down into the bowl of his pipe with his thumb, then struck a match. 'Ours have flown the coop long since. Eldest boy's in Australia, settled. Married with a couple of kids. Other lad's in the job, London, Fraud Squad at the Yard. We get to see him once in a while.' Guiseley took the pipe from his mouth and laughed. 'Hear him talk, you'd think I was an old dinosaur. I told him, what he does, white-collar crime, lief as not be with one of them financial outfits in the City, making real money.'

'And the girl? You had a daughter, too, I thought.'

'Married this Asian bloke, wholesaler of some sort, big place the other side of Bradford.' He looked at his pipe and struck another match. 'Esme goes over to see them sometimes.'

Elder stayed silent and a moment later Guiseley's wife came through from the house with a tray, a pot of tea and proper cups, cheese scones. Her hand when Elder shook it, though small, was calloused and strong and, whatever her husband might claim to the contrary, Elder would have bet good money at least half the garden work was hers.

A few polite exchanges and she went back inside to look after the shop.

Guiseley indicated Elder could do the honours with the pot.

'Now,' he said after his first taste, 'you've not come out of politeness and I doubt you've took up social work, so you'd best tell me what it is you want.'

'Susan Blacklock.'

'Aye. Should've guessed. Sticks in the craw, don't it? Ones you never put to bed.'

He supped more tea and stared out across the grass.

'If I asked you now,' Elder said, 'thinking back, what would you say happened?'

'Same as I would've forty-eight hours after she went missing and no sign. She's dead. Some bastard's killed her. Though I am surprised the body's not turned up, I'll grant you that. Some small room for hope there, if that's what you're after.'

'I don't know,' Elder said.

'That business down in Gloucester, Fred and Rosemary West, all them bodies they were digging up, carrying off to be identified, dental records and the like, I kept half-expecting she'd be one of those. Easy enough for her to have gone off on her own, hitched a ride, one end of the country to the other, near enough. It's what kids do, given a half a mind.'

Elder poured hot water from a jug into the pot, swirled it round a little and refilled their cups. In his mind's eye, he saw his daughter, Katherine, rucksack on her shoulder, walking towards him down the lane.

'That pair as were put away,' Guiseley said. 'McKeirnan and Donald. You still think it was them?'

'Until someone convinces me otherwise.'

Guiseley nodded and fiddled with his pipe.

'The files on the case,' Elder said, 'I'd like the chance to look through them.'

'You don't want much then.'

'I thought maybe there was a favour you could pull, somebody you could call.'

'You know,' Guiseley said, 'when you came up here,

57

the way you put yourself about, you put up a lot of backs.'

'There was one girl already dead, another likely gone the same way. There wasn't a lot of time to be polite. Observe protocol.'

'Even so.' With the air of someone who's been backed into a corner, Guiseley sighed. 'Give me the chance to make a couple of calls. I'll see what I can do. No promises, mind.'

Elder nodded. He knew, grudging or not, Guiseley would do what he could.

'Thanks, Don.'

'It'll cost you. A couple of pints at least.'

9

Shane Donald stepped out of the station and stood on the lower step, looking around. Uncertain. Great pillars behind him, like it was the entrance to Buckingham Palace or something, some stately home, not poxy Huddersfield station. His travel warrant still in his pocket, the one they'd given him when he'd left prison that morning. Duffel bag over one shoulder, two carrier bags: all the things he owned.

He'd put on weight inside, filled out; muscle on his arms and legs, quite hard. Strong, even though he might not have looked it at first glance. He liked that. Taller, too, five eight or nine. Hair cut short and fine stubble sandpapering his face.

No longer a kid.

They'd given him a map, hand-drawn, how to find the hostel, instructions written down. He could always ask someone, he supposed, but he'd rather not do that. Keep yourself to yourself, avoid looking anyone in the eye: one of the things he'd learned inside. Just one. And there were others, too. Keep yourself to yourself, but if you can't . . .

He stepped out from the kerb and crossed the street.

◆

The probation hostel was in a large Victorian building, detached, set back off one of the broad tree-lined roads slowly rising out of the town centre. Several of the others, close by, looked to have been turned into guest-houses, small hotels.

Donald had checked his piece of paper several times on the way out there, fidgeting it in and out of his pocket, folding and unfolding and then folding it again; he was looking at it again now, wanting to be certain of the number.

As he stared up at the house, someone moved behind one of the upstairs windows and he felt a sudden urge to turn and run, go back the way he'd come and keep on going. Lose himself. He'd done it before.

The front door opened and a man was standing there, sandy-haired, forties, a grey cardigan unbuttoned over a faded green shirt, grey trousers, sandals.

'Shane Donald? Good. Excellent.' Walking towards him now. 'You're joining us today. I thought you'd be here pretty much round now. Though with the trains the way they are these days, you can never tell.'

He held out his hand.

'Peter Gribbens. Assistant manager. I'm to be your key worker.'

There was peppermint on his breath and his eyes were a twinkling blue.

◆

The interior smelt faintly of disinfectant. Music was playing somewhere, somebody's stereo, just the bass clearly audible. Movement. The sound of television or maybe radio. Clatter of cutlery being laid. Voices raised in anger, shrill laughter and then quiet. Higher up in the house, someone using a vacuum cleaner.

'Come on,' Gribbens said, moving towards the stairs. 'I'll show you to your room, give you a little time to settle in. Then I expect you wouldn't mind a cup of tea. And we can have a little chat.'

The room was on the second floor, high-ceilinged, square; there were single beds on opposite sides, a wardrobe in dark wood, embossed at the centre and deeply scarred, twin chests of drawers. The window was barred.

'Don't worry about that,' Gribbens said, following Donald's gaze. 'All the windows were like that when we moved in, the upstairs ones at least.' A suggestion of a laugh. 'It's not to keep you in.'

One bed was made but not too evenly, a few possessions clustered near it, magazines and an alarm clock on a straight-backed chair.

'Your room-mate is Royal. Royal Jeavons. He's been with us almost two months. He'll show you the ropes.'

Royal, Donald was thinking, black then, got to be.

Gribbens retreated to the door.

'Come down just as soon as you're ready. My office is on the ground floor, across from where we came in. My name's on the door.'

Donald sat down on his bed and stared at the floor.

◆

Peter Gribbens's office was long and narrow, one of several which had been partitioned off from a larger room. One wall was dominated by a chart, names and

61

dates in different colours, arrows and asterisks in black and red. On another were clustered more than a dozen framed photographs, in most of which Gribbens stood smiling in the company of colleagues or with disparate groups of his charges, mugging 'Cheese' for the camera. On his desk were piled folders, manila or plastic in different colours, several notebooks, two jars crammed with pencils and pens; to make room for a tray holding two mugs, sugar and a packet of biscuits, Gribbens's laptop computer rested on top of a telephone directory. Behind the desk, a tall window looked out on to a lawn with shrubs to each side and an ivy-clad wall at the foot.

'Shane, Shane, come on in. No sense letting this get stewed. Sugar, yes? One or two?'

Donald sat in the empty chair, accepted his mug of tea and looked around uneasily.

'Here. Have a biscuit. Chocolate digestives, no expense spared.' Again, the beginnings of a laugh that failed to follow through. 'You must be hungry, coming all that way. Changing trains. I expect you had something on the journey. A sandwich, something of the sort. Never mind, there'll be a proper meal soonish. No complaints about the food here, that's one thing. No complaints at all. Like Oliver Twist, most of our lads. Coming back for more.'

The biscuits were slightly soft, chocolate coming off on Donald's fingers. He didn't know whether to lick it off or risk wiping it away on the underside of the chair.

Gribbens opened one of the folders, then flipped it closed. 'The thing is, while you're here there are certain rules . . .'

Donald looked back at him attentively and let his mind go blank.

'Under the terms of your licence . . . Abide by the rules and regulations . . . Avoid contact with anyone involved in criminal behaviour . . .' The voice went on and on and then stopped. For the first time, Donald noticed the ticking of a clock.

'Shane?'

'Yes?'

'You understand all that? What I've just said.'

'Yeah.'

'Good.' Gribbens shuffled another piece of paper across his desk. 'Any special dietary requirements? You're not vegetarian, for instance?'

Donald was shaking his head.

'Nothing you're allergic to? Wheat? Nuts? No? Good, good. How about religious affiliation?'

'What?'

'Your religion. You know, Catholic, Church of England.'

'No, nothing.'

'Just Christian, then. We have quite a few who . . .'

'No, I said. Nothing. I don't believe in nothing.'

Gribbens ticked the requisite box and pushed the paper away. 'Your probation officer will see you tomorrow. Just to make sure you're settling in.' Gribbens got to his feet. 'All right, off you go. You'll find some of the others downstairs. There's a pool table, television.'

When Donald was at the door, Gribbens called him back.

'It's important that you try and make this work, Shane. That we all do.'

◆

63

Royal Jeavons was sitting on his bed, head back against the wall, headphones in place, CD Walkman close to hand. He opened his eyes briefly when Donald entered, a few seconds, nothing more. Donald crossed to the window and looked out, the backs of houses, lower down the silhouettes of trees. The paint on the bars had been chipped away with time, smeared with the droppings of birds. He went across to his own bed and sat. He was trying to remember what time it was: he didn't have a watch.

Jeavons was stocky with thick muscles at the neck, a shaven head, wearing sweat pants and a matching top. Trainers without socks.

'Fuck you lookin' at?' Jeavons leaning forward a little now, eyes still closed.

'Eh?'

'Fuck you lookin' at?'

'Nothing.'

'Nothin'?'

'Yeah, nothing.'

'Calling me nothin'?'

'No.'

'What?'

'I'm not.'

'Not what?'

'Calling you nothing.'

'No?'

'No.'

'Then that's cool, innit?' Jeavons looking now, full across at Donald, looking now and smiling. Broad face breaking into a wide grin.

'New, right?'

'Yes.'

'In today.'

'Yeah.'

''Safternoon?'

'Yes.'

'Don't give away fuckin' much.' Jeavons shutting off
the player, lifting the headphones clear. 'But that's okay,
man, that's cool.' Moving forward, stretching out a hand.
And Donald rising to meet him, hoping it wasn't going to
be some fancy high-five shit, but no, just a quick old-
fashioned handshake, two of Jeavons's fingers the thickness of his entire hand.

'Royal,' Jeavons said, splitting the word decisively in
two. 'Royal Jeavons.'

'Shane. Shane Donald.'

Jeavons nodded, stepped away. 'So, Shane. You had
the lecture, right? Gribbens.'

'Yes.'

'An' he ask you if you a Christian, right?'

'Yeah.'

Jeavons laughed and shook his head. 'Told him I was
brought up Baptist, right? Pentecostal Baptist. And he's
askin' me was it the full, like, immersion, like when I was
baptised, and I says, yeah, this pool, innit? South London.
Which is true. Thought he was gonna grab hold of my
hands and ask me, you know, kneel down on the carpet
and pray. Huh! Some sad motherfucker, but least he plays
it straight an' that's more'n you can say for some. Once
in a while, he'll turn a blind eye, too. Say maybe you
comin' in late, somethin', yeah? I mean, he's got this
lecture, right, you just have to stand there for that and say
you're sorry when he's done. See, he love that. That sorry

shit.' Jeavons laughed again. 'Give that man some genuine-soundin' repentance and you got him, eatin' out your hand, innit?'

He punched Donald on the upper shoulder, playful, no bad feeling, not hard enough to raise a bruise.

'You an' me, we're gonna get on, man. Just so's you don't snore too loud and don't make too much noise when you come.'

10

Rob Loake had filled out and then some, the centre button of his blue suit straining to be free. Seated behind his desk, he wore a pale blue shirt, striped tie, the long-suffering expression of a man for whom piles are a way of life.

'You know what you're asking for's against the rules?'

Elder allowed his weight to shift, almost imperceptibly, from one foot to the other.

'No way it's bloody on.'

'Then why am I here?' Elder said.

Outside, traffic moved with a steady hum.

'Don Guiseley's a mate of mine, a good skipper. He always reckoned you was worth the time of day. Me, I don't think you're more'n shit on a shoe.'

Elder nodded, said nothing. When the phone went, Loake had the receiver in his hand before the second ring. He spoke tersely, then rose to his feet. 'Something important I've got to attend to. You can wait here.'

Elder waited some seconds after the door closed before stepping around to the other side of the desk. The Susan Blacklock file sat there, three files to be precise, each thick to overflowing. Tension tightening in his stomach, he began to leaf through, skimming what seemed tangential and seeking out the rest.

There was a long statement taken from Trevor Blacklock, transcriptions of a series of interviews, officers probing for signs of tension between Susan and himself – a father who had been too distant from his adolescent daughter or possibly too close? Trevor Blacklock's responses were sometimes angry, at others almost evasive and it was clear that for a while he had been regarded as a suspect. Yet it seemed to Elder that the feelings Blacklock expressed about Susan were akin to those between most fathers and their teenage daughters: bewilderment, exasperation, love. And his alibi – after helping Susan's mother with one or two jobs around the caravan after lunch, he had driven the car into Whitby to have an almost threadbare tyre replaced prior to their journey home – had been checked and double-checked and deemed, as far as possible, watertight.

Elder looked at his watch. A little sweat had collected in the palms of his hands and along his scalp. Footsteps came towards the door and paused outside before moving on.

When interviewed, the woman working in the holiday park shop had said that Susan had seemed especially preoccupied that afternoon, nervous even. Apprehensive.

Elder wrote the name Christine Harker down in his book, and several minutes later added that of Kelly James, a local girl Susan had got to know over the course of several years' holidays.

He was still reading when Rob Loake came back into the room, not quite closing the door behind him. 'You know how it is, took longer than I thought.'

'Yes, it can happen.' Closing the file, Elder stepped around the desk.

'No time now for a chat.'

'No.'

'You can find your way out?'

'Yes.'

Cigarette smoke was sour on Loake's breath.

Sometimes, Elder thought, as he crossed the car park, you can be too close to really see what's there, fail to recognise what's right before your eyes. Believe, all too readily, what you've been told. What you think you've seen.

He knew the drill: go back to basics, assume nothing, look with a fresh eye. With any luck he could be back at the coast before midday.

◆

Kelly James was now Kelly Todd.

Mondays, Wednesdays and Fridays she worked as a beautician – facials, manicures, pedicures, waxing. When Elder went into the shop, she was just finishing a half-leg, underarm and bikini wax on a dental technician bound for ten days' bed and half board on Ibiza.

'Just take a seat over there,' she called. 'I'll be with you in ten.'

Elder thumbed through an old issue of *Vanity Fair*. Ten became fifteen. The radio seemed to be playing the same song, over and over again.

'Here we are, sorry it took so long.' She was swathed in a fuchsia wraparound, her face made up to high-gloss perfection. 'Susan Blacklock, that's what you said.'

'Yes.'

'They've not found her, have they?'

Elder shook his head.

'Poor girl. It sounds awful, I know, but I've not thought of her in years.'

They sat on the steps at the rear of the shop, a view along a narrow alley, a ginnel, Elder supposed: a few dustbins, geraniums at back windows, the inevitable seagulls. Kelly had produced mugs of instant coffee and nursed hers now with one hand, cigarette in the other.

'Somebody killed her, didn't they? Nobody stays away that long, else. Disappears and never gets back in touch. Don't matter what's upsetting you, getting you down, what kind of rows you've had. You send a postcard, don't you? A phone call. Eventually. Don't fret, I'm all right.' She took a long drag on her cigarette, holding the smoke down in her lungs.

'And were there?' Elder asked. 'Things getting her down, I mean?'

'Oh, just the usual. Pocket money. Clothes. Who she could see, who she couldn't.' Kelly sipped her coffee. 'There'd been this lad the year before. Back home where she lived. Bit rough, by the sound of him. Older than her. Well, when you're fifteen who wants to waste their time coppin' off with some mucky little tyke with spots? Anyhow, her mum and dad, they'd sort of freaked – maybe it was worse, her being the only one. Laid down the law. Her dad especially, after that he was on to her all the time, by all accounts. Wanting to know where she was, who she was with.'

'And you think this might have been enough for her to want to leave home?'

Kelly watched a near-perfect smoke ring till it fragmented into the air. 'No, not really. Like I say, it was just normal teenage stuff. Something to moan about, feel sorry for yourself. She wasn't above that, Susan. Bit dramatic, in her own way. Oh, not shouting and screaming all over the place, don't get me wrong. No, quiet, she were that. What I mean, she seemed to like makin' out things was worse than they really were.'

'And this lad, the one all the fuss had been about, was she still seeing him, do you think?'

'No, I'm pretty sure. She would have said.'

'Did she talk about anybody else? Boyfriends?'

'Not really, not in as many words. Some bloke there was, maybe fancied her, something to do with this drama club. I don't think they'd ever, you know, done anything about it. Susan waiting for him, most like, to make the first move. You know what girls are like.' She grinned. 'Some girls.'

'And you can't remember his name?'

Kelly stared at her long fingers holding the cigarette. 'No, I'm sorry. I don't know if she ever said.' She smiled and shook her head. 'Not being a great deal of help, am I?'

Elder shrugged. 'You can't tell what you don't know.'

'I suppose not.'

Elder left his coffee half finished and thanked her for her time, told her where he was staying in case something occurred to her later. It was always possible, once things got stirred up freshly in your mind.

'Her poor mum,' Kelly said, 'not knowing like that, for certain I mean, it's not fair, is it?'

'No, it's not fair.'

Passing back through the shop Elder realised it wasn't that they were playing the same song, more that all the songs sounded the same. Just the sort of remark, he realised, his dad would have made about the Beatles and the Stones.

◆

Christine Harker was still working in the holiday park, behind the counter in what was now the Everydays Convenience Store. 'Just helping out. You know how it is, once in a while. Otherwise, I've got a nice little job down in town. Fruit and veg. Afternoons. Puts a few bob in my pocket. Mind you, I do miss *Countdown*.'

She was a short woman, generously built, late fifties, Elder guessed, with the sort of all-purpose permed grey hair that would suit for another twenty years or more. Her eyes had lit up the instant he had mentioned Susan's name.

'She's turned up, then?'

Hope turning to disappointment as she read the expression on Elder's face.

'I always thought she would, you know. Daft really. Against all, you know, the odds, but it's what I've always wanted to hear. How she'd run off somewhere, London perhaps. Settled down. Kids of her own.' She smiled. 'See it on the telly, that Sarah Lancashire, someone like that, her daughter'd disappeared, it'd all turn all right in the end. Hugs and tears. Only life's not like that, is it? Real life. Sometimes you forget. Life, they just bloody go and that's an end to it.'

Elder stood aside while several small purchases were

made: cigarettes, a can of Coke, tissues, a plastic ball. Listened to Christine Harker joking with her customers, he wondered about the bitterness she'd just shown and what had happened to her own children when they were fully grown.

'When you talked to the police,' Elder said, the shop quiet once more, 'you said that Susan seemed different that afternoon.'

'I know. And she were. I'd swear to this day. Pre-occupied. As if her mind was somewhere else. Sort of day-dreaming, I suppose.'

'And you've no idea . . .?'

'No.'

'Nothing she said?'

'That was it, she didn't say a thing. Not really. Just handed me the chocolate bar and her money, waited for the change. I must have made some remark, something about her going back soon. Back home, you know. She just sort of nodded and then she was on her way. I wondered if she'd had another falling out with her dad, but I never liked to ask. Besides, it would have been too late then, she'd gone.'

'Another falling out?' Elder said.

'Oh, it was nothing special, I don't suppose. Not compared to some of what you get up here. But no, a couple of days before it'd been, the pair of them going at it right outside here, hammer and tongs. Crying she was and telling him to leave her alone. "You got no right to talk to me that way. No right." And him coming back to her, "Yes, I have. As long as you're under my roof, I've every right." I don't know what it were about, something she should or shouldn't have done, I dare say. In the end she run off, back towards the caravans, and he went after her, cursing and swearing. Next day I saw them, they was right as rain.'

For a moment she looked away. 'It never does any good, does it? Carrying on. Get to a certain age, no matter what you say, they'll do what they're going to do and you just have to let them get on with it. Hope for the best.'

Half-smiling, she shook her head. 'You got any kids?'

'One. A girl.'

'How old?'

'Sixteen.'

'Then you'll know.'

Elder thanked her for her trouble and bought a Mars Bar to keep him company on the way back into town. Where the path angled away from the spur of cliff beyond Saltwick Nab, a few iris petals showed blue among the grass.

11

Helen Blacklock's house was tucked away in a part of the town Elder didn't really know. A small terraced two-bedroom on one of the narrow streets feeding off the hill that climbed steeply up towards the main Scarborough to Whitby road. From the upstairs window he guessed there would be a partial view of the estuary, the marina, the dock where ships from Scandinavia until recently had unloaded their timber.

Helen was standing outside the front of the house, bucket by her feet, rubbing a cloth back and forth across the living-room window. A small transistor radio, resting on the ledge, was quietly tuned to Radio 2.

He stood on the pavement, waiting for her to become aware of his presence and turn around. When she raised her head she saw his reflection, clear in the newly polished glass.

'What are you doing here?' No hostility, just surprise. 'Probably not just passing, eh?'

'Probably not.' He smiled and it earned him nothing in return.

She was wearing black trousers and a loose-fitting black top, her hair pulled off her face and held by a narrow band of cloth, blue-black. Traces of dark make-up smudged her eyes, as if left over from the night before. The hand that held the cloth was broad and raw, fingernails bitten back.

'How did you know I'd be in?'

'I didn't.'

'I do work, you know.'

'I'm sure you do.'

'One of them places on the quay. Doughnuts. Sticks of rock and candy floss.'

'You're not working today.'

'Not unless you count this.'

'I thought we might talk,' Elder said.

'I thought we were.'

'No, I mean . . .'

'I know what you mean.'

An elderly woman wearing a winter coat despite the temperature, went slowly past pushing a wicker shopping trolley and Elder stepped closer to the house and out of her way. 'Susan's disappearance, I've been going through the files.'

A strand of hair had worked its way loose and Helen reached up and pushed it back into place.

'I'm not saying I've found anything new, startling. I don't want you to think that. I may not come up with anything significant at all. It's just that sometimes when you go back over things, I don't know, I suppose you read them in a different way.'

She was staring at him, waiting. The last thing he wanted was to get her hopes up again without reason.

'I thought if we talked, if I could ask a few questions . . . if you didn't mind. It just might help.'

'Here,' she said, holding out her free hand towards him.

'What?'

'Take hold of that hand. Go on.'

He did as he was asked: the bones were firm, the skin less than smooth, the grip strong.

'You don't have to tiptoe round me,' she said. 'I'm not made of glass.'

No, Elder thought, flesh and blood. He followed her inside the house.

◆

The interior was small and snug and crowded with furniture that had most likely come with her from where she had lived before – the three of them, Trevor and Susan and herself – pieces she'd not wanted to part with, couldn't afford to replace. Dark orange curtains at the window, a patterned carpet on the floor, muddy brown. The faint, pervasive smell of tobacco.

'You'll have to take as you find, isn't that what they say? Just let me get shot of this stuff and I'll get kettle on. You'll have a cup of tea?'

'Yes, thanks.'

'Sit yourself down, then. I'll not be long.'

There were two small views of Whitby on the wall, watercolours, dried flowers in a vase; a photograph of Susan, framed, above the fireplace, another, showing her standing between her parents, on top of the TV. In the first she was wearing a purple top, long legs in tight white jeans. Pink flip-flops on her feet. A bright day, she was squinting a little against the light, eyes averted from the camera, angled away. The edges of her auburn hair afire.

There would be others, Elder was certain, preserved

77

carefully, chronologically arranged; school reports, too, certificates and thank-you notes and birthday cards and pieces of artwork going back to those on which Susan could only just write her own name: hand prints and potato prints, smudges of now fading colour, butterflies with broken wings. Bits and pieces of a life.

'Here we are.'

Helen walked slowly into the room, a mug in each hand, and Elder took one from her, a view of the Abbey with a hairline crack down through the glaze.

'Thanks.'

He smiled and she responded, just a little, with her eyes.

'It's cosy,' he said, sitting back down.

'Cramped, you mean.'

She had taken the band from her hair and now it fell almost to her shoulders, framing her face. Crow's feet etched quite deep, a slight puffiness beneath the eyes. The vestiges of make-up, he noticed, had been wiped away.

'What was it you wanted to know?'

The tea was weak, as if the bag had been removed too soon. 'That last day,' Elder said, 'anything you can remember. Up to when Susan left the caravan.'

'Anything?'

'Yes. Take your time.'

Helen cradled her mug in both hands. 'We got up late that morning, I remember that. Trevor was always like a bear with a sore head when that happened, even on holiday. Liked to be up and doing things – even when there were nothing special to do. He went out for a walk, I think. Picked up a paper on the way back, *Express* most

78

likely, once in a while the *Mail*. I had breakfast waiting when he got back.' She drank some more tea. 'After that we went to Robin Hood's Bay. In the car, you know. Just for an hour or so. Trevor, he used to like mooching round in rock pools when the tide was out, which it must have been, I suppose, and Susan and me, we sat on a bench up above the beach. Chatting, I dare say.'

'Can you recall what about?'

'This and that. Could've been anything. Most anything. Susan's college, where she was going, we talked about that a bit, I know.'

'And was she worried about it? Starting college?'

'No, not a bit. Looking forward to it. Siobhan and Lynsey, her friends from the drama group, they were going there too. She'd not made friends easily, you see, Susan, not all the way through school. I mean, she rubbed along, but that was it really. Then when she got involved in all this drama stuff, things seemed to start going better for her. They'd be going off to plays. All over. Leeds. Manchester. London, once. Newcastle-on-Tyne. Four in the morning, near enough, that time, by when they got home. Trevor had been all for calling out the police, he were that worried.'

'But everything was all right?'

'Oh, yes. One of them Shakespeare plays, went on for hours. And then they had a puncture on the way back down.'

'And Susan . . .?'

'Oh, she'd loved it. Had a wonderful time. An adventure. You could see it in her eyes.'

'And these friends of hers, they'd have been there as well?'

'Siobhan and Lynsey. Yes, I imagine. They were pretty inseparable, that last year.'

Both girls had been interviewed, Elder knew. Probed about any relationships Susan might have had with boys, relationships she might, for whatever reason, have kept from her parents. A few tales of parties and underage drinking aside, momentary crushes and the usual furtive fumbling, all of the questioning had yielded nothing.

'When you were talking,' Elder said, 'the two of you, that morning, she didn't seem as if there was something troubling her?'

'No. No. Why d'you ask?'

'The woman in the park shop, she said she'd seemed a little – what was it? – preoccupied.'

Helen looked down at her hands and then up again. 'I don't know what about. I really don't.'

'She also said she heard Susan and her father having a tremendous row, just the day before.'

Helen looked at him steadily. 'It's news to me.'

'But you're not surprised?'

'Not really, no . . .'

Elder waited.

'They were always really close, Susan and Trevor, when she was young. Mummy, let Daddy do it. Let Daddy. Daddy. I'll be honest, I used to get jealous sometimes. I mean, I'd be the one lugging her round the shops in the buggy, pushing her on the swings. Reading the same stories over and over again. Putting up with her moods. What? Seven, eight hours a day. And then he'd come breezing in at supper time and she'd be all over him. How's my little girl then?'

80

Ash fell from her cigarette and, without looking, she brushed it from her skirt.

'It all changed when she went up to secondary. She seemed to pull away. And Trevor resented it, you could tell. The way he looked at her sometimes, as if – I don't know – as if he felt betrayed. As if she'd turned against him.'

'And do you think this was all a part of her growing up, puberty if you like?'

'I suppose so.'

'It wasn't due to any difference in him? The way he was with Susan? Something he'd done?'

'Done?'

The word hung between them, inexplorable.

'No,' Helen said. 'It was Susan who changed. She became closer to me, for one thing. Almost like we were, well, sisters, I suppose.'

'And Trevor felt shut out.'

'Yes.'

Elder was thinking about Katherine, about Katherine and Joanne. The pair of them walking ahead of him, heads together, arm in arm; disappearing for hours into a succession of shops, finally emerging with flushed faces and bags crammed with spoils; hushed conversations on the settee at home which would either explode into giggles or shut off the instant he entered the room.

'How did he react to this?' Elder asked. 'Trevor.'

Helen drew on her cigarette. 'Part of the time he made out he didn't care. Other times, he cared too much. Fussed around her, asking questions – school, friends – forcing himself upon her almost. When he did that, of course, she closed herself off all the more. He'd live with that for a while, you know, pretend he hadn't noticed. And then – it could be any little thing, sometimes it didn't seem to be anything – he'd explode. Real, real anger. Once a month, once a week, less, more. It was like living with a time bomb in the house, never knowing what was going to set it off.'

'He hit her.'

'No. No – well, once or twice. A few times, maybe. When she was twelve, thirteen. She'd wind him up, knowing full well what she was doing. You know how kids can. When he couldn't take it any more he'd lash out. Didn't know what else to do. Once, I remember, we were at my parents', Sunday lunch. He reached right across the table and slapped her face. You can picture the to-do there was about that. Susan ran off screaming, my mother hurrying after her, trying to calm her down; my dad up in arms, trying to lay down the law. Trevor, finally he slammed down his knife and fork and stormed out. Whenever they came to visit after that, he'd find some excuse to be out of the house; either that or he'd feign a headache, lay down upstairs with the blinds drawn till they'd gone.'

'And this was all when she was younger? Hitting her, I mean.'

'I told him if it didn't stop . . . if it didn't stop, I'd leave him. We'd leave him. Susan was coming on fourteen. He knew I meant it, you could tell. I suggested he got help. Talked to someone, a therapist, whatever, if he couldn't control it himself. And, give him credit, that's what he did. He never raised a hand to her after that.'

'But he did still get angry?'

Helen wasn't looking at him now, but was gazing,

82

unfocused, at the floor. 'Every so often, yes. Over things he thought important.'

'Boys?'

'Boys, yes. Or if he thought she'd been lying to him, being deceitful.'

'And was she?'

Helen looked at him now. 'I expect so. Girls are. Usually they have to be.' She stubbed out her cigarette.

'Trevor,' Elder said. 'Are you still in touch?'

'No. Not really.'

'You haven't got an address?'

'Tamworth, somewhere.' She got to her feet. 'I'll get it for you.'

'Those girls you mentioned, I don't suppose you've got addresses for them, too?'

Helen shook her head. 'I don't think so. Not any more. They were really good about keeping in touch at first, Siobhan especially. One of the lads, too. Rob, I think it was. Used to send cards on Susan's birthday, little things like that. But after a while, well, you know how it is – but just let me go and see.'

While she was out of the room, Elder looked more closely at the family photograph and thought about Trevor, off on his own searching for starfish or whatever, while mother and daughter gossiped and giggled like the best of friends.

Helen came back holding a small address book, slightly the worse for wear. 'Here we are, Siobhan Hansen. And that's Trevor's, there. Siobhan's though, it's a good few years out of date, mind. I doubt she's there any more. You could always try the school, though. The big comprehensive. Chesterfield. Used to be the grammar school a long time back. The drama teacher, Mr Latham, he might still be there. I suppose one or two of them might have kept in touch with him.'

'All right, thanks.' Elder noted the addresses down in his book.

Helen walked with him the short distance to the door. 'How much longer will you be around?'

'Oh, another day possibly, I'm not sure.'

She looked as if she was about to say something more, but changed her mind. Whether her wrist brushed his arm or the other way around, it was almost certainly accidental. She watched him for some moments, but turned away before he reached the corner of the street.

12

Pam Wilson had promised her dad she would never follow him into probation, no matter what. It had not been a difficult promise to make. Watching him leave for the office each morning of her childhood at around seven, sometimes as late as seven thirty, urging his arthritic Vauxhall over the hills and out of the county from Todmorden into Huddersfield and then returning back each evening at a similar hour, paperwork with him, had convinced Pam that no one in his or her right mind would opt for a career as a probation officer, overworked, under-appreciated and seriously underpaid.

She and her then best friend, Julie Walker, had sworn on their shared fifteenth birthday that they would dedicate their lives to buying designer clothes, dating only Italian boys, drinking Bacardi and finding jobs that would pay them sufficiently to afford a penthouse flat in the centre of Leeds before they were twenty-five. After taking a degree in business studies, Julie was now, at the grand old age of thirty-seven, marketing manager for the country's second-biggest-selling brand of multi-flavoured potato-based snacks, with an annual income in excess of 70K, excluding bonuses, a leased company car and a water-level dockside apartment on the Thames. Pam thought it had looked somewhat over-the-top in the pages of *Hello!* magazine, Julie holding hands on the white leather settee with Darren What's-His-Name, who'd made his name at Highbury and now was lucky to get off the bench at West Ham.

Pam, meantime, having switched courses during her first year at university, trading history for psychology and sociology, had toyed with the idea of a fast-track career in the police, hated that, rebounded somehow into selling advertising space on television, something for which she was temperamentally unsuited, then spent nine months as a trainee manager in a department store before signing on for a TEFL course with a view to teaching English somewhere warm; after catching a bad case of hives and something infinitely worse and more personal in Barcelona, flat broke and despondent, she had moved back into her old room at home and accepted a post as trainee probation officer.

It was something about which her father never missed an opportunity to tease and chide her. Most usually in the car park, mornings after she'd followed him in her rusting Toyota on the journey to Huddersfield.

Now, at thirty-seven, she drank bitter in preference to Bacardi, the only words of Italian her last date had known wouldn't have stretched far beyond *espresso* and *Di Matteo*, and she was living just along the valley from her parents, in a narrow terraced house in Hebden Bridge. And, although she might not always have admitted it, she found working in probation satisfying. Challenging, frequently; frustrating, certainly; yet strangely satisfying.

Pam would not have been first choice as Shane

Donald's probation officer; not that she lacked the necessary experience, but given the nature of Donald's offence, his history of violence towards women, a male officer would normally have been given the job. But several months earlier, at the time it had been necessary to become involved in the plans for Donald's release, Dennis Robson was on leave of absence with a stress-related illness, Terry Smith had ricked his back on the badminton court, and that left Pam holding, as it were, the baby.

The first time she had met Donald she had been surprised at how much younger than his thirty years he appeared; had surreptitiously checked, in fact, his date of birth on the papers in his file. Since then, the several-days' stubble he had affected, together with his close-cropped hair, made him seem, if not exactly older, certainly stronger, more self-contained. He had answered Pam's questions with a minimum of fuss, brief and to the point, grudgingly polite. Conscious of the magnitude of what he had done. Contrite. Serious about making a new start. Pam thought experience had taught her who to believe, to recognise when the wool was being pulled over her eyes. With Shane Donald she had never been sure.

Risk. How much was attached to his release? None that an uneasy feeling, deep in her gut, could testify to, rationally explain. And others, other professionals, had assessed, weighed in the hand, decided what was appropriate, correct.

On the way to the hostel and her third appointment of the morning, she picked up a coffee and a doughnut and gave herself ten minutes, parked in a lay-by rereading

Donald's file. Low educational attainment, dysfunctional home, victim of abuse, easily led. At the trial, Donald's barrister had alleged that her client was, in his own way, as much a victim as the girl he and McKeirnan had raped and murdered. Pam was less sure. There wasn't a lot she hadn't come across, but, given a little imagination to fill in the gaps, what Donald and his companion had perpetrated on the young women they'd held captive still brought out goose-pimples along her arms; made her look round with a slow chill of apprehension, sitting there alone in her car, a single woman who'd failed to take the elementary precaution of locking the doors.

By the time she pulled the Toyota in to the kerb outside the hostel and parked, she was back in control. Checking the mirror to make sure there was no stray icing round her mouth, she set off towards the front door: five ten and close to a hundred and fifty pounds, strong shoulders and upper arms from playing volleyball, a loose-fitting pale grey suit over a black polo-neck, hair which had once been blonde but had darkened with age cut spiky and short, a leather bag, A4 size, over one arm.

'Pam.' As was his habit, Peter Gribbens greeted her at the entrance, hand outstretched. 'Good to see you.'

'You too, Peter.'

'Let's go into my office, you can talk to Shane in there.'

'If you're sure you don't mind.'

The first time they'd met, Gribbens had asked to which denomination she belonged; on the second, he'd invited her to join him and his lady wife for a day's ramble along the Pennine Way. Drawing a blank on both fronts, he'd since retreated behind the slightly blustering cheeriness that was his norm.

88

'How's he been getting on?' Pam asked.

'Oh, quite well, I think. Quite well. He's quiet, keeps himself to himself. So far, at least. No signs of any aggression. But then, it's early days, early days.'

'Well, the sooner you wheel him in . . .'

'Ah. Yes. Yes, of course.'

When Donald stepped into the room, Gribbens closed the door behind him.

'Shane, come on in. Sit down.'

He did as he was asked, his gaze passing quickly from Pam's face to the window behind her, the walls, the scuffed toes of his shoes.

'So, how do you think you're settling in?'

'All right, I s'pose.'

'No problems with the other residents?'

Donald shook his head.

'How about the staff?'

Donald blinked and chewed on a nail.

'Shane?'

'No, there's nothin'. 'Sfine.'

'You're sure? Because if there's anything bothering you, now would be a good time to say.'

'No, like I said, it's okay.'

'And your room-mate? I assume you're sharing a room?'

'Royal, yeah. He's good. Leaves me alone.'

'All right. Now, there are just a few things about the terms of your licence we ought to go over again, just to make sure they're clear. See if there are any questions you want to ask. Okay?'

Donald nodded. Rules and regulations. He knew about rules, knew the games you had to play. Do this, do that.

89

He had been aware of the clock almost immediately this time, the small click that came with each movement of the hands. Report to me regularly, Pam was saying. Try not to be late. Respect the hours the hostel lays down. If there's every anything seriously worrying you, talk to your key worker first and then to me, all right, Shane? All right? Donald fidgeted a little on his chair.

'What it all comes down to,' Pam said, 'you have to avoid doing anything which breaks the terms of your licence. Anything at all.'

She was coming down hard on him, she realised that, not the best way to keep him trusting her, not at all, but each time she looked at him, that whippet face, the way the skin was picked and sore around his fingernails, she couldn't prevent the images rising in her mind. What he'd done with those hands.

'Shane? You do understand?'

'Yes. Yeah, of course.' And then he smiled his quick and thin-lipped smile and it was Pam who looked away.

'We'll help you to find a job,' she said, recovering. 'Help you to ease yourself back into the day-to-day, but a great deal has to be down to you. This is a chance you've got, a chance in a way you've earned. It's up to you to make it work.'

Donald mumbled something she didn't catch, didn't understand.

Pam shuffled one of the pages from his file in front of another. 'Your sister, Irene, have you been in touch with her yet?'

A shake of the head.

'But you will?'

'Yeah, tonight. Tonight. I was goin' to ring her tonight.'

Donald's elder sister and her family lived close by in Marsden, Pam knew. Somewhere she had driven through numerous times on the way into Oldham and Manchester, little more than a village filtering away on either side of the A62. Irene had been the only member of the family to have visited Donald with any regularity during his time in prison, her presence in the area one of the reasons Huddersfield had been chosen for his relocation.

'We talked about it, didn't we?' Pam said. 'How it would be good for you to spend time with her, her family. Arrange for you to stay for a weekend.'

Donald was remembering Irene's husband, Neville, the look of fierce contempt on his face the last time they had met.

'I daresay Irene might persuade your mother to come down and visit before too long. How would you feel about that?'

Donald didn't say.

'Shane?'

'Yeah, it'd be all right, I suppose.'

Donald's mother hadn't been to see him in prison more than half a dozen times, Pam realised. Perhaps she was ashamed, ashamed at what he'd done. Felt herself in some way to blame.

'There's just one more thing I wanted to mention,' Pam said. 'Make you aware of. One or two of the local papers, near where Lucy Padmore lived, they've been carrying stories for a while now about your release. It's mostly been pretty hostile, I'm afraid. Lucy's father, he's made threats, what he'd do if he found out where you are.'

Donald's hand was at his mouth, teeth tugging a small flap of pink skin from near the edge of his thumb nail.

91

'If it doesn't get taken up nationally,' Pam said, 'and I can't see any reason why it should, there's no reason anyone here should know. But if I were you, I'd be careful who you talk to, say as little as possible about how you offended, just in case. All right?'

A quick nod.

Pam pushed her papers together and dropped the folder down into her bag.

'I'll see you in my office, then, Shane, a week today. Eleven thirty. The details are on my card.'

When Donald left, Gribbens was hovering outside. Once she'd gone over the salient details of the interview, Pam needed a few words about one of the other residents, and then she could be on her way. A quick sandwich and then back to the office, a case conference on a habitual shoplifter pencilled in for two. Before any of that she needed a cigarette. When she'd agreed to share the house in Hebden with a rabid non-smoker, she'd embraced it as an opportunity to give up. The packet of Marlboro Lights in her glove compartment was only there for emergencies. A quarter of a mile along the road, she pulled in and switched off the engine, wound down the front windows midway and lit her first cigarette in almost two months. What had disturbed her most about the interview with Shane Donald was not that for most of the time he had refused to look her in the eye, but that the one time his eyes had settled on her face his mouth had twisted into a smile.

13

Most crimes against children, Elder knew, were perpetrated within the family. Uncle. Step-parent. Mum or dad.
Trevor Blacklock had been interviewed on six separate
occasions inside a week. Someone had had an instinct, a
feeling, but Blacklock had never been cautioned, never
been charged.

The house was in a small crescent, part of a newish estate
near the western edge of Tamworth, garages and front
lawns, semi-detached. The rose bed by the fence looked
well-established; tubs either side of the front door held
geraniums, white and a mixture of reds. Elder had tele-
phoned the previous evening and been greeted by Trevor
Blacklock's brusque 'Hello'. At the first mention of Susan's
name the line had gone dead. When Elder had dialled again,
moments later, the phone had been disconnected.

By now, a little after ten, he assumed Blacklock to be
at work; the sliding door to the garage had been pulled a
third of the way back down, no sign of a car inside. Tins
of paint were neatly stacked along one side; on the other,
a selection of garden tools were clipped to the wall. In
some neighbourhoods, Elder thought, those would have
been liberated by now.

A woman's face showed for a moment at one of the front windows, peering out.

Elder walked up to the door and rang the bell.

She was small, slight, almost bird-like, mid-thirties, a cap of dark hair and brown, nervous eyes.

'I don't suppose there's any chance Trevor's still here?' Elder said.

'Oh, no. He's been gone a good couple of hours. More.'

'Not one for a lie-in, then?'

For an instant, she smiled. 'Chance'd be a fine thing. If he's not in by eight, the garage's hollering down the phone.'

'Shame,' Elder said. 'I was just calling on the off chance.'

'You're a friend, then?'

'More a friend of Helen's, really.'

'Helen?' And then, 'Oh. Oh, I see.'

'I could always call by where he works. Just to say hello.'

'Trevor and Helen, they've not really been in touch . . .'

'No, I know. A shame, isn't it? If you'll just give me a few directions, I'll be on my way.'

There was a child's bike, Elder noticed, leaning up against the hall doorway behind where she stood.

◆

The showroom took up most of the frontage, shiny new cars with men in shiny suits patrolling in between; potted plants with shiny leaves. Reception was off to one side, a shallow curved desk behind which a brittle blonde talked briskly into a telephone, tapping at a computer keyboard with her free hand.

Elder waited until, with an expression of distaste, she set the receiver back down. 'Some people,' she said, 'expect you to work miracles.'

Almost immediately the phone rang again and she put the caller on hold.

'Trevor Blacklock,' Elder said. 'I was wondering where I could find him?'

'Parts. Through that door there, round past the first bay and it's on your right.' A pink nail pointed the way.

A framed certificate was attached to the wall: Trevor Blacklock had gained the gold standard in Parts Management in the company's national training scheme. Blacklock himself stood behind the counter wearing a yellow short-sleeved shirt, his name taped to the breast pocket, just in case there should be any doubt. He was fifty, Elder thought, fifty-two; they were of an age.

'Yes, sir?' Blacklock said. 'How can I help?' The fingers of his left hand toyed with the computer keyboard, ready to begin the search.

'I wanted to ask a few questions,' Elder said. 'About Susan.'

Blacklock stepped backwards and both hands gripped the counter hard. 'How the hell did you get here? How did you know where I was?'

'It doesn't matter.'

'Yes, it does.'

'All right, I asked. I asked your wife. Partner. Whichever it is.'

'You've no right.'

'Look, I don't see why you're getting so het up. Ten minutes of your time, that's all I want.'

'No.'

'Why not?'

'Because you've no bloody right.'

'Listen,' Elder said, his voice level and even, trying to bring things back under control. 'I'm not a reporter. I'm not the police.'

'I know who you are.'

'Then you know I was involved with the investigation when Susan disappeared.'

'I know you lied.'

'Never knowingly.'

'*I'll find her*, that's what you said.'

'I know.'

'So is that what you've done? Is that why you're here now?'

'No.'

'Then get out of here and leave me alone. I've nothing to say.'

A mechanic came in for some front brake pads; a customer wanted replacement wiper blades for an N-reg Vauxhall Corsa. Elder turned on his heel and left.

◆

He gave it one more try that evening. The six o'clock news would just have been finishing and dinner, in all probability, standing ready by the microwave or simmering on the stove.

It was the wife who came to the door, brisk and businesslike now, a little flour adhering here and there to her hands.

'My husband doesn't have anything to say to you . . .'

And then he was there himself, standing behind her,

changed out of his work shirt into a comfortable check, nothing comfortable in the tightness round his mouth and eyes.

'What happened to his daughter all those years ago is something Trevor will always regret. But that was in another life. His life now is here with us. I only hope you can understand.'

It sounded like a prepared statement, a release for the press. And as if to round things off, the perfect newscast moment, a girl of seven or eight, the very image of her mother, appeared in the doorway between them.

'Daisy,' the woman said, 'please go back inside.'

Instead the girl leaned against Blacklock and, automatically, his arm went about her, fingers stroking her hair.

They were still standing there when Elder climbed into his car and switched on the ignition, slid it into gear and began reversing away.

14

'Neutral ground then,' Maureen Prior had said when
Elder had phoned and suggested meeting in the Arbo-
retum, the inner city park that stretched across the centre
of Nottingham, from the eastern edge of the general
cemetery and the Mansfield Road.

It was not Maureen that Elder met first, though, but
Charlie Resnick, Detective Inspector, hands in the
pockets of the shapeless beige raincoat that he wore in all
weathers; Resnick making his way down past the circular
bandstand towards the exit on to Waverley Street. From
there he could walk up through the cemetery to Canning
Circus and the station where his CID team had its office.

'Charlie.'

'Frank.'

The two men stood at roughly equal height, an inch or
so above six foot, Resnick the heavier by a good stone
and a half.

'So,' Resnick said, 'how's retirement then?'

'Not so bad.'

Resnick looked unconvinced.

'You must have your thirty years in by now, Charlie.
You should try it. See if it suits.'

Resnick shook his head. 'I'll soldier on a bit longer yet.'

'Die in harness, eh?'

'Hopefully not that.'

There was a smear of something yellow, Elder noticed, that had dried on the front of Resnick's shirt, close alongside his tie.

'Devon, isn't it?' Resnick said. 'That you've hived off to.'

'Cornwall.'

'What brings you back here, then?' Resnick asked.

'Oh, you know . . .' Elder gestured vaguely.

Resnick nodded. 'Ah, well, best be getting on. Good to see you again, Frank.'

'Charlie. You, too.'

Elder stood and watched him walk away, still light on his feet for such a heavy man. He'd not quite disappeared from sight when Maureen came down the main path from the rose garden, striding briskly.

'Talking over old times?'

'Something like that.'

Maureen nodded. 'I just worked with him the once. Liked him. A good copper.'

'I'm surprised he's still up at Canning Circus, still a DI.'

'Not as if he didn't have the chance. Chief Inspector, Major Crime Unit, back when they were setting up. What I heard, more or less handed to him on a plate.'

'And he turned it down?'

'Too much admin, most likely. Paperwork. Still likes to get out and about, does Charlie. Get his hands dirty.'

'I can understand that.'

'Besides, you remember that DC of his, Kellogg, Lynn Kellogg?'

Elder thought perhaps he did: round-faced, soft-spoken, stockily built, late-twenties.

'They got it together a few years back, just about when the Crime Unit was being set up. Kellogg was in line for a sergeant's post. Could have proved awkward, the pair of them, you know . . .'

Elder knew. He'd seen that sort of thing happen and fall apart.

'Upshot of it was Resnick turned the job down, opted to stay where he was. Kellogg made the jump to Major Crime. This was before the unit was split up on to two sites. Done all right for herself, too. Inspector now, acting up, out at Carlton.'

The other site, where Elder and Maureen had been stationed, was some thirty minutes' drive out of the city at Mansfield, now in a new building which resembled nothing as much as a second-rate hotel.

'And they're still together?' Elder asked. 'Resnick and Kellogg?'

'As far as I know,' Maureen said, and then, seeing Elder's rueful grin, 'What? What's so funny?'

'Resnick. I'd never have thought he was the sort.'

'What sort's that?'

'You know. Younger women. Bit of intrigue. Romance.'

'You don't approve?'

'No, it's not that,' Elder said, though, in truth, he was less than sure. 'It's more I always took him for a bit of a sad bastard, really.'

'Maybe that's part of the appeal.' Maureen grinned. 'That and being cuddly. Not like some I could mention.'

'Let's walk,' Elder said briskly. 'I wanted to talk about Shane Donald.'

◆

There was not a great deal new that Maureen had to say. Both local papers were continuing to run the story of Donald's release, refusing to let it die. For their part, Lucy Padmore's parents had collected several thousand signatures demanding statutory life imprisonment for all murderers, life meaning life. David Padmore was still telling anyone who would listen just what he would do to Donald should he get the chance.

'How long do you think it will be before the whole affair goes public?' Elder asked. 'Plastered all over the tabloids. Reporters doing their damnedest to track Donald down.'

'You never know, he might be lucky.'

Elder didn't think good luck and Shane Donald were acquainted, never mind the best of friends.

'How did you get on up in Yorkshire?'' Maureen said. 'Manage to turn up anything new?'

He ran down his progress for her, such as it was, the largely abortive visit to Susan Blacklock's father, the couple of friends from her old drama group he was still trying to track down.

For a while afterwards Maureen was thoughtful, saying nothing.

'What?' Elder asked eventually. They were standing towards the eastern edge of the park, near the battery of guns that had been brought back from the Crimea.

'You don't think there's a danger she'll get traumatised

all over again, Susan's mother, you dredging this all up now?'

'Of course I do.'

They walked on, under the tunnel beneath Addison Street and up the other side.

'You didn't come down just for this,' Maureen said. 'We could have had this conversation on the phone.'

Elder smiled. 'It's Katherine, she's running tomorrow. The Club County Championships out at Harvey Hadden.'

'You're staying over then?'

'That's the idea. I was going to book into one of those bed-and-breakfast places on the Mansfield Road.'

Maureen made a face. 'Tinned tomatoes and stewed tea with the sales reps over breakfast? Why not give Willie Bell a ring? He's got this place near Mapperley Top, lives there on his own. He takes in lodgers sometimes, on the force, you know. Likes the company, I think, as well as the cash. Nothing fancy, but it's clean. Far as I've heard.'

Elder knew Willie Bell. A DS who'd come down from Dumfries and Galloway ten years since and had still to lose the soft Scots burr to his voice; he'd been married once, Elder seemed to recall. But then so had they all.

'If you've got a number for him,' Elder said, 'I'll get in touch later.'

Taking her mobile from her bag, Maureen pressed *menu* then *phone book* and then *call*. 'Here,' she said, handing it across. 'Why not do it now?'

15

Pam Wilson stood in Peter Gribbens's office, mid-morning, looking at the photograph on his desk. Gribbens and his wife. Vanessa, was it? She thought it was Vanessa. The pair of them in walking gear and half way up some mountain somewhere, .the Lake District probably, both beaming God-given smiles, all right in this particular part of His garden. She'd asked him once, Gribbens, after one of his charges had absconded, taken his trust and shoved in back in his face, how he managed to stay so positive, smiling even, day after day after disappointing day.

'I pray,' he'd said, without a moment's hesitation. 'Ask the Lord for strength and pray.' Then added, laughing, 'And Marmite, of course, toast and Marmite. That and a good, strong cup of tea.'

Pam had never liked Marmite, not even as a child. Marmite soldiers her dad had lined up around her plate. And as for the rest . . . one visit to Sunday school and a now totally implausible pre-teen crush on Cliff Richard do not a Christian make.

The door opened and Shane Donald sidled in.

'Shane. Come on in. Take a seat.'

'What's wrong?'

'What do you mean?'

'I was supposed to be seein' you at your office, that's what you said.'

'That's right.'

'Well then.'

'I was passing, that's all. And I've got what might be good news.'

She sat down and waited for Donald to do the same, his eyes never really seeming to focus, blinking out from beneath slightly lowered lids. Pam this morning wearing a black cotton jacket over a loose grey top, black cords and an old pair of weathered blue Kickers she'd had for years.

'The news. It's about a job. One of the supermarkets, the big ones, they've got a vacancy . . .'

'Not for me.'

'What do you mean?'

'They won't take me on.'

'Why do you say that?'

'You know why.'

'Tell me.'

'Not once they know what I done.'

'They won't. Not in any detail. None at all.'

'They'll know I've been inside.'

'Of course.'

'Then why . . .'

'Shane, look, we've talked about all this before. And besides, I've spoken to them. They know me. They've helped out before. It's part of their policy.'

'Yeah?'

'Yes.'

'This job, what is it then?'

'Oh, working in the store mainly, stacking shelves, that kind of thing. Collecting trolleys from the car park once in a while, making sure they're in the right place. Helping out generally.'

Donald was fidgeting on his chair, chewing his nails, looking at the floor.

'It's a start, Shane . . .'

'It's bollocks, that's what it is.' The sharpness in his voice took her by surprise. 'It's a job for kids jackin' off school.'

'Shane, like I say, it's a start, that's the important thing. Prove you can hold this down and then we'll see. See what else you might go on to. All right?'

No answer.

'Shane?'

Suddenly he was looking at her, his eyes unwavering. 'Is that it?' Donald said.

'What do you mean?'

'All you wanted to see me about?' Half out of his chair.

'No. Not, not really. I was wondering, your sister . . .'

Slowly, he sat back down.

'If you'd been in touch with her?'

'I said I would, didn't I? What's the matter? You don't trust me?'

'No, it's not that at all. I just wanted to know how you got on, what arrangements you'd made. I was interested.'

'I'm meeting her in town, some café.'

'Instead of going round.'

'That's what I said.'

'The first time, I suppose it's a good idea.'

Donald snorted. 'It's him, isn't it? That cunt, Neville.'

'Irene's husband, d'you mean?'

'That cunt, yeah.'

'Shane, please . . .'

'What? What's wrong?'

'Your language, it doesn't help.'

'Language?'

'Yes.'

'About him?' Donald laughed low in his throat. 'You've met him, right?'

'Once. Yes. Briefly.'

'Then you know he's a cunt.'

Instead of counting to ten, slowly inside her head, Pam was remembering a lecture on Suitable Forms of Address in a Multi-cultural Society – when speaking to clients at all costs avoid 'nitty-gritty', 'good egg', 'gobbledegook', 'egg and spoon'. As far as Pam could recall, nothing had been said about the word 'cunt'.

'Shane,' she said, 'why do you feel that way about him? Your brother-in-law?'

'Why? 'Cause he hates my guts, that's why. 'Cause he don't want Irene to have nothin' to do with me. 'Cause he wishes I was dead.'

'I'm sure that's an exaggeration. And we know Irene wants to help, don't we? We just have to hope Neville will come round with time.' She eased back her chair. 'When are you meeting her?'

'This afternoon. Three o'clock.'

'Good. And the interview at the supermarket's Monday morning. At eleven. I'll come with you to that, if you want.'

◆

The café was near the old market hall, small and low, with slatted-wood chairs and round tables that wobbled the instant they were touched. The windows, front and back, were frosted over with steam. Plants trailed haplessly from plastic pots in varying stages of decay. Out of place and out of time, a small CD player splurged out songs of sea and surf: 'California Dreaming', 'California Girls', 'Surf's Up', 'Surfin' USA'.

'A total wank, all that,' Donald remembered McKeirnan saying. 'A total fuckin' wank.'

Himself, he didn't care either way.

'Shane, over here!'

And there was Irene, heavily up to meet him – God! She'd put on some weight. Never pregnant again, was she? Not at her age.

'Shane, it's lovely to see you.'

Kisses all round his face and hugs fit to break his back.

'All right, all right. Okay. That'll do.' Donald, embarrassed, pushing her away.

'Pleased to see you, aren't I?' Irene's face bright with smiles. 'Here,' pushing some money into his hand. 'Get yourself something to drink. Eat, too, by the look of you. Starving you at that place, are they, or what?'

'Looks like you got enough for both of us.'

'Thanks very much.'

She sat with a cigarette, stirring sugar into her tea and waiting for him to get served. Her baby brother. When she'd heard the evidence at the trial, what he and that other bloke had done, she'd felt sick to her stomach; vomited later until the back of her throat was raw.

'So what's it like?' she asked as soon as he'd sat down. 'Are they treating you okay?'

'Yeah, all right. I'm fine. How 'bout you and the kids?'

'Oh, you know.' The oldest, Irene thought, was not much older than Shane had been when he'd gone inside; the second, a girl, was less than a year younger than the one they'd murdered. Murdered and the rest.

'You think I'm going to let him come within a mile of here?' Neville had said. 'Within a mile of our Alice? After what he did.'

And he'd seized Irene's arm and swung her round, twisting it up behind her back, forcing her towards their thirteen-year-old, who stood, uncertain and half-terrified, beside the kitchen door.

'Look at her. Go on, take a good look at her. Go on. Now think back on what he did, your precious bloody brother. And tell me you want him here, in our home.'

Releasing her, he'd slammed through the door, leaving mother and daughter facing one another till Vicky reached out a hand and then, when Irene put out her own hand to meet it, spun away and followed her father into the other room.

'Your place,' Donald said. 'He's not going to let me come, is he?'

'No, love. No,' she said quietly. 'I'm afraid he's not. Not for a while, anyway.'

'I am their uncle, you know. Family. Don't that count for nothin'?'

Less than steadily, Irene lit one cigarette from the butt of another. She'd told herself she wasn't going to cry. She was not.

◆

Donald watched *EastEnders* and *The Bill*, then played pool with Royal Jeavons, winning two games out of five, the best he'd done. When he'd mentioned the supermarket job, instead of dissing him in some way, Jeavons had surprised him. 'Shit, man, it's not cool, but it's a job, right? Not the rest of your life. Six months, innit? After you was inside how long? No. Check off the days, count the time, you know how it goes.' Not long after that Jeavons had got into conversation with a bunch of the others, backslapping and laughing, and Donald had drifted away.

'Everything okay, Shane?' Peter Gribbens met him on the stairs. 'Saw your sister today, I believe. How did that go?'

'Great, yeah. Just great.'

'Off to spend a weekend soon, eh? All the family together.'

'Yeah. Soon.'

'Capital. That's the stuff.'

Donald slammed the door closed and tore the sheets and blanket from the bed, hurled the pillows across the room and turned the bed itself over on its side; he pulled the drawers from the chest and spilled their contents on the floor, tried to overturn the wardrobe and failed, finally threw himself against the wall and smacked his head against it hard. Punched himself in the face. Once, twice, three times, more.

He was on his knees, blood running from his nose, a cut above his eye, when Royal Jeavons came into the room.

'Shit, man. Oh, shit.'

He righted Donald's bed and sat him down, head back

to stop the flow of blood, went back downstairs and returned with some ice wrapped in a towel which he placed over the swelling around the eye. 'Here. Hold that in place.' With a flannel and paper towels, he cleaned Donald up as best as he could. Disappeared again for several minutes and came back with aspirin. A plastic cup of water from the sink. 'Swallow these.'

He set to rights the chest of drawers, then collected the bedding from where it was strewn across the room.

'Best lie down now, right?'

When Donald was curled on the mattress, knees pulled up towards his chest, Jeavons spread first the sheet and then the blanket carefully over him.

'We're gonna have to make up some story for this, you know that, don't you? Tripped and fell downstairs, something Gribbens is gonna swallow. Let's hope it don't look so bad in the mornin', innit? Now you get some sleep.'

Back at his own side of the room, cross-legged on his bed, Jeavons reached for his Walkman and slipped the headphones in place over his head.

16

Katherine was drawn in the outside lane, Elder feeling the
tension in his stomach as, along with other runners, eight
in all, she jiggled and stretched, waiting for the starter to
call them to their marks. Three hundred metres, less than
a complete circuit of the track. Katherine's hair tied back
behind her, her competitor's number lifting a little in the
May breeze. And now they were moving to their places,
a final stretch from Katherine, reaching high above her
head before easing her feet down into the blocks and then
leaning forward, fingers splayed, just nudging the edge of
the line, shoulders tense and arms taut, eyes focused and
head perfectly still. The gun, sooner always than Elder
could anticipate, and they were off, Katherine well away,
but so were they all, fifteen metres, twenty-five, thirty.
The stagger making it impossible to judge which of them,
if any, had the early advantage.

Katherine, by virtue of her position, was first into the
bend, the rest stretched in an almost perfect half-chevron
behind her. The national standard was 40.70 seconds,
41.60 the entry standard required for the English Schools
Championships. The figures drummed into him.

One of the three black athletes, muscular and strong,

was gaining ground now in the second lane; tall, with pale skin and long, flowing hair, the girl immediately inside Katherine was matching her stride for stride; the three of them with a clear space between themselves and the rest as they came out of the final bend and into the straight. Elder aware that he was shouting Katherine's name, loud above the noise of the crowd that had gathered close to the finishing line. The black runner forcing ahead, two strides, three, and then Katherine coming back at her, drawing level with twenty metres to go, mouth open, chest pushed forward, head back; the two of them, neck and neck, head to head and stretching for the line until the tall girl surged between them, breasting the tape, hand punching the air in triumph.

All around Elder excited voices, recounting the finish of the race, and all of his attention upon Katherine as she squatted near the side of the track, head bowed, staring at the ground.

◆

'She did well.'

Elder turned at the sound of his wife's voice, tense again but in a different way.

'Don't you think so?' Joanne said. 'She ran well.'

'Yes, she did.'

She was wearing a leather jacket, artfully creased and aged, a bleached blue T-shirt and what looked like new blue jeans, red-and-white Nikes on her feet. Green eyes. Pale lipstick on her mouth, pale pink. Either she'd been spending time on the sunbed or she and Martyn had been off to where? Sardinia? The Bahamas? Tenerife?

'She was unlucky,' Elder said.

'Second place.'

'It was close.'

'You think she could have been third?'

'We'll have to wait for the announcement.'

'Yes.'

People moved around them, changing positions, waiting for the next event, the next race.

'I didn't know you were here,' Elder said.

'Of course I'm here.'

'I didn't see you.'

'No.'

'Joanne . . .'

'Yes?'

'It doesn't matter.'

She looked older, he thought, no obvious make-up masquerading the tiny lines crinkling away from the corners of her eyes: older and all the better for it. He would have reached out for her if he could.

'You here long, Frank? Just up for this or what?'

'A couple of days probably, two or three.'

'Where are you staying?'

'Mapperlcy Top. Friend of a friend.'

'You'll see Katherine?'

'I hope so.'

'I would say come round, Frank, only . . .'

A shake of Elder's head, a smile around his mouth. 'It's okay.'

She took a pace towards him and he stood his ground. 'Why don't you meet Katherine when she's changed? I'll wait at the car.'

'You're sure?'

She nodded. 'Of course.' And then, 'You're looking well, Frank. That Cornish air, it must suit you.'

'Something like that.'

He was thinking of the first time he had seen her, a little over twenty years before. A day off and he had gone into Lincoln. Wandering aimlessly up the cobbled street towards the castle, passing time really, little more, not looking where he was going; Joanne had stepped out of a coffee shop and bumped right into him, the impact knocking her nearly off her feet. Elder's hands had reached out and caught her, surprise and anger on her face changing quickly to a smile.

'Goodbye, Frank,' she said now.

Foolish to stand there and watch her walk away.

◆

Katherine's face was set into a scowl, sports bag slung over her shoulder, her hair still damp from the shower. Elder took her into an awkward embrace, a hug from which she instinctively turned, his kiss missing her face and just catching the back of her head.

'Well done.'

'Don't joke.'

'I'm not.'

'You saw what happened.'

'You came second.'

'I clocked the same time as the girl in third.'

'You were second, a close second.'

'I fucking lost.'

'Katherine.'

'What?'

114

Elder shook his head. The reproof had been out of his mouth before he could think.

'I had the race,' Katherine said, 'and I lost it.'

Elder held his tongue; in the face of her anger, he didn't know what else to say.

'I got past Beverley. I was cocky. I didn't think, I wasn't aware. I eased off.'

'No.'

She cocked her head, questioningly. 'What? You were running and not me?'

'No. I was watching. And it didn't seem to me . . .'

'I eased off.'

'Okay, if you say so.' He reached for her hand and she pulled away.

'Your mum's in the car.'

'Yeah, right.'

'I'll walk down with you.'

'Suit yourself.'

They reached the edge of the car park in silence, Katherine acknowledging one or two of the other athletes with a curt nod on the way.

'So what's next?' Elder asked. 'Running, I mean.'

'There's an inter-counties next month. The English Schools – always assuming I'm selected.'

'You will be, surely.'

'Not necessarily.'

'You were well inside the qualifying time.' Hers had been announced as 40.43.

'You know what the record is, English Schools?'

Elder shook his head.

'38.35. Run like I did today and I'll get creamed. I won't even get through the heats.'

'Then you'll run faster.'

'Oh, yeah? And how'm I going to do that?'

Elder shrugged. 'Train. Toughen up.'

There was little humour in Katherine's laugh. 'Dad, you're full of shit.'

'Thanks.'

'My pleasure.'

Dipping his head he kissed her on the cheek and this time she let it happen. The faint, acerbic taste of sweat that hadn't quite washed away.

'I could meet you somewhere tomorrow. Lunch, maybe?'

'I don't think I can.'

She read the disappointment, clear on his face.

'How about coffee?' she said. 'I could do that.'

'All right.'

'I've got to go and get this book from Waterstone's. They've got a place upstairs, I could meet you there.'

Elder shrugged. 'Anywhere.'

'Eleven thirty, then. Okay?'

And with a swing of her bag she was away, Elder hesitating, but only until Joanne, getting out of the Range Rover to greet her, had folded her arms around her, Katherine dropping her bag by her side. *It's Mum,* Katherine had said. *You should have loved her more.*

I should have loved you both more, Elder thought as he moved away. Loved something else less – the job, myself. Maybe I loved you both as much as I could. A melancholy thought, but not necessarily untrue.

17

Donald was immediately awake, not knowing what had woken him or why. No sound. Nothing other than the occasional acceleration of a car on the slope of road outside, the creak of a board as the house settled and shifted in its own time. Outlines in the room were clearer now: bulky, angular furniture, the covered shape of Jeavons in the opposite bed. Goose-pimples along Donald's arms and he wondered why. In prison, the first years especially, he had woken often sheathed in sweat, a nightmare of body parts and objects glistening with semen, blood and shit. Metal and glass. Jagged. Smooth. Screams and laughter. McKeirnan's laughter. The therapy had helped, that and the medication, allowed him to offload, come to terms. Sleep. But not now.

He reached out and checked his watch: two seventeen.

Pulled the covers high over his shoulder and turned back to face the wall; the already familiar resistance of the mattress beneath his hips and arm.

'Shane.'

The voice so soft it could have come from somewhere inside his own head, his own brain.

'Shane.'

117

Still soft. Insinuating.

'Shane.'

Holding his breath, Donald swung back around. It was someone else, not Jeavons in the bed.

'Who . . .?'

Where was Royal? Why wasn't he here?

'Wakey-wakey, Shaney. Rise and shine.'

A torch flicked on, held below the chin, lighting up the face, and Donald recognised him then, one of a bunch of four or five who hung together, clustered in corners, spat out remarks, made jokes, dared others to stare them out, answer back. Clayton? Carter? Claymore? Cleave? That was it, he thought. Cleave.

'No guardian angel, Shane, looking after you. Not tonight. Downstairs with mates of mine, watchin' videos. Porno.' Cleave laughed. 'Better'n layin' here listenin' to you whimper in your sleep. Mind you, surprises me, Shane, after what you done, you can sleep at all.'

Cleave's voice not soft now, hardening.

'No conscience, Shane? No fucking conscience? That what it is?'

In one quick and supple movement, Cleave was out of the bed and on his feet, T-shirt, briefs, Stanley knife in his hand, the blade extended.

'There's people looking for you, Shane, you know that? The father of that girl you killed. He wants to find you. Do you harm.'

With one sweep, Cleave sliced through the sheet Donald was holding, opening it from near top to bottom, stem to stern.

'Like that,' Cleave said, 'the sound of your guts spilling out.' And laughed. 'Your tripes.'

118

Moving fast, he brought the blade upwards until it was under Donald's nose, the intersection with his upper lip, the first dribble of blood seeping down into his mouth, the smallest of cuts.

'Next time,' Cleave said and laughed again. A quiet laugh. Mocking. 'Next time, unless . . .'

He backed away and from underneath Jeavons's pillow pulled a newspaper, folded flat. 'Here.' Shaking it open, he held up the torch so that Donald could read. 'My brother sent me that. He comes from down there, see, knew about you, what you were inside for, what you'd done. And he's been down the pub when her old man's been hollerin' on about what he'll pay to know where you are. Padmore, yeah? Five grand, he reckons. More. And why d'you think, eh, Shane? Think he wants to shake your hand?' Another laugh, a touch more pressure on the blade. 'No, Shaney, he wants to kill you, that's what. Hurt you first. Hurt you bad. What you done to his little girl.'

Cleave stepped away. Not far.

'One phone call, that's all. All it'd take. Five grand. And why shouldn't I? Eh? One call. All that money, that cash. And me a model citizen. Seein' you get what you deserve.'

'Don't.' Donald's voice was faint and unsure.

'What? What's that?'

'Don't. Please don't.'

Cleave sniggered. 'Please. I like that. Please. But what you gonna do for me, eh? What'm I gonna get for not turnin' you in? Eh, what, Shane, what?'

'I don't know.'

'What? Speak up?'

'I don't know.'

'I tell you what,' Cleave said, kneeling now beside the bed, his face close to Donald's own. 'You can get me money, that's what you can do.'

'I haven't . . .'

'What?'

'I haven't got any money.'

'You can get it, though. Got a sister, ain't you? See, I know. Nothin' goes on in this place I don't know. You can get money from her.'

'No.'

'Sure you can. Beg for it, borrow it, steal it if you have to. I don't care. Just so long as it's there. Long as you do what I ask, what I tell you.' The blade moved from Donald's nose to rest against the eyelid, just above the eye. 'My slave, Shane, that's what you're going to be. Get me money, clean my shoes, fetch my tea. I've always wanted one of those, a slave, a – what do they call them? That film I saw 'bout public schools. A fag, that what it is?' He laughed. 'You'll be a fag, all right. I give the word, you're going to get down on your knees and suck my cock, lick my arse, do anything I want. Right, Shane? Right? Otherwise, I'm going to make this call. Let Lucy Padmore's dad know exactly where you are. And you don't want that, do you, Shane? Do you, eh? Shaney, eh?'

'No,' Donald said quietly. 'No, I don't.' And closed his eyes.

◆

When Elder arrived on the upper floor of the bookshop, Sunday morning, Katherine was already sitting there, knees up, in a chair against the window, reading a magazine. A tall *latte* and *pain au chocolat* on the small table close by.

Elder ordered filter coffee and a muffin and joined her. More than half of the other seats were already taken. On a low seat, a woman sat with a book and an orange juice, unselfconsciously feeding a baby at her breast. At one of the other tables, a bespectacled man pecked away at the keyboard of his laptop. A middle-aged couple riffled through the sections of the Sunday paper, passing them to and fro, pausing to read from items which caught their fancy.

'Is this a regular haunt?' Elder asked.

Katherine shrugged. 'Not really. It's just somewhere to go.'

'And you need that?'

'Of course. Yes. Sometimes.'

'Are things difficult then, at home?'

'No.'

'But if . . .'

'Don't push it, dad, okay?'

Okay. He broke off a piece of muffin and it crumbled in his hand. The coffee was fresh, maybe not quite as strong as he'd hoped.

'I'm sorry about yesterday,' Katherine said, 'after the race. I was in a foul mood.'

'It's all right.'

'Yeah, well, I shouldn't've jumped down your throat like that.'

'You were upset. Angry.'

'I shouldn't have been angry with you.'

Elder ate a piece more muffin, offered some to Katherine, who shook her head. 'Are you really doing something at lunch-time?'

'Really.'

'When we've finished this, can we go for a walk at least? Just, you know, around. It's a while since I've been here, you know. Things change.'

'Okay.'

Outside, they walked along Bridlesmith Gate, passing close by Cut and Dried, one of Martyn Miles's hairdressing salons, the one which Joanne, as far as he knew, still managed. Neither of them referred to it or glanced in its direction. Low Pavement, Castle Gate and the subway carrying them beneath the steady traffic along Maid Marian Way. To the Castle then, a quick walk around the grounds, a turn around the bandstand, chatting sporadically but easily, nothing important, not really, this and that. He bought Katherine an ice-cream and for a moment she was a child again. Dad, can I have a treat? When can I have a treat?

Leaving the Castle, they went up a string of narrow streets and round on to Upper Parliament Street, past what had still been a large Co-op department store when Elder had last come this way. Five minutes later and they were dropping down towards the Old Market Square, the usual coven of heavy drinkers stretched out on one of the raised patches of grass.

'Will I see you again?' Elder asked. 'This trip, I mean?'

'That's up to you.'

'I'll phone.'

'Call me on my mobile.'

'Same number as before?'

'Same number.'

'Okay.'

He kissed her on the cheek and she kissed him back, a

squeeze of his arm and she was away. Elder crossed the square and began walking up King Street to where there he knew there was a Pizza Express. The Odeon in the city centre had closed down, as had the ABC, but there was a new multiplex apparently where the *Evening Post* building had been. He wanted to chase up some of Susan Blacklock's old drama group but that would have to wait till after the weekend. He'd pass the time watching a film instead.

In the event he fell asleep in row G, barely disturbed by the smell and persistent rattle of popcorn, the almost permanent undertow of whispered voices.

◆

His room in Willie Bell's house had a three-quarter-size bed – a double if you're on good enough terms, as Willie explained – a book shelf partly stacked with old Rothmans' Soccer Annuals and back copies of *Penthouse* and *Police Review*. There were two upright chairs and a small square table, a narrow but deep armchair with dodgy springs, and a built-in wardrobe inside which a dozen or so metal hangers jangled whenever the door was pulled open. A small television set stood on a wooden chest in the corner, an alarm clock with luminous hands on the floor beside the bed. The window looked out on to an array of rear gardens, lights burning behind half-drawn curtains and coloured blinds at the back of the houses opposite.

As a welcoming gift, Bell had placed a bottle of Aberlour on the table, along with a single thick-bottomed glass.

Elder sat for a while, listening to the sounds of Bell's own TV rising up from below; the muffled bass tones of music through the party wall of the house next door; dogs sporadically barking, one setting off another until they all fell quiet and then, high and unworldly, the cry of a fox, a pair of foxes in rut.

He picked up both bottle and glass and carried them downstairs.

A few hours later both men were comfortably settled in the front living-room, the remnants of a take-away curry piled to one side, the Aberlour two-thirds gone. Willie Bell had been holding forth on Partick Thistle and Kilmarnock; the duplicity of women, wives in particular; the beauty of the farming country into which he had been born. Elder nodding and from time to time contributing the odd word.

When the phone rang, Bell picked it up and growled his own name; after listening for a moment, he passed it across.

'Shane Donald,' Maureen said, 'he's done a bunk. We've just been officially informed. He's unlawfully at large.'

18

Pam slipped the lock behind her and set off along the terrace to the path that would take her quickly up above the town. Trainers, grey sweat pants and matching hooded top. When she'd first moved into the house in Hebden Bridge, she had persevered with her morning run, hills or no. But after stumbling twice on the uneven ground, her left knee, already weak, was liable to go out at the least excuse, so now it was this, the briskest of thirty-minute walks, arms swinging wide across her chest, pumping to push her heart rate up. The first part of her route skirted a small wood, after which a narrow lane, edged on one side with bilberry bushes, lifted her on to an old track, largely overgrown and running east to west, which still climbed until it levelled out and she would pause and turn, the whole valley below her, breathing in long, slow draughts of air.

Mill chimneys, long disused, stood tall above the rows of houses, densely packed, the canal running through them like a thread. Across the valley, the fields rose sharply, cross-hatched with low stone walls, farm buildings sparsely set down and exposed on the north-facing slopes.

To the right, rising above a cluster of distant rooftops,

rose the church tower at Heptonstall, burial place, so her house-mate Danny had informed her, of the poet Sylvia Plath. Said with some solemnity as though he was expecting her to set out on an instant pilgrimage, be impressed. But Pam had read some Plath at university, an adjunct to second-year psychology, 'Lady Lazarus' and 'Daddy', hysterical and overheated in Pam's estimation. The poor woman terrified. And then to end it all as she did, life too much to bear at thirty, her head in an oven, gas full on. Why several of Pam's fellow students revered her as some kind of feminist icon and kept posters of her alongside those of Virginia Woolf and Janis Joplin in their rooms, she'd never properly understood. Martyrs all, maybe, in a way. But role models, not on your life.

She turned and set off briskly along the track; another few hundred metres and she would scale a wall, slip through a sheep field, climb a gate and begin her descent.

◆

Shane Donald, Gribbens had phoned her from the hostel the morning after he had gone missing. Something had set him off, panicked him perhaps. Gribbens had spoken with his room-mate and learned nothing; he would talk to the other residents and find out what he could. Scarcely any money, few clothes, Gribbens thought he might not get too far; with any luck he could even change his mind, see sense, come back.

By now the police would know that Donald had absconded and be on the lookout for him, though with what degree of purpose she wasn't sure. People remembered, though, what Donald and McKeirnan had been convicted

126

for, the details albeit hazy and magnified with time. It wasn't lodged in the folk memory like Brady and Hindley or the Yorkshire Ripper, Mary Bell, those boys who had killed poor Jamie Bulger. But for some, in certain parts of the country in particular, they were still there in the shadows where parents' imaginations strayed, nights when their teenage daughters were late home, last bus and last train gone.

'What you did, Shane, you and Alan, how do you feel about it now?'

'It were wrong, weren't it? Course it were. Dead wrong.'

As Pam turned the key in the front door, she made up her mind that she would clear something from her crowded schedule, pay a visit to Donald's sister, see what, if anything, she knew.

◆

Behind the unclipped hedge, the meagre patch of garden was home to several children's bicycles – mostly missing some crucial element like a wheel or handlebars – an upturned pram, assorted toys. Plans for a flowered border had foundered in dog shit and neglect. The front door was partly open, the bell no longer worked.

Pam called out to announce herself and after several moments Irene appeared, apron over a man's shirt and crumpled skirt, slippers on her feet, the kind Pam's mother wore when she was alone, pink and comfortable with pom-poms over the toes.

'I don't know if you remember me?' Pam said, showing her card.

'It's Shane, isn't it? He's got hisself in trouble again.'

'He's gone missing from the hostel, I'm afraid.'

'Daft wee sod. You'd best come in.'

When the children, five of them, had left that morning it had been like a hurricane. Plates, socks, school books, coloured mugs and magazines, odd trainers and discarded clothes were strewn higgledy-piggledy on every chair back and surface and across the floor. A small child with wide dark eyes and tangled hair remained behind, beneath a ratty blanket on the settee.

'That's Tara, she's off sick,' Irene explained. 'Tara, pet, d'you want anything to drink? Some juice? A glass of milk? Hang on while I put kettle on, make this lady and myself a drop of tea.' And then, over her shoulder to Pam. 'If I said I'd stopped for two minutes since seven this morning, I'd be a liar. And Neville, he's no help. Sets 'em off, that's what he does. Shouts till they're screaming and moaning, the eldest yelling back at him, then out he goes and slams the door. Leaves me to it. Milk, I daresay, and sugar. One or two?'

'No sugar, thanks.'

'Suit yourself.'

Pam cleared space on a chair and sat down. When she smiled at the little girl – five, Pam thought, five or six – the girl pulled at the blanket and buried her head.

'You've not come looking for him here,' Irene said, passing Pam her tea. 'Waste of a journey that. Not set foot in this place, not with Neville the way he is. Won't let him near the kids, you see, that's what it is. I know when we talked before, about Shane coming out of prison, well, I thought I could change his mind. Neville. Thought I could talk him round. But he won't budge. After, you know . . . well, you can understand.'

Pam thought that she could. 'I just thought you might have some idea,' she said, 'why Shane might have left the hostel, where he might have gone.'

'Me?'

'You talked to him, just the other day. I thought he might have given some clue.'

'No, love. Didn't say a great deal about anything, to be honest. Not his way. Asked about the kids an' that. Oh, said as how you was fixin' him up with some job. Supermarket. He did say that.' Irene drank some of her tea. 'There's biscuits if you'd like, I should've said. Digestives and there might still be a few custard creams.'

Pam shook her head. 'No, thanks, I'm fine. The hostel, did he say anything about how he was settling in?'

Irene gave it thought. 'Bloke he was sharing with, okay he said, especially for a black. That was about all.'

'He didn't give any indication that he was thinking of running away?'

'No. No. Not a one.'

'And you haven't any idea, Irene, have you, where he might have gone?'

'No, love. I'm afraid I've not.'

'How about home? Sunderland?'

'Last place he'd go. Last place on earth, I should've thought.'

'And are there friends . . .?'

Irene reached for and lit a cigarette. 'Knew him as well as you should, that's not a question you'd ask. Not the sort as makes friends easily, our Shane. Better for him maybe if he did. Unless they're like that rotten bastard, of course. The one as led him on.'

Pam nodded and tried some more of her tea, weak and

over-milked. 'If he does get in touch with you . . .' she began.

'He'll not.'

'But if he does, please tell him to contact me. I can help. It might not be too late to straighten things out. Otherwise I'm afraid he's going to be in real trouble.'

Reaching out, she set a card down on the arm of Irene's chair.

For no apparent reason, the little girl began to snivel, then to cry.

'I will help him,' Pam said, on her feet. 'It's my job.'

'For Christ's sake, shut it, Tara,' Irene said. 'I'm not putting up with that row the rest of the day.'

She walked Pam the length of the short path and through the missing gate.

'He had a bastard life, you know. Shane. Everyone on to him. Growing up. Runt of the litter, you know how it is. If he'd topped hisself before now I'd not've been surprised.'

Pam nodded and said goodbye. When she turned the car around at the end of the street and drove back past, Irene was still standing there. Pam waved and got no response.

'I thought she'd never fucking go,' Shane Donald said, the moment his sister got back inside the house. 'Thought you were going to sit there gassing for hours. Interfering bitch.'

◆

Donald had waited, watching the house, until Neville and the kids, all except Tara, had gone. Irene opening the door

130

to him, a gasp of surprise before hustling him inside, his clothes in a state from sleeping rough, face and hands grimed with dirt; running a bath and then breakfast, bacon, egg and beans.

Shaven-haired, jumpy, Donald twitched at each new sound. Thirty years old and still, save for what lived in his eyes, looking seventeen. Her baby brother. How many years had she pulled him, sobbing and broken, into her arms? Ssh, Shane. Ssh, pet, it'll be all right. She reached out for him now, fingers barely touching his arm before he pulled away.

'This bloke at the hostel,' she said, 'the one as threatened you. Couldn't you tell somebody? You know, somebody in charge.'

'Jokin', right? Imagine what'd happen to me if I did that. Be lucky to get out of there in one piece. 'Sides, wasn't him, only be someone else.'

'Suppose, you know, you'd paid him, given him some money . . .'

'What money?'

'Come to me, like he said.'

'And what?'

'I'd've given you what I could.'

Donald laughed. 'Bingo money? A tenner? Fifty quid? How long d'you reckon he'd keep his mouth shut for that? When someone's offerin' his brother five fuckin' grand.'

'You don't know if that's true. He could've just been saying that to wind you up.'

Angrily, Donald pushed his plate and mug away. 'I saw the paper, didn't I? Her father mouthing off.'

Irene looked at him then. 'Here,' she said, reaching

across the table, 'I'll just clear these pots away.' Anxious to be free from his gaze; not wanting him to see the tears in her eyes and know they were not for him but for someone she had never seen.

◆

He followed her upstairs while she was sorting through her husband's old clothes for whatever was halfway suitable, whatever he might not miss.

'Where will you go?'

'I dunno. Wales, maybe.'

'For God's sake, what for?'

'This bloke inside, he reckoned you could live dead cheap. Just pickin' up the odd job, like.'

'You'll let us know?'

'Hm?'

'Where you are? Send a postcard or something?'

'Yeah, course.'

So far Irene had found a pair of jeans that would be all right with a belt, rolled up; two shirts, three T-shirts, a jumper with paint down one sleeve, assorted dodgy underpants and socks. Neville's feet were huge; the shoes Shane was wearing would have to do.

'She was your age, wasn't she? The girl. Lucy.'

Shane stared at her until she looked away. When he got up and left the room, she finished stuffing the clothes down into an old sports bag.

'Another cup of tea before you go?'

'No, thanks.'

The probation officer's card was in Irene's hand. 'Here.'

'What's that?'

'Take it.'

'What for?'

'Maybe you should go and see her.'

'Yeah. And maybe I should just turn myself in.'

'Shane, she might be able to help.'

'Help put me back inside, you mean.'

'No. She said she'd be able to straighten things out.'

'Yeah? And how's she hopin' to do that?'

'I liked her. For one of her kind. She's straight, I reckon. You could trust her.'

'You think?'

'It's got to be better than just goin' off to Wales or wherever. Somewhere you don't know.' She put her hand on his and this time he didn't pull away. 'You should try. The probation officer. Give her a chance.' She squeezed his hand tighter. 'Promise me, Shane. Promise, yes?'

'I've got to go.'

'Here.' She pushed a twenty-pound note and a packet of Silk Cut into his hand. Hugged him and awkwardly he hugged her back. There were two cheese-and-pickle sandwiches and a Mars Bar tucked down inside his bag. He had already taken the sharpest of the small knives from the kitchen drawer; that bastard Cleave had got the better of him in the hostel and he wasn't about to let it happen again.

'Go on then,' Irene said. 'You better go.'

And closed the door so that she would not have to see him walk away.

'Mum!' Tara shouted from the other room. 'Mum, I want a drink.'

'Coming.'

◆

When Neville arrived home from work the two eldest were upstairs playing Eminem on their tinny stereo and shouting along; Alice was sitting with Tara on her lap watching TV; Brian was out back, kicking a ball up against the wall. Irene sat on the settee, a can of Strongbow in her hand, cigarette in her mouth, tears streaming down her face.

'Fuck this for a game of soldiers!' Neville shouted. And without bothering to close the front door behind him, he set off down the pub.

◆

Pam's early-morning walk on the tops seemed to belong not just to another day, but another time altogether, almost another country. Her frustrating visit to Shane Donald's sister aside, most of her hours had been spent chasing down clients who had missed their appointments or trying not to lose her cool with those who had managed to arrive. Plus, the ACO had taken her to task for what he obviously considered shoddy paperwork and then, as she was leaving his office, dropped another hint about her furthering her career with an MBA. In the midst of all that there had been a phone call from Gribbens at the hostel: some kind of intimidation seemed to have been behind Donald's abrupt departure, but so far he'd failed to uncover precisely what kind and who was responsible.

At five minutes past seven, she finally switched off her computer, dropped a couple of files down alongside the Nick Hornby in her bag for late-night reading, switched off the lights and headed for the door.

The ACO, she was glad to see, was still at his desk, while everyone else had jumped ship. Her car sat at the far side of the almost deserted car park, close against the wall.

Inside, she turned the key in the ignition and automatically switched on the radio, punching through the stations and finding nothing to claim her attention before returning the car to silence. Her shoulders were stiff and tight and there was an ache low in the small of her back. What she needed was a swim followed by a sauna, maybe a good massage, some tender loving care. What she did was flick open the glove compartment and reach for her cigarettes. The radio again and this time she chanced on something part-soul, part-jazz, a woman's voice, a saxophone. Inhaling deeply, she leaned further back in her seat and closed her eyes.

'Don't move,' Shane Donald said, a whisper inside her head.

For a moment, she thought it was fantasy, a dream.

Then the tip of the knife pressed sharp against the nape of her neck.

19

Elder had arranged to meet Katherine in the city centre after she'd finished her training and at quarter past the hour he was still there, pacing up and down between the stone lions at one end of the square. All around him, girls in skimpy dresses, abbreviated skirts and halter tops, chattered, giggled and smoked, before heading off to one of the nearby pubs with their mates. Some stood on their own – young men and women both – pretending not to check their watches, feigning nonchalance until the person they were waiting for walked into view.

Twenty past.

Twenty-five.

He had made a quick call to Maureen earlier and caught her just as she was coming off shift: no news of Shane Donald so far. But then, as she said, early days. They made a tentative arrangement to meet for a drink the following evening, when he got back from his meeting with Paul Latham, the drama teacher at Susan Blacklock's old school. Maureen brisk but not unfriendly, businesslike on the phone.

His mind moved from Maureen to Maddy Birch, with whom he'd worked – what? – fourteen or fifteen years before. A good officer in her way, Maddy, if lacking Maureen's single-minded drive. A good copper and a woman, he had picked her to work with him interviewing Donald for that very reason, because she gave off a certain warmth, a softness even, a suggestion that she cared. Whereas with Maureen most of the time gender was forgotten, not an issue unless she chose it to be.

To his right a girl with dark, curly hair and high heels, a woman really, threw her arms around the neck of a grinning man and kissed him on the mouth.

He wondered where Maddy Birch was now, a DI somewhere most probably in one of those small towns in or around the Wolds, Market Rasen or Louth. Or maybe she'd chucked it in, got married, two kids on a nice estate outside of Lincoln, ferrying them back and forth from school to Guides or whatever in a four-by-four. One night, late, the pair of them more than a little drunk after someone's leaving do, they had stumbled into a doorway and he had found his hand against her breast. When they separated, moments later, breathless, he had seen, illuminated in the shop light from across the street, the amusement bright in the green of her eyes.

'Dad! Dad!' It was Katherine, sports bag on her shoulder, hurrying towards him past the fountains. 'Dad, sorry I'm late.'

◆

When they headed up into King Street from the square, Katherine had assumed her father to be aiming for Pizza Express, but instead Elder led her across the street to Loch Fyne Oysters, something of a treat.

'What's this in honour of?' Katherine asked.

'Nothing special,' Elder said. 'Why?'

'It's just . . .' She gestured vaguely with her hands.

'What?'

'Nothing, Dad. Nothing, okay?'

They were seated across from one another in a high-backed booth, the restaurant already three-quarters full. The waitress brought them their menus, ran through the day's specials, and left them to decide.

'Anyway,' Elder said, 'I bet you've been here with your mother scores of times.'

'She and Martyn prefer Sonny's.'

'I see.'

Elder asked for a beer and Katherine, after a surreptitious glance at her father, a glass of house white. Each studied the menu with care.

'All right,' Katherine said, leaning forward suddenly. 'I'll tell you. Bringing me somewhere like this, a bit special, it's as if . . . It makes me think you're going to, I don't know, make some great announcement or something.'

'About what?'

'I don't know.'

'Well, such as?'

'You're leaving the country, maybe. Emigrating. New Zealand. Canada. Or you've met someone. You're getting married again.'

'I'd have to get divorced first.'

'Don't joke.'

'I'm sorry. I didn't know it bothered you.'

'What?'

'Me being with someone else.'

138

'Are you?'

'No.'

'Well then.'

'In fact, I seem to remember you saying it was a good idea.'

'That was different.'

'How so?'

'That was going to bed with someone, that's all. I thought it would do you good.'

Despite himself, Elder was smiling. 'Thanks very much.'

'I didn't mean anything really serious. You know, living together. Moving in.'

'And if I were, whatever you'd call it, part of a couple, something permanent, would that really matter?'

'To me, you mean?'

'Yes.'

'Of course.'

'But why?'

'Because it would change things.'

Elder reached for her hand. 'Things have changed, sweetheart. They changed three years ago.'

'I know.'

Katherine had crab and then roast cod; Elder a small bowl of mussels followed by halibut steak.

'Well,' Katherine said, raising her glass. 'I've got something to celebrate even if you haven't.'

'Tell me.'

'The inter-counties. I've been selected.'

'Excellent.'

'Just don't say I told you so.'

'I told you so.'

Katherine poked out her tongue and for a second she was transformed, in Elder's eyes, back to barely twelve, long-legged, hair twisted in a single plait, school uniform askew.

After coffee, they stepped out on to the street and almost collided with a couple laughing, walking arm in arm.

'Sorry,' Elder said automatically and as the man raised a hand to signify okay he caught sight of Katherine, stopped and grinned.

'Hi, Kate.'

'Hi.'

He was in his twenties, Elder guessed, leather jacket and jeans, the girl with him a little younger, spiked hair above a dark green bandana, cream silky trousers, spangly top. The man's grin broadened as he looked from Katherine to Elder by her side.

'Oh, this is my Dad. Dad, this is Alan. He teaches at our school.'

'Good to meet you, Mr Elder.'

Elder nodded.

'Well, got to be going. Have a good evening.'

They stood a while and watched them cross the street.

'Does he teach you?' Elder asked.

'No.' Katherine shook her head. 'Modern languages, French and Spanish. Mostly lower down the school.'

'Nice-looking girl he was with,' Elder said.

'Yes,' Katherine said. 'She's in the upper sixth.'

20

Pam didn't know how long she had been in that position, leaning back against the headrest on the driver's side, the point of Donald's knife not quite steady against her skin. Time enough for her breathing to have steadied, the tune on the radio to have changed to something more languorous and inappropriate. All of the time willing herself not to look too obviously towards the probation offices where a single light still burned. Diagonally across the car park the ACO's Volvo waited. If he were to call it a day and come out now, he would surely see her there, her silhouette behind the wheel, walk over to ask if she were all right.

But nothing happened. No one came or went.

'Shane,' she said quietly, keeping her voice as even as she could. 'Please, put the knife away.'

As he leaned forward, Donald's breath was warm on the side of her neck, her ear. 'Not on your life.'

'But there's no need.'

'I don't trust you.'

'But you're here.'

'Irene said you'd help.'

'I can. So I can. But not like this.'

She started to turn and with a small jump of Donald's hand, the knife point punctured her skin.

'I told you.'

'I know, I know.'

She could smell him in the small space of the car, his sweat, his fear meshing with her own.

'Shane, look, there's nothing I can do. To harm you. Why don't you just put away the knife and we can talk. Talk sensibly. We could go back inside, my office . . .'

'No!'.

'All right, all right, we'll talk here. Only you have to put away the knife.'

'How do I know I can trust you?'

'Because you can.'

'You're lying.'

'No, Shane, I'm not.'

'First chance you get you'll turn me in.'

'That's not true.'

The music on the car radio was replaced by the station signal and then a man's voice, smug and earnest, selling life insurance.

'Shane,' Pam said, 'I'm going to move.'

'No.'

'I have to. My back, it's really hurting me. I just want to sit up, that's all. There.'

She could see his face in the mirror now, off-white, anxious, a film of sweat above his eyebrows, along the bridge of his nose.

'Shane,' she said, addressing the reflection. 'Your sister said I could help you and she was right. But you do have to put down the knife first. All right?'

'Street Life' started up through the small door speakers, perky and bright.

'Shane?'

She held her breath as the pressure of the blade lessened and then disappeared.

'Okay, I'm going to turn round now.'

'No!'

'Well, let me turn this off at least. Then we can hear ourselves properly.'

Mid-syllable, the singer's voice disappeared. There was silence in the car, the outside sounds of passing traffic distant and remote.

'So go on then,' Shane said. 'Tell me. If you're gonna help, tell me what you can do.'

Lies collided inside Pam's head as she hesitated, unsure what to say. His situation was difficult and getting more so by the moment. This ludicrous business with the knife. What was he thinking? And even if she were to keep silent about that, even then, the consequences of what he had done were severe.

'Look,' she began, 'there's one thing you have to understand. After what you did, leaving the hostel, breaking curfew, your licence will have been revoked. There's nothing anyone can do about that.'

'You mean I have to go back inside.'

'Yes.'

The side of his fist slammed against the car window. 'Then what's the fucking point!'

'The point is I can help you sort it out, what happened, what it will mean. Try and find a reason for what you did. Help you explain.'

Donald said nothing, shifted a little in his seat.

143

'When you left the hostel,' Pam said, 'was that because someone had threatened you in some way? Because if it was, if you thought you were really in danger, well, that would be a reason, wouldn't it?'

'And make it okay?'

'Not exactly. But I'm sure it's something the Parole Board would take into consideration.'

'You'd tell them.'

'Yes, I suppose I could try and . . .'

'You'd tell them. Speak up for me. Explain.'

Pam drew breath. 'I'd make a report . . .'

'I don't want a fuckin' report!' The knife was back, close to her face.

'All right, all right. I can speak to them directly, I'm sure I can. But, Shane, listen, this is important. You have to put the knife down now. For good. Give it to me. And then you have to go – I'll come with you if you want – you have to go to the nearest police station and turn yourself in.'

'No.'

'Shane, listen. The sooner you do that, the better it will be. Then we can sort out exactly what happened and I can try to help you explain. But you have to hand yourself over to the police. You have to. There isn't any choice.'

Neither of them had heard the approaching footsteps until they were almost at the car, the ACO calling Pam's name as he bent towards the window, hand outstretched to tap upon the glass. Even as Donald's right hand was opening the offside door, his left was reaching across the seat to snatch her bag. Moments later he was scrambling over the low wall and out of sight, the ACO shouting at shadows and Pam leaning forward, head against the windscreen, hands gripped fast around the wheel.

◆

The ACO accompanied Pam to the police station and remained with her, solicitous, while she made her statement. Despite her assurances that she was all right, no more than a little shaken up, the police doctor had examined her, applied antiseptic cream and an Elastoplast to the back of her neck and suggested she take a couple of Nurofen. Pam had been to the cash point that lunch-time, which meant there had been not far short of a hundred pounds in her purse, alongside the usual selection of plastic. She could cancel the credit cards, of course, would do as soon as she got to a phone. An hour, perhaps a little more since arriving at the station, she was sitting with a cup of tea and a cigarette when tears started to run, soundlessly, down her face and she began to shake. The ACO patted her gently on the top of her shoulder but, careful in these matters, abstained from holding her hand.

Newly appointed, the police superintendent was eager for his officers to get to grips with something other than Friday night drunk and disorderlies, taking and driving away, street-corner dealing and the usual spate of unresolvable domestics. Having a convicted murderer unlawfully at large and quite possibly still on your patch was one thing, him coming after his probation officer with a knife was another. Robbery and grievous bodily harm. Catch the little bastard and sling him back inside and he'd be in incontinence pads and fighting off Alzheimer's before he got the right side of the Parole Board again.

All of the extra activity that ensued was not lost on the local crime reporter, who promptly pulled in a few favours, not least from the detective sergeant with whom he regularly shared a jar after hours, and then arranged for a photographer to snatch a couple of candid shots of Pam as she left the station, still looking a little dazed. The reporter was a stringer for one of the nationals, which, along with several of its rivals, had been keeping half an eye on the local furore about Donald's release, waiting to see if it blossomed or faded on the vine. And now the news editor, mindful of circulation wars and the doctrine of market share, sent hacks scurrying through the files, ferreting out as many tasty details of the original crime and resultant trial as would play well in the current climate. All right, sixteen-year-olds didn't jerk the paedophile cord as strongly as when the victims were barely adolescent, but there was enough of it there in the shadows to add a little bite to the Why Release These Monsters angle. Several ounces of sexual prurience whipped up with a pint or so of righteous indignation and you'd tapped in to the heart of middle England.

So, he bellowed across the news room, get your sorry arses up there, Huddersfield, get a story out of that probation officer and, unless she's a complete dog, lots of pictures; while you're there, check out the hostel, see what you can worm out of the other inmates. Oh, and our stringer reckons this lad who's bolted's got family up that way, a sister, something like that. Let's get our hands on her before somebody else does. Then there's this Padmore who's been shooting his mouth off all over the local Notts. press, the one whose girl was raped and murdered. Let's see what we can do to freshen that up a little, give it a new angle. Last up, this Donald, what about the bloke who arrested him? How does he feel seeing his work go to waste? And what sort of a depraved bastard did he reckon Donald for anyway? Okay, what are you still standing there for? Let's move it.

21

A traffic accident had closed the motorway north, an articulated lorry slipping its load and causing a twenty-three-car pile-up and blocking all three lanes; the tailback was already at fourteen miles and counting. Diversions had been posted. Elder settled for the back lanes that sent him scuttling through Langley Mill and Codnor, the twisting camber of the road testimony to the disused mine shafts that burrowed higgledy-piggledy below ground. Due north then through Alfreton and Clay Cross till, close to Wingerworth, he could see Chesterfield's famous crooked spire leaning above the rooftops.

He had arranged to meet Paul Latham in the old market square – medium height, medium build, medium sort of bloke really, flower in the buttonhole, that ought to do it, not a great call for that sort of thing in Chesterfield, always excepting funerals, that is. In the event, Elder picked him out easily, sitting on one of the corporation benches, head in a book: rose-pink carnation, unfashionably long hair curling up against the collar of his pale corduroy suit, a soft leather shoulder-bag close by.

'Mr Latham?'

'Paul.'

'Paul, then. Frank. Frank Elder.'

Latham's grip was firm and quick.

'It's good of you to make the time.'

Latham smiled. 'Either this or some benighted version of macaroni cheese. Mounds of chips.'

'What do you suggest?'

'No shortage of pubs. Though not while you're on duty, I dare say.'

Elder shook his head. 'I've not been that for years.'

'I thought . . .'

'Sorry, perhaps I should have made myself more clear. I retired from the force a while back. This is just . . . well, personal, I suppose.'

'I see.'

Elder wondered if it were his imagination, or had Latham looked relieved on learning the visit was unofficial?

'A pub would be fine,' Elder said.

They found a corner where they could talk, Elder giving in to the thought of food and ordering a Melton Mowbray pie to accompany his half of bitter, Latham settling for a fruit juice and some KP nuts.

'Drama, then, that's what you teach?'

'That and a bit of English. Media studies too, I have to teach that now.'

'Looking at advertising, newspapers, stuff like that?'

Latham laughed. 'Mostly watching old episodes of *EastEnders*, then justifying it with some sociological waffle.'

He was still quite boyish when he laughed, Elder thought, good-looking in an arty kind of way. Difficult to pin down his age, but not as young as first impressions suggested. Somewhere close to forty-five. Which would have made him thirty when Susan Blacklock disappeared, possibly a year or so younger.

'You remember Susan?' Elder asked.

'Of course.' Latham's face took on a serious bent. 'A lovely girl. Special.'

'In what way?'

'Ah. Where to start? She had a good brain, for one. She was able to understand things with more maturity than most. Relationships, for instance.'

'Relationships?'

'Between characters.'

'You mean in drama, plays?'

'She could get beneath the text, between the lines.'

'And this made her special?'

'For someone her age, yes, I think so. Especially when you consider her background.'

Elder looked at him sharply. 'I don't think I understand.'

'Usually, when you come across something like that, scratch the surface and you'll find dad's a writer, mum's some leading light in rep at least. But in Susan's case, well, if you've ever met her parents you'll know what I mean. Perfectly nice people but I doubt if they've got an original idea between them, and if there's a book in the house that isn't Catherine Cookson or Tom Clancy, I'd be surprised.' Latham tipped another palmful of nuts into his hand. 'Nothing amiss with that, don't get me wrong, but it's not the kind of background to foster creative thought and understanding.'

Elder could feel Latham getting under his skin. 'How do you account for it, then, this skill, if that's the word, that Susan had? Was it some kind of intuition or what?'

'Something she was born with?' Latham chewed thoughtfully. 'I think that's true as far as it goes. It was a gift. Some kind of throw-back, possibly. But that wouldn't account for everything. No, she was alert, eager to learn, immersed herself in whatever we were doing, worked damned hard. It was as though . . .' Fingertips pressed together, for a moment Latham's eyes closed tight. 'It was as though she didn't want to be where she was and drama – acting, theatre – that was a way of releasing her, taking her somewhere else.'

'Where exactly?'

Latham smiled. 'Who knows?'

Elder persevered. 'She was different to the others then, her friends? What were some of their names? Siobhan. Lynsey.'

'It's a matter of degree. Seriousness. It was all more of a game for them. Not that they were devoid of talent, mind. Siobhan even went on to drama school, fashioned some kind of a career.' He lifted his glass. 'She turns up in *The Bill* every once in a while, usually playing some tart.'

'And is that what Susan wanted, do you think, to be an actress?'

'An actor? No, I don't think so.'

Elder used his knife to augment a slice of pork pie with mustard. 'Susan, you never heard anything from her after that summer? A postcard, the odd phone call, anything like that?'

'No, not a thing. If I had, I'd have informed her parents, the police.'

'Of course.' Elder chewed, then swallowed down some beer. 'And Siobhan? Lynsey?'

'Yes. They've been pretty good about keeping in touch, both of them. Christmas cards, you know. A note from Siobhan if she was in something, bit of radio, a telly.'

'You've got addresses for them, then?'

Latham gave it some thought. 'Lynsey, I'm not so sure. But Siobhan, yes, I think so. Somewhere in London. But how up to date it is, I'd hesitate to say. They lead a bit of a nomadic life, you know, actors.'

'You wouldn't mind letting me have it, all the same?'

Latham hesitated, uncertain.

'I can always track them down some other way,' Elder said. 'This would make it easier, that's all.'

'Very well.' Latham scrambled in his bag and came up with a bulging Filofax; five or six addresses beneath Siobhan Banham's name had been crossed out and replaced. 'Here you are – London, NW1.'

Latham uncapped a ball-point, pulled a sheet of blue paper free from the back of his organiser and wrote the address down in a neat, slightly curlicued hand.

Elder thanked him and slid the address down into his top pocket.

Latham looked at his watch. 'I really did ought to be getting back. First lesson, Tuesday afternoon. Third-year drama. If I'm not there on time they'll have dismantled the hall.'

Outside, Elder offered his hand. 'The boys in the group, was Susan interested in any of them?'

Something passed across Latham's face, impossible to define. 'Interested?'

'You know, girlfriend, boyfriend. Attraction. Friendship. Sex.'

152

'Not as far as I was aware.'

'And you would have known, I mean, had it been anything serious.'

'Not necessarily.'

'But you must have seen quite a lot of them out of school, theatre trips and so on. If there'd been something going on . . .'

'I might have noticed, I suppose. But no, no, I'm sorry, I'm afraid I can't help you there.'

Elder held his gaze.

'I'm wondering why you ask?' Latham said.

'Oh, nothing special. Curiosity, I suppose. Trying to fill in a few gaps.'

'I see. Well, as I say, I must . . .'

'Third-year drama, you must get back.'

'Yes.'

'Thanks again for your time.'

Elder watched him move briskly away, sidestepping the lunch-time dawdlers and window-shoppers, women with pushchairs, young men grazing on take-away burgers and battered chicken, small children who would neither be bullied nor cajoled. He was thinking of what Latham had said about Susan Blacklock wanting to be released, taken somewhere else. Wasn't that what all children, all young people, wanted at some stage of their lives, teenagers especially? All those day-dreams: fantasies in which we are foundlings, the parents we have grown up with not our real parents at all.

He was almost at the edge of the square, heading back to where he had parked the car, before the newspaper headlines caught his eye. *KILLER AT LARGE. PROBATION OFFICER HELD AT KNIFEPOINT*. He rummaged in his

153

pockets for some change. High on the right of the page was a photograph of Shane Donald as he had been in 1989, and, blurred beneath the fold, a picture of himself leaving the court after the guilty verdict on Donald and McKeirnan had been returned.

◆

Maureen excused herself from her colleagues when she saw Elder enter the bar.

'You've seen this?' he asked, slapping the newspaper with the back of his free hand.

Maureen nodded. 'They didn't even catch your best side.'

He bought her another half, a Jameson's and a chaser for himself, and they managed to find themselves a spot where they didn't have to shout above the electronic cackle of games machines or the sports channel on the overhead TV.

'You know what sticks in my craw?' Elder said. 'The way they come on all holier than thou, as though they're doing some kind of public service. Making the likes of Shane Donald into a media celebrity.'

'And driving him further underground into the bargain.'

Elder nodded. 'To say nothing of dredging up all the details of what happened and splashing them all over the inside pages.'

'Sells papers.'

'Without a doubt. I wonder what it does to the victims' families?'

'According to the *Post*, Lucy Padmore's father's angry enough already; this'll just about send him ballistic.'

Elder was thinking about Helen Blacklock, reading possibly about the horrendous things that had been visited upon Lucy and imagining her own daughter suffering in the same way.

'How goes your own little inquiry?' Maureen asked.

When he'd finished giving her an abbreviated account of his meeting with Paul Latham, her face creased into a smile.

'What?'

'Didn't exactly get your vote for personality of the month.'

'Not exactly.'

'You think there's any more to it? Other than the two of you not hitting it off?'

'I don't know.'

'But you'd like to think there might be.'

Elder shrugged and tasted his whiskey. 'Anything definite would be good.'

'You'll go and talk to that woman in London? The actress.'

'I'll give it a shot.'

He asked Maureen about her current case load and they chatted about the job through another round of drinks, one or two other off-duty officers wandering over to exchange a word, bid Maureen good-night, cast an eye over her companion.

'Grist to the rumour mill come morning, I dare say,' Elder remarked.

'Good luck to them,' Maureen said.

'Another?' Elder asked, pointing towards her empty glass.

'Best not.'

'Maddy Birch,' Elder said. 'Name mean anything?'

'DI, isn't she? Lincolnshire somewhere. Your old patch. I've run across her a few times in the past. Nothing recent, why?'

'Oh, no special reason. Just thought you might know where she was stationed.'

Maureen angled back her head and laughed. 'Feeling horny, Frank?'

Elder had the grace to blush as he was reaching for his coat.

Outside a light drizzle of rain was falling. 'You don't fancy something to eat, I suppose?' Elder said.

Maureen shook her head. 'No, thanks.' And then, smiling, 'Should've asked me before you started on about Maddy Birch. Mind you, answer'd still have been the same. Good-night, Frank.'

◆

He picked up a doner kebab with chilli sauce at the take-away not so far from Willie Bell's home. Wherever Willie was it wasn't there. Elder found a beer in the fridge, tipped the food out on to a plate and sat down in front of the TV. On a street illuminated by neon and watered down with artificial rain, a couple of New York cops were rousting druggies in shop doorways, talking fast out of the sides of their mouths. He had Katherine's mobile number in his wallet, but it was probably too late to call. And it wasn't Katherine he was thinking of but Joanne. At the athletics stadium, the blue of her T-shirt, fit of her jeans. *I would say come round, Frank, only* . . . Joanne, Maddy Birch – what was it, Elder wondered, about green eyes?

156

He finished his kebab, switched off the set and went upstairs to bed.

◆

First thing next morning, Pam Wilson was doorstepped outside her house and although she pushed her way past the reporters, refusing to speak, she knew they would find ways of putting words into her mouth. By eleven, Irene had invited one compassionate young newsman in for a cup of tea and before the quarter-hour thought better of it. By then it was some twelve or thirteen minutes too late. Come afternoon, her husband, Neville, had been offered an exclusive contract for his story, a murderer in my family, or something similar, and signed on the dotted line.

Of Shane Donald there was not a sign.

22

Four hours, near enough, that's how long it had taken him to get a lift, hanging around the lorry park, asking drivers who, more often than not, brushed past him without so much as a word. Manchester, mate. Manchester. Come on. If he'd been some tart with fishnet stockings and a skirt up her arse, like the one he saw scrambling up into the cab of an eight-wheeler carrying auto parts, there'd have been no problem. But instead there he was, hands in pockets and shoulders hunched, rain needling into his face. Give us a lift, eh? Bastard. Bastard. Bastard. Cunt.

Earlier, he'd warmed himself up in the cafeteria, meat pie and chips, a packet of fags, tea with plenty of sugar. The cash he'd found in the probation officer's bag would last him a while if he was careful, eked it out; fat chance he had of using her credit cards, forge the signature well as he might. No way some boss-eyed shop assistant was mistaking him for Pamela Wilson, her name scrawled large across the strip on the reverse. First chance he got, he'd sell them, let somebody else take the risk of getting caught.

In the end it was some foreigner who picked him up, Dutch, three times a week he made the journey, Rotterdam to Immingham and then the M180, M62, Leeds, Bradford, Manchester and back. Glad of the company. Inside the cab the usual photographs, torn from the pages of soft-porn magazines. They hadn't been on the road five minutes before the driver pushed a cassette tape into the deck. 'Blues. You like blues?'

Donald didn't know.

'Fabulous Thunderbirds. I saw them in Holland. Just last year.'

'Oh, yeah.'

'Listen to this. "Look Whatcha Done".' He cranked up the volume a little more. 'Kid Ramos. Some guitar, huh? You like it?'

Donald thought it was like a circular saw working through his head.

'Okay, so what kind of music you like? Come on, you have to talk, yes? Keep me awake. What kind of music?'

'I dunno.'

'Yes, you must.'

The Dutchman pulled out to overtake another lorry and the spray from the road washed across the windscreen like a wave. Donald remembering those evenings in the caravan, McKeirnan telling him, sit down, sit fucking down and listen to this.

'Eddie Cochran,' Donald said. 'That's who I like. Gene Vincent and Eddie Cochran, stuff like that.'

'Yes.' The Dutchman's face broadened into a tired smile. 'Eddie Cochran, "Fifteen Flight Rock". I know this.'

Donald thought it was twenty, 'Twenty Flight Rock', but he couldn't be bothered to argue. He closed his eyes and feigned sleep.

He must have slept in earnest. Next thing he knew he

was being shaken awake, the driver leaning towards him, shouting in his face. 'Come on, you have to wake up.'

The lorry's indicator flashed off and on, reflected on the surface of the road.

'We are here now. End of journey.'

They had pulled some little distance off the motorway and stopped by the entrance to a small industrial estate, the buildings, most of them, shadowed in darkness.

'Come. You have to go now. I will get into trouble.'

Donald yawned and rubbed his eyes with both hands. It felt cold, a chill running up through him. In the half-light he could see a uniformed guard approaching the gate.

'Where the fuck are we?'

'Manchester.'

The Dutchman reached past him and pushed down the handle, opening the cab door.

'Goodbye, Eddie.'

'What?'

'Eddie Cochran,' the Dutchman said and laughed.

The bag his sister had given him in one hand, Donald jumped to the ground and moved aside as the lorry juddered forward. At least it's not fucking raining, Donald thought. By the time he'd worked his way back on to the main road it was.

On either side, warehousing, blank and featureless, was interspersed with empty, chain-fenced lots.

'Where the hell am I?' Donald said to no one. 'Manchester? This isn't any soddin' Manchester.'

At the first roundabout, there were signs to Oldham, Rochdale, Stalybridge, Ashton-under-fucking-Lyne. When, after what seemed like the best part of half an hour, the first car appeared and Donald stepped off the kerb, arm out and thumb angled forward, the driver veered sharply towards him and skidded through a standing puddle of water, soaking him from the waist down.

'Fucking bastard!' Donald shouted after him. 'Fucking cunt!'

Manchester City Centre, the sign read, twelve miles.

◆

Both the chief and the ACO had urged Pam to take some time off, go away, a short break, a little holiday; stay home if you must, paint the bathroom, varnish the stairs. All of those appointments in her book were suddenly, it seemed, less important; they could be rescheduled, dealt with by other staff, indefinitely postponed. Had she thought all this was primarily out of concern for her well-being, rather than that of the service, she might have been better pleased. As it was, she needed to work, to sit there at her desk, have that distraction.

When the two uniformed officers came in, her first thought was that Donald had been found, that something – she didn't know why she thought this, or what she feared, except that she was sure it was something bad – had happened to him. But when they opened what looked like a grey bin-liner and lifted out her bag, she knew it was something altogether less.

'You recognise this?'

'Of course.'

'It's yours?'

'Yes.'

'The one that was stolen?'

'By Shane Donald, yes.'

'There isn't room for doubt?'

Pam looked again at the bag. 'No. No, none at all. Where was it found?'

'I don't know if we can . . .' one officer began.

'Motorway services,' the other said. 'M62 west. The men's toilets. Stuffed down the back of the cistern.'

'I don't suppose my purse was there?'

'Afraid not.'

'If we could ask you to identify the contents?' the first officer said.

From a separate bag, her belongings spread slowly across the centre of her desk. Appointments book, address book, files, her copy of *How to be Good*, several dog-eared letters she'd been meaning to reply to but had never found the time; tell-tale shiny blue paper from too many bars of Cadbury's Fruit and Nut; a lighter and matches but no cigarettes; two black Bics and a stub of pencil; tampons, business cards, postage stamps, keys.

'That's all yours?' one of the officers said.

Pam nodded. 'It's all mine.'

'Sorry about the purse,' the second officer said. 'Hope there wasn't too much cash inside.'

'Enough.'

He smiled sympathetically.

'Never mind,' Pam said brightly. 'Perhaps it's gone to a good cause.'

Neither of the officers seemed to appreciate the joke, if joke it was.

'There's no news, I suppose?' she asked. 'About Donald, I mean.'

'Can't really say, miss.'

Miss? What had he been doing, reading her hand for signs?

'Not likely to tell us, even if there was.'

'I can keep the bag now?' Pam asked. 'My stuff?'

She could. The two men nodded, mumbled and left. Tweedledum and Tweedledee. She doubted if either of them was as much as twenty-four or -five. Their visit not the only thing lately to make her aware of her age, conscious of her mortality. A knife being held, albeit shakily, against the skin, against the neck, will do that to a person, Pam had found.

She hated it; hated him. Donald. The way he'd made her feel then. Vulnerable. Afraid.

The way he was making her feel now.

◆

He had bought a bacon roll, two rashers nicely greased and ketchup running down the edges of the cob; tea in a lidded polystyrene cup and a Twix. There was a park across from the parade of shops, benches here and there along a narrow path, a broken roundabout and some kids' swings, patches where the grass had been kicked to mud. At the far end, a brick-built toilet stood close against the road. The bench Donald chose was grafittied over like the rest, one of the wooden slats missing at the back. He sat minding his own business, washing down the last of his roll with a final swig of tea, thinking about McKeirnan. In his place, now, what would McKeirnan have done? What would he have been doing now?

A pair of magpies screeched down from the trees and hopped about on the ground nearby, disputing over a

163

piece of shiny paper that had blown there from one of the overflowing bins.

The truth was, of course, McKeirnan would never have got himself there in the first place.

Alan McKeirnan who could talk his way out of most things, turning on the blarney, the crack, the charm. Not that he was Irish nor anything like it, not really. Oh, a couple of generations back maybe, his grandad or his great-grandaddy over from County Wicklow or so, slaving on the railway, digging out some bloody great canal, whatever job it was called for muscle and but little brain. McKeirnan's father though, he'd been in the building trade, a brickie by day, playing guitar and singing by night. Pubs the length of Kilburn High Road, Harlesden, Royal Oak. Sometimes with two or three other fellers, sometimes by himself. 1959, three years before Alan was born, he'd auditioned for this rock-and-roll group, Johnny Kidd and the Pirates. Bass guitar. Kidd had pulled his amp lead out mid-number, laughed in his face and then, so the story went, felt sorry for him and hired him as his roadie. For a while. Johnny Kidd and the Pirates.

When McKeirnan got really drunk, really into it, late at night and smashed on pills, it was their records he'd put on, their songs he'd sing, thrash along to, playing air guitar. 'Please Don't Touch', 'Shakin' All Over', 'Linda Lu'.

'My godfather, you know,' McKeirnan used to say. Drunk and a little exhausted, three in the morning and the booze all but gone, stretched out on the floor with a spliff in his hand. 'My fucking godfather, Johnny fuckin' Kidd.'

It wasn't true.

McKeirnan had told him the truth one day, the two of them setting up on a fair site at Cleethorpes; a clear blue morning, Donald remembered, cold, not a cloud in the sky. 'He asked him,' McKeirnan said, 'my old man asked him, come, you know, to the church, the christening, and Johnny said – that wasn't his real name, that was Fred, Frederick, Frederick Heath – anyway Johnny said sure, sure I'll be there and then, of course, he never came. Didn't matter, my old man said, he told me he'd do it and that's good enough. Anyone asks you who your god-father is, you tell 'em, Johnny Kidd; tell 'em that and watch their faces change. Course, Johnny was already dead by then, killed in a car crash when I was only four. Somehow my old man always managed to forget that.' McKeirnan's laugh was sour. 'Probably never even asked him at all, lyin' cunt.'

A mother was pushing a small child on one of the swings; a bunch of eight- or nine-year-olds were chasing a ball. A couple of men wearing long coats and woolly hats were sitting three benches along, passing a bottle of cider back and forth between them. Cars, Donald noticed, would pull up at the kerb alongside the toilets, stay parked for five or ten minutes, then drive away.

McKeirnan's father had ended up like that, Donald remembered, worse still, sleeping rough on a bench in Kensal Green, sneaking into the cemetery at night and sheltering from the weather. Cheap cider, cans of lager, four for the price of three. The occasional bottle of port. Miniatures of whisky. Anything. He was dead by the time McKeirnan was barely twelve years old. His mother a memory and little more. For a year or so, he was passed

165

around the family like old washing, borrowed clothes. Then foster homes, forever running away. Fairgrounds became his natural home.

'Johnny Kidd now, I'll tell you,' McKeirnan had said, another occasion this, watching the tide go out at Camber Sands. 'Johnny, he had the right idea. Got himself killed well short of thirty, car crash, bang! Like Eddie Cochran, James Dean. Before he got tired and old.' McKeirnan had paused to light a cigarette. 'Cochran, the crash that killed him almost did for Gene Vincent too. Bust up his already busted leg. Poor bastard was already trying to drink himself to death, should've ended it there. I saw him once, you know, some uncle of mine took me to this rock show, Lowestoft, somewhere like that. Great Yarmouth. I was eight or nine. This fat bloke came out on stage with a brace on his leg. Black leather. Face puffed up so you could scarcely see his eyes. Pathetic. Few months later he was dead from ulcers. Ulcers. What kind of a fuckin' death is that?' He grabbed Donald by the front of his shirt. 'I'm alive past thirty and you're still here, you find me, right. Fuckin' find me and do me in, I don't care how. Yeah? You promise? You fuckin' promise?'

Of course, Donald had given his promise. What else could he do?

And now McKeirnan was way past thirty. Close to forty and locked up inside a prison where he had not spoken to anyone, by way of what might pass for conversation, in years.

If he were here, what would McKeirnan do?

Another in the ever-changing parade of cars passed slowly along one side of the park before reversing to a halt. On his feet, Donald watched as a man wearing a blue suit got out of the car, locked it and looked around quickly before disappearing into the Gents.

◆

Donald stepped inside and walked towards the urinals, the man in the suit the only other person there. Donald stood two places along and unzipped his fly. After a couple of moments he glanced sideways towards the man and the man winked. He was fiftyish, Donald guessed, with a round, reddish face, overweight. The man winked again and Donald nodded back.

Without zipping himself up, the man backed away and entered one of the cubicles, leaving the door ajar. Donald could see him in there, playing with himself, trousers below his knees.

Donald spun around, moving fast, swung his foot and kicked the door back hard. The man shouted and tried to rise, but by then the knife was inches from his face.

'No! Don't! Please.'

'Pockets, empty 'em now. Now!'

A fumble of wallet, cash, keys.

'Put 'em down, down on the floor. Now push 'em, with your foot, over here.'

Donald scooped up the wallet and the money, kicked the house keys back against the wall.

'Car keys.'

'No, I can't.'

The knife jabbed fast towards his eyes and the man flinched, shielding his face with his forearm. Donald kicked him in the chest.

'Car keys, now.'

He snatched them from the man's hand and jumped backwards, slamming the cubicle door shut as he went. McKeirnan had let him drive a few times when he had been either too tired or too drunk and Donald wondered if he would remember how. It took him several minutes to get the car started and figure out the gears, and all that time the man in the blue suit sat in the cubicle weeping, trousers bunched around his shoes.

23

Give or take a few minutes the train to St Pancras was on time. Elder had spent the journey reading or gazing out through the window, endeavouring to blank out the pervading babel of mobile phones. After several days of fairly miserable weather, the fault apparently of something that did or didn't happen over the Azores, the morning was bright and sunny, the grass shining like silver in the fields. The book he was reading was *A Kestrel for a Knave* by Barry Hines, about a boy from a pit village who trains a hawk. They'd made a film of it which Elder had never seen. Puny and put upon, the boy is bullied at school and half-ignored at home; without the hawk, the kestrel that learned to come to his glove and that he grew to love, he would have had nothing. Drifted. Become what?

Growing up, Elder thought, whatever kind of family we come from, we need something extra, important. For Katherine it was running, for Susan Blacklock it had been drama, and for Shane Donald . . . for him it had been Alan McKeirnan. Fairgrounds and early rock-and-roll and the doling out of pain. Sex and pain. Control. And now, after thirteen years in prison, half a life, almost, of institutions, he was on the run. Out there somewhere on his own. Wreaking what harm?

On the fields the sun still shone as brightly, feathering the trees; a small child, riding a tricycle at its mother's side, stopped and waved at the passing train. Elder closed his book and closed his eyes. In less than twenty minutes they would arrive.

◆

The area of London Siobhan Banham lived in seemed a good way from the nearest tube; the streets around St Pancras and King's Cross were jammed fast, the line waiting for taxis long and slow. Elder checked his *A–Z* and decided he would walk. The prostitute at the corner of Goods Way scarcely glanced up at him as he passed; seventeen, Elder thought, eighteen at most, bruises round her neck, long-sleeved top hiding the tracks on her arms.

A strange miscellany of car-repair shops lined one side of the street and in amongst them premises selling second-hand office furniture and dubious antiques. A small park gave way to the St Pancras Hospital, then some new office buildings and the entrance to a garden centre, the road rising above a canal. Flats now, low blocks in yellowing brick, leading to terraces of late-Victorian houses and then Camden Square. South Villas led off from the top end: solid properties long since divided into flats. Siobhan lived in the third house along, second floor, the name Banham printed in neat purple ink amongst others alongside the door.

'You're not the plumber?'

'Afraid not.'

'Then you must be the policeman.'

'Guilty as charged.'

'Come on up.'

Siobhan was shorter than Elder had anticipated, with pale skin and a shock of startling red hair. Scarlet, Elder would have ventured had he been pushed. She was wearing jeans and a long and loose white collarless shirt. Her feet were bare.

'Every time I switch on the washing machine, I flood the kitchen floor,' she explained on the way up the stairs. 'You don't know anything about washing machines, I suppose?'

'Sorry. Bit of a launderette man myself.'

'Oh, well. Come in, come in.'

A white cat sat curled on a low settee over which brown-and-orange striped material had been draped, brightly coloured cushions scattered along its length. Narrow Indian rugs lay on polished boards. A metal table, painted grey. Books and CDs on shelves, in boxes, at intervals across the floor. Theatre posters on the walls. On one of them, the Gate at Notting Hill, Elder spied Siobhan's name near the top of the cast, the list alphabetical.

'Nice place,' Elder said.

'Yes. It's great. I can't afford it, of course. Shared till a month ago. Tina got pregnant and decided to go home to Kirkwall. Can you imagine what it's like living on Orkney?'

'No.'

'Neither can I. Tea or coffee?'

'How about tea?'

'I'm sorry to be such a cliché, but all I've got is herbal. Peppermint or camomile.'

Elder smiled. 'The coffee isn't dandelion?'

'Lavazza, actually. One-hundred-per-cent Arabica beans. Speciality of the house. And I've got one of those little octagonal pots I can make it in.'

'Then coffee it is.'

'All right, just make yourself at home. Don't mind Vanessa, she won't bite.'

Vanessa looked as if anything more vigorous than stretching out a paw would be too much to contemplate. Having surveyed Elder with one baleful eye, she went back to feigning sleep.

Siobhan paused at the kitchen door. 'I could turn that off if it's bothering you.'

Elder, who had been only vaguely aware of music playing, shook his head. 'No, it's fine.'

By the time she returned, almost seven or eight minutes later, the music, some kind of stringed instrument, probably Middle-Eastern – was there such a thing as an *oud*? – had wound its way around Elder's brain.

The coffee was good, strong and not bitter, and Elder drank his with a little milk, Siobhan lifting the cat on to the floor so that she could sit, cross-legged, at one end of the settee while Elder sat at the other. After inspecting the underside of her tail for several moments, Vanessa jumped back up, circled and lay between them, her claws flexing in and out of a small blue cushion.

'When you rang,' Siobhan said, 'work aside – I always think whenever the phone rings, those seconds between picking up and whoever's at the other end responding, I always think it's my agent telling me I've got a call back from the RSC or someone's broken a leg and would I please hurry along to the National. Instead of which, if it is about work, it's either a British Council tour of Shakespeare to Croatia and Kazakhstan or forty seconds as a sex-starved sheep herder on *Emmerdale*. The last thing I did – this isn't my natural hair colour, you know, I dyed it for the part – was a stage version of *Gone With the Wind* at Battersea Arts with a cast of four and a dozen assorted puppets. Don't ask about the puppets.'

She pushed both hands up through the maze of her hair and shook her head from side to side. 'Now, sorry, what was I saying?'

'When I rang.'

'Oh, yes. Well, I thought it was probably to do with Susan. Before you'd even said. She'd been in my mind, I suppose. Seeing it on the telly, the news, about that man escaping, absconding, whatever. Loose, anyway. On the run. Shane Donald, is that his name? When Susan disappeared, they thought he'd killed her, didn't they? The police. You. Is that what you thought? What you thought had happened?'

'It was a strong possibility, yes. Donald and McKeirnan. Everything suggested . . .'

'But was it what you thought? What you felt inside?'

Elder only answered after a pause. 'Yes.'

'And now?'

'Now I don't know. I still think it's possible but . . .' He shrugged. 'I just don't know.'

'Poor Susan,' Siobhan said.

'You were close. Good friends.'

'Yes. Not as much as I was with Lynsey. Lyns and I had been mates since we were in nursery. But yes, that year, I'd say we were close, the three of us. About as close to Susan as you could get.'

173

Though far from loud, the sound Elder's cup made when it touched down in the saucer was clear and distinct.

'Go on,' he said.

'I don't know. It was just something about her. She'd let you get so close and then . . .' Siobhan raised both hands, palms outwards, fingers spread.

'Some people are like that,' Elder said. 'Private.'

'Yes.'

'So there were things she kept to herself?'

'I suppose so.'

'Family stuff?'

Siobhan swung her legs round and the cat raised her head from where it had been nestling and looked aggrieved.

'Partly, yes. I mean, Lynsey and I were in and out of one another's places the whole time. We'd known each other longer, of course, but even so. If we went to Susan's house more than a couple of times in the year, I'd be surprised.'

'Why do you think that was?'

'I think she was a bit, not ashamed exactly, but embarrassed. Not that she had any reason to be. It wasn't as though she lived in some slum. And her mum, her mum was nice as can be. Ordinary, you know, but nothing wrong with that.' She laughed. 'Better than a mother who downs gin and tonics like they're going out of style and is forever dragging you off to auditions.'

'And Susan's father?' Elder asked. 'What impression did you have of him?'

Siobhan drank some more coffee while she thought. 'It's difficult to say. I mean, he just wasn't there a lot of the time, working I assume, and when he was, well, he was okay, I suppose. That's all you could say. I think he ignored us as much as he could.'

'How about with Susan? What was he like with her?'

Siobhan pushed out her bottom lip. 'Pretty normal. She was quiet around him, though, I did notice that. Walking on eggshells, you know? As though she didn't want to set him off.'

'Set him off?'

'I heard him shouting at her once. Lyns and I turned up early to go to this thing and he was really carrying on. A proper screaming match. You could hear him outside, down the street.'

'Do you know what it was about?'

'Oh, some boy. Someone Susan had a bit of a crush on. A right yob, too. No wonder her old man was wetting his knickers. Not that he needed to have bothered. It was all over more or less before it'd started. He dumped her and then there were the usual tears and wailing and soon after that she was over him. Had fun with us instead. Look . . .'

Startling the cat, she sprang to her feet and fetched a photo album from one of the shelves. 'I thought you'd like to look at these.'

In the first photograph, the drama group was gathered in front of the school minibus before setting out: Susan Blacklock stood at the far right, half a pace from the rest. There were eight girls and four boys in all; Paul Latham, wearing a baggy off-white suit, front and centre, smiling. In most of the others – outside the Royal Shakespeare Theatre at Stratford-upon-Avon, on the pavement in front of the Roundhouse in London – Susan stood close together with Siobhan and a dark-haired girl Elder presumed to be Lynsey.

'Yes,' Siobhan said when he asked. 'That's Lyns.'

There were pictures of the three of them as a trio,

175

singly or in pairs – laughing, making faces at the camera, miming tears. Siobhan with fingers at the corners of her mouth, stretching it wide; Lynsey poking out her tongue. Silly hats, badges, garish clothes. Three girls, three young women having the times of their lives.

'Do you still see a lot of her?' Elder asked. 'Lynsey.'

'I did. Until about a year ago. She met this bloke who does stand-up and followed him back to Canada. Toronto.' She smiled. 'Not the end of the earth, just seems it.'

'You miss her?'

'Oh, yes.'

'You've not been over? To visit.'

Siobhan looked at him. 'You know what it's like, when you think you know someone really well; they're your best, your closest friend, and then they fall for someone who seems to epitomise everything you thought you both despised? And you think how could they? And then, after a while, you start to think perhaps you never really knew them that well at all.'

When she finished speaking Elder thought she was close to tears, certainly upset.

'You want some more coffee? I think there's a little left in the pot.'

While she was out of the room, Elder traced back through the album. In one photograph, mid close-up, Susan Blacklock was looking directly at the camera, serious yet smiling. Beautiful, Elder thought. For that moment. Beautiful.

'Who took this?' he asked when Siobhan came back into the room.

'I'm not sure. It could have been . . . well, it could have been anyone . . . but I'd say Mr Latham, probably.'

176

'Why do you think that?'

'Oh, the way she's standing, you know, like it's a proper photograph. Not just another snap.'

'She liked him then, Latham?'

'Of course she did. We all liked him. Adored him, practically.'

'You fancied him?'

Siobhan laughed out loud. 'Not in a million years.'

'Why not?'

'You just didn't.'

'Because he was a teacher?'

'God, no. It wasn't that. Lyns and I both had this thing about Selvey, taught maths. We'd follow him around, hide notes inside his register, phone him at home sometimes. Sit around late at night talking about him, what it would be like, you know . . . The pain of it was he was knocking off this slapper in the lower sixth all the time. All came out when she got pregnant, took an overdose and had to be pumped out, lost the baby. She works in Marks now, Sheffield. I bump into her from time to time when I go home.'

'And the man? Selvey?'

'Changed schools. Deputy head somewhere in Derbyshire, that's what we heard. Inspector of schools by now, most likely.'

Elder closed the album and rested it against the back of the settee. 'So if Paul Latham wasn't out of bounds as it were, in your imaginations at least . . .'

'Why didn't any of us fancy him? I think we were all sure he was gay at first. You know, drama, dressing up. All that flapping of hands. Exaggeration.'

'But he wasn't?'

177

'I don't think so. I don't think he was anything really. Sexually, I mean.'

'He's not married.'

'He wasn't then. Not unless he kept her hidden in the attic. He had this cottage a little way out of town, on the way to Matlock. Everything just so. You could have eaten your dinner off the floor.'

'You went there, obviously?'

'He had a summer party, every year.'

'And that was all?'

'Lynsey and I went over a few times with a couple of the others, after rehearsals. Just, you know, chilling out.'

'And Susan?'

'She might have been with us once or twice, yes, probably was.'

'How about on her own? Do you know if she ever went there on her own?'

Siobhan was shaking her head, amusement vying with surprise. 'You think they were having an affair, don't you? Susan and Paul.'

'Isn't it possible?'

'No.'

'Can you be sure?'

'Even if she hadn't said – and she would, girls don't keep that kind of stuff to themselves, secretive or not – don't you think one of us would have noticed something, spending all that time together? After school, weekends, being shaken around in the damned minibus.'

'Yes, I suppose so.'

'Anyway, as I say, he wasn't the type. The two of them – it doesn't make sense.'

Elder remembered what she'd said about her best

friend falling for a Canadian comic but chose not to remind her. 'What about the boys in the group,' he said, 'is it possible she had a crush on one of those?'

Siobhan reached for the album. 'This couple here, denim jackets and jeans, they were gay. Not quite out but not exactly in the closet either.' She laughed, remembering. 'Not till they came to the end-of-year party tarted up like twin versions of Boy George. Mind you, I wouldn't mind betting they're married now, kids, mortgage, the whole bit.' She cocked her wrist and attempted a Kenneth Williams voice. 'Just a phase, love. Just a phase.' Laughing. 'Someone we were going through.'

The laughter merged with a small fit of coughing, for which she apologised. Pulling herself together, she indicated one of the photographs.

'Now Rob there, Rob Shriver, he was the heartthrob of the bunch if anyone, but he'd been dating Linda Fairburn since year three. D'you know they're married with three kids, still together, happy as the proverbial in some mock-Georgian paradise in Macclesfield. Every Christmas I get this chain letter along with photos of the children. You know, those dreadful things in flimsy card frames, kids saying cheese in their school uniforms. Enough to make you throw up. Except it's sweet, really.'

'How about him?' Elder asked, pointing towards a tall lad with longish hair and rimless spectacles, standing to Susan's left.

'Stephen. Stephen Makepiece Bryan. Our tame intellectual. Read Brecht every day before breakfast. Reckoned Mozart and Jimi Hendrix were God. Gods. And Shakespeare, of course. But, no, come to think of it, he and Susan got on pretty well. Both only children, I think that was part of it. And she did go with him to a concert once. Something classical. I can remember Lyns and I teasing her about it. But for all that, I don't think there was anything, you know, physical. Stephen was probably too much in love with himself to waste it on others.'

'Do you ever hear from him, Stephen?'

'No, but I think Rob and Linda do, I could give you their number if you like. Or why don't you try that site on the web – Friends Reunite, is that what it's called? He might be listed on there.'

'Okay, thanks. Maybe I'll do that. Now, I should be going. I've taken enough of your time.'

Siobhan made a mock bow. 'My lord, 'tis mine to give withal.'

'Shakespeare again?'

'Walkers crisps commercial, more like. Let me get you that number and then I'll come down to the door.'

The sky had clouded over a little and offered the possibility of rain. Things change.

'You don't recall anything about getting back late from a theatre trip to Newcastle?' Elder asked. 'The minibus breaking down. A puncture.'

Siobhan thought then shook her head. 'Not specially. That sort of thing happened all the time.'

'This would have been really late. Three or four in the morning.'

'No, sorry. The only thing special I can remember happening at Newcastle, we drove all the way to see the National's *Lear* and the safety curtain got stuck. They had to abandon the whole performance.'

'You don't know when this was? I mean exactly?'

'No. I'm sorry.'

Elder took a step away. 'Thanks again for the coffee. And the chat.'

'I enjoyed it.'

'Take care, then.'

Elder raised a hand and set off down the street. At the corner of the square he checked his watch, thought about the times of the trains home and quickened his pace. Home, a funny word to use. A rented room and little beyond his clothes and a few books that were his own. Was he going back down to Cornwall when all this was over, and if not what exactly was he intending to do? Where was he going to go?

For now St Pancras would do.

One step at a time.

24

If it hadn't been for the car, Gerald Kersley would never have gone to the police at all. Debit and credit cards he could get stopped, the cash he could spare. But an almost-new Renault Vel Satis without a scratch on its satin finish . . . there was no way he could claim on the insurance without officially reporting the loss.

The uniformed officer at the local station noted down the details laboriously.

'And when you stopped at the park, sir, to use the Gents, that was at approximately a quarter past?'

'Yes.'

'Less than half an hour after you'd left home?'

'Curry I'd had last night, I was caught short, you know how it is.'

'Yes, sir. Of course,' the officer said. The park toilets were a well-known haunt for cottaging, something the police were mostly happy to turn a blind eye to, other than when some virtuous citizen rousted the chief constable with a complaint.

'And you left the car for how long, sir? Ten minutes?'

'Less. Much less. Five at most.'

'So whoever took the car was pretty swift, knew what he was about . . .'

'They do, don't they?'

'There isn't any way you might have accidentally left the keys in the car?'

'Good God, no. I'm not a fool.'

'No, sir.' The officer doing his best not to smirk.

It was found a day later, wrapped around a lamppost south of Stockport. Shane Donald had managed to get himself lost, got turned around and ended up driving south-east out of Manchester instead of south-west as he'd intended. Giving it some welly along a rare stretch of open road he'd had to swerve to avoid a post van and lost control. A few bumps and bruises and a cut to the forehead aside, he'd got out of it lightly, grabbed his bag and legged it, slightly limping, away.

Half an hour or so later, Donald then stumbled upon a rare piece of luck, a small travelling fair setting up on a patch of waste ground, dodgems and an antique Whirlatilter, a few roundabouts and sundry stalls, a large inflatable slide which small children scrambled up with the aid of criss-crossed ropes, before rolling and tumbling noisily down, shrieking all the way. Five goes for two pounds, no adults or shoes allowed.

Donald wandered around until he got into conversation with the man who seemed to be in charge, bragged a little about his past experience and was set on, collecting money at the base of the slide, a task he shared with a surly Croatian, turn and turn about.

His hair cut short and from a distance looking almost bald, Donald could have been any young man between nineteen and thirty, only the plaster over his cut forehead to distinguish him from the rest. What resemblance he had to the photographs that had so far appeared in the newspapers was negligible at best.

It was towards the end of that first day, evening really, lights on all around, the sweet burnt smell of onions from the hot-dog stall, that he noticed the girl standing at the centre of the six-sided darts stall. Score fifty and over to win a prize, no doubles, bull's-eye counts twenty, own darts not allowed. She stood blinking out, her skin purplish in the coloured neon light, surrounded by soft toys and stetson hats, a set of darts with green flights in her hand.

'You wanna go?'

Donald shrugged his shoulders, shook his head. He had been hovering around the stall for quarter of an hour now, maybe more. Wandered off and come back with a bag of sugared doughnuts, stood around some more.

'Come on, have a go, why don't you? I'm not gonna charge, am I?'

There was an accent of some kind in her voice, not strong, vaguely northern. He set the doughnut bag down and accepted the darts from her hands. They were light, of course, as he knew they would be, the centres drilled out. All but impossible to aim. He scored seventeen and she offered him a teddy bear, pale orange, button eyes and a black thread mouth. Instead of refusing he said thanks and tucked it down inside his belt.

'Here,' he said, holding out the bag dark now with grease. 'Have one of these.'

She had a silver stud, he could see now, small, to the left of her nose. Her hair was clipped short. When she bit into the doughnut, sugar freckled her upper lip.

'My name's Angel,' she said. 'What's yours?'

'Shane.'

There were small gangs of youths roaming around, shouting and pushing at each other, drinking out of cans. When one of their number, having failed to get two out of three darts to as much as stick into the board, started mouthing off at Angel, calling her a cheating cunt and more, Donald faced him down and told him to move on and, to his surprise, the youth, after offering to punch him out so as not to back down in front of his mates, did exactly that.

'Thanks,' Angel said. 'But you needn't've bothered. I get that all the time on here. And worse.'

''Sall right,' Donald said.

When the fair closed down around two, he finished cashing up at the slide and came back to help her pack away, bolt down the sides.

'Thanks,' she said again.

''Sokay.'

'You smoke?' she asked.

'Yeah. Why not?'

Angel rolled a narrow spliff, struck a match and got it going, then passed it across. They walked over to a small incline at the edge of the site and sat down.

'Where you staying? You staying here or what?'

Donald shrugged. 'Thought I'd scrounge a blanket, kip down on the ground. 'Snot cold.'

She accepted the spliff back from him, held the smoke in her mouth and then drew it down into her lungs. She was not long out of school, Donald guessed. Sixteen. Seventeen.

'How about you?' Donald asked.

Angel pointed over towards one of a small cluster of caravans. 'I'm sharing with Della. She sort of took me in. Few months back now. She's okay.'

Donald nodded. 'You're not really called Angel,' he said.

'Yeah. Angel Elizabeth Ryan.'

'I thought you were takin' the piss.'

'That was my dad.'

They sat and smoked, listening to the occasional flurry of laughter from elsewhere on the site, the sound of a car on the road at their backs, going past with its radio playing.

'Shane . . .'

'Yeah.'

'You gonna stick around or what?'

'He said I could carry on workin' the slide if I wanted.'

'You goin' to?'

'While, maybe. Few days, why not?'

'What's this from?' she asked, not quite touching the plaster on his head.

Shane grinned. 'Crashed a car, didn't I?'

She moved her face in front of his and when she kissed him her lips felt dry and cracked; her tongue was quick and wet and then she pulled away. He could feel the goose-pimples all along her arms. They smoked the joint right down to its end and then Angel scrambled to her feet, brushing the dirt from her jeans.

'I'd best be getting in.'

'Okay.'

When she'd gone, he turned and unzipped and pissed where he stood, a long curving stream that seemed to go on and on. By the time he'd finished, she was walking back towards him, a blanket over one arm.

'Here, Della says you can have this.'

When he tried to kiss her again, she turned her head away.

'See you tomorrow.'

'Yeah. Reckon so.'

He was still thinking of the kiss, the exactness of it, when he fell asleep.

◆

Donald worked the slide for two more days, helping out on the dodgems once or twice, giving Angel a hand to put up and take down her stall. The fair's owner, Otto, was a traveller from several generations of travellers; the fair itself had belonged to his father and uncle before him. Most of the people who worked it now were family: sons, nephews, cousins. Della, who had more or less adopted Angel, was Otto's sister.

One of the cousins gave Donald a sleeping-bag and told him he could bed down in the back of the truck that pulled the Whirlatilter. On the second night, Della invited him into the caravan for supper, thick stew with meat and potatoes and a bottle of raw red wine. Glasses of white spirit that made Donald choke. Otto joined them at one point, drank mightily, tore off a piece of bread and wiped it round the almost empty pot.

'Good boy!' he said, gripping Donald hard on the shoulder. 'Good boy, huh?'

I'm thirty years old, Donald thought, not a boy. He said nothing.

The following day Della walked across to the slide when he was working, her skirts trailing in the dust and dirt. Early in the afternoon, it was still quiet, a few young kids, mothers with buggies or babies slung across their chests.

'Angel,' she said, 'she's had one hell of a life, you know that?'

Donald nodded, though in truth he knew nothing, only what he'd guessed.

'Mother on drugs, no good; father never there; foster homes, in care. Run away all the time, police bring her back. When I found her, six months now, she was skin and bones. Hates herself. Cut herself with razor. Not now. Now that has stopped.'

She moved closer and caught hold of Donald's arm.

'You harm her, make her start again, I cut you here.' Releasing his arm, her hand moved fast between his legs. 'You understand?'

'Yeah.'

'Yes?' Twisting harder.

'Yes.'

'Good.' When she stepped away, Donald's eyes were watering and his crotch was sore.

'You've been in prison,' she said. Not a question. 'Inside. Maybe a long time.'

'Yeah, I . . .'

She made a chopping movement with her hand. 'No. Just so you know I know. Your business for now.' She moved close again, breath warm on his face. 'Angel, you be good to her or you answer to me.'

◆

That night Angel came to him in the truck while he slept.

At first he thought the pressure against his body was part of a dream. The sound of the zip slowly sliding down. As she slipped into the opening of the sleeping-bag he felt her feet and legs cold against his, the sharp bones of her knees. She was wearing a white T-shirt and a pair of skimpy cotton pants. When he tried to talk she kissed his cheeks, his lids of his eyes, the corners of his mouth. He felt himself go hard against her and when she felt it too she drew in a little gasp of air.

'Take it easy,' she said, as suddenly he moved, pushing a hand between her legs. 'No. Stop, stop, stop.'

'I thought . . .'

'Here.' Her small fingers tightened about his wrist and then, when he was still, she moved his hand back beneath her, easing the edge of damp material aside.

'There. Now slowly . . . slowly . . . slow!'

Shifting position slightly, she eased down against him and he felt her gradually opening against his fingers, warm and damp.

'Slowly, Shane. Slowly, for fuck's sake. Please, please, please.'

When she came, she sank her teeth into the flesh of his upper arm and broke the skin.

'Jesus!'

'What?'

'That hurt.'

'I'm sorry.'

Gently, she kissed the half moon on his arm. Their legs, inside the sleeping-bag, were fast in sweat. Angel unglued herself and, peeling her T-shirt over her head, rolled away until she lay naked on her back on the bed of the truck.

'You're beautiful,' Shane said, knowing he should say something.

Her small breasts, when she lay like that, almost disappeared; he was surprised by the thickness of the hair that grew between her legs.

'You haven't got anything, have you?'

'What? What d'you mean?'

'A condom, what you think?'

Donald shook his head. He had thought she meant HIV, some disease.

'Here then.' Twisting towards him, supple, she took him in her mouth.

'You don't have to . . .'

But within moments he had come and she had swallowed him, most of him, and leaned forward against him then, her face against his chest. Without moving her, Donald turned slightly inward on his side and closed his eyes, her heart beating against him.

He woke, without knowing that he had slept, one arm numb where his weight had pressed it down on the metal ridge of the truck floor. Slowly turning, he shivered and fidgeted the zip of the sleeping-bag back up. There was a light on inside one of the other caravans and already the sky was beginning to lighten at its eastern edge. He wondered how long Angel had stayed with him before she had gone back. He was trying to remember, moment by moment, what had happened, when he fell asleep again without meaning to.

When he saw her again, a couple of hours later, crossing the site from Della's caravan towards her stall, she raised a hand in his direction and smiled quickly without ever breaking stride.

25

When Shane Donald didn't turn up again within forty-eight hours, handcuffed and crestfallen, when he didn't commit some heinous crime, national interest waned. His brother-in-law's exposé, even with the imagination of an otherwise bored sub-editor to add spice, was put on hold. Pam Wilson found that she could lift her head above the parapet without fear of cameras being thrust in her direction. One of the broadsheet nationals, which might have been thought to know better, ran an in-depth survey of sexual crimes involving pairs of malefactors and their youthful victims.

Elder rang the number Siobhan had given him for Rob Shriver several times and on each occasion was politely informed that neither Rob nor Linda Shriver could come to the phone right then, but inviting him, should he choose, to leave a message for either of them or, indeed, for any or all of Matthew, Dominic or Eliza. Twice Elder demurred and on the final occasion he left Willie Bell's number.

When he tried his daughter's mobile, thinking they could meet up for a coffee or a meal or maybe even a visit to the cinema, he was automatically transferred to her home number and before he could think to ring off, Joanne had come on the line. There was an awkward pause followed by one of those halting conversations in which each asks the other questions to which they scarcely care about the answers. They kept it up for several minutes before Elder thought he heard a door opening in the background followed by a male voice and then it was Joanne saying, 'I'll be sure to tell Katherine you called,' and that was that.

Elder could remember when he and Joanne – mostly Joanne, but with him propping up his end willingly – had talked for hours about anything and everything. Politics to fashion by way of films and books and friends. And plans! To carry out even half the plans Joanne could conceive within a twelvemonth would have taken as many years. Some, as Elder was wont to point out, were impractical, pie in the sky – let's open a shop, a boutique, a fashion salon of our own, a small hotel; go and live in America, Lisbon, the Balearic Islands, anywhere but where we are – and for the most part they depended upon him quitting the police force and becoming something other than what he was: the flatfoot detective she'd met in Lincolnshire when she was just nineteen, had married a little over six years later, and had finally persuaded to head for the big lights of London seven years after that.

You married the wrong man, he used to tell her jokingly, but both of them came to believe it was true. Perhaps if she'd met Martyn Miles years earlier it would never have happened. Except that Martyn Miles probably wouldn't be seen dead in Lincolnshire – or, rather, that's the only way he would consent to being there – and if

Elder and Joanne had never married there would be no Katherine.

A thought Elder refused to countenance.

Take away the rest, everything, and Katherine made it all worthwhile.

Hungry, he opened a large tin of baked beans, added Worcester sauce, and ate from the saucepan with a spoon. He was rinsing out the pan beneath the tap when the phone rang and he picked it up.

'Hello, this is Linda Shriver. You left a message asking one of us to call.'

Elder thanked her for getting back to him and explained what he wanted.

'And this is to do with Susan Blacklock and why she disappeared?'

'Yes.'

'I see.'

There was a pause at the other end of the line.

'You knew her, of course,' Elder said.

'Yes. Yes. Not as well as Rob and the others, but yes.'

'And you didn't like her.'

'Why do you say that?'

'I don't know. Just a feeling.'

She laughed, brittle and just off-key. 'You should be a detective, Mr Elder.'

'Thank you,' he said, and then, 'Would you mind telling me why you felt that way about her?'

She thought before replying. 'I never . . . it's difficult, because I was never really a member of that little group, only through Rob and of course that was never the same . . . but I don't think I ever . . . I want to say believed her, but that's not really what I mean.'

'You didn't trust her?' Elder suggested.

'I don't know if it's quite that, either, though that might well be part of it. No, it's more I never really believed in who she was, as though it was all a front. All this wonderful drama, blah, blah, blah. As if it was just something she was doing for show.'

Elder remembered the photographs. 'Isn't that what they were all doing, in a way?'

'Yes. I know what you mean.' She laughed, warmer this time. 'I'm afraid I haven't explained myself very well. All I'm doing is tying myself up in knots.'

'That's okay.'

'I wouldn't fare very well, would I, in an interrogation? Someone like you would let me waffle on, positively encourage me, and then, when I was totally confused, pluck the truth right out of the hat.'

'Which is?'

Linda laughed, louder and more nervously this time. 'I was jealous of her, of course.'

'Because she was interested in Rob?'

'God, no! Half the damned school, the female half anyway, were throwing themselves at him, but most of the time I don't think Susan even noticed he was there. It was Rob who was infatuated with her. I'd catch him gazing after her sometimes, like some sorry dog that can't get his bone. Or whatever. I even told her once. It was at some party or other, think I'd probably had a drink or two, Dutch courage, anyway I told her if she ever . . . well, ever anything as far as Rob was concerned, I'd have her eyes out. I'm sorry, that's awful, isn't it? After what . . . you know . . . what might have happened.'

Elder didn't reply.

'Anyway,' Linda said, 'all that happened was she looked like I was something the cat had dragged in then she walked away.'

'And you waited for him to get over it?'

'Something like that.'

Elder heard a small clink of glass against glass. More Dutch courage, he thought.

'Do you know if Susan was involved with anyone?' he said. 'Anyone at the school?'

'I don't think so. She and Stephen, Stephen Bryan, they used to spend quite a bit of time together, but I don't think there was anything to it.'

'Are you sure?'

'No. But I don't think Stephen was interested in girls. Still isn't, as far as I know.'

'You mean he's gay?'

'I don't think it's that simple. Rob still sees him from time to time and he's never said anything one way or the other.' She paused. 'Of course, if there had been something going on between Stephen and Susan, it would explain why she wasn't interested in Rob.'

'Yes,' Elder said. 'Of course.'

'Look, I ought to be getting Rob's dinner ready. And the boys will be back from Scouts. I'll ask Rob to phone you after we've eaten, shall I?'

'If you would.'

'And Mr Elder, all of that stuff about him and Susan, there's no need, is there . . .?'

'Absolutely not.'

'Thank you. Thank you very much.'

◆

Almost as soon as he'd put the phone down, it rang again.

'Hello, Dad?'

'Yes.'

'Mum said you called.'

'Yes. I thought we might meet up or something.'

'Tonight?'

'Yes.'

'Okay, I can do that. Great.'

'The only thing is . . .'

'Now you can't.'

'There's this call I'm expecting. I . . .'

'Why don't you get a mobile, Dad? Join the twenty-first century like the rest of us.'

'Kate . . .'

But she was gone. Elder thought about the bottle of Aberlour upstairs in his room; then he thought about Linda Shriver, sipping white wine while she waited for her husband and her sons to come home. Better the kettle, a cup of tea, an improving book. He'd finished *A Kestrel for a Knave* and thought he might try some Dickens. He'd picked up a copy of *David Copperfield*, which looked as if it might be interesting. Bulky though, not easy to carry around. But seated in Willie Bell's one seriously comfortable armchair, it kept him occupied, more or less, until Rob Shriver called back, almost an hour later.

'Hello, this is Rob.'

He sounded tired, Elder thought, just in those four words; tired, world-weary, older than he should have been, older than he was. Perhaps he had too much responsibility, a stressful job, maybe the commute in and out of Manchester or wherever was getting to be too much of a strain. Perhaps it had simply been a bad day.

Elder wondered if he was about to make it worse. 'It's about Susan Blackwood,' he said.

'Yes, Linda told me.'

I'll bet she did, Elder thought.

'You haven't any news?' Rob Shriver asked.

'No, I'm afraid not. I wish I had.'

'Yes,' he said heavily, and then, picking himself up, 'Was there anything particular you wanted to know? I don't know if I'll be able to help, it was all a long time ago, but, of course, if I can.'

'When I was talking to Siobhan . . .'

'Siobhan Banham?'

'Yes. She told me about an occasion when you all went to the theatre in Newcastle to see the National . . .'

'No.'

'Sorry?'

'She's wrong. If it was Newcastle it wouldn't have been the National, it would have been the RSC.'

'You're sure?'

'Positive.'

'But it might have been *King Lear*?'

'Oh, you mean the performance that never was. Safety curtain came down and wouldn't go back up. We bought pizza and ate it in the bus on the way home.'

'You'd have been back early then?'

'Half-nine. Ten. Ten thirty at the latest.'

'And you were dropped off how, all together at the school?'

'Usually that was what happened, yes. But no one would have been expecting us back so soon. Some of us called our parents, I remember, and got picked up. That's what happened in my case, certainly.'

'And the others?'

'I'm not sure. Latham drove them home, I suppose.'

'I see. Well, thanks for your time.'

'That's all?'

'I think so. For now.'

'I see.'

'You don't have a contact number for Stephen Bryan, do you?' Elder said. 'Or an address? Siobhan thought you might.'

'Yes, I've got them both here somewhere. If you'll hang on.'

The receiver banged slightly when it was put down. In the background Elder could hear voices, the fall and rise of distant conversation, family gossip.

'Here it is,' Rob Shriver said. The address was in Leicester, no more than forty-five minutes' drive away.

'Look,' Shriver said, his voice lowered suddenly, 'if you do find out anything about Susan . . . I appreciate it's unlikely after all this time, but could I ask you to let me know?'

'If I can.'

'And Linda, it only upsets her, maybe if I gave you the number of my mobile . . .'

'Go ahead.'

'You do understand?'

'I think so.'

Elder wrote down the number, thanked him again and broke the connection. How was it possible to maintain a crush on someone for thirteen years, a passion even? Someone you've not seen in all that time? As easy as it was, perhaps, to nourish jealousy, feed it every now and again, watching it grow.

Was Elder thinking about Rob and Linda Shriver or about himself and Joanne?

He didn't think he could spend any more time that evening with *David Copperfield*; he'd read enough to know things would get worse before ever they got better. Half an hour later he was in bed and, surprisingly, asleep, only to be woken in the small hours by the late return of Willie Bell in his cups, slamming doors and treating the neighbours to a raucous version of 'Dancing Queen', transposed for the occasion into a Scottish rant.

26

At night he lay awake and waited for her to come. It was colder now and he had two blankets spread across his sleeping-bag. There was movement always: even on the edges of the city it was never quite still. And sounds. Smells. The smell of popcorn and hot dogs that lingered, diesel fumes and what seemed like burning rubber, slow-burning rubber, smouldering somewhere distant.

He listened for her and sometimes thought he could hear the catch of the caravan door as she pushed it shut; sometimes he heard her steps as she approached, and sometimes, like tonight, it was like the first night when she had surprised him, even though he had been sleeping then and now he lay waiting.

How long had it been? A week? Less than a week.

Angel lifted the doubled edges of the blankets and drew down the zip of the sleeping-bag far enough to allow her to slip inside.

'Be careful,' she said. 'I'm cold.'

'Doesn't matter.'

'It's cold outside.'

'Not in here.'

'Be careful of my feet, they're freezing.'

''Sall right.'

'No. They're like ice.'

'I'll soon get 'em warm.'

'Don't touch them. Don't let them touch you.'

'Don't be stupid. Put them against me.'

'You're sure?'

'I said so, didn't I?'

'All right. Only don't say I didn't warn you.'

'Ow! Jesus! They're like fucking ice!'

'I told you.' Laughing.

'Get them fuckin' off me.'

'All right, all right, all right.'

By now she was laughing so much she was rolling a little from side to side, as much as the sleeping-bag allowed, and the laughter came close to tears and then both laughter and tears became coughing and he was holding her as she rocked forward against him, the harsh barking sound from her mouth and the hard small knots of her spine.

This had happened before and it frightened him.

'You okay?'

'Yes . . . yes . . .' She was struggling to catch her breath and stop the persistent coughing which was hurting her chest.

'You should go to the doctor, you know that, don't you?'

'It's all right.' Quietly. 'I'll be okay. Just give me a minute. Just . . .'

She turned away, turned as much as she could, and he followed her face with his face, wanting the fit of coughing to be over.

'Angel, you're okay, yeah?'

'Yes. I'm fine.'

He kissed her and moved his hand across her. She was wearing a sweater over her T-shirt and he ran his hand up under both of them until it reached her breast. For a moment, as he touched her, she arched her back and then, settling, she wrapped her legs around his and said, 'How are my feet now?'

'Warm.'

'Really?'

'Warm enough.'

◆

The day before she had come running to him, running like a young girl across the fairground, arms waving in the air. So excited that at first she could scarcely speak.

The fair was moving on and Shane could go with them. She had asked Otto and it was all right. The Croat was going north to Scotland with his girlfriend, who was one of Otto's nieces, and Shane could run the slide all by himself. Not only that, Otto was willing to let them rent the caravan his niece and her Croat had been living in, it wasn't expensive, not too expensive, she was sure they could afford it between them and if they couldn't then Della had said she would help.

'Well?' Angel had said. 'T'rrific, eh?'

'Maybe.'

'What d'you mean, maybe?'

'Yeah, I suppose . . . I dunno.'

'But what's wrong? What's wrong with it? I thought you'd jump at the chance. Jump at it.'

He wouldn't look in her eyes.

'You only want to fuck me for four nights and that's it. That what you're saying?'

'No.'

'Then what is?'

'I dunno.'

'What do you want, Shane? Just tell me. We're leavin' the day after tomorrow and you're gonna do what? Say goodbye and thank you very much. Get me in the truck for a last feel, a last fuck.'

'Stop it.'

'That what I am, Shane, just some stupid fuck, a slapper, a slag, a cunt for you to come off in, a tart, a whore?'

'Stop.'

'Is that all I am to you, some stupid little fucking whore?'

'No.'

'No, Shane?'

'No, I swear.'

'Then prove it.'

They went to Otto together, Shane afraid that he would start asking more questions now, as if he were Angel's father, though he knew she had no father, not really, and Otto knew it too. Otto would want to know about his family, where he had worked, where he had been, why he had been in prison. If Della knew that he had been inside, then Otto would also. But instead of this Otto told stories and joked and teased them, trying to embarrass them as if they were children. And then he poured all three of them a drink and talked to Shane, man to man, about the rent, the responsibility for the slide, all the while Angel watching and smiling.

'Where is it we're going?' Shane asked.

'Angel didn't tell you?'

'No.'

'I didn't know,' Angel said.

'Newark.'

Shane couldn't believe it. 'You're putting me on.'

'Newark-on-Trent. Five days. It is a good place for us, you'll see. But you know it, maybe?'

He knew it right enough.

It was where he had first seen Alan McKeirnan, the rain driving hard, almost horizontally, across the open space where the fair was being pitched. 'You gonna stand there like a fuckin' statue,' McKeirnan had called out, 'or lend a hand?'

Of course he couldn't go back. Not there. It would be lunatic, stupid. Back where it had all started, where they would be on the lookout for him, where he was known. Smack in the backyard of that bastard who was out to get him, get even for what had happened to his daughter, swearing vengeance, what he wouldn't do.

'What's the matter, Shane?' Angel had asked once they were outside Otto's caravan.

'Nothing. Nothing's the matter, why?'

'You went all quiet, that's all.'

'I was thinkin'.'

'What about?'

'For fuck's sake, Angel,' he had said, rounding on her. 'Why can't you ever leave me a-fuckin'-lone?'

The rest of that day, that's what she had done. Steered clear and when he'd seen her, laughing with the other lads, those who worked the fair and those that were simply hanging round, passing time, it had gnawed at him, like a rat at his insides. But Newark, Mansfield,

Worksop, Notts., how could he go back there? And where after that? Gainsborough. Lincoln. Louth. Then Mablethorpe, Ingoldmells, Skegness, Sutton on Sea: up and down that North Sea coast, backing trailers and caravans in and out of winding coastal roads, the mist drifting in off the sea. McKeirnan spotting Lucy Padmore on the front at Mablethorpe, fair hair catching the sun as she turned unknowingly towards them. 'There,' McKeirnan had said, nudging him. 'There's the one.'

◆

He lay now on his back, head and shoulders clear of the sleeping-bag, smoking a cigarette. Angel was curled against him, arms and legs across him, head against his chest. He could hear the faint rasp and sigh of her breath, feel the movement of her ribcage against his side. It was never really dark there, Shane thought, a dull yellowish light always, one or two stars only shining through. McKeirnan had tried to tell him something once about the stars, but almost as soon as he'd told him, pointing out shapes that were difficult to make out, Shane had forgotten their names and McKeirnan had sworn at him, angry, and told him again how he was next to useless. Useless. Maybe Angel, Shane thought, knew something about the stars.

She stirred against him and her breathing changed and he knew she was awake.

'Shane,' she said eventually. 'You are coming with us, aren't you? You are?'

Shane didn't answer; closed his eyes.

27

Somehow Willie Bell was up before him, already several slices of toast to the good, arguing with the *Today* programme on the radio before switching to Radio 2 and harmonising along with Neil Diamond as he poured fresh water into the pot. 'Tea's here, help yourself to anything else.'

Elder filled his cup and sat at the far end of the kitchen table, riffling through last night's *Post*.

'Sleep well?' Bell asked.

'Not so bad.'

'You've got rid of the dreams then?'

Elder slid the paper aside. 'What dreams are these?'

'First couple of nights here you were calling out something dreadful. Of course, you could've sneaked some woman back in, you crafty bugger, in which case I'd not like to know what the two of you were up to, but without that I'd say, no, you were dreaming right enough. Not pleasant either. A wonder you didn't wake yourself up.'

Elder nodded. Since leaving Cornwall he'd thought he'd left the dream behind.

'I'm going into the city,' Bell said, 'if you want a lift.'

'I wouldn't mind. My daughter says I have to buy a mobile phone.'

Bell laughed. 'Be a new haircut next. Something more fashionable in the way of clothes.'

Twenty minutes later they were heading south towards the centre, progress slow in the morning traffic.

'This little investigation of yours,' Bell asked, 'how's it going?'

'Not sure to be honest,' Elder said. 'A few facts, half-truths, suspicions – things that didn't come out first time around. But as to whether it's leading somewhere . . .'

'Sounds like police work to me.'

'I suppose so.'

'You miss it?'

'Sometimes.'

'You not think that's why you're doing this, on account you can't let go?'

'Can't let go of the case or can't let go of the job?'

'You tell me.'

Elder didn't know. 'You can drop me,' he said, 'anywhere near Trinity Square. As long as that's not going out of your way.'

He hadn't realised the biggest drawback about purchasing a mobile phone was standing in the middle of the shop while some young man in a cheap suit ran through his spiel. Sign on the dotted line and he could walk out with something state of the art that would enable him not simply to make and receive calls and text messages, but access the internet, send emails and faxes, transmit visual images and download material on to his personal computer. And all while, as Jimmy Durante would have said, his left foot could be cracking walnuts. His dad's one party piece that had been, sitting at the piano with a paper cup in front of his face singing 'I'm the Guy Who Found The Lost Chord' like Jimmy Durante. A comedian with a raucous voice and a big nose, who ever thought of Durante today? When had he last thought of his father?

Elder cut off the salesman in mid-flow and told him he wanted the simplest phone possible, no trimmings, no extras, pay as you go. Charged and ready to use.

'I'm afraid we don't do that,' the salesman said.

'Do what?'

'Sell phones ready charged.'

'You do now,' Elder said.

Back out in the street, he tested it by calling Stephen Bryan's number in Leicester but only succeeded in getting his machine. Leave a message or try my mobile. Elder tried the mobile and after a longish pause was informed it was switched off but if he wished he could leave a message. He left a message. There was no knowing when or even if Bryan would get back to him and he didn't want to waste another day.

A brisk walk along Clumber Street and Bridlesmith Gate took him to the Broad Marsh Centre and then the station. If he changed trains at Grantham, he could be in Newcastle in well under three hours. At the AMT stall in the concourse he bought coffee and a muffin. *David Copperfield* was bulking out his coat pocket. Buying the muffin had made him think of Katherine. Perhaps he would call her from the platform, hoping for her approval. And there were a few others he ought to let have the number too, no point in having one otherwise. Maureen, certainly. Willie Bell. And Helen Blacklock? He wasn't sure. According to the screens high on the wall

208

above the entrance, his train was due in seven minutes, expected on time.

◆

When Elder arrived in Newcastle, the weather, which had passed through several permutations on the way up, settled into an all-encompassing blue. He checked with the newspaper vendor in the station forecourt and confirmed the theatre was but ten minutes' walk. Past the new shopping complex and there was Gray's Monument, like a smaller version of Nelson's Column. The Gray after whom the tea was named, Elder wondered, or had that been a relation?

The Theatre Royal was near the top of the street on the right-hand side, a grand building whose fluted columns seemed mainly to have resisted the incursions of pigeons or late-night graffiti artists. Having no joy at the front, Elder went in search of the stage door. A few words of explanation, a joking aside or two, and the assistant house manager was summoned and duly appeared, a busy dark-haired young woman who introduced herself as Rebecca.

With as little folderol as possible, Elder explained what he wanted.

'Thirteen years ago, you say?'

'Thirteen or fourteen.'

'And you want to know this why?'

'It's just for verification. That's all.' He could see her wavering. 'But it is important. Otherwise I wouldn't be taking your time.'

She sighed and pushed a stray hair away from her eyes. 'Follow me.'

The office was along a high, narrow corridor, the smell of recent paint still coming off the walls.

'All the house manager's notes are computerised now,' Rebecca explained. 'Have been for the past five or six years. Before that everything was entered by hand in one of these.'

Pulling open the centre drawer of a bottle-green cabinet, she revealed a mishmash of stiff-backed books, spiral bound.

'Help yourself. Whatever you're looking for, it's either in there or nowhere at all.' Lifting one out, she traced a finger line through the dust. 'Should have been turfed out ages ago.'

Elder was glad that hadn't been the case.

'Can I get you anything? Coffee? Some water?'

'No, thanks. I'm fine.'

It didn't take him so long to find what he was looking for. November 1987. A Tuesday. The RSC. *King Lear*. During the routine operation of the safety curtain before the performance, the mechanism jammed and the fault could not be rectified, causing the performance to be cancelled. Patrons were offered a refund or an exchange.

When Rebecca drifted back in to see how he was getting on, he was idly leafing through the book.

'A couple removed their clothes in the middle of Act Two and threw them down from the upper circle?'

'That's nothing. How did you get on?'

'Fine. Is it possible for me to get a photocopy of this page?'

'I don't see why not.'

Five minutes later he was back out on the street, the copy thoughtfully slipped inside a manila envelope by

Rebecca, along with a programme for the theatre's current season. 'Four in the morning, near enough, by when they got home.' Helen Blacklock had said. 'Trevor had been all for calling out the police, he were that worried.' According to Rob Shriver they had arrived back in Chesterfield by around ten. Which left six hours unaccounted for. Paul Latham driving Susan Blacklock home.

◆

Latham was in the school hall, supervising an after-hours drama group of twelve- and thirteen-year-olds. Right then, they were in pairs, building an improvisation around the theme of mistaken identity; some worked intently, head to head, others relished the opportunity for shouting and gesticulation. Elder was certain the teacher had seen him, standing at the back of the hall near the door, but he gave no sign. At the end of the exercise, he got everyone sitting in a circle and asked some of the pairs to share what they'd been doing. Applause, laughter, groans, a few parting words from Latham and they were picking up their coats, changing out of their soft-soled shoes, heading off in boisterous twos and threes.

'I didn't think,' Latham said, pitching up, 'I'd be seeing you again so soon.'

They had half the length of the hall between them.

'I thought we should talk,' Elder said.

'Go ahead.'

'Here?'

'Why not? Whatever it is, I can't imagine it's very

private. And anyway, there's only the cleaners to over-hear.'

Elder moved a couple of paces closer. 'It's about Susan.'

'Of course.'

'Susan and yourself.'

'Listen,' Latham said, 'I helped you before and I was glad to.'

'That night you drove back early from Newcastle, when the play was cancelled, was that when it started?'

Elder thought one side of Latham's face twitched slightly, but he wasn't sure. 'I don't know which particular fantasy you're entertaining . . .'

'Or was it already a going thing by then? I bet you couldn't believe your luck, an excuse to spend all that time together.'

'You know, I'm surprised you were able to get in so easily,' Latham said. 'They're so much stricter about all that kind of thing nowadays. Strangers on the premises. Or did you show somebody an old – what are they called? – warrant card. Is that what it was?'

'Six hours,' Elder said. 'Six hours with the minibus all to yourselves. Or did you take her back to the cottage? Time enough, I'd have thought.'

'I think,' Latham said, moving in the direction of the door diagonally across from where Elder stood, 'I'll see if I can find the caretaker. He might even want to call the police.'

'Wait,' Elder said.

Latham broke his step but nothing more.

'This isn't a game, you know,' Elder said. 'An impro-visation.'

'Isn't it? What a pity.'

When Latham emerged into the school car park forty-five minutes later, Elder was leaning against the side of his own ageing Ford, waiting. Latham hesitated, then turned and marched towards him; when he stopped, a few metres short of Elder, his arms were folded across his chest.

'I meant what I said. I suspect you thought I didn't, but I assure you I did. If you continue to harass me I shall go to the police.'

'I don't think so,' Elder said.

'Then you're wrong.'

'Mr Latham, I know that on the night the play was cancelled you and your group were back in Chesterfield by between half past nine and half ten at the latest. There's testimony to that effect. I also know that, according to Susan Blacklock's mother, you didn't bring her home until four the next morning.'

'That's what she says?'

'It is.'

'Then she's wrong.'

'I don't think so.'

'She's distraught, she's obsessive, in her state she'll say anything.'

'I believe her.'

'That's your privilege.'

'Why not tell the truth? After all this time what harm can it do?'

'Harm?' Latham smiled. 'You must think I'm very stupid.'

'Misguided, I prefer to think.'

Latham's arms came down to his sides, hands tight like

213

fists. 'What you're suggesting, that I had an improper relationship with one of the pupils in my care, it's untrue. It's something I would never countenance, something indeed I would condemn.' He moved a pace away. 'Should you ever have any evidence to support such an allegation, I'm prepared to refute it in the presence of my solicitor. Until then, I'll thank you to leave me alone.'

Elder reached down through the open window of the car and picked up the Polaroid camera he'd borrowed from Maureen earlier. The flash went off in Latham's face and he wasn't fast enough to block the shot with his arm.

'Thanks,' Elder said and, getting into the car, he turned the ignition, engaged gear and drove away, the image of Paul Latham becoming smaller and smaller in his rear-view mirror.

28

Shane had sold Pam Wilson's credit and debit cards, all of Gerald Kersley's save one. The money was stashed in a sock at the bottom of his sports bag. Even Angel didn't know where it was. Getaway money. Mad money. McKeirnan had taught him that. No matter how low you go, always keep a little something back. Then if you're right down to the wire and needs must . . .

There were other things McKeirnan had taught him too, things that had stuck, unlike the names of constellations, the names of the stars.

Always keep the advantage, never give everything away.

Always have something that will give you the edge. Like a blade, a knife. And if you have to use it, use it first. Take the upper hand. Hold your temper, keep it for when it matters. Don't waste it in situations where all it's going to do is get you into trouble. There'll be trouble enough, you'll see.

And then there had been McKeirnan's advice on women, on girls: never mind what they say, they all like a bit of this, a bit of that, they love it. A bit of rough. And this . . . and this . . .

With Angel in the sleeping-bag it had been different, little room to move, what could you do? But now they had the caravan: space, privacy. They'd arrived at the Newark site late at night, no thought of doing anything other than downing a few beers, smoking the odd joint, some good stuff going round – amphetamines, a few Es. Shane having a good time, getting high, starting to look at Angel in that way and even though she'd said no to taking more than a spliff or two herself, he figured that didn't matter. Once they got back to the caravan everything would be okay.

The moment they were inside, he grabbed her from behind and threw her down, yanking her skirt high over her behind and driving his hand between her legs. When she shouted he clamped a hand across her mouth and when she bit his finger he slapped her face. He grabbed for her again and she knocked his hands away and he punched her, hard, to teach her who was boss; pushed her back to the floor and squeezed hard at her breast, falling across her and forcing his fingers up inside, despite the fact that she was tight and dry.

'Shane! Shane! Shane! You're hurting! You're hurting! What the fuck d'you think you're doing?'

Gloating, he pushed harder and she caught hold of his wrist and held it fast.

'Shane. Stop, stop, stop. For God's sake, stop.'

Shane rocked back on his heels, breathing hard.

Tears were running down Angel's face, tears mixed with snot. Gingerly, she pulled her legs up close together and her skirt back down.

'I'm sorry,' he said, an interval later. 'I'm sorry, I thought . . .'

'You thought what?'

Shane turned his face away.

'You thought I'd like that? You thought that was what I wanted?'

'Yes.' His voice barely heard.

'Oh, Shane.'

She leaned slowly forward against him, resting her face high on his chest, the top of her head beneath his chin and the last of her tears warm on his neck. Then she leaned back again and slapped him with her open hand across one side of his face, slapped him as hard as she could. Not once but twice.

'Don't you ever try that with me again. Ever. Understood?'

And though his face stung and his eyes were watering and she had raised a weal over his cheek-bone with the nail of her middle finger, Shane did nothing. Said nothing. Stayed where he was. Even when Angel went outside and closed the door.

McKeirnan's rules. But McKeirnan was inside, likely facing another ten or twelve years before he could even think about asking for release. And Shane, here he was, free sort of, outside at least. The fuss there'd been, that had mostly died down. As for the police looking for him, didn't they have better things to do? Of course, coming back this way he'd been taking a chance, but if he kept himself pretty much to himself, stayed out of trouble, maybe he'd get away with it. Why not? After all the shit that had been handed down, wasn't he due a little luck? And he had Angel, didn't he? At least he thought he did. Wasn't that proof enough?

He thought she was never going to come back that

night. Considered going out after her, talking her round, but no, she was most likely in Della's caravan and just about the last thing he'd wanted right then had been the wrong side of Della's tongue.

So he lay there, restless, his head still abuzz. Despite the way Angel had reacted, he was thinking about that moment when he had grabbed her and thrown her down and when he did that he was remembering being with McKeirnan, McKeirnan and the girl. Lucy. All the things they had done. The pictures blurred yet clear enough in his mind. He felt himself growing hard and he was thinking he'd have to bring himself off when the door to the caravan opened and Angel stepped back inside.

In the dark he turned away from her silhouette. He could hear her taking off her clothes and he thought most likely she'd sleep in the chair or even in the old sleeping-bag on the floor, but instead she climbed in behind him and he held his breath as she settled in beside him, her back towards him, their skins, their spines barely touching.

'Angel,' he said softly, minutes later. But she said nothing and after a little while more he thought she was sleeping and that was when she started talking, telling him in a small clear voice of what had happened to her first when she was seven and then again when she was nearly eleven and when she was thirteen, and the anger inside Shane welled out of him and he lay there rigid, his fists clenched, wanting nothing more than to go and find them, the men who had done those things to her, and cut them, cut them until they bled and the blood had drained out of them and they were hanging upside down on a butcher's rail with hooks where their pricks had been.

218

And in the morning, when she was still sleeping, he found his knife and took it to the sink and cut deep into the flesh of his left hand and held it there, watching the blood run out.

'What happened to you?' Angel asked, once she was up and awake, looking at the plaster on his palm.

'Nothin'. Accident.'

'Fancy a cup of tea?' Angel said, moving past him.

'Yeah, why not?'

There were still a few splashes of blood high inside the metal sink and Angel washed them away while she was waiting for the kettle to boil.

◆

Everything was fine until later that day. Neither Shane nor Angel said anything more about what had passed between them the night before; Angel went to ready her darts stall and Shane began to wash down the inflatable. Music was coming from the dodgems, even though there were no visitors yet on the site and none of the dodgems were working. The music made Shane feel pretty good, some of it stuff he remembered hearing in prison, songs that might have been by Queen or Abba, and then it was Elvis – 'All Shook Up' and 'Teddy Bear' and 'Loving You' – Shane singing along as he worked and remembering then what McKeirnan had said about Elvis Presley, that he should have died when he was young and lean, not fat and old, and Shane not knowing whether that was right or wrong.

By now the first punters of the day were beginning to trickle through, kids mostly, small groups of them, ten-

and eleven-year-olds, then younger ones with their mums and once in a while their dads, and Shane was busy taking the money and doling out change, making sure everyone going on got shot of their shoes before they climbed the rope-ladder the first time, trying to keep in mind how many goes each kid had had and calling them back down if they tried to sneak another for free or getting the extra money out of their parents which was better still.

Time passed quickly like this and he was able to forget everything about what had happened before and what might go wrong again.

Early evening he saw that Angel was taking a break and sitting with four or so of the others, mostly lads who worked the fair and another he didn't recognise. It took him a little time, but eventually he managed to collar somebody else to spell him on the slide and he wandered over and joined them, Craig from the dodgems making the introductions. 'This is Brock,' and Brock, at closer sight, was one of those fat-bellied, bearded rockers who liked to call themselves Hell's Angels. Shane had come across a few of them inside and more when he'd been with McKeirnan. This one had tattoos the length of his arms and around his neck and a snake and a death's head side by side on the belly which hung fat and white over his belt, his T-shirt rising up as he leaned back and laughed and belched and laughed again.

'Here,' he said, tossing Shane a can of Heineken from the batch at his feet.

Shane caught it and snapped it open and when he did the beer squirted out over him causing Brock to laugh some more.

'Fuckin' waste,' he said. Then, leering at Angel, 'What

220

we should've done was pour it over girlie here and have ourselves a show.'

'Don't think about it,' Angel said and Shane bit his tongue.

Another beer or so on and Brock and Craig tired of discussing the respective merits of Nortons and Kawasakis and somehow the subject got back to Angel, how she wouldn't know she'd really been had until she'd gone low round the bend with her legs stretched round the pillion of a Harley 750.

'In your dreams,' Angel said and got up to leave.

Which was when Brock made a clumsy grab for her and she half-stumbled avoiding him and Shane, quick to his feet, told the biker to keep his fucking hands to himself.

'If I wasn't having such a good time,' Brock told him, 'I'd wrench your miserable fucking head off your fuckin' neck and shove it up your arse.'

At which Craig and the others hollered with laughter, Brock himself louder than the rest, especially when Shane turned and started to walk away, hoots of derision following him on his way.

Angel, not sure what he was doing, half-heartedly tried to intercept him, but Shane pushed her aside and went straight to the caravan, coming back out again almost immediately and walking fast back towards the group he had just left, quickening his pace still more for the last ten metres before sticking his knife into Brock's belly and slicing upwards through the loose, pale skin.

Brock stared up at him, open-mouthed, too astonished at first even to scream or shout, both hands clutching at his abdomen as if to hold it together. Shane spat in his face and turned away, one arm around Angel, leading her back towards their caravan, no one following them, no one, for those moments, daring to.

Inside the caravan, Shane dropped the knife on to the floor between them.

'You didn't have to do that,' Angel said.

'Yeah,' Shane said. 'Yes, I fuckin' did.'

He was reaching things down from the narrow shelf and stuffing them into his rucksack – T-shirt, thin sweater, underwear.

'What are you doing?'

'What's it look like?'

Angel turned away, eyes closed.

As he moved towards the door, Shane's arm brushed hers.

'You're coming back?' she said.

'Maybe, yeah.' Stooping, he picked up the knife and slid it down into his bag. 'Tell Otto a couple of days, okay?'

Rather than see him walk away, Angel pushed the door to the caravan quickly closed.

29

Elder received his first-ever text message on Saturday morning. It was from Katherine. When he had added the necessary vowels and consonants and applied a leavening of common sense, it appeared she was running in a three-way club meeting at Loughborough that afternoon. Why didn't he come along?

Katherine was competing in the two hundred metres and the four-by-one-hundred relay, neither perhaps her best events, but good speed training and besides, there were other athletes to accommodate. There was a small crowd but a good track and the weather conditions were near perfect: not too much heat and the kind of wind that could only be called a light breeze. Katherine had drawn the outside lane in the two hundred, fine if you liked cruising into the bend, the sense of being out there all on your own, but less good in that, unless you turned your head, you had no real idea for ages where the other runners were, and turning your head was something you just shouldn't do.

Past the halfway point and with the stagger starting to unwind, it looked as though Katherine's lead was unassailable; midway down the straight and with the tape in sight, suddenly there were three of the other runners pulling back on her; in the last moments of the race Katherine glimpsed them in the corner of her eye and dug deeper, pushing for a final surge that didn't quite materialise. A dead heat for third, Elder thought, nothing to separate her from the Loughborough Harriers athlete, and then, when the announcement was made, Katherine had been pushed into fourth place by five hundredths of a second.

He was standing with her when the result came over the loudspeakers and, remembering what had happened at the Harvey Hadden Stadium, feared it would send her into the doldrums at best, but no, she seemed philosophical enough.

'That's what I've got to work on, my speed through that final third.'

In the relay, she was running the third leg, her team with a slight lead when she took over the baton, that lead marginally increased by the time she'd handed over to the athlete on the final stretch, who cruised home with several yards to spare, arms aloft.

The meeting over, Elder bought a can of Coke and sat with his book and tried to keep his mind from straying elsewhere: Helen Blacklock up in Whitby, hoping for news, a knot in her stomach tightening every time the phone chanced to ring; Shane Donald still somewhere at large.

'Dad.' Katherine was walking towards him with two of the other girls, one of whom Elder thought he recognised from the relay team. 'Any chance we can give Ali and Justine a lift back?'

'I don't see why not.'

Elder scrambled to his feet, Katherine made the slightly more formal introductions and they shook hands. A few hiccups with the one-way system and they were heading for the A60 that would take them through Bunny and Ruddington to Nottingham.

'What are you doing later?' Elder asked, inclining his head towards Katherine in the front seat.

When she didn't answer right away, one of the girls in the back seat piped up. 'She's got a hot date, Mr Elder.' Both girls laughed.

'Is that true, Kate?' Elder asked.

'Of course it's not,' Katherine retorted. 'They're just being stupid.' But she was blushing despite herself, his mature daughter reduced to twelve or thirteen.

'How about you, Dad?' Katherine asked a short while later. 'What are you up to?'

'Oh, nothing special.'

'No villains to catch?'

'I don't do that any more, remember?'

'No?'

Elder didn't respond.

'Mum's home, you know,' Katherine said. 'And I'll bet you anything she'll be on her own. Why don't you give her a call?'

'I'll think about it.'

They both knew that was all he would do.

◆

Maureen said that she would meet him in the Chand, a curry house near the foot of the Mansfield Road, somewhere between a quarter to ten and a quarter past.

'Sorry it's a bit vague, Frank; someone I've got to see.'

An informant, Elder guessed. Unpaid overtime where Maureen was concerned. 'Don't worry,' he said. 'I'll take a book.'

'Okay. And Frank . . .'

'Yes?'

'We're not talking anything but business, understood?'

'Understood.' He knew he should have kept his thoughts about Maddy Birch to himself.

Arriving at the restaurant around ten, Elder ordered poppadams and chutney and a bottle of Kingfisher and propped open his book: not the best judge of character, Copperfield was getting in a right tangle over the behaviour of his best friend, who had just eloped with the young and vulnerable niece of a Yarmouth fisherman. Yarmouth. In his mind's eye Elder travelled north along the contours of the North Sea coast: Great Yarmouth, Cromer, Skegness, Mablethorpe, Cleethorpes, Bridlington, Scarborough, Whitby.

'You look a bit of a sad git, you know, Frank, sitting there like that,' Maureen said. 'Just a book for company.'

'I've done worse,' Elder replied, slipping the envelope he was using for a bookmark into place.

Maureen sat and when the waiter appeared at her shoulder ordered a pint of lager. 'Same again?' she asked, indicating Elder's almost empty glass.

'This'll last,' he said, with a shake of the head.

Maureen smiled. 'Prudent as ever.'

'You know me.' From the plastic bag at the back of his chair he withdrew the Polaroid camera and set it down. 'Thanks for the loan of this.'

'Any result?'

Opening the book again, he took a single photograph from inside the envelope and passed it across.

'Hm,' Maureen said, 'not bad-looking in an arty kind of way.'

'Apparently.'

'Tell me about it,' she said.

Pausing only so that they could place their orders, that's what he did.

'So now,' she said, when he had finished, 'you've got a reason for disliking him, but no proof.'

Nodding, Elder lifted the picture of Paul Latham away as their food arrived. Chicken rogan josh, lamb pasanda, pilau rice, sag aloo, more poppadams and a peshwari naan.

'The team looking into Susan Blacklock's disappearance, they didn't question Latham at the time?'

Chewing, Elder shook his head.

'So if he was having it off with her, no reason he's going to come forward, jeopardise his career.'

'Maybe not.'

'He just sits tight, hopes it will all blow over without he becomes involved. Must have thought he'd managed it till you came nosing around. And even now, you don't know it for a fact. I mean, suppose he did take her back to that – what? – cottage of his. Five or six hours with an attractive girl. For all you know they could have been reading all the damned play they'd missing seeing. That and drinking cups of tea.'

'It's possible,' Elder agreed.

'Any damned thing's possible, Frank. One thing this job teaches you. Any damned thing at all.'

The lamb was tender, not too heavily spiced, the rogan josh slippery with tomato and rich.

227

'Even if he was shagging her,' Maureen said, 'it doesn't mean he had anything to do with her disappearance.'

'I know that.'

'But you've got a feeling.'

'Something like that.'

Maureen grinned. 'You've been wrong before.'

'Thank you very much.'

'Seriously,' she said, 'what are you going to do now?'

Elder shrugged. 'Take the photograph up to Yorkshire, tout it around. See if it rings any bells.'

Maureen put down her fork. 'Maybe you should have done that before you confronted him.'

'I dare say.'

They were quiet for a time, concentrating on the food. The restaurant was filling up now, approaching closing time. Elder asked Maureen about work. A father of three who had killed his wife and children, then tried to kill himself and failed. A suspicious death where the body had been exhumed. A shooting, probably drugs related, in St Ann's. The kidnapping of a five-year-old boy in the north of the county, a ransom demand the parents had complied with before contacting the police, their money taken and the boy not yet returned. It was clear from the way Maureen recounted the story she suspected one of the parents of being somehow involved.

'Busy then,' Elder observed.

'Overstretched not the word,' Maureen said.

Elder leaned back as the waiter reached down to clear away their plates. 'Coffee?'

'Go on then.'

It had just arrived, together with several foil-wrapped mints and the bill, when the phone started to ring.

228

'Yours or mine?' Maureen asked with a smile as she reached inside her bag. Somehow the idea of Elder with his own mobile phone amused her.

She listened for several moments, face becoming grave.

'Right,' she said into the phone. 'I'll be in.'

And then to Elder, as, rising, she fished for her wallet and some money to pay the bill. 'A girl's gone missing. Just sixteen. Last seen at Rufford Country Park just before four this afternoon.'

30

Emma Harrison had left her home in Beeston, on the outskirts of Nottingham, at a little after nine fifteen that early June morning. Her mother had driven her and her younger sister, Paula, into the city centre, the express purpose being to buy Paula some new shoes. Emma she was dropping off near the Friar Lane roundabout, close to the Old Market Square where she was meeting her friends Alison and Ashley. Emma, her mother had thought, not always at her best before noon on a Saturday, had been in a particularly good mood that morning, polite and cheerful. At one point in their relatively short journey, as they were passing along University Boulevard, Mrs Harrison had asked Paula to please stop kicking the back of her seat, to which Paula had replied that she was not and had promptly done it again. It had been Emma who had smoothed the situation over, bringing a smile to her mother's face at the same time as preventing her younger sister from descending into the kind of ten-year-old sulk that could have jeopardised the whole expedition. She's growing up, Mrs Harrison had thought, maturing, accepting responsibility.

'You won't be late back?' Mrs Harrison said, leaning

across from behind the wheel. She had pulled over on a double yellow line, partly blocking the inside lane.

Emma ducked her head back down towards the open car window. 'Mum, we've been through all this. Alison's dad's meeting us and then dropping me off, okay?'

'All right. But don't forget your father and I have got tickets for the theatre. You're looking after your sister.'

From the back seat, Paula let out a mock groan of anguish.

'Okay, Mum. Don't worry.'

'Bye then. Have a lovely time.'

For a few moments, as she eased back out into the traffic, Mrs Harrison glimpsed her elder daughter in the rear-view mirror, before losing sight of her, intent upon manoeuvring into the lane that would take her to the car park off Derby Road.

Emma walked back towards the underpass, glancing at her reflection in the glass shop front to her right, denim skirt and a flowered halter top, her fair hair fastened in a high pony-tail, pink sandals, a small beaded bag from Accessorize over one shoulder.

Alison and Ashley were already waiting, swinging their legs near the fountain, Ashley with a rucksack full almost to overflowing with provisions her mother had insisted she take with her: sandwiches and crisps, bottled water, sun cream, an extra cardigan and a plastic waterproof that folded away inside a book-size bag.

'For heaven's sake, Mum,' Ashley had complained. 'We're catching a bus, not crossing the Atlantic. Besides, there's a perfectly good café there.'

'Save your pocket money,' her mother had replied, shooing her out of the house. 'Spend it on better things.'

On weekends and bank holidays through the summer there were special buses that went out to Rufford Park, then on to Clumber Park and Newstead Abbey. At Rufford that day, besides a sculpture trail that went down through the gardens and towards the lake, there were four local bands playing live in the grounds. Alison had assured them the singer with one of them was the spitting image of Robbie Williams. Robbie Williams before he got too old. It was going to be a great day out.

They spent the first half an hour or so mooching around the shop in the old stable block, nearly but never quite buying bangles and rings and hand-painted cards and other arty things; then Alison wanted to go the café because she'd seen these boys heading in that direction; but when they got there, she'd decided she didn't like them at all, also very Alison, so they sat on stools by the far wall laughing and joking and teasing Alison so much that in the end she stormed off to the toilet in a temper.

Once Alison had calmed down and they'd all made up, Emma suggested following the sculpture trail down through the gardens but the others had outvoted her and they'd walked off in the direction of the lake instead, sitting on a bench to eat Ashley's sandwiches and feeding the crusts to a growing crowd of noisy geese and ducks.

'C'mon,' Alison had said, jumping up. 'The music's starting.'

The first band were awful, Emma thought, dead folky, the kind of thing her parents listened to when they'd had people to dinner and were sitting round afterwards pretending not to be smoking dope. After that it was a real boy band, Boyzone with acne, and all the little eight- and nine-year-olds and their grannies were going crazy and loving it and Ashley said let's go back to the café, but Alison had staked out a good place and didn't want to lose it, so they split up for a while, Emma borrowing Ashley's spare cardigan because it was clouding over and she was getting goose-pimples with only her halter top.

The queue to get served in the café took for ever and so did the one for the loo and by the time the two of them had pushed their way back to where Alison was sitting, the third group were already into their second number. 'See what I mean?' Alison shouted above the volume. The singer, Emma thought, looked more like Gareth Gates than a young Robbie Williams, and she supposed he didn't sound too bad, but it was the bass player with dyed white hair and tight snake-skin jeans who was sexy, seriously sexy, and she nudged the others and they all laughed, knowing what she meant and before long they were jumping up and down and dancing on the spot and it was as great as they'd hoped it would be. Truly great.

As the band came to the end of their final number, the drummer throwing his sticks out over the crowd while the singer milked the applause and the bass player stood to one side looking beautifully cool, Emma decided she had to go to the loo again and Ashley said, looking at her watch, they ought to hurry, the bus left in twenty minutes, so they agreed to meet up at the bus stand on the far side of the car park to catch the four o'clock. By Ashley's watch it was three forty-one.

Neither Alison nor Ashley saw Emma again.

When she hadn't turned up with ten minutes to go, the two girls ran back and checked the toilets and the café and the shop but there was no sign. Back at the bus-stop they begged the driver to wait and he did so for a couple of minutes, Alison and Ashley hoping against hope that Emma would suddenly appear.

The driver told them he had to go.

'What are we going to do?' Ashley asked.

'We'll have to get on,' Alison said. 'This is the last one.'

As soon as the bus had pulled in at the Victoria bus station they told Alison's father what had happened. Tight-lipped, he drove them to Emma's house and immediately Emma's parents took her younger sister, Paula, across to a neighbour and drove out to Rufford themselves to look for their daughter.

At a little after nine thirty that evening, they went into Nottingham Central police station and reported Emma missing.

◆

That night the dream returned with a vengeance. Soft flesh that pressed and slithered against his own, something alive that twisted beneath his feet and broke as he climbed the stairs. Threadbare, the blanket thrown across the bed, his hand gripping its greasy hem, eyes averted, breath held against the stench; at the moment of jerking it back to reveal what lay beneath, thank God, he woke.

The scream that faded on the air was Elder's own.

The T-shirt in which he slept was clammy with sweat; his skin burned hot and cold.

In the bathroom he stripped off and towelled down, splashed cold water on his face; the features that looked back at him from the mirror were older than he recognised and knew too much.

Below, Willie Bell was sitting at the kitchen table, whisky bottle open, Elder's glass already poured.

'The lassie out at Rufford Park?' Willie said.

'I dare say.'

'Perhaps she'll be home this morning, draggin' her tail behind her.' Willie said.

'Perhaps.'

Neither of them believed it to be true.

31

The sun broke through the clouds at the exact moment
Elder crested the hill, lighting up the ribbon of road that
curved sharply downwards before climbing again in a
straight Roman line between heather and gorse. He had
phoned Helen Blackwood before leaving Nottingham,
quick to assure her that he had discovered nothing new,
nothing major, but he would like to talk to her nevertheless; if she were free that evening, maybe he could buy
her dinner.

'Come here,' she said, 'why don't you? Long as you're
prepared to risk my cooking. I'm off work at six, give me
time to pick up a few things on the way home – say eight
o'clock?'

'Okay.'

'That's not too late for you?'

'No, it'll suit me fine.'

Now he would have the bulk of the afternoon to see
what memories, if any, his Polaroid of Paul Latham
might unlock. As outside chances went, he realised, this
was further afield than most.

◆

'Tell you what,' Kelly Todd said, 'why don't you let me do your hands? Then we can talk at the same time.'

Elder was not immediately taken with the idea, she could see.

'It's not poofy, you know. There's all kinds of blokes have it done now. All sorts, you'd be surprised. Come in here to pick up their wives and while they're waiting I slip them down into the chair. Besides, I've had two cancellations this afternoon and I'm dead bored. Go on, just get shot of that jacket. That's it.'

Elder sat down and unbuttoned his shirt cuffs and began to roll back his sleeves.

Wearing pink today, bright lipstick in a similar shade and with her hair piled high and clipped in place, Kelly rolled the trolley holding her paraphernalia into position and took a seat facing him.

'Look there, you see,' she said, taking hold of one of Elder's hands, 'these nails, they're in a right state. Bite them, don't you? Some of them. Well, most men do.' When she smiled, she looked younger by years, almost carefree. 'There's no law against using a nail-file, you know. In the privacy of your own bathroom, of course.' She laughed and her laugh was surprisingly light, Elder could smell the mixture of tobacco and mint on her breath.

'Just let me have that hand again. There.' She slid his fingers down into a bowl of lukewarm, soapy water. 'You've not found anything then? Susan?'

'Nothing definite, no.'

'No, I doubt you'd be back here if you had. Besides, there'd have been something in the paper. If there'd been a body, I mean.'

Elder nodded.

'I'll be honest, after all this time I'm surprised you're still looking.' Removing his hand, she began to pat it dry. 'That girl who's just gone missing, Nottingham way, it was on the news this morning, that's nothing to do with you, is it?'

'No, not really.'

'Poor kid. Sixteen, isn't she?' Kelly shook her head. 'Crying shame.'

'She could still turn up, it's early days.'

She stopped what she was doing to look at him. 'You have to believe that, don't you? At first, anyway. Bit like the parents, I suppose.'

'Kids go missing all the time, youngsters. All right, they might be sleeping rough somewhere, but mostly they're not . . . something terrible hasn't happened to them, they're alive.'

He knew the figures, knew that statistically, no matter how far the media lined its pockets fermenting things, serious offences against children and young people were decreasing. Between 1988 and 1999, in England and Wales, the annual number of five- to sixteen-year-olds murdered dropped from four per million to three. The number of under-fives murdered fell from twelve per million to nine. In the same period incidents of gross indecency with a child were down by over twenty per cent. And most child deaths, he knew, took place inside the home rather than outside it. Rarely on the edge of a cliff or the shrubbery of a park. Most of those who abused or attacked children were members of the child's own family, a fact too highly charged for most people to entertain or comprehend.

'You still think Susan might be alive somewhere, then?' Kelly said. 'Living a different life?'

Elder sighed. 'I don't know.'

'Hold still. Just let me get to the cuticles on this hand.'

A girl poked her head round from the hairdressing side of the salon and asked Kelly if she wanted a cup of tea.

'Oh, go on then.'

'Tea?' the girl said in Elder's direction.

'No, thanks.'

It was time for Elder's other hand to soak. 'When we talked before,' he said, 'you mentioned someone in Susan's drama group who might have had a bit of a crush on her.'

'That's right, yes.'

'Rob doesn't ring any bells? Rob Shriver?'

Drying his right hand, Kelly gave it some thought. 'No. No, I'm sorry. You didn't come all the way up here to ask me that?'

'No.' Swivelling in his chair, he reached round into the inside pocket of his coat and took out an envelope. 'In there.'

Carefully, Kelly drew out the photograph. 'Looks a bit startled, doesn't he?'

'Do you recognise him?'

Kelly shook her head. 'I don't think so. I'm sorry.'

The girl brought in a mug of tea, set it down on the edge of the trolley and went away again without speaking.

'Who is he?'

'He ran the drama group Susan belonged to.'

'A teacher?'

'Yes.'

'And you think they might have been . . .' Her expression finished the sentence for her.

'It's possible.'

239

Kelly picked up the Polaroid again and studied it closely. 'Yes, I suppose so.'

'What do you mean?'

'Looking at this – I mean, I don't know what sort of a bloke he really was, of course, could've been a right bastard – but no, he looks, well, sympathetic somehow. You can imagine it, her falling for someone like this. It's the eyes, you see. There. Look. The eyes.'

Elder looked. Sympathy wasn't necessarily what he saw. 'She never mentioned him, Latham, when she was talking about school or anything?'

'Never. Not as I remember.'

'And you've not seen him before?'

'I'm sorry.'

'Ah, well.'

'Here,' Kelly said, 'let me put this back in its envelope before it gets polish on it or something. Then I just want to see to these nails, squarish I think, buff them up and they'll look a treat. Feel better, too, you see.'

◆

Christine Harker was working her afternoon shift at the greengrocer's near the harbour bridge, the sides of her green overall darkened by the constant rubbing of her hands. When Elder entered, she recognised him right away, acknowledging him with a nod of the head before continuing to serve a middle-aged woman – a woman roughly the same age as herself – with onions, courgettes, potatoes and cabbage.

'How are things?' Elder enquired, once she'd tendered the woman her change.

240

'Mustn't grumble.'

'I wondered if I could show you a photograph?'

Christine Harker's eyes narrowed. 'Of course.'

She held the Polaroid between thumb and middle finger, Elder waiting for her to dismiss it instantly, but the disavowal didn't come. The longer she studied it, the more something inside Elder began to tighten and turn.

But then, 'No,' she said. 'I don't think it is.'

'You don't think it's who?'

'The man I saw her talking to.'

'Go on.' Elder's innards gripped fast.

'I thought of it after you were here a week or so back, up at the holiday park. Talking to you, it jogged the memory somehow. I should have got in touch then, I suppose. In case it was important, you know.'

Another customer came into the shop and an assistant in an overall similar to Christine's came out from the back room to serve.

'You saw Susan talking to a man,' Elder guided her.

'Yes. The day before she disappeared it would have been.'

'The day after you heard her and her dad, Trevor, having a row.'

'Yes. That's who I thought it was at first, her dad. But no. Somebody older, fortyish maybe. Trevor's age or thereabouts, but not him.'

'Where was this?'

'Just up by the main entrance to the site. Standing there, talking to him. I was a way off, just coming out of the office.'

'And did you – this might be difficult to answer – how well did you get the impression they knew one another?'

241

'Oh, I don't think I could say.'

'Were they standing close to one another or not?'

'Normal, you know. Like you and me. I thought he was asking her directions, to be honest, either that or something about the site.'

'You didn't see him come in, though, into the park?'

'No. No. He turned and walked away.'

'Off down the coast path? To a car, what?'

'I didn't see a car. But then he didn't look like a hiker either, no rucksack or anything like that. Of course, if he'd had a car it could have been parked back up the road a bit out of sight.'

Elder nodded. 'You say he didn't look like a walker – how was he dressed?'

'Just sort of ordinary, as I remember. Beige sort of trousers – they might have been those, what d'you call them? Chinos. That and a shirt. Like I say, ordinary.'

'And when he moved away, Susan, what did she do?'

'I don't know. I mean, it was only a few moments I saw them. If it hadn't been for that set-to with her dad the day before, I doubt I'd have given it as much attention as I did.'

'So could she have followed him, when he turned away?'

'No, I don't think so. At least, I never saw her. She was just stood there when I walked back down towards the shop.' She gave Elder an apologetic smile. 'That's the best I can do, I'm afraid.'

'No, it's fine. You've done well. Especially after all this time.'

Christine Harker smiled. 'Gets that way, don't it. As you get older, I mean. Ask me what I was doing day before yesterday and I'd draw a blank.'

Elder smiled in return. 'I wonder, did you mention this to the police when they interviewed you?'

'I'm honestly not sure. I mean, I might have. It was all a bit of a blur at the time. I really don't know.'

There had been no reference to it, Elder thought, in the case notes he had read.

'Can I ask you,' he said, 'to look at the photograph again?'

She did so, taking her time, not rushing, but again she shook her head. 'No, it's not the same. This man, for one thing, he may not be any younger, but somehow he seems it. I don't know if that makes any sense. It's not what he's wearing even, not from what you can see. His hair, maybe.' She shook her head. 'I can't explain it better than that. I'm sorry.'

'You shouldn't be. Like I say, you've done brilliantly. If more witnesses had your recall the job would be a lot easier.'

A job I don't really have any more, he thought as she walked with him to the door.

'I don't think I've been a lot of help,' she said again.

'Not at all.'

'Tell me one thing,' she said, concerned. 'If I had remembered this at the time, made more of it say, would that have made a difference? To finding Susan, I mean?'

'It's hard to know. But on balance, no, I'd say probably not.' Briefly, he rested his hand on her shoulder. 'You've nothing to reproach yourself with, don't worry about that.'

The bridge was about to be raised to let a tall-masted boat through into the inner harbour and Elder was going to have to wait before being able to cross. Stepping back on to the cobbled road by the old Customs House, he looked up the Guiseleys' number in his notebook and transferred it to his mobile phone, which was proving useful after all.

Esme answered on the fourth ring, surprising Elder by recognising his voice right off.

'I don't suppose Don's around?' Elder said. 'I was hoping I'd catch him.'

'If you're in Whitby,' Esme said, 'you might be in luck. I've told him he's got to pick up a few things at Safeway, and when he does that he usually has a pint or two in the Board. It's near the foot of the steps.' A smile came into her voice. 'He's either in there or he's slipping around.'

'Okay, Esme. Thanks.'

If Don Guiseley was surprised to see him it didn't show. 'You can top this up if you've a mind.'

Elder nodded and went to the bar where he ordered a pint for himself and a half which he poured into Guiseley's glass.

'Taken a shine to this part of the world, then?' Guiseley said.

'Not exactly.'

Guiseley worked tobacco down into the bowl of his pipe with his thumb. 'Still chasing shadows?'

'That what I'm doing?'

'You tell me.'

Succinctly, Elder told him of his suspicions about Susan Blacklock and Paul Latham, about the meeting between Susan and a so-far unidentified man the day before she disappeared.

Guiseley held a match to his pipe, then laid the

matchbox across it and drew hard; dissatisfied, he shook out another match and tried again. A bit like fishing, Elder thought, smoking a pipe: most of the fun was in the preamble, rather than the thing itself.

'The business with the teacher,' Guiseley said finally, 'I'll buy that. Commonplace, I don't doubt. There was a bit of a trend for it the other way round a while back, d'you remember? Women teachers in their thirties, married most of them, takin' off with lads of fifteen or sixteen. Papers were full of it. Mind you, not hard to see why. Four or five times a night at that age, bloody women must think they'd died and gone to heaven, some of 'em.'

He chuckled and swallowed down some beer.

'You'd have your work cut out, mind, proving anything after all this time. 'Less you can scare a few witnesses out of the woodwork, of course, turn up a few mucky photographs. But even if you did, though, on its own, what does it mean? A bit of hanky-panky for the pair of them. For the lass, a modicum of heartbreak, I dare say. Tears before bedtime. I doubt we're talking grand passions here. Life and death. Or is that the way your mind's heading?'

'I don't know.'

For a moment, Guiseley glanced over his shoulder, attracted by some small commotion down on the beach. Two small dogs in conflict over the same ball, their owners trying to prise them apart, threats and harsh words. The ball, meanwhile, forgotten, floated out on the tide.

'She'd've been in love with him, of course. Thought she was. But the other way about? Unlikely, for all that.'

'But not impossible,' Elder said.

'Okay, say that's right. He loves her, she's turned his life around; he's besotted and for her it's just a bit of fun. He gets all serious and she doesn't want to know. It frightens her, she's out of her depth. She tells him she doesn't want to see him again.'

'And then what?' Elder said.

'You tell me.'

Elder stared back at him.

'You think he killed her,' Guiseley said.

'I think it's possible.'

'How? Why?'

'Because of what you said. She's saying it's over and he won't accept it. She's written him a letter, let's say, while she's off with her parents on holiday. He follows her up here, wanting to change her mind. They argue, fight, maybe what happens is an accident, a rush of temper, I don't know.'

Guiseley was back to fiddling with his pipe. 'You needed the woman, didn't you? Harker, is that what you said her name was? You needed her to identify him and she didn't.'

'She was a good seventy metres away, possibly more.'

'She's a good witness, you said so yourself.'

'It doesn't mean he didn't meet her another time.'

'And it doesn't mean that he did.'

'I know,' Elder said. 'You don't have to spell it out.'

'Hang about,' Guiseley said, rising slowly to his feet. 'My turn to get them in.'

The pub was still fairly quiet, a smattering of early-evening drinkers, regulars, gathered around the bar. A few visitors, out-of-towners sitting around the periphery. Music, low and pointless, papering over the cracks.

'One thing,' Guiseley said, returning. 'One thing you should ask yourself: if when you'd met him, this Latham, he'd turned out to be a grand chap, salt of the earth, dedicated, friendly, the sort of bloke you could see yourself spending time with, a few pints of an evening, much like this, would you still be going after him the way you are?'

Elder sipped his beer, sipped then swallowed. 'I think so, yes. If I thought it likely he'd harmed her. Yes.'

Guiseley released a sigh. 'Well, you know your own mind, of course. But I will tell you this. If I were your commanding officer, me a super and you a young DI, I'd say where's your evidence, lad, imagination aside? I'd reckon you were flying a kite, head in the clouds instead of down on earth.' He laughed. 'And you'd be calling me an old fool, behind my back at least.'

'No,' Elder said. 'No, Don, you're not that. Not a fool, at least.'

Without a ready change of subject they continued to drink in silence.

32

By the time Elder arrived at the house, some minutes after eight, Helen Blacklock was sitting out on her front step, smoking a cigarette. A glass of wine, half-empty, alongside her.

'I'm sorry I'm late.'

'It's all right.' She smiled at him warily with her eyes.

'I met up with somebody, got to talking . . .'

'It's all right.' Her face was slightly flushed. The first glass, Elder wondered, most likely not.

'I like to sit out here of an evening.' She laughed. 'Gives the neighbours something to think about.' She drew on her cigarette and stubbed it out against the underside of the step.

'It's a nice evening,' Elder said.

There were martins swooping low over the house, round and down and round again in shallow loops; martins or swifts, he was never sure which. Swallows he could recognise.

'I suppose we'd best go in,' Helen said.

He offered her his hand, but she ignored it and got to her feet with just a little help from the adjacent wall.

'I'm not drunk, you know.'

'I know.'

'Nor rusted with age.'

'No.'

He followed her inside.

The smell of tobacco he'd noticed before was almost lost beneath the scent of polish; Helen had run a duster over the surfaces, tidied round. The settee she'd pushed closer to the side wall so as to extend the dining table on which two places were set, a small vase of flowers between.

'Let me have your coat.'

'Thanks.'

She disappeared with it and when she returned it was with an opened bottle in her hand.

'You're going to join me, I hope?'

'Why not?'

She poured wine into his glass and then refilled her own.

'I hope it's okay.'

'I'm sure it will be fine.'

'Cheers, then.'

'Cheers.'

She was wearing a blue dress, blue and white, short sleeves and a squarish neckline, the skirt slightly flared; white shoes with a low heel. The dress was tight at the waist and Elder thought she might not have worn it for some little time. Above her eyes, her make-up was bluish grey; the lipstick round her mouth, dark red, had smudged against the glass.

'Do you want to talk now or later?' Helen asked.

'Silence doesn't seem such a great idea.'

'That's not what I mean.'

'I know.'

'So which?'

'Later. Later, I think.'

'Okay, take a seat. Dinner won't be long.'

Elder sat at one end of the settee. The wine was red and reasonably spicy; he had no idea what it was but to his palate it was more than okay. The framed photograph of Susan above the fireplace was still there, but the other, that had shown her with her parents, a touch awkwardly between them Elder had thought, was no longer on top of the television. Possibly Helen had moved it while dusting and not got around to putting it back. I think your sixteen-year-old daughter was most probably screwing her teacher, how did you slip that easily into the conversation? After the main course? With the dessert?

'A top-up?' Helen asked, popping her head round the door.

'Not quite yet.'

'Just be a couple of minutes now.'

'All right.'

It was pasta: penne with a meat-and-tomato sauce, broccoli and a green salad. Ready-grated Parmesan cheese in a small tub. Garlic bread. Halfway through, Helen interrupted a conversation about holidays with a yelp.

'Melon. I forgot the melon. I bought it for a starter and it's still out there in the bag.'

'It doesn't matter.'

'It's a waste.'

'Maybe we can have it for dessert.'

'I bought something else for dessert.'

Elder smiled sympathetically and finished his wine

250

and then nodded when Helen offered to replenish his glass. A drop more for herself and the bottle was empty.

'I should have brought a bottle with me,' Elder said. 'It was thoughtless, I'm sorry.'

'No, you're my guest.'

'Even so, isn't that what you're supposed to do? Wine or flowers or something?'

'I don't know,' Helen said, and laughed. 'I forget.'

'Yes.'

'You too?'

'When Joanne and I were together we used to go out quite a bit. If we could find a babysitter. Friends of hers mostly. She preferred not to spend too much time in the company of police officers.'

'Apart from you,' Helen said.

Elder didn't reply.

'You went to see Trevor, didn't you?' she said.

'He told you.'

Helen shook her head. 'No, she did.'

'His wife?'

'The chipmunk. That's what I always call her. To myself at least. Anyway, reading the riot act she was, over the telephone. What right had I to send people round to bother her Trevor, get him all agitated, worked up? He had to take a day off work, apparently, after talking to you.'

'That's just it, he didn't. He wouldn't talk to me, refused point-blank.'

'He wants to pretend it didn't happen,' Helen said.

'That Susan disappeared?'

'That she ever existed.'

They ate the rest of the course without saying very

251

much, after which Helen collected the plates and carried them into the kitchen, returning with raspberries and vanilla ice-cream in separate bowls and two pieces of cheese, Swaledale and Lancashire, on an oval plate with crackers and celery.

Elder thought she might have used the opportunity to shed a few tears.

'It's a little girl you had, wasn't it? I remember you talking about her once, back you know . . . She'd have been what? Eighteen months when Susan disappeared?'

'Two. Around two.'

'Grown-up now, then.'

Elder nodded. 'Sixteen.'

'The same age as . . .'

'Yes.'

'Before, when you were talking before, something you said . . . you and your wife, you're not together any more?'

'Not for a while now.'

'And your daughter . . .'

'Katherine.'

'You still see her?'

'Not as much as I'd like. Though that's my fault, I dare say, much of it.'

'But you do see her?'

'Yes.'

Elder finished off his ice-cream and berries, cut a slice of Lancashire and ate it with a cracker. Helen pushed raspberries around her plate, toyed with the ends of her hair.

'It wasn't very good, was it?'

'What?'

'The dinner.'

'It was fine.' The pasta, some of it, had stuck together, the broccoli had been overcooked. 'Really, I enjoyed it.'

Helen didn't look convinced.

'I'll just get this out of the way,' she said some minutes later. 'I can make coffee, if you'd like.'

'Thanks, yes, that'd be nice. But let me give you a hand with these.'

'You stay there. There's no need.'

'No, it's all right.'

Helen slid the dishes into the sink and was turning away just as Elder advanced towards her, empty glasses in his hands.

'I told you not to bother.'

'No bother.'

He reached past her to set the glasses down and as he leaned back again, his face close to hers, close enough, she kissed him, or he kissed her, it scarcely mattered which, they were kissing; Elder with his eyes shut tight as her mouth moved over his, his tongue on hers and her breathing loud and ragged and when he touched her his fingers accidentally found a small place at the side of her dress where the seam had split and the tips of his fingers were touching skin.

'Frank.'

She spoke his name which he hadn't known she'd known and for an answer he kissed the side of her face and on down into her neck and she said his name again only louder this time and he moved his hand against her and felt a few more stitches give and now he had hold of her inside her dress, the flesh moving easily beneath fingers and thumb, and she was kissing the corner of his mouth and the bridge of his nose and his eyes and as he moved against her she went awkwardly backwards and then down, half-stumbling, on to her knees and he went with her, still holding her, and she pulled at the open collar of his shirt and when the button refused to give she bit the underside of his lip, not hard, but hard enough and he moved his hand from inside her dress and touched her breast and she jerked back and clipped her head against the wooden edge of the sink and said, 'Frank, I'm too old to do this on the kitchen floor.'

He got to his feet, suddenly embarrassed, but she took his hand and led him to the stairs and there was a moment when, as the old nursery rhyme says, they were neither up nor down, and when he might have pulled away, pulled back, come to his senses, had second thoughts; but she turned, mid-stair, and bending her face towards him she kissed him full on the mouth and long and after that there were no questions nor doubts nor hesitations.

'Don't close the door, Frank,' she said, once they were inside the room. 'It will be too hot.'

Kicking off her shoes and crossing past the end of the bed – a double bed with a patterned quilt in shades of green and white pillows resting up against a plain head-board – she drew the curtains closed.

Elder stooped to take off his shoes.

'Frank, help me with these.' She stood with her back to him while he fidgeted three round pearl buttons through their holes and unsnagged a loop of material from a small hook at the top of the dress. And then, stepping out of the dress, she stood facing him in knickers and a peach-coloured bra. Her thighs were stocky and round and her belly swelled and hung down a little and her breasts were wide and full.

'Don't stare, Frank. It's rude.'

He smiled and got to unbuttoning his shirt and when she asked him if he wanted help with the rest said he did not.

'Wait,' she said, when he was down to his boxer shorts. 'Let me do that.'

Sitting on the edge of the bed she lowered them till the elastic was just below his balls and took him quickly in her mouth, licking away the first drops of come, before taking the head in her mouth again and washing her tongue across it so slowly Elder was frightened he would finish there and then. Relinquishing him with a grin, she licked him deftly from tip to stem and then lay back on the bed, legs parted and knees slightly raised.

He made a channel through the wet cotton of her knickers with his tongue, then eased the material aside and, as she raised herself from the surface of the bed, ran his tongue back along the salt, pink line between the curls of dark hair, relishing the taste as she opened herself up to him, the slick salt taste and musky smell.

When she thought he might stop she set her hand on the back of his head and held him there, rocking back and forth against his face until, with a barely muffled scream, holding him fast between her legs, she came. And shook. And came again.

Perspiration ran down into Elder's eyes and made them sting.

Releasing him, Helen angled herself round until, with a little manoeuvring on Elder's part, they were lying sideways and face to face across the bed.

'Jesus, Frank.' She kissed the sweat from his eyebrows and tasted herself on his mouth and on his chin. 'Jesus, that was . . .' She laughed and held him. 'I forget what that was.'

She smiled and laughed some more and Elder reached around and unfastened her bra and kissed her breasts which were fleshy and loose with nipples that were dark and large and which he kissed and teased between his teeth and when he slid one leg between hers she said, 'Wait, just wait,' and when Elder rolled away disappointed she said, 'I don't suppose you've got a condom?' He shook his head and she pushed herself off the bed and half-walked, half-hopped to what he assumed was the bathroom, returning moments later with a silver foil-wrapped rectangle. 'I daren't guess what the sell-by date is on this.'

◆

Not so very much later they were sitting up in bed, leaning back against the pillows, Helen smoking a cigarette.

'Well,' she said, 'did the earth move for you?'

'What?'

'Isn't that what they say? If it's really good. The earth moved.'

'I don't know.'

She smiled. 'I must have read it in some magazine. A hundred and one ways to describe your orgasm.'

Elder half-turned towards her, his hand on her arm. 'How would you describe it?'

Helen laughed. 'I think half the street's got bloody subsidence, that's what I think.'

He laughed with her and kissed her and they fooled around a little but their hearts weren't in it, what they

256

really wanted to do, both of them, was cuddle and that's what they did.

Elder didn't know which of them fell asleep first except that when he woke it seemed to be full dark outside and Helen was lying across him, a faint line of dribble running from one corner of her mouth down along his chest. Without waking her, he pulled the covers around her and kissed the top of her head and already he was thinking about what had happened and what, if anything, he had got himself into. Helen stirred against him and settled and he closed his eyes and imagined the distant rise and fall of water and tried not to think at all.

He must have fallen asleep again because when he opened his eyes Helen was coming back into the room wearing a towelling dressing-gown and holding a tray. She had been down to the kitchen and made tea and toast and carried it back, pot, cups, small plates, milk, sugar, butter, the whole works. In one pocket of her dressing-gown she had two teaspoons and a knife; in the other a small pot of black cherry jam.

'I just love this, don't you? Toast and jam and tea in bed. In winter, when it's really cold, I steel myself and run downstairs and make it, then fetch it back up here.'

'It's not just for after sex, then?'

'If it was I'd've starved long since.'

The tray was balanced on the bed between their legs and Helen was leaning down now to pour the tea.

'It was great, though,' he said, bending forward to kiss her shoulder. 'Thank you.'

She looked at him. 'Don't be grateful, Frank.'

'I'm sorry. I didn't mean . . .'

'I don't want to be thought of as social services, that's

257

all. Now drink your tea before it gets cold. And try not to leave crumbs in the bed.'

When she was through pouring them both a second cup, she said, a smile in her eyes, 'So was there something you wanted to tell me or was this what you really came round for?'

'No, there was something. I mean, it's not definite, I don't have any absolute proof, but I thought you should know all the same.'

'For heaven's sake, know what?'

He told her his suspicions about her daughter and Paul Latham, the circumstantial evidence and Latham's denials. For some little time, Helen said nothing and then when she did it was, 'I hope he was good to her, that's all.'

'That's all?'

'It was nearly fifteen years ago, Frank. What's the point in getting angry now?'

'I would have thought if he was taking advantage . . .'

'If.'

'What do you mean?'

'I mean I don't think it's ever that simple, is it? And besides, look at us. We're not exactly in a position to judge.'

'We don't have ties or responsibilities and we're old enough to know better.'

'And you don't think Susan was? Old enough to know what she was doing.'

'No.'

'Tell me again, Frank, how old's your daughter.'

'That's got nothing to do with it.'

'How old?'

'Sixteen.'

258

'And that's got nothing to do with it?'

'No.'

'Oh, Frank.' She leaned in against his arm. 'How old do you think I was when Susan was born?'

'I don't know.'

'I'm forty-seven, Frank. Work it out.'

'That's different.'

'Why?'

'Trevor wasn't twice your age.'

'No, Trevor wasn't.'

'Well, then . . .'

'Frank.' She rolled on to her front, one leg over his, rattling the contents of the tray.

'Yes?'

'I don't want to talk about this now.'

'All right.'

He lay there for a while, holding her, and felt his eye lids closing. 'If I'm going . . .'

'You're not.'

'It's the waste of a perfectly good B and B.'

'Shut up.'

On his way to the bathroom, Elder lifted the tray from the bed and set it on the floor. 'You can use my tooth-brush,' she called after him.

When he came back to the room five minutes later, she was asleep.

Elder climbed into bed carefully beside her and lay there for a while, listening to all the strange sounds that strange houses make until he could hear nothing at all.

33

Elder woke up not knowing where he was. Helen was already dressed and down in the kitchen, preparing breakfast. Last night's melon had been sliced open and set on plates. The kettle had recently been boiled and bread cut for toast. More toast.

'You talk in your sleep,' she said. 'Did you know that?'

'Have I said anything incriminating?'

'Not yet.'

The look that he gave her chilled her even as it made her laugh.

'God, Frank. Relax. I'm not expecting anything of you, you know.'

'I'm sorry, I didn't . . .'

'Two grown-ups, remember? A rare bit of fun. Rare for me, anyway. I'm not going to fall apart on you, don't fret. Now, there's coffee, if you want. Instant. Or there's tea.'

'Tea.'

'Okay, sit yourself down next door. I'll bring it through.'

It was still a little short of eight o'clock, the living-room quite bright with early sun. Seagulls squawked and shrilled overhead. The voices of people passing in the street outside. The photograph of Susan Blacklock above the mantelpiece looked back at him unjudging. It had all the makings of a warm day.

'You're going back this morning.'

'Yes.'

'Back to where?'

'Nottingham, I suppose. For now, at least.'

'And then?'

'I don't know.'

Helen set down cups and plates, then pulled out a chair for herself. Her hair was tied back and she looked older than the night before.

'Your daughter?'

'That's part of it.'

The melon was sweet and the juice trickled down around his chin.

'What?' Helen said.

'Hm?'

'You had a dirty grin on your face.'

'Oh, just remembering.'

There was marmalade as well as jam to go with the toast, Safeway's own brand.

'This Latham, the teacher, you thought there might be more to it than just the two of them copping off?'

Elder nodded. 'I thought it was a possibility, yes.'

'And now?'

He shook his head. 'I'll pass on what I know to the police, the local force. The case is still open, after all. Whether they decide to take it any further's up to them.'

'And there's nothing else? Nothing else you've found?'

'Not really, no.'

'This Donald,' Helen said, 'Shane – Shane Donald – him as did a runner. Recent.'

'What about him?'

'When Susan – you know – you fancied him for it, didn't you? Thought him and that other chap . . .'

'McKeirnan.'

'That's it, McKeirnan. You thought they might have been involved.'

'I thought it was a possibility, yes.'

'And now?'

Elder shook his head. 'I don't know.' He looked into her eyes and then away. 'I'm sorry.'

'What for?'

'Letting you down.'

'Don't be silly. You tried. Did your best. You still cared.'

'I made you a promise.'

A wry smile came to Helen's face. 'Men do. All the time. Then spend the rest of their lives regretting it.'

When breakfast was over they both knew he was anxious to be gone. At the doorway, she slipped her arms around him. 'Last night, it was lovely, you were right.'

'Don't be grateful,' he said.

She grinned and made a face.

'I'll see you,' he said.

'Really?'

This time she didn't stay to watch him walk away.

◆

Rob Loake kept him waiting and then some. It was warm, flaming June and the inside of Loake's office was warmer, some kind of rules and regs about ventilation Elder didn't understand. There were dark patches beneath the arms of Loake's shirt and his striped tie had been pulled down to half-mast, the top two buttons of the shirt undone.

'Bastard, isn't it?'

Elder shrugged noncommittally.

'All right for the fucking Algarve, but this is fucking York.' He seemed genuinely aggrieved.

'I'll not take too much of your time,' Elder said.

'No.'

Elder told him about Latham and Susan Blacklock, what he knew, what he surmised. Succinct as Elder was, Loake managed to look at his watch not once but twice.

'And none of this came out at the time?' Loake said when he'd finished.

'As far as I can tell Latham was never questioned.'

Loake leaned towards him. 'Maybe if you hadn't been so keen pointing us at Shane fuckin' Donald, he would have been.' His expression was close to satisfaction.

Elder let it ride.

'What do you expect me to do now?' Loake asked.

'Nothing necessarily. Though I'd have thought there was one question that should be asked.'

'Why didn't he come forward at the time?'

'Yes.'

Loake made a sound somewhere between a groan and a sigh. 'I should've thought it was bloody obvious. He didn't want his nuts cut off by the education committee for screwing under-age girls.'

'That's one reason, agreed.'

'Okay, mastermind, what's the other?'

'Ask him.'

'Fuck you, Elder!' Loake was on his feet double-quick. 'Coming in here telling me how to do my fucking job.'

Elder took an envelope from his side pocket and slid it across the desk. The veins at the side of Loake's forehead were standing out for fine weather.

'I've written it all up in there, dates and so on. If you do decide to have a word with Latham you might find it useful.'

'Elder . . .'

'If I see Don I'll tell him you were asking for him. And I'll see myself out.'

Why was it, Elder asked himself, the older he got the stronger the urge to throw a punch became? It was as well he'd taken retirement when he did. He was almost back at this car when his mobile phone rang. It was Maureen Prior. Someone answering to Shane Donald's description had tried to use a stolen debit card in the centre of Nottingham.

34

They met in a small café off Bridlesmith Gate, one of the few that hadn't yet been squeezed out by Starbucks and Caffè Nero. Maureen, who had been in court that morning, sat sober and smart in a grey suit, the skirt an efficient length below the knee. Elder, who was wearing shapeless trousers and a faded blue shirt, was feeling slovenly and under-dressed by comparison, uncomfortable in the heat. They hadn't been sitting there many minutes when Maureen took off her suit jacket and folded it neatly across the back of the adjacent chair.

'It was Dixon's in the Victoria Centre,' Maureen said. 'Saturday. Trying to buy a CD Walkman. Not cheap.'

'How sure are we it was Donald?' Elder said.

'Pretty sure. We got quite a good description from the young Asian guy who served him. Early twenties, hair cut really short, trainers, jeans. Skinny as a rake.'

Unless he'd changed a lot in prison, Elder thought, Donald could be mistaken for early twenties, no problem.

'Apparently the assistant had been watching him for some little time. Thought there was something shifty about him, nervous even. Seems he'd been in the shop earlier, looking around. Assistant thought he was out to nick something if he could. Asked if he wanted any help, got no for an answer. Half an hour later, he came back in again, asked to listen to the Walkman. Said okay. Everything was fine until the machine refused his card. The assistant asked him if he'd like to pay some other way, but by then he was already on his way out of the store. That was when he checked the number against the list of stolen cards they keep near the till. Bingo.'

'Gerald Kersley.'

'Exactly. Kersley was robbed in a public toilet in the Greater Manchester area a couple of days after Donald absconded. Car keys. Wallet.'

'There's nothing else to connect them?'

'Only circumstantial. Timing's spot on.'

Elder picked up his cup and lifted it to his mouth before realising it was empty.

'You want another?' Maureen asked.

'No, it's okay.'

Elder shook his head and looked around. Not so many years before he would nip in here sometimes to meet Joanne on her lunch break, the salon she managed no more than minutes away. He pictured her sitting across from him where Maureen was now, picking at the salad on her plate and chatting away while Elder enjoyed a bacon sandwich and brown sauce. Nowadays it was all *focaccia* this and *focaccia* that.

'That card,' Elder said, 'it could have changed hands half a dozen times by now.'

'I know.'

'And the description, it could be half the population almost, between eighteen and thirty.'

'Yes.'

'Without a recent photograph . . .'

'CID in Huddersfield, they got hold of one from somewhere. Prison service, maybe. Probation? They were going to use it on some leaflets when he went missing, you know, fliers, but somehow never got around to it. Anyhow, they're emailing it down. Probably sitting on the computer up in Mansfield now.'

'How soon can we get hold of a copy?'

'Just about as soon as we've finished this and walked to Central Station. I'll call my office and get it sent on.'

While Maureen used her mobile, Elder finished the last of his coffee. If it was Donald, why wait till now to use one of the stolen cards? And why on earth would he choose to return to the very part of the country where he and McKeirnan had operated before?

'All right,' Maureen said, slipping the phone back into her bag and reaching for her coat. 'We're on. If you're interested, we can check on the search for the missing girl while we're there.'

'Emma Harrison, is that the name?'

'Yes.'

'Still no trace?'

Sombre, Maureen pushed through the door and out on to the street. 'You think it could be Shane, don't you?'

Elder shrugged. 'Turning up here . . .'

'If it is him.'

'Okay, if it is him. Turning up here the weekend this Emma disappears. Same age, near as damn it. Same age as Lucy Padmore, Susan Blacklock.'

'Same age,' Maureen reminded him, 'as most girls reported missing.'

'Coincidence, then?'

Maureen shook her head and set off along the pedestrianised street that would lead them to Trinity Square and the central division police station at the corner of Shakespeare and North Church Streets.

◆

Maureen signed Elder in at the desk and spoke on the internal phone to one of the office managers on the third floor. Because the operational base of the Major Crime Unit was divided between two sites, both away from the centre, it was sometimes necessary to beg space or facilities at the city force's headquarters. After holding for a few minutes, Maureen was informed there was an office with a computer temporarily empty on the third floor. Within minutes, she was downloading the image on to the screen.

Elder held his breath as the likeness of Shane Donald appeared, Shane staring at the camera, pugnacious, vulnerable, a haunted look far back in his eyes – what he had experienced in prison, Elder guessed, what he had gone through. Then and before. The aggression that he saw, the challenge in his expression, they were new. It had been there, of course, to a degree, but previously it had been hidden, submerged, waiting for Alan McKeirnan to set it free. Now that anger, the aptitude for violence, was closer to the surface. Volatile.

'You recognise him?' Maureen asked.

'Oh, yes.'

'Not changed a great deal?'

'No, he's changed.'

Maureen moved the cursor and clicked the printer into action.

The portrait lost some of its definition in the process, some of its texture in the transition from colour to black and white.

'I can get a colour copy later,' Maureen said. 'This will serve for now.'

'You want to try it out on the bloke from Dixon's?'

'If that's okay with you.'

Maureen switched off the printer, moved the cursor to the top of the screen and clicked the mouse to shut the computer down. 'Let's see if they've turned up anything on Emma Harrison on the way out.'

◆

There were four uniformed officers, two detectives and three civilians in the incident room, the majority of them accessing new information and building up a database, or using HOLMES, the Home Office computer system, to prioritise lines of inquiry. Both Elder and Maureen knew this to be, in many ways, the most important function of all – prioritise wrongly and a vital piece of information could be shuffled back into the middle of the pack and not investigated for several days. Days which could prove crucial.

Photographs of Emma Harrison were pinned to one wall, together with copies of the poster which had been printed in its thousands and widely circulated. On the adjacent wall were a general map of the area in which Emma had gone missing, and a plan, blown-up and more detailed, of Rufford Abbey and Country Park, areas marked in different colours to indicate the progress of the search.

The initial supposition had been that, having missed her bus, Emma would have attempted to hitch a lift or had befriended and accepted shelter from someone she had met at the concert. Either way, she would turn up the following morning, a little shamefaced and bedraggled, but safe. When this didn't happen, the scale of the incident was raised to that of a fully-fledged missing persons inquiry. Something Emma's father was angry had not been done initially. 'She's not stupid,' he said. 'If all that had happened was that she'd missed the bus, she'd have phoned.'

Though Emma's mobile had recently been taken from her, after numerous rows about excessive use and spiralling costs, and she was waiting to exchange it for another model which allowed her to pay for calls as they were made, there was no shortage of regular telephones in the central area of the park.

The senior of the detectives, a worried-looking detective inspector with shirtsleeves rolled back and rimless spectacles, got to his feet as Maureen Price entered, Elder in her wake.

'Gerry.'

'Maureen.'

'Gerry, this is Frank Elder, he retired a couple of years back. Frank, Gerry Clarke.'

'Frank. I've heard of you.'

Elder shook the proffered hand. 'All good, I hope.'

'Frank was involved in a similar disappearance quite a few years ago,' Maureen said.

'You'll know what a bastard it is,' Clarke said. 'The parents at home, twitching every time the phone rings, tearing out their hair, fearing the worse and not wanting

270

to admit it. And us here, every hour as passes . . . well, you do know.'

Elder knew all too well.

'There's still no sign?' Maureen said.

'Not as much as a sighting, not one we'd take seriously, and that's strange in itself. You could look at it as a blessing, in a way. Half your personnel running about all over the county, else. Folk getting in touch just to break the monotony a lot of the time. Get their name in the paper, face on the telly. Not that we haven't had our fair share of calls, but up to yet it's manageable.'

'Which way are you thinking?' Elder asked.

Gerry Clarke shifted his balance right to left. 'No big rows at home, undue pressure at school, boyfriends, usual things you're looking for, this kind of scenario. My betting she's either gone off with someone she met at the concert – and we're appealing to everyone who was there to get in touch – or she's still somewhere here.'

He led them across to the map of Rufford Park on the far wall.

'How big?' Elder asked.

'Couple of hundred acres, give or take.'

Elder whistled softly.

'Lot of ground to cover,' Maureen said.

Clarke nodded. 'We've pulled in officers from across the county. Plus volunteers, local. At first we concentrated on these areas here, the old stable block and the gardens that run down behind this sort of orangery affair. Lots of walls criss-crossing, quite thick shrubbery and this stream running down to one side. Then you've got the old abbey off to one side, most of that's empty inside now, pretty much a shell and not the safest of places to be clambering around. We've got people going back through there now.'

'This area,' Maureen said, 'over here?'

'The Broad Ride, that's what it's called. It's a track leading down past these trees to the lake. There's a path that runs right round the water, you can see there, but it's narrow and in places pretty overgrown, that far side especially, not easy to penetrate.' He took off his glasses and rubbed at the bridge of his nose. 'You could hide a body there for a long time without it ever being found.'

'And the lake?' Elder asked.

'We've got 3D scanners due on site later today. Any unusual objects or air pockets under the surface of the water, they should show them up. And there's a team of divers standing by.' He sighed and slid his glasses back into place. 'We'll drag it if we have to.'

Maureen thanked him and said that if and when he had any news she would like to be informed. They all knew that after forty-eight hours with no sign the chances of finding Emma Harrison were slipping away. And any clear indication that what they were dealing with was abduction, then the Major Crime Unit would be officially involved. The next time she spoke with Detective Inspector Gerry Clarke her interest could be more than casual.

◆

Salim Ratra was busy selling one of the new Philips DVD machines that records as well as plays, something of a bargain at a fraction under five hundred pounds.

'Do you understand all this stuff?' Maureen asked.

Elder laughed. 'In our house the only one who could work the VCR was Katherine. I think she first got the hang of recording *EastEnders* when she was four.'

In our house, he thought, not a phrase he used much these days.

As soon as Salim had put through the paperwork on his sale he came over to where they were waiting. Maureen took the printout of Shane Donald's photograph from her bag. 'It's not a great copy, I'm afraid.'

It was good enough.

'That's him,' Salim said, an edge of excitement lifting his voice. 'Him, innit?'

'You're sure?' Elder asked.

Salim smiled. It was a winning smile, Maureen recognised. 'See that bloke was just here, right, with his wife. Buying the Philips, yeah? Two weeks ago he come in on his own, sniffin' round, askin' all these questions, right, should he go for the Samsung, multi-region playback with the handset hack, or maybe, push up to the Denon ASV-700 with the surround sound? Come back in an hour ago, less, recognised him the minute he walked through the door. My customer, my sale, right? Faces, names, it's my job. How I make it work. And that, that's the one was in here Friday with the dodgy card, you can take my word.'

◆

Elder and Maureen stood on the broad pavement outside the Victoria Centre, people hurrying past on either side. Buses waiting three in line for the lights to change at the corner of Milton Street. Elder's shirt was sticking to his back and it wasn't just the temperature, though it was still in the high twenties and the air was thickening with all the hallmarks of a coming storm.

'There doesn't have to be a connection,' Maureen said, cautiously.

'I know.'

'Shane Donald shows up in the city on Friday and the day after a girl disappears a bus ride from the centre. Coincidence.'

'Emma Harrison,' Elder said. 'She's the same age as Susan Blacklock when she went missing, the same age as Lucy Padmore when they killed her, Donald and McKeirnan. And you've seen the photographs: Emma, she's got fair hair, long fair hair. The same as the others.'

'Frank, a lot of sixteen-year-olds go missing, statistically I'll bet half of them have got fair hair. Maybe more. There's nothing to link Emma Harrison to Shane Donald, nothing.'

'Aside from the fact that he was here.'

'If it's true.'

Elder took a pace forward, out of the path of a young woman pushing a double buggy. 'You'll talk to Gerry Clarke?' he said.

'Both of us, eh?'

As they crossed towards Trinity Square the first drops of rain could already be felt.

35

It was Harold Edge who found the cardigan. Harold, seventy-two years old and a founder member of the East Notts. Senior Ramblers, straight-backed still and eyes like a hawk. Wednesday morning he had set out with Jess, his border collie–labrador cross, and caught the bus from Newark towards Lincoln, alighting some five or six miles out of the town and setting off on a route that would take him, via a series of footpaths and old, unmarked lanes through Norton Disney and back around to town. A good day's hike.

The rucksack on his back held an Ordnance Survey map, compass and binoculars, a bar of Kendal Mint Cake, two cheese-and-pickle sandwiches, an apple and an individual size Melton Mowbray pie. There were chocolate drops for Jess, a bottle of water for them both and a fraying copy of the *RSPB Book of British Birds*. Only recently had he taken to using the German-designed anti-shock walking pole one of his nieces had bought him three years before.

Harold had been walking for close on an hour and had paused at a field edge to check directions. There was supposed to be a path leading off from the far side, but could he see a gap in the hedge, could he buggery? Then there it was, more than a little overgrown with hawthorn but large enough for a man to squeeze through single file, a narrow stile to climb and then once down on the other side the way was clear.

It was Jess, in truth, who found it, the cardigan that is. Sniffing around in the bracken that had grown up around the hedge bottom, tossing her head and barking so loud that Harold thought she had unearthed a rabbit hole or something, maybe even a badger set, but instead it was a dash of colour, something purple. 'Here, girl, here. Good girl.'

Carefully Harold used the ferrule at the end of his walking pole to free the material from the thorny branch on which it had become caught and lift it up into sight. A girl's cardigan, he thought, not in bad nick either. A mite too fancy to belong to a regular walker, he could see that. He could spread it out across the hedge, leave it in case whoever had dropped it came back, but somehow that seemed to him unlikely. With care, he folded it instead and placed it inside his rucksack. One or other of the charity shops in town would be grateful for it, he was sure.

It wasn't until he was home that evening, watching the local news while he ran a nice relaxing bath, that he made a connection between his find and Emma Harrison. When she was last seen, the newscaster said, Emma had been wearing a halter top in a floral print, a blue denim skirt, pink open sandals and a purple cardigan.

Harold turned off the bath, refolded the cardigan inside a double sheet of newspaper, placed his parcel inside a plastic shopping bag and carried it to the local police station forthwith.

The area in which Harold Edge had been walking was, for the most part, gently undulating farmland. North of the village of Norton Disney and above the narrow road, little more than a lane, which ran east from the A46, was a wood and, running close to the village itself, the River Witham, making its long arching journey towards The Wash. There was a small quarry to the east and the rest, dotted here and there with farm buildings and the occasional bungalow, was fields. There had been one quite heavy fall of rain in the past four days, otherwise it had been dry and warm; the cardigan was dry to the touch when it was delivered over, with only some small suggestion of dampness where one of the arms had twisted underneath itself. There was a clear pull – not exactly a tear – on the left side where it had snagged against the hedge and caught fast.

Ashley Foulkes immediately identified the cardigan as the one Emma had borrowed and burst into tears; her parents confirmed that it was hers. Constable Eileen Joy, who had been appointed liaison officer with the Harrison family, gave them the news.

The main focus of police attention was redirected from Rufford Park towards the area around Norton Disney. Officers from the Nottinghamshire force were joined by others from Lincolnshire, personnel from the Royal Air Force base and a significant number of civilian volunteers. The land would be searched a field at a time, moving gradually outwards: each building, every hedgerow and gully, each barn. The scanners that had been readied for use on the lake at Rufford were redeployed alongside the River Witham.

If Emma Harrison had been following the path that Harold Edge had taken, had climbed the stile, squeezed through the narrow gap in the hedge on her own, where on earth had she been going and why? And if, as seemed more likely, she had been with somebody else, was this voluntary or was she being forced? Was she, in fact, being carried? And if so, how far? The spot was some distance from the road, the nearest point a car could reach. It would take someone of considerable strength to carry her that far. That far and beyond.

Detectives were making a fingertip search close to the spot where the garment had been found, examining the ground for footprints, taking photographs, looking for evidence along the edges where the hedge overlapped the stile.

It was now four days, give or take, since Emma Harrison had last been seen.

◆

When Elder and Joanne had moved back from London in 1997 – Katherine eleven and about to start at secondary school – Bernard Young had been a detective chief inspector in the Major Crime Unit, noted for his collection of tropical fish, a certain degree of outspokenness and his penchant for high-flown literature and three-piece suits in various hairy strands of Harris tweed. Stand downwind of him on a hot day and you could imagine yourself luxuriating in the warm stench of some Highland bothy.

Now he was Detective Superintendent Young, the senior officer at the head of the unit, with a significant hike in pay and an office that afforded a view out over the car park and adjacent rooftops, a fraction of sky. On a cabinet to the side of the room, the shelves of which housed uniform editions of Shakespeare, Fielding and Smollett, fresh water hissed through a six-by-three-metre tank in which the overflow of his fish collection was currently disporting itself, small darting movements of orange and gold glimpsed through glass.

In the room that afternoon, aside from the superintendent himself, were two detective inspectors, Maureen Prior and Gerry Clarke, and, at the superintendent's invitation, Frank Elder.

Bernard Young's suit jacket hung from a hanger behind the office door and the buttons of his waistcoat, all but one, were undone.

'I'd like to think,' he said, 'that young Emma was out enjoying the countryside of her own free will when she crossed that field, yomping through the buttercups and cow shit without a care in the whole wide fucking world. I'd like to think someone sprinkled fairy dust on her eyes that sunny Saturday afternoon and she's been wandering around in a blissful trance ever since. Except this isn't *Midsummer Night's* fucking *Dream*. And sooner or later we're going to find her poor sodding body.' He looked from one to the other of his colleagues. 'Unless one of you's about to disagree?'

Nobody did.

'Right. Then she's there because someone's taken her there, that's what we assume. Someone she's met out at Rufford or later. She might have gone with him initially of her own volition – most likely did – or she might have been under duress from the start. She might have known him or she might not. So far there's too many unknowns, too much we don't know.'

Maureen started to say something but thought better of it.

'Gerry,' Young said, 'what you've put in place would be hard to improve upon . . .' Clarke moved a hand across his face to disguise a rising flush of embarrassment. 'So all search operations will remain under your control. Maureen, tracking down and interviewing known offenders, that'll be your priority. Sex Offenders' Register for starters. Anyone convicted of sex or violent offences and recently released back into the area from prison.'

Maureen nodded. Before filleting them out, they could be looking at around eight hundred names, possibly more. And how many detectives would she have at her disposal? If she were lucky, very lucky, and if other forces came up trumps, there could be thirty or forty. Overtime guaranteed for the first week, but after that . . .?

'It should go without saying, but I'll underline it anyway. Co-operation between the two of you's essential, no withholding, open access at all times. Anything important, any developments, I want to know almost as soon as you do yourselves. And all statements to the press, the media, are cleared through me. No grandstanding, understood?'

'Understood, sir,' Maureen said.

'Right, sir,' Clarke said.

'All of which brings us to Frank here. You both know him. You, Maureen, as well as I do if not better. You've worked with him and successfully, not so many years back now. It was Frank who was largely responsible for putting McKeirnan and Donald inside and now, as we all know, Donald's on the loose. More than that, he was in the area just one day before Emma Harrison disappeared. Of course, that may be no more than a coincidence and if I were a betting man I'd say it probably is. But then I take a look at that picture of young Emma and bring to mind the face of the lass those two bastards killed. Peas in a pod, maybe not, but fruit from the same tree.'

He paused to take a breath, sip a little water from the glass on his desk.

'I've talked to the ACC about this earlier and I'm offering to take Frank into this investigation as a civilian consultant. He knows Donald probably better than anyone and he's worked this kind of case before. Added to which, the unit's already up to the gunnels and we need every bit of good help we can get. Frank knows his way around, knows the way we work, I doubt he'll be getting under our feet.'

Elder knew full well that before the super had spoken to the assistant chief, Maureen Prior had spoken to him.

'Comments? Observations?'

'I think it's a good idea,' Maureen said without hesitation.

'Gerry?'

'No skin off my nose,' Clarke said. 'From what you've said, he'll be mostly working Maureen's side of the fence, anyway.'

'Right,' said the superintendent, automatically beginning to rebutton his waistcoat. 'It's yours, Frank, if you want it.'

'I'll do what I can,' Elder said.

◆

Paul Latham was waiting for him near the enquiry desk, looking awkward and out of place. The trademark suit, pale corduroy, was still the same, but his shoulders sagged and the life had gone from his eyes.

'You're not easy to track down,' Latham said.

'What do you want?'

'Aside from giving you the satisfaction of knowing I've been suspended, I'm not sure.'

'Okay,' Elder said. 'If you want to talk, let's not do it here.'

They found a nondescript pub with metal ashtrays and coasters advertising a beer that was no longer brewed. '*Big Screen Sports Here*' proclaimed a notice, but Elder couldn't imagine big crowds. He ordered a half of bitter for himself and wished that he hadn't; Latham had a large gin and tonic, the better half of this deal if nothing else.

'So what's on your mind?' Elder asked.

'Aside from finding another job, you mean? Outside of the teaching profession, of course. Not an easy task when you're my age and all of your working life has been spent in schools.'

'I'm sorry,' Elder said, though he wasn't sure if he meant it, even then.

'Are you?'

Elder sipped some more bitter and lightly grimaced. 'What happened?'

'That thug you sent round, that's what happened.'

'I didn't send anybody anywhere.'

'That member of Her Majesty's constabulary, fine upholder of the law.'

'Loake.'

'The very same. Detective Inspector Loake. Who

282

marched right into the middle of one of my classes and more or less accused me of being a paedophile in front of thirty twelve-year-olds. Oh, I've written to his chief constable and my MP and the Police Complaints Authority, not that it'll do a scrap of good. To all intents and purposes, I've been sacked, my contract discontinued; I've been almost completely ostracised by colleagues I've worked with, some of them, for over ten years. I suffered the indignity of being escorted from the premises and instructed not to set foot on school grounds again without written permission, which, of course, I won't get. My union representative assured me that I have the right to appeal, at the same time as ostentatiously looking at his watch. My time, it seems, as a member of the noble profession, is up.'

'Noble?'

'That's what I said.'

'What's so noble about seducing fifteen-year-old girls?'

'Seducing? Is that what happened?'

'You tell me.'

'We became very close, Susan and I. We were friends.'

'Yes,' Elder sneered.

'Believe what you will.'

'She was in your care,' Elder said.

'And what? I hurt her? Caused her pain?'

'Probably.'

'I don't think so.'

'You abused your trust.'

'The trust that mattered was the one between Susan and myself, and I never abused that; I never lied to her, never exaggerated my feelings, told her anything that wasn't true.'

'You took advantage . . .'

'God! You're a self-righteous prig.'

'If you or anyone like you ever came near my daughter . . .'

'You'd what? Tar and feather me and have me frogmarched through the streets? Cut off my balls and throw them to the dogs? Hang me, perhaps? But no, I've read the placards; hanging's too good for the likes of me.'

'You're being ridiculous,' Elder said.

'Am I? Does it never occur to you that what happened between Susan and myself was considerate and loving and that maybe, just maybe, it was what she needed at that stage of her life?'

'No.'

'Just as, if your daughter had a relationship with an older man, that could be what was right for her?'

'No.'

Latham lowered his head, picked up his glass and swallowed down more gin.

'Susan,' Elder said. 'When did you see her last?'

'On the last day of term. They'd mostly left, Susan's year, their exams were over, some of them were already off on their holidays or had started summer jobs. Susan came in to say goodbye. She was going off to college in September, a different life. There was no way in which we were going to carry on seeing one another, we'd discussed all that. She gave me a card, it was very sweet, a quotation from Shakespeare, the sonnets. I still have it, you can see it if you like. *For Paul with love and thanks for everything*. I never saw her again.'

'And you've no idea what happened to her?'

'None.'

Elder continued to stare at him.

'You think I'm lying?' Latham asked.

'No.' Elder pushed his beer away, unfinished. 'I've got to be getting back.'

'I'll stay here a while longer.'

Elder nodded and got to his feet.

'What happened with Susan,' Latham said. 'I don't regret it. Not at all. No matter what's happened to me since.'

With the merest of nods, Elder left him sitting there, staring into an all but empty glass.

36

When Elder's marriage had broken down he had put as much distance between himself and the wreckage as he could. For the first few months Joanne had lived in a sort of limbo, seeing Martyn Miles more openly, staying over sometimes, but mostly returning home to face the unmade bed and Katherine's reproachful stare. Some small part of her, she realised afterwards, was waiting for Elder to get back in touch, argue, concede, find a way through, set things to rights. He had done it before.

When this didn't happen she put the house on the market and Martyn traded up his flat for something larger in the same area: a new architect-designed house set amongst largely fading nineteenth-century splendour. At the front, white concrete presented a curved, almost featureless face to passers-by; to the rear, a wall of sheer glass separated a hundred metres of landscaped garden from the double-height living-room with its spiral staircase and expensive prints.

Within minutes of meeting her, years before, in a salon he owned in London, Martyn had touched Joanne's arm and a charge had run through her, reflected in her eyes. And in that moment she had known that unless she turned and walked away, sooner or later she would sleep with him, no matter how hard she tried to convince herself otherwise. Of course, she didn't walk away, she stayed. As if aware of a tacit agreement between them, Martyn withdrew, did nothing to pursue her, their relationship professional and beyond reproach. Elder, meanwhile, worked longer and longer hours, became less and less a part of Joanne's life, beyond the drab and ordinary, the back turned in bed, the everyday. In the end it was almost trite – a party, a little too much wine and what began in the back of a hired car ended on a circular bed with a mirrored wall mimicking the sweated thrashing of their limbs.

After that there were so many promises made and broken; promises to Frank, promises to herself. Sometimes she and Martyn would go for months without being alone together, without touching; when he was trying to get established in America they were out of contact for almost a year. He had other women, she knew, girls – still married, a husband more or less in her bed, how could she complain? With time, the fire between them cooled as these things do.

By the time she moved to Nottingham, she and Martyn were business partners and good friends. He looked after the salons in London, everything else was increasingly down to her. When, occasionally, he travelled up and stayed, they would have dinner together, nothing more. And then, like flicking a switch, it changed. She wanted him, like a sudden illness inside her. A fever. And Martyn responded, excited by the change. They saw each other more and more, took risks; once she phoned him in the middle of the night, slipped out of the house and made love to him on a neighbour's path, naked beneath an old raincoat of Frank's she grabbed from behind the door.

Elder had to find out. For quite some time she was sure he knew but for whatever reason didn't want to say. More and more she gave him opportunities and more and more he turned away. And then, suddenly, she was telling him, confessing, and it was as if he had never known at all. The words as cold and hard as stone, as glass. *Frank, I've been seeing him again . . .*

◆

He had not been to the house before. He knew of it, where it was, had driven past it several times; once, thumbing through a lifestyle magazine someone had left in a beach café in Cornwall, he had found an article about it, colour photographs, an interview with the architect. In one of the pictures, an interior shot, there was Martyn, hands in the pockets of his loose white suit, posing barefoot in front of the spiral stairs. In another, he and Joanne sat side by side on a leather sofa, holding hands.

That afternoon he had been introduced to the other members of the inquiry team and noticed no more resentment than he had expected. Some faces he had known from before, others had been new. He read through the interviews conducted with members of the public who had been in the band tent that Saturday afternoon, then secluded himself with a monitor and the CCTV tape from the craft shop at Rufford Park. Footage showing Emma, Alison and Ashley earlier in the day had been noted and marked, the three of them laughing as they moved from one section to another, picking up this, trying on that.

And there was brief footage of Alison and Ashley later, hurrying, almost running round the aisles in their last frantic search for Emma before the bus departed.

What Elder wanted to see was something else.

Shane Donald.

After almost two hours, there was only one section he kept going back to: a man standing at the very edge of the camera's range and for no more than seconds, enough to glimpse an arm, a blur of face, the arm again and then the back as he turned – a dark shirt, short hair, nothing more – turning in response to something shouted or said. No more than an impression, impossible to recognise. But there on camera, in the middle of the frame, her face quite animated, a slender girl with light hair, holding something in her hands – a piece of jewellery, a necklace, bracelet, it was difficult to tell – holding it up as if to say, hey, look at this, and then the camera swivelled away and when it moved back both girl and man were gone.

Was it Donald? Elder asked one of the technicians to transfer the image on to disk so that it could be blown up, sharpened, printed off. He was still thinking about it with part of his mind as he stood at the front door, waiting for a response to the bell.

Joanne's face registered surprise, then relaxed into a smile.

'Frank, you could have phoned.'

'And give you time to leave?'

'Martyn's not here.'

'Shame.'

Joanne hesitated just a moment before stepping back from the door.

'You'd best come in.'

The hallway was pale wood, spotlights sunk into grey walls, a tall single flower in a tapered vase.

'Come on through.'

He followed her into the living-room, the raised ceiling and faint blue-grey paint making it seem afloat in space. Outside, at intervals on the stone patio, lights burned inside silvered lanterns, though it was not yet dark.

'Can I get you a drink? Some wine? A beer.'

'A beer might be nice.'

Elder watched his reflection closely in the sliding glass, as if not trusting what he might yet do.

'I hope this is okay.' She handed him an open bottle, cold to the touch, condensation already forming on the sides. 'It's Martyn's favourite. French, I think.'

Elder let the remark pass.

She stood there, a glass of white wine in her hand, not quite at ease, surveying him.

'I've seen you look better, Frank.'

'I've felt worse.'

She was wearing a skirt in a creamy colour that was most probably called taupe or ecru, a violet top that clung to her perhaps a touch more snugly than it should, and Elder hated her for being as beautiful as she was.

'So, Frank, to what do we owe the honour?'

'We?'

'Martyn's out, some meeting or other . . .'

'You said.'

'Katherine's not back yet from training. Often she hangs out afterwards with friends.'

'Just you and me, then.'

'Like old times.'

'No.'

Joanne sighed, as if already tired of the game they were nearly playing. 'What was it, Frank?'

'This girl who went missing locally, a few days back . . .'

'It's all over the news. Emma something.'

'Harrison.'

'What about her?'

'I'm involved in the investigation. A consultant. As from today.'

'Why you?'

'Something I was involved in before, there might be a connection. Nothing's definite.'

'Oh, Frank.' She half-turned away. 'I thought that was all over.'

'Maybe it never is.'

Joanne sat on the sofa, head down, glass of wine held lightly in both hands.

'I thought you should know,' Elder said. 'It means I'll be around for a while. Longer than I'd expected.'

'So?'

'It's not so big a town, Jo, you know that.'

'I know.'

'Because of Katherine, if nothing else, I wanted you to know, that's all.'

'You'll be able to see a little more of her.'

'Yes.'

'She'll like that.'

'I hope so.'

Joanne tried for a smile that didn't quite arrive.

'Do you want another beer?'

'I've hardly started this.'

'I think I need some more wine.'

Neither of them moved. Faintly, the sound of a car negotiating the curve of the street outside. Something – a cat? – moved along the far edge of the patio, distracting Elder's attention. When he turned back into the room, Joanne was on her feet, empty glass in hand. The front door opened and then closed.

'Frank! What the fuck're you doing here?'

Martyn Miles grinned from just inside the doorway, suit jacket thrown back over his shoulder, one finger through the loop at the collar holding it in place. His hair was tousled as though he'd been driving with the top of the car down, and his cheeks were flushed.

'You and Jo, just like old times.'

'I said that,' Joanne observed.

Elder said nothing.

'Sorry to come home early and disturb your little tête-à-tête.' Martyn draped his coat across the back of a perspex chair, lowered himself down on to one end of the sofa, kicked off his leather slip-on shoes and swung round his legs. 'I don't suppose, sweetheart, there's any chance of some coffee.'

Joanne stared at him for a moment, barely hostile, before turning away.

'And a couple of aspirin while you're about it.'

Elder drank some more of his beer.

'For God's sake, sit down,' Martyn said. 'You make me nervous. Or maybe that's the point.'

Elder angled a chair towards the sofa and sat.

'You came round to see Katherine, no doubt,' Martyn said.

'Actually, I called round to say I'm staying in town for a bit.'

Martyn looked at him carefully. 'That's nice. You must come to dinner.'

'Probably not.'

They said nothing else until Joanne came back carrying a tray; coffee, water and aspirin for Martyn, wine for herself.

'I was just saying, Frank must come to dinner one evening. Soon. You don't mind me calling you Frank?'

'Fucking my wife must give you some privileges.'

'Except she's no longer your fucking wife.'

'Frank,' Joanne said, 'I think you should go.'

'I should never have come.'

'Why don't you phone next time, it might be easier?'

'Yes,' Martyn said, slightly drawling his words. 'Send an email. You do know about email?'

Neither of them moved when Elder crossed the room towards the door.

At the end of the short drive, an ageing 2 CV was parked behind Martyn Miles's Audi convertible, and Katherine was leaning back against it, being kissed by a tall youth in dark blue sportswear, one of her arms round his neck.

Elder coughed and slowed his pace.

'Spying, Dad?' Kathcrine said, stepping clear.

'Not exactly.'

'Dad, this is Stuart. Stuart, my father.'

The two shook hands.

'Stuart trains with me sometimes.'

'I see.'

'I'd better be going,' Stuart said. His accent was local without being overstated.

The engine fluttered into life and made its usual sewing-machine sound as it pulled away.

'Serious?' Elder asked, with a nod in the direction of the departing car.

Katherine grinned. 'He might be.'

'I feel sorry for him then.'

'Don't,' Katherine said, and then, 'You've been to see Mum?'

'Yes.'

'About time.'

'I don't think so.'

'You didn't have a row?'

'Not exactly.'

Slowly, Katherine shook her head. 'Is Martyn here?' Elder nodded.

'Well, that makes a change, anyway.'

'What do you mean?'

'Nothing.'

'Kate . . .'

'Nothing. I didn't mean anything.'

A car went sedately past on the opposite side of the road, headlights full on. The dark was starting to crowd in about them now, filling in the spaces.

'What I came to tell your mother, I'm going to be here for a while, helping out with this investigation into the girl who went missing.'

'I know.'

'How can you?'

'We had the local radio on in the car. It was on the news.'

'Jesus.'

'You're famous, Dad, let's face it. Infamous, anyway.' Smiling, she reached up and kissed him on the cheek. 'I'll call you.'

'Do that.'

Quickly he hugged her, then stepped away. Her hair smelt fresh and slightly lemony from her shower. He would go back and, if Willie Bell was out, read some more *David Copperfield*, get an early start in the morning.

37

They sat outside a small café close to the river's edge. It's smack in the middle of the town, Pam Wilson had said on the phone, turn right at the lights and you're there. There's a little car park close by, a bookshop across the street. You can't miss it.

The traffic had not been as fierce as Elder had imagined and he had arrived early, no sign of anyone answering the probation officer's description inside the café or out. He thought the bookshop, which seemed mainly to sell remainders, might provide him with something to read when he had finally laid *David Copperfield* to rest. But fifteen minutes of shuffling between heavily loaded tables and packed shelves still left him empty-handed; each time he picked out a book and turned it over to read the summary on the back, flipping it open perhaps to try the first few sentences on his tongue, only resulted in him, undecided, sliding it back.

Back out on the narrow pavement, he recognised her from across the street. A biggish woman with short, jagged hair, wearing a loose and faded T-shirt, running shoes and jeans. Seeing him crossing the street towards her, she got to her feet and held out a hand.

'Pam Wilson.'

'Frank Elder.'

'You found it okay, then.'

'No problem.'

She looked directly at him without avoiding his gaze. On the table in front of her were a mug of coffee, some kind of fancy croissant, a blue disposable lighter and a packet of cigarettes.

'Do they come out,' Elder asked, nodding in the direction of the café, 'or what?'

'You order inside, they bring it out.'

He asked for a regular coffee and resisted the array of cakes and pastries.

When he got back outside and sat down, Pam had lit a cigarette and was squinting slightly as the smoke drifted past her eyes.

'You don't mind sitting out here?'

'No, it's okay.'

'I like to take advantage of the weather when I can. Indulge my vices at the same time. One of them, anyway.'

'How are you feeling?' Elder asked.

'Me? I'm fine.'

'But you are still off work?'

'A few days' well-deserved holiday.' She put down her cigarette and broke off a piece of croissant. 'Sick leave, actually.'

'It can shake you up,' Elder said.

'Tell me about it.'

'He threatened you with a knife.'

'He held it against the back of my neck.' Reaching round, she touched her skin below the hairline. 'None too steadily, either. He was probably as frightened as me.'

'You were frightened because of what you thought he might do?'

She drew smoke down into her lungs. 'I knew what he'd done before.'

A waitress brought out Elder's coffee, set it on the table and walked away. A young mother was sitting close by the wall that separated them from the river, her child asleep in its buggy. Traffic moved slowly at Elder's back.

'Donald, you think he's capable of doing the same – similar – again?'

She looked at him for what seemed a long time. 'Yes. I think I do. I did then, certainly, that evening in the car.' Abruptly, she laughed. 'Stupid, isn't it? I'm brighter than him, bigger than him. Heavier, certainly. Fitter. I could have knocked the knife out of his hand, slapped his face and overpowered him. Instead I sat there like a victim, waiting to be hurt.'

'Yet you recommended him for release,' Elder said.

Pam shook her head. 'Not my decision alone. And if I'd wanted to argue against it, I wouldn't have had anything concrete to back it up. Whenever I saw him he'd make all the right noises, tell me what he knew I wanted to hear, how he was sorry, understood the seriousness of what he'd done – oh, you know the kind of thing.'

'And you didn't believe him?'

'I didn't know. That's just it, I didn't know. It was just a gut feeling, that's all.'

'Sometimes that's all you need.'

Pam took one more drag and then stubbed out her cigarette. 'I'm giving them up again tomorrow. Or is that the day after?'

'How about today?'

'All right. Here, take them.' The pack was in her hand, held out towards him. 'Go on, take them.'

'You can always go into the shop around the corner and buy more.'

'So what's the answer?'

Elder shrugged. 'Keep those, know they're there but don't light one up.'

She smiled. It was a good smile, Elder thought, generous and open. He wondered how Shane Donald had been able to get so far under her skin. 'I've tried that,' she said.

'It doesn't work?'

'Most of the time.' She broke off some more croissant and put it in her mouth. Behind them, the baby had woken up and started to cry. 'When I went to see him at the hostel, Donald, we sat there going through the usual rigmarole and then at the end of it he smiled and when he did that – I don't know, it just got to me, it was as if he was acknowledging that it was all a game and he knew and underneath nothing had changed. He hadn't changed. Given the same opportunity he would do the same things again.'

She reached for her coffee mug but it was already empty.

'Right after that, it was when I had my first cigarette in months.'

'And you still believe that?' Elder asked. 'Now. That he would hurt someone. Like before. For the sheer pleasure, the charge, the thrill.'

'I think he could.'

Elder leaned away and she read the movement well. 'You don't agree.'

'I don't want to.'

'Because of this missing girl?'

'Maybe.'

Pam smiled. 'What does your gut feeling say?'

Elder shook his head. 'I haven't laid eyes on Donald for close on thirteen years. You have. But when I did know him, back then, it was his friend, it was McKeirnan, I'm sure, who took the lead, initiated everything.'

'Prison changes people,' Pam said. 'Not always in the way we want. Sometimes it breaks them, sometimes it only serves to make them hard. Maybe what Donald did was grow up inside. Maybe he doesn't need someone like McKeirnan any more.'

◆

By the time Elder had driven back down the motorway, they'd found the place where Emma Harrison had been held.

It was an out-of-work roofer who made the first discovery, a pink sandal with a single band of leather, slightly worn down sole and heel. It was nestling amidst a thick clump of thistles towards the southern edge of a meadow that had been left for pasture, the sun catching it just at the moment that the volunteer searcher made his slow way across the field, right to left, head down. Even in the adrenaline rush of his discovery, he had known enough, had watched enough TV – *Taggart*, *Dalziel and Pascoe*, *Frost* – to know better than to pick it up, handle it, obscure whatever prints might be importantly in place. Instead he marked the spot carefully with the small rucksack he was carrying and hurried to the nearest uniformed officer, a young constable from Ollerton pacing in his shirtsleeves, the tips of his ears and the back of his neck reddening from the sun.

A quick, uncomfortable task to confirm the sandal as Emma's, one of a pair bought early that spring.

A line on the map connecting the two finds, cardigan and sandal, suggested the direction that had been taken. A path that led through one more swathe of meadow, dipping at its furthest edge towards a stream running meagrely along the hedge bottom; fifty metres more and the hedge was halted abruptly by a length of fencing, mostly broken down. An overgrown track led towards what had once been a farm, a smallholding, little more. The main building had been boarded up and, at some later date, set fire to, blackened timbers meshed with crumbling brick. The second of two barns was sturdy, its door secured by a padlock that was easy to break. The stink brought tears to the eyes, phlegm to the back of the throat. Blood, dried vomit, human excrement. At first the officer feared the bundle by the far wall might be a body, but it was straw and sacking filtered through with ash. A length of chain bolted to an upright; rope hanging from the roof. Discarded in one corner, wadded into a ball and also stained with blood, lay Emma Harrison's halter top.

By the time Maureen Prior arrived, shortly after Gerry Clarke, and only a little in advance of the media, the immediate area had been sealed off. Forensic experts and Scene of Crime were gathering to perform their tasks. Generators were already in position to provide the extra lighting that would be necessary. Bottles of water, flasks of tea.

Plastic covering on her shoes, Maureen stood alone in

the centre of the barn, looking at the chain, the rope, the stains darkening the already dark floor. Thinking about a fifteen-year-old girl. Imagining.

Later, she would be sick; later when she was alone and unobserved.

Now she turned and stepped back out into the sun.

'Okay, Gerry,' she said. 'Let them get started.'

◆

'Do we know how long she was held there?' Elder asked.

'Best guess is two days,' Maureen said. 'Three at most.'

For a long moment Elder closed his eyes. 'Days and nights,' he said.

'Yes.'

They were walking alongside the Trent, following the broad curve of the Victoria Embankment past the Memorial Gardens and towards the old viaduct, the worn expanse of the recreation ground to their right, dog walkers and the sporadic shouts of casual footballers. Along the river, a narrow boat eased through the water with an even rise and fall of oars.

'There are tyre tracks leading in and out,' Maureen said. 'It's been so dry lately, they're not clear and it's difficult to know how long they've been there. It's going to be tomorrow at the earliest before we know if there's anything distinct enough to be of use.'

'The lane into the farm,' Elder said. 'In the other direction, where does it lead?'

'Left and you're back on the A46, then it's south towards Newark, north to Lincoln.'

'And if you go right?'

'Lincoln again. Or skirt the city and finagle your way east.'

'To the coast.'

'Yes.'

Elder was silent for some little time.

'What are you thinking?' Maureen eventually asked.

Elder shook his head as if to clear the thoughts from his mind. They walked on a little further, level with the bowling green, and then Elder paused.

'If we assume whoever's keeping Emma prisoner has a vehicle, then why all this traipsing across fields?'

'I've been thinking about that, too. Suppose the barn wasn't his first choice. He takes her somewhere else, then, for whatever reason, has to move on.'

'On foot, though. Why on foot?'

'It would make sense, wouldn't it, if, having abducted her, he wanted to get rid of the vehicle in case it had been seen.'

'In which case we should have found an abandoned car somewhere. Car or van.'

'Perhaps we still will.'

They resumed walking.

'If he takes her with him,' Maureen said, 'from the barn, it means she's still alive, right?'

'Maybe.'

'Frank, what other reason could there be?'

'I'm not sure.'

When they reached the viaduct they stopped again. Directly north, above the no-longer-new housing of the Meadows, they could see the outline of the castle and the rounded roof of the Council House. Ahead of them, as they turned, were the floodlights of both the Forest and

County grounds, on either side of the Trent beyond the bridge.

'You still think it could be Shane Donald?' Maureen asked.

'I was thinking,' Elder said. 'All this toing and froing across open land, then the items of clothing, the cardigan first and then the sandal, whoever it is, what if he's leaving a trail he wants us to follow?'

'He wants to be caught?'

'Not necessarily. Not necessarily that at all.'

◆

At the evening press conference, Bernard Young kept as close to the facts as he could. Yes, we are assuming that the building in question is where Emma Harrison was held. No, we have no clear indication as to where she might be at this present time, but we are continuing to follow up a number of leads.

'What specific inference,' asked the correspondent from one of the broadsheets, 'should we draw from the involvement of former Detective Inspector Elder with the investigation?'

'None,' the superintendent said, 'other than the fact that he is an experienced professional with significant experience in similar cases. And as you well know, in cases such as this, we not infrequently call in assistance from a variety of outside agencies.'

'Frank Elder,' put in the local crime reporter, 'led the hunt for McKeirnan and Donald, didn't he?'

'He was a member of that investigating team, yes.' Not altogether liking which way this was heading, the detective superintendent was on his feet.

'And Shane Donald, as I believe, having been released from prison, is still unlawfully at large, isn't that correct?'

'No further questions,' the superintendent said, stepping clear.

'There will be a press conference,' the public relations officer announced into the microphone, 'at eleven tomorrow morning. In the event of any major new developments, you will, of course, be informed.'

◆

'Our daughter,' Ronald Harrison said, 'is she alive or dead?'

Slowly, the liaison officer shook her head. 'We don't know, Mr Harrison. I'm afraid we just don't know. But we must hope for the best.'

38

Hope dies hard and sometimes fast. The burned-out wreck of a four-year-old Honda Civic, reported stolen from the railway station car park at Retford on the day before Emma Harrison disappeared, was found on an old travellers' encampment between the River Trent and the A1, north of Newark. The charred remains of a sandal resembling Emma's were discovered in the boot. The other sandal.

After careful examination of the lane leading to the barn where Emma had been held, Scene of Crime officers identified the partial tyre tracks of what they believed to be a medium-sized van moving both in and out; the tracks corresponded, as far as they could determine, to those of a white Ford van fitted with new radial tyres which had been stolen from outside a house in Newark, while the owner was inside removing the mechanism from inside a large sofa bed, prior to carrying it down stairs. The van had not, so far, been found.

At a little before ten on Saturday morning, two boys, aged twelve and fourteen, staying with their families on a camp-site near by, were riding their bikes around on the sands north of the small town of Mablethorpe on the

Lincolnshire coast. Heading back across the dunes, the older boy, showing off, sent his bike into a spectacular skid, the arc of his rear wheel gouging deep into the sand and uncovering the shallow grave in which Emma Harrison had been buried.

'Mablethorpe,' Maureen Price said, when she heard the news. 'Isn't that . . .'

'It's where Lucy Padmore's body was found,' Elder said. 'Fourteen years ago.'

'Buried on the dunes.'

Elder nodded, stone-faced. 'On the dunes.'

The Sundays had a field-day: from broadsheet to tabloid, they filled their pages with fact and supposition, reporters filing stories rich in overelaborate detail and prurient surmise. There were diagrams showing where the body had lain, interviews with the boys who found the grave; sketch maps which traced Emma's presumed movements through those last six days. Photographs of Emma were culled from different sources, others showed her parents shielding their faces from the cameras as they hurried into the hospital to identify their daughter. Column after column was devoted to memories of Emma by her friends. She was always so full of energy, full of life; everyone loved her, everyone. She will be remembered in our prayers, the local vicar assured anyone who cared.

We might wonder, said the archbishop, if we are not all in some way reaping the harvest of a society in which sex and commerce are ever and ever more closely linked and in which the sexualisation of our children and young people is increasingly accepted without question or rebuke.

Speculation as to the identity of her killer was rife. The usual tactic of naming and shaming paedophiles was tawdrily trumpeted. Elder's presence as part of the investigation team compounded the interest aroused by the coincidence of two young women being buried on the same stretch of coast. The more horrific details of Lucy Padmore's abduction and murder were refreshed for our memory. Those papers who had begun to put together pieces about Shane Donald when he absconded from the probation hostel had a head's start on their rivals. *IS THIS THE FACE OF EMMA'S KILLER?* one shrieked in type three centimetres deep. Lucy Padmore's father offered a reward leading to the killer's capture, a sum instantly matched and improved upon by a national daily.

Elder stood on the edge of the dunes, staring out across the expanse of grey, cold sea.

'Do you think it's him?' Maureen asked.

'I don't know.' His voice was sharp, harsher than he'd intended. 'I'm sorry, I . . .'

'No, it's okay.'

Neither of them spoke again for some little time. Each knew for now they were dealing with conjecture, little more: the post-mortem had still to determine the exact cause of death. Detailed forensic examination of the body and the burial site, the barn and the burned-out car might uncover DNA evidence incontrovertibly linking Donald to the crime. Other leads, other clues. Equally, officers might find a match with one of the known offenders who were still being methodically checked out as part of the ongoing investigation. Computers would cross-check information with the CATCHEM system, in which statistics from four decades of offences against children were stored. But all this took time and waiting left a vacuum into which thoughts tried repeatedly to filter down.

'When Donald and McKeirnan took Lucy Padmore,' Elder said eventually, 'it was here. Mablethorpe. What they did to her they did here. Whoever took Emma, it was the best part of eighty, a hundred miles away. When he held her prisoner that was still a good way off, seventy miles, say. And yet he risks discovery driving her here when he could have left her in that barn in Nottingham-shire. Why?'

Maureen organised her thoughts. 'It's a question we should ask a profiler, a forensic psychologist. And will. But if there's a pattern . . . I don't know, maybe it's something he has to recreate. A sort of fetish, I suppose.' She looked around. 'Something about this place.'

Elder was remembering standing there before, the same wide spread of sand, the same fall and rise of waves, the selfsame spot or so it seemed.

'If it is Donald,' Maureen said, her voice tugged at a little by the wind, 'what are the chances he'll do it again?'

'If it is,' Elder said, 'as long as he's at large, they must be high.'

◆

It's a truism, perhaps, that prison changes everyone who passes through the system, prison officers, prisoners, probation officers, everyone; at the same time it cements within some people aspects which will never change. During his time at Gartree Alan McKeirnan seemed to Elder to have become a waxwork of his former self, a carapace of the man he had watched insolently smiling in the dock and who had been sent down for life. Forty years of age but looking older – ageless – McKeirnan walked stiffly, escorted, into the small and airless room, a tall, thin figure dressed in grey and black.

'Gimme a cigarette.'

Elder shook one loose and lit it for him, passing him across the pack.

'You took your time,' McKeirnan said. 'The boy's been gone a while now.' He laughed, a metallic, rusted sound. 'Big boy now, out there on his own.'

'You're worried about him?' Elder asked.

McKeirnan's eyes seemed to have sunk back deep into his head.

'You sound worried about him,' Elder said.

'Shane, no.'

'Concerned?'

'No concern of mine.'

'Your boy, it's what you said.'

'Not any more.'

'But you're responsible.'

'Me? What can I do, in here?'

'You did it a long time ago.'

McKeirnan stared back at him with flat, dark eyes.

'A girl's been killed,' Elder said.

'We have television, you know. Some do. Sky News. CNN. BBC News 24. The screws at least. Things pass around.'

'Then you'll know who I'm talking about.'

'Sixteen, wasn't she? Such a shame. Pretty, too.'

'You know where she was found?'

'Freeze your balls off that coast, most weeks of the year.'

'Would Shane go back there?' Elder repeated
McKeirnan looked away.
'Would Shane go back there?'
'He might.'
'Why? Why there?'
'Where he come of age.'
'And d'you think this could be him?'
'Is he on his own?'
A movement across Elder's face told him he was not.
'He'd never do it on his own,' McKeirnan said.
'How can you be sure?'
'Anything else you want to know,' McKeirnan said, 'it's gonna cost.'

Elder took a second packet of cigarettes from his pocket and set it down on top of the first.

'No. I mean really cost you. Big.'
'I'll not bargain,' Elder said.
'Then what makes you think,' McKeirnan said, 'I'd waste myself on the likes of you?'

'Because it's Shane out there. Your boy. Your protégé. Because he's out there and you're not.'

'And good luck to him,' McKeirnan said, raising an imaginary glass.

Elder scraped back the chair, starting to rise.

'Wait,' McKeirnan said, extending his hand. 'Wait a minute, wait.'

Slowly, Elder sat back down.

'Tell me,' McKeirnan said, leaning forward, lowering his voice. 'Tell me what he did to her, the girl. Then maybe I'll tell you what you want to know.'

Elder stared hard into his face. 'Go to hell, McKeirnan.'

McKeirnan laughed the same raw, ugly sound.

The fair had finished in Newark after the weekend, laid low for a day, packed up and driven north to Gainsborough, an ungainly market town just across the border into Lincolnshire. Another patch of muddied wasteland, another day of offloading and laborious setting-up. Donald kept his head down, pitched in, did his bit and no more. In the evenings he was quiet, preoccupied. One day when Angel woke up, his side of the bed was empty and Shane nowhere to be seen: the second time he had gone off without warning. No note, no explanation. After the flare-up with Brock, the incident with the knife, he had been gone for two whole days.

While Shane was away, Della, serious-faced, called Angel over to her caravan and sat her down. One of the newspapers was open on the small table, Shane's blurry image staring out.

'Here,' Della said, steadying Angel's arm before she fell. 'Here. Sit yourself down. Take a sip of this.'

Angel read each page, each column several times, speculation about what had happened to Emma Harrison, speculation and a little fact.

'What's all this got to do with Shane?' Angel asked, her voice a whisper.

Della turned the page and read the summary of Shane's trial, the account of the ordeal Lucy Padmore had undergone at his and McKeirnan's hands. Inside her something twisted and caught. She was pale when she left Della's caravan, her skin the colour of a winding-sheet, a shroud. For the first few steps, her legs threatened to undo her, cast her down.

Late that evening, when Shane reappeared, Angel read the expression on his face and held her tongue.

That night, instead of making love, he clung to her and as she lay there in the dark she imagined she heard the small, constant movement of his lips; had she not known him better, she might have thought he was saying his prayers.

Come morning, he was quiet and still, a touch withdrawn, but closer to his usual self.

Grateful, Angel dipped her head to kiss his neck as she passed behind him on her way out.

Still she waited until she and Donald were next alone and away from others' eyes.

'Look,' pushing the newspaper before him. 'That's you, isn't it? You cut her. You hurt her. You did all those . . . those things to her and then you killed her.'

Donald snatched the paper from her and buried his face in it, then let it fall.

'Yes,' he said.

'Oh, Christ!' Angel cried. 'Oh, Christ!'

The next morning they were both gone.

39

The post-mortem was inconclusive as to the exact cause of death: the injuries the body had received, the time spent in warm weather in a shallow grave. At some point in her ordeal, Emma's life had given out. The probability that she had been already dead when she made her last journey to the coast was high, but difficult to prove.

The van was found illegally parked outside an antique shop in Louth, one of several that permeated the town. This time there were no souvenirs, no obvious clues; the vehicle had been wiped meticulously clean inside and out. A preliminary trawl suggested there would be no fingerprints, possibly not as much as a stray hair. Whoever had been careless enough – or content – to lead them to Emma Harrison's body was leading them no further.

Detectives examining the spot where Emma had been found were having no more luck. The boy's bicycle had inadvertently ploughed up some of the area around the grave and the coarse dry sand revealed little else; what signs there were suggested that whoever had spent time there with the body had been wearing some smooth covering, possibly common-or-garden plastic bags, over his shoes, much in the same way as the officers themselves.

As a site, the barn seemed likely to prove more fruitful, but such had been the state of the interior, that the process of sorting and identifying was more than usually painstaking and slow.

While Maureen Prior's team continued to track down and eliminate the most likely offenders, officers under Gerry Clarke, now freed from the task of finding the missing girl, attempted to evaluate and respond to the calls that were coming in as a response to the flurry of media publicity and the promise of financial reward. Overweight and lonely women who rarely walked further than the corner shop and wanted their five minutes in front of the television cameras. Couples who stuck a pin in a map and claimed to have seen someone resembling Shane Donald struggling with a girl, playing the odds much as they bought tickets for the lottery or backed a rank outsider at a hundred to one.

Elder stayed pretty much in the background during much of this, assessing the information as it was processed as best he could, feeling frustrated despite everything, too far from the centre of the investigation.

He was kicking his heels in the corridor, contemplating yet another cup of nondescript coffee, when Helen Blacklock got through to him on his mobile. 'You're okay?' she said and then, after an awkward pause, 'I tried calling you before . . .'

'Yes.'

'Left messages.'

'Yes, I know.'

Another pause and then, 'You'd rather I hadn't called.'

'No. Not at all.'

'Then you're busy.'

'Yes.'

'This girl, the one they found, Emma . . .'

'Yes.'

'You don't know . . .'

'No. We're still pretty much in the dark, I'm afraid.'

'And Donald?'

'Helen, we're still investigating, doing what we can.'

'You don't want to talk about it.'

'It's difficult.'

'Yes, of course. I understand.' He could hear her breath, close to the phone, as she drew on her cigarette. The one she'd lit before dialling. 'I'm sorry, I shouldn't have phoned.'

'No, it's okay.'

'Goodbye, Frank. Some other time.'

When the phone went dead, he felt guilty, without being a hundred per cent certain why.

◆

It was late on Monday afternoon when one of Clarke's young DCs flagged a call made by a man who gave his name as Craig and claimed to have been working with Shane Donald on a fairground in Gainsborough, and what did he have to do to claim the reward? By midday Tuesday no one had responded and it was only when the constable who'd taken the original call brought it directly to the DI's attention, that action was taken.

'Maureen, it's Gerry. Is Frank around?'

Elder was less than a dozen feet away, staring at names on a computer screen.

'There's something you both might want to follow up

on. I'll give you the details. May be nothing, you never know.'

Less than ten minutes later, the sun bright and high at their backs, both Elder and Maureen were in an unmarked saloon, driving north.

◆

Craig was working the dodgems, swinging his way from car to car, not tall, five six or seven, thick dark hair with something of a curl, a sleeveless denim shirt that showed off the muscles in his upper arms, patched jeans. They watched him amidst the blare of music, joking with the kids, chatting up the girls. Wasn't many a night he didn't end up copping a feel at least, out there in the grass around the fairground's edge.

Neither Elder nor Maureen looked like punters exactly, standing where they did, waiting for the ride to end. 'Craig,' Maureen said, approaching him quietly, not wanting to make a fuss. 'It is Craig, isn't it?'

His eyes pale blue and nervous, flitting from one to the other, uncertain.

'I think you wanted to talk to us. About Shane Donald.'

'Not here.'

The caravan he shared with three others smelled of stale air, stale beer and cigarettes. A sweet undertaste of dope. Sweat and spliffs and skinning up. Four men under thirty living close together.

'Can we open a window or something?' Maureen asked.

'They're stuck,' Craig said, the merest hint of apology.

They settled for an open inch or two of door. Craig

317

cracked a can of Special Brew, reached for his tobacco and his papers.

'This reward,' he began.

'Just tell us,' Maureen said, 'what you know.'

Without too much embellishment, he did exactly that: Shane appearing outside Manchester, not so long back, and getting hired on. Then taking up with Angel . . .

'That's her real name?' Elder asked.

'Far's I know.'

'Go on,' Maureen said.

Craig told them about the time Shane had attacked his friend, Brock, unprovoked, with a knife. 'Crazy, fuckin' crazy. Just sliced him up for no reason. Walked right over to him and cut him. There. Had to take him to the hospital, wait half the night while they sewed him up.'

There'll be a record, Maureen was thinking, easy enough to check.

'And this was out of the blue?' Elder asked. 'No provocation?'

Craig backed down a little under his stare. 'He might've said something, I don't know.'

'What about?'

'About the girl.'

'He was defending her?' Maureen said.

'If you like, yeah. 'Cept it was nothin', nothin'. Brock, what he said. Nothing.'

'Donald evidently didn't think so,' Elder said.

'Yeah, but he's fuckin' crazy, i'n't he, like I said. I always knew it, right? Right from the first time I saw him. Somethin' about his eyes, the way he don't look at you, you know, head on. Dunno what she sees in him, Angel, 'cept she's a bit of a scag herself.'

'When did you last see them?' Maureen asked.

'Sunday. Sunday night. Last thing. In the morning they was gone.'

'You don't know where?'

Craig pulled a stray flake of tobacco from his lip and shook his head.

They asked him how long the fair had been in Gainsborough and where it had been before. At the mention of Newark, Elder and Maureen exchanged a glance. They asked how much time Donald had spent away from the fair – say, in the past week. Craig had some idea he'd gone off the previous weekend, after attacking Brock, maybe once since then, he wasn't sure. There didn't seem to be a great deal more he could tell them that would be of use.

'Thank you for getting in touch with us,' Maureen said, preparing to leave.

'That's it?' Craig said. 'That's all?'

'For now. We'll want to talk to some of the others, of course. Before we go.'

'What for?'

'Oh, corroboration, that's all.'

'But I was the one as told you, right? Told you where he was.'

'Where he'd been.'

'Yeah, but, leading to the arrest, that's what it says. The reward. Information leading to the arrest . . .'

'And conviction.'

'Yeah, and conviction. Okay.'

'All a long way off,' Maureen said, pushing open the door.

'But he done it, right. The girl.'

319

'We don't know,' Elder said. 'We just don't know.'

'Hey! It said so, in the paper, black and fuckin' white.'

◆

Della had no reason to trust the police. When she had read about Shane Donald, her only thought had been to tell Angel, warn her; after that, let the pieces fall where they may. Life dealt the cards and all you could do was play them, close to your chest as you could. It had dealt her a man she had loved, a woman also; a child who had died. Now she lived in her caravan and travelled with the fair; sometimes she told fortunes, dealt the tarot, gazed into any future but her own.

For Elder and Maureen Prior she made tea, black and strong.

'She saw something good in him,' Della said. 'She'd not have gone with him otherwise. Not like she did. I've known her a while now and she's not been like that before, not with anyone. Not like she was with him. She loves him. And I thought she might never trust anyone enough to do that again.'

'How old is she?' Maureen asked.

'Seventeen.'

'And you don't know where they've gone?' Elder said.

'No, and I don't know if I would tell you if I did.'

'It might be for the best,' Maureen said.

'What? Prison? Can you imagine what would happen to someone like Angel if she was shut away in prison? Him, too, for that matter.' Della shook her head. 'My God, no. Let them have happiness while they can.'

320

'But you told Angel about Donald,' Maureen said. 'Warned her.'

'I wanted her to know, that's all. I wanted her to choose.'

'Let's hope she chose wisely.'

'He won't hurt her,' Della said.

'You seem certain.'

'He loves her, too. In his way.'

'Would he hurt somebody else?' Elder asked.

Della looked at him squarely. 'I do not think it was him, if that is what you're asking. I don't think it was him, killed that poor girl. They have been here working. Both of them.'

'We need to find them,' Elder said. 'Nevertheless.'

Della looked back at him without speaking.

'Does she have family?' Maureen asked. 'Angel?'

'None she would go to.'

'None at all?'

'She was in foster homes, I think. Liverpool, somewhere. And then, I think, Stoke-on-Trent. That's all I know.'

'And a name? Aside from Angel.'

'Angel Elizabeth Ryan, that's what she was baptised.'

'The caravan they stayed in,' Maureen said. 'Is it all right if we have a look?'

Della was about to say no, but then shrugged. 'Why not? It can't do them any harm.'

They appeared to have taken what was theirs and left. There were a few magazines, the crumpled pages of a newspaper, a pair of laddered tights, two odd socks, a stained T-shirt that could have belonged to either one of them, several tea bags, a bottle of milk going off, a tin of

321

beans, two almost empty plastic bottles of shampoo, a Lil-lets box with one tampon still inside, a comb missing several teeth and, squeezed tight behind the edge of the mattress where it had fallen, a strip of film.

It had been taken in one of the instant photo booths that were found in stations and the like, four pictures one above the other; Shane and Angel with their heads jammed close together, smiling, squinting, mugging for the camera. In one Angel was kissing the underside of Shane's chin; in another, she was staring at him, her face angled upwards, while Shane's gaze was fixed firmly on the camera, brazening it out. Thirty and seventeen, they could have passed for twenty-one or -two and fifteen or even less.

◆

The sky was losing light as they drove back, Maureen at the wheel.

'How long have we known one another?' Elder asked. They were just going past the Marton roundabout, heading south.

'Total? Five years, six maybe.'

'And we worked together for what? Three of those?'

'Where are you going with this?' Maureen asked.

'Five years,' Elder said, 'and all I know about you is you're good at your job, prefer your whisky with water, draught bitter over anything out of a can. I've a vague idea where you live, but I've never seen inside; I don't even know if you live with someone else or if you live alone.'

'That's right,' Maureen said.

'And doesn't any of that strike you as strange?'

'What is this?' Maureen asked. 'Is this about Joanne? Has she been getting to you in some way? Getting under your skin?'

'You see, you know everything there is to know about me, just about.'

'You choose to tell me, that's why.'

'And you don't.'

'That's correct.'

One night, on a journey not dissimilar to this, but longer, down from Scotland, in fact, and in rain, he had unburdened himself about Joanne's affair with her boss and Maureen had listened, saying little, making no comment at all when the story was over, though Elder had been able to sense her disapproval radiating through the small space around them, all the more fierce for being unspoken.

'Do you think it's him?' Maureen said.

'I don't know.'

'Everything seems to point that way.'

'I know.'

'But you're not convinced?'

Elder shook his head. 'Something about it – I don't know – it doesn't feel right.'

'If he's not guilty, why run?'

'Wake up to find your picture all over the front pages, headlines accusing you of murder, what would you do? Give yourself up, hope it sorts itself out?'

'Not if I were Donald I wouldn't.'

'Precisely.'

A few miles further on, Elder said, 'Guilty or not, he'll have to be reeled in.'

Maureen nodded. 'If they stay together, it'll be easier.

I'll get on to social services, see if we can't get some kind of history, a list of foster homes at least. She might just remember one of them kindly enough to think of it as a place to go, a place to stay.'

'They'll need money,' Elder said. 'Soon, anyway. They'll either steal it or try to find work. We should try and check out any small fairs, seems it's what they both know.'

It was darker now, dark without ever becoming really black, the sky largely bereft of stars, the moon a sliver in the corner of one eye. Had Maureen been right, Elder wondered, had that evening with Joanne – less than an evening, barely an hour – had that got to him in some way he'd failed to recognise at the time?

Like old times.

No, it hadn't been that.

'Where do you want me to drop you, Frank?' Maureen asked as they came close to the city's edge.

'Anywhere. It doesn't matter.'

'I can pass near Willie Bell's if that's where you're going.'

'That'll do fine.'

Before she had turned off the main road, Maureen's phone rang. She identified herself, listened, acknowledged and broke the connection.

'Gartree. McKeirnan wants to see you.'

'I'm only just back from seeing him. And much good it did me.'

'Well, he wants to see you again. He says it's important. Seems he's been getting some interesting post.'

40

The postcard showed a length of concrete promenade, tapering into the distance like some vast utilitarian defence against the sea; a few huts selling plastic buckets, spades, black-and-white footballs inside yellow mesh, Bob the Builder T-shirts, mugs of tea and ice-cream for the beach. Families sheltering behind wind-breaks on bleached-out sand. And then the sea, spreading like dead grey skin towards a grey horizon. '*Welcome to Mablethorpe*' in bright red cheery type.

McKeirnan held up the card between finger and thumb for Elder to see. When Elder reached out to take it, McKeirnan moved it swiftly out of reach.

'You said this was important,' Elder said.

'It is.'

'Then don't play games.'

'C'mon,' McKeirnan said, 'now you're here, what's the rush? Relax. All the time in the world.'

'That's you,' Elder said.

'And you? Detective Inspector Frank Elder, retired. What is it now? Bingo? Bowls? Senior citizens' discount at the massage parlour Friday afternoons?'

'Don't fuck with me, McKeirnan.' Elder looked at his

325

watch. 'If I get up and leave, I'm not ever coming back. No matter what.'

McKeirnan held his gaze for maybe thirty seconds longer, then reversed the card and slid it across the dulled surface of the table for Elder to read.

'*Alan – Having a lovely time. Wish you were here.*'

The handwriting, in blue biro, was uneven, somewhat rushed, sloping slightly downwards left to right. The final full stop pressed hard enough to make a small indentation on the other side. There was no signature.

'So what?' Elder said.

'Look at the postmark.'

It was dated Saturday, the day Emma Harrison's body had been found.

'Coincidence,' Elder said.

'You think?'

'Tell me otherwise.'

'You're the detective. Least, you were. You tell me.'

'You're saying it's from Shane?'

'Am I?'

'McKeirnan . . .'

'No, I'm not.' A smile, deep in McKeirnan's eyes. 'Not Shane. Not exactly.'

'Riddles, McKeirnan.'

'And you don't like to play.'

'I don't like to be jerked around by the likes of you.'

'Poor baby.'

Elder sat on his hands. Controlled his breathing. Counted to ten.

He picked up the card and looked at it again. 'You're claiming there's a connection with the death of Emma Harrison.'

'I am.'

'You'll need to be more specific than that.'

McKeirnan smiled. 'He did her, that's the thing.'

'How do you know?'

The smile became a grin. 'He promised me.'

'Who?'

McKeirnan leaned back in his chair. 'Remember what you said before? When you were here. How you wouldn't bargain? Well, now you will.'

'And you told me, I'm washed-up, retired. Even if I wanted to, there's nothing I can do.'

'I'm not unreasonable,' McKeirnan said, 'no grand ideas of pardons, early release. But if I've, what, another six years to do, I want them easy. I want out of this place. I want to be reclassified. Category C.' He laughed. 'I want to get ready for the outside world, get prepared.'

He leaned forward again suddenly, his face close to Elder's, skin stretched tight across the sockets of his eyes.

'The girl, he didn't kill her right away, did he? Kept her for a while, a day or two. Things he had to do. To her. You don't have to tell me what they were, 'cause I know. You, you can only imagine, but I know. And I know something else. It won't stop there. Not with one. He'll do it again. Unless.'

'What you're asking,' Elder said. 'I don't have the power.'

'Then get me someone who has.'

◆

'How do we know he's not bluffing?' Bernard Young asked. They were in the superintendent's office, early afternoon. Young yanked open one of the drawers of his desk and slammed it shut. 'Christ, I hate being held over a barrel by scum like that. Hate it.'

The silence in the room caught and held: only the sounds of four people breathing less than easily, of water refreshing itself in the fish tank to the side. The constant blur of traffic moving back and forth. The muffled trills of telephones.

'For what it's worth,' Elder said, 'I believe him.'

Bernard Young swivelled his chair away and back again. Less than half an hour before he had come from a particularly awkward session with the ACC. The need for an early result, the reputation of the force. Some catnip at the Home Office had been badgering the chief constable. Down in London, a team of high-flyers from the Met were already sharpening their pencils and the toes of their boots, ready to step in and review the way the investigation was being conducted. And then there were the faces of Emma Harrison's parents, turned towards him, eviscerated as their daughter.

'All right, Frank,' he said, 'tell me how you see it.'

Elder cleared his throat. 'We have to assume McKeirnan knows who sent the card. And knows him well. Which could mean they've corresponded on the internet – I assume he's allowed some kind of access, monitored some of the time – or there've been letters going back and forth. My guess, the amount of censorship in McKeirnan's case would be practically nil. But I think it's more than either of those. I think it's someone he knows, someone he's talked to face to face, which means a fellow prisoner.'

'In which case,' interrupted Gerry Clarke, 'we can track him down ourselves.'

'Go through all the prisoners aged thirty and younger who've been released from Gartree within the last – what? – five years.'

'Why under thirty?' Clarke asked.

'That's part of it,' Elder said. 'I'm sure. *Not Shane, not exactly* – McKeirnan's words.'

'Couldn't he be lying to protect Donald?'

'I don't think so.'

'Why not?'

'For one thing I doubt there's any love lost between them. And for another . . .' He was remembering the expression on McKeirnan's face. *He did her, that's the thing. He promised me.* The relish with which he'd said the words.

'No,' Elder continued. 'I think this is somebody new, someone who, for whatever reason, wants to do McKeirnan's bidding. Wants his approval. Whoever this is, he wants to be like Shane Donald. McKeirnan's acolyte. His helper. Disciple. The postcard is a way of testifying, showing he's made good, kept the faith, kept his word.'

'Why now?' Maureen asked. 'Why act now?'

'If Frank's right, that's simple, surely,' Clarke said. 'Whoever it is, it's because he's only recently been released.'

'Agreed,' Elder said, 'and not only that. It's because Donald has been, too. And he knows Donald's on the run. He wants to put us off the track, assume that Donald's to blame.'

'But wants McKeirnan to know the truth,' Maureen said.

'Yes.'

Bernard Young leaned forward, elbows on his desk. 'Gerry, if we do the follow-up ourselves and let McKeirnan go hang, how long before we can expect a result?'

'Well, first, we need a list from Gartree of all the recently released prisoners who might have come into contact with McKeirnan. Cross-check it against the lists we're already working on of offenders with a profile of violent or sexual crimes. Start off with Nottinghamshire and Lincolnshire, South Yorkshire maybe, take it wider if we need to. Once we've got all that information on to the computer, we just might get a match by the end of tomorrow. More than one, probably. Maybe a dozen.'

'To be traced and checked,' Maureen said.

Clarke nodded his head.

'So we could be looking at another two or three days, possibly more.'

'Possibly, yes.'

'All right,' Young said. 'Belt and braces time. Gerry, get the search started, stress the urgency. If you get there first, all well and good. Meantime, I'm going to speak with the ACC and then the governor at Gartree. The Home Office, if I have to. Maureen, you and Frank be ready to leave within the hour.'

◆

McKeirnan looked Maureen Prior over with a tired leer.

'Putting it to her, Frank?'

'Sit down, McKeirnan,' Maureen said.

Taking his time, he sat. Neither of them would be there if he weren't in the driving seat, and he knew it.

'We need to know,' Elder said, 'who sent the card.'

'When we've agreed . . .'

'No promises, that's not how it's going to work.'

'Then it's not going to work at all.'

With a lazy scrape back of his chair, McKeirnan got to his feet. He was almost across the room, the prison officer primed to unlock the door, when Maureen called him back.

Ignoring the smug look on his face, she waited until he had sat back down.

'This is what we can do,' she said. 'Put in a report to the governor saying that you've been particularly helpful with inquiries we're carrying out as part of an ongoing investigation. We'll stress that you were the one who came forward, volunteering information without first being asked. Our recommendation will be that, in view of this responsible behaviour, you should be reassessed and, all other things being equal, recategorised as a Category C prisoner.'

'That's it?' McKeirnan said.

'That's it.'

McKeirnan rocked his chair back on to its rear legs and smoothed the fingers of his left hand across the fist of his right.

'You've got five minutes to decide,' Maureen said. 'One's almost up.'

McKeirnan eased the chair back down. 'All you want's the name?'

'It's a start,' Elder said.

'Two minutes,' Maureen said, without looking at her watch.

'Okay.'

She took a pad from her pocket and swivelled it towards

331

him; uncapped a ballpoint and set it down close by his hand. 'Write it down.'

Looking at her, McKeirnan ran his tongue along his lower lip, then picked up the pen. 'How do I know the minute you walk out of here, you won't go back on everything you've said?'

'You don't.'

McKeirnan slowly grinned, then carefully printed two words at the centre of the first blank page and pushed it back. When he released the pen it rolled to the edge of the table and bounced to the floor where it lay unclaimed.

Adam Keach.

'Tell us about him,' Elder said.

'Look him up, his case notes, file, whatever. You can do that.'

'Something else. Tell us something else.'

McKeirnan smiled. 'He'd follow me round, beg me to talk about it. What we did. Found ways of paying me. Saying thank you.' He laughed his abrasive laugh. 'When I get out, he said. I'll show you what I can do.'

Maureen replaced the pad of paper in her bag.

'One other question,' Elder said. 'Susan Blacklock.'

'Who?'

'Susan Blacklock, she went missing the same summer Lucy Padmore's body was found.'

'You asked me about her before.' McKeirnan shook his head. 'I dunno no more now'n I did then.'

'The North Yorks. coast, McKeirnan, Whitby. You and Donald were there.'

'We went to a lot of places, me and Shane.'

'What happened to her, McKeirnan?'

'I said. I don't know. I'll tell you one thing, though. If

you still haven't found her, whoever buried her buried her deep.'

'All right,' Maureen said to the prison officer. 'We're through here. Lock him back up.'

◆

Adam Keach was born in Kirkby in Ashfield in 1978, the middle of three boys. When he was eighteen months old his mother was convicted of fraudulent deception in regard to benefit payments; his father already had a long list of petty offences and was known to the local police and probation service. Social services were alerted when Adam's younger brother, Dean, was treated at Mansfield Community Hospital for severe bruising and abrasions to the arms and legs; a social worker visited the house on two occasions and satisfied herself that the children were not in danger. No further action was taken. At the age of fifteen, Adam was suspended from school for stabbing a fellow pupil in the back of the hand with the sharpened shaft of a Bic pen; at seventeen, he and his elder brother, Mark, were twice questioned regarding the theft of a computer and a Game Boy from a neighbour's house without any charges being brought. Finally, not so long after his nineteenth birthday, he was sentenced to three years for aggravated burglary; after attacking a fellow prisoner with a length of pipe and almost taking out his eye, the sentence was doubled and Keach was moved to Gartree prison where he met Alan McKeirnan.

Adam Keach was finally released back into the community in late May, two weeks, approximately, from when Emma Harrison disappeared.

◆

At that evening's press conference, Bernard Young went out of his way to stress that, although the investigation was still moving forward on several fronts, they were still most anxious to trace the whereabouts of Shane Donald, who was now believed to be in the company of one Angel Elizabeth Ryan. There was a number for members of the public to call with any information concerning either of those individuals and all such calls would, of course, be treated as confidential.

Two sets of Angel Ryan's foster parents had been traced and were being questioned, while a third was still being sought. Sightings of the pair of them in places as diverse as Rotherham and Hull and Hest Bank near Morecambe Bay were being followed up.

The longer they could keep their search for Adam Keach from the media, the better they believed their chances of finding him before he found another victim.

41

It was the second night Shane and Angel had spent sleeping rough, this time in a doorway at the back of a parade of shops not far from the centre of Crewe, old newspapers spread beneath them for insulation, coats and each other's bodies for warmth – the temperature merciful in that it didn't fall into single figures. For breakfast they drank milk and ate bread that had been left early outside a café up the street. Angel had cut her hair short, almost as short as Shane's.

Much of yesterday she had spent sitting cross-legged outside Crewe station, a cardboard box open on the pavement and a sign that read 'Starving and Homeless, Please Help'. All that she had collected had been two pounds fifty-five in coins and a used train ticket, someone's idea of a joke. Once, when she'd cadged a smoke, a man in a well-cut suit had handed her the almost full packet with a grin; a woman had given her half a cheese-and-salad sandwich, a youth of no more than sixteen or seventeen had fetched her a large coffee from the station buffet and presented it to her with a solemn bow. Station staff had scowled but not moved her on.

Towards the end of the day, Shane had gone off alone,

returning a couple of hours later with almost fifty pounds in assorted notes.

'Where d'you get this, Shane? All this money?'

'What's it matter?'

'Tell me.'

'You don't want to know.'

When she had finally plucked up the courage to ask him about Emma Harrison he had said the same. The same until he was cuddled up against her in the doorway, his breath warm and sour against her neck, the side of her face. 'That girl, I never touched her. Don't know who she is. This stuff they're sayin', the papers an' that, it's lies.' His hand slipping beneath her arm to touch her breast. 'You believe me, right?'

'Yes,' Angel said. 'Yes, of course I do.' Desperately wanting to.

A few moments later, she felt his body relax behind her and realised he was asleep.

◆

The day before, Angel had been round to the house where her foster mother used to live – Eve Branscombe, the only one she'd really liked, the one she'd called Mum – and found she'd moved on. The woman who'd answered the door had been a bit shirty at first, as if Angel were about to pull some elaborate con about collecting for charity, but then she'd relaxed when Angel had explained – not the truth, of course, not all of it, but enough to gain the woman's sympathy. She'd asked Angel in and given her a cup of tea and some biscuits, bourbon or rich tea; written an address down on a scrap of paper, uncertain of the number, but the road she thought was right. I hope you find her, love, good luck.

They were going to try today. Angel washed herself as thoroughly as she could in the public toilets, put on a fresh top, creased but clean, and combed her hair; Shane needed a shave and the sole was starting to come away from one of his shoes.

They caught a bus and then walked. The street they were looking for was a cul-de-sac in a small new estate, some of the houses still unfinished and surrounded by mounds of dirt and piles of bricks, as if the builders had run out of money part way.

No one had heard of a Mrs Branscombe at the first house they tried, but next door thought she might live at number twelve. There was a hanging basket by the front door, pink and purple fuschia and scarlet geraniums trailing down. The door itself was mostly pebbled glass; the bell played a four-note tune.

The woman who came to the door looked to be in her early sixties, short and plump, slippers on her feet, a floral apron tied over a plain blouse and skirt. She blinked at Angel and started to say something and then choked on her words.

'Angel,' she finally managed.

'Mum.'

As Shane looked on, embarrassed, they fell into one another's arms. When Angel finally introduced him, tears in her eyes, Mrs Branscombe shook Shane's hand and said it was a pleasure to meet him and invited the pair of them in.

'Eve,' she said. 'You can call me Eve.'

The living-room was at the rear, small and squarish

337

with a door that opened out into the garden. A two-seater settee and an armchair, matching; china dogs along the tiled mantelshelf above the flame-effect gas fire.

'You two sit right there while I put the kettle on. Angel and me, we've got a lot of catching up to do.'

After several cups of tea, a ham sandwich and some slices of Battenberg – shop, of course, but almost as nice as home-made; I'll say this for it, it's a lovely marzipan – Eve Branscombe listened with interest to Angel's bowdlerised tales of working here and there with a small travelling fair. And if Shane said little, well, he was shy in company, a lot of young men are.

'And now you're just travelling, is that right? A little time to yourselves. A holiday.'

'Yes, Mum,' Angel said, 'that's right.'

'Where you heading next then?'

'We're not sure. We thought we might stay around here for a few days. I'd like Shane to get to know where I grew up. The town, you know.'

'You were happy here.'

'I was.'

Shane was afraid there might be more tears.

'You don't do fostering now, then?' Angel asked.

'No, love, not any more. Getting too old for it. It's just me on my own now.' And then, aware of the way Angel was looking at her, she said, 'There's a spare room upstairs. If you wanted to stay for a bit. It's not big, of course. Only a single bed. But I daresay you won't mind cuddling up.'

'Thanks, Mum. That'd be great. Wouldn't it, Shane, eh?'

'Yeah, great.'

'That's settled then.' Eve kneaded her hands into her thighs as if working dough. A few minutes later, when the last pieces of cake had been passed round, she said, 'It's tiring work, travelling, isn't it? Sticky, too. If either of you wanted a bath, there's plenty of hot water.'

◆

Every time they moved in the bed, it creaked. The mattress was a notch above wafer thin.

'This used to be mine, you know,' Angel said.

'More comfortable, sleeping on the fuckin' street.'

'Shane, that's not true.'

'True enough.'

'And besides, she's doin' us a favour, right?'

'Right,' Shane said grudgingly.

They were talking in whispers, not wishing to be overheard. At a few minutes short of ten, Eve Branscombe had switched off the television and announced she was off to bed. 'I can't stomach watching the news nowadays. Always something terrible, earthquakes and murders. You're welcome to stay up yourselves, of course, long as you like. There's plenty of milk if you want a bedtime drink.' She smiled a soft round smile. 'Just make yourselves at home.'

About the last thing Shane and Angel had wanted was to tune in to the news. They had sat there for perhaps another fifteen minutes, listening to the sounds from the bathroom upstairs, then gone up to bed themselves.

'How long did you live with her anyway?' Shane asked.

'Three years, a bit more,' Angel said. 'From when I was nine to when I was twelve. Getting on thirteen. She

339

gave me a bike for my twelfth birthday, I remember that. Second-hand, it was, but I didn't care. I had to leave it behind when I moved.'

'Why did you? Move, I mean? You were getting on so well, how come you didn't stay?'

Angel fidgeted with the uneven ends of her hair. 'She had this boy as well then, Ian. Older than me, just a couple of years. He started . . . you know, he started tryin' to mess around with me. I tried to tell Mum but it was difficult. She really didn't listen. Everything else she was fine about, everything else but . . . but that. In the end I had this piece of glass and I cut him. They took me away. Mum, she didn't want them to, she wanted them to give me another chance, but no, they weren't having any. That was when I went into a home, a children's home. I started cutting myself there.'

She moved closer to Shane and he kissed her, just friendly at first and then something else. For the second time, Shane slid a hand down towards the crack of Angel's backside and for the second time she told him, 'Don't.'

'What's the matter? You getting your period or something?'

'No, it just . . . it just doesn't seem right.'

'Why not, all of a sudden?'

'Here, in this bed.'

'What's wrong with it?'

'Mum'd hear us.'

'She's not your fuckin' mum.'

'You know what I mean.'

'And she thinks you're some virgin, does she?'

'Now you're being stupid.'

'You're the one being fuckin' stupid.'

'Oh, Shane . . .'

'Yeah?'

'Let's not row, eh?'

Shane breathed out slowly. 'Okay, okay, I'm sorry. It's just . . .'

'I know.'

After a while he rolled onto his back and she brought him off with her hand.

◆

In the morning, Eve Branscombe asked them how they'd slept, ushered them into the snug kitchen where two places were laid for breakfast, gave them cornflakes and then boiled eggs, two each, and plenty of toast, a slice of which, for Angel, she cut into narrow strips.

'Soldiers, remember?'

'Course.'

'Well, eat up. There's more toast if you want it. Tea's in the pot.'

'Aren't you having anything, Mum?'

'Oh, I've had mine.'

Just a few minutes later, Shane realised he needed the toilet. He found Eve on the upstairs landing, standing beside the telephone, receiver in her hand. A copy of that morning's *Mail* was on the small circular table, folded open to a photograph of himself on page two.

'Bitch!'

Fear flooded her eyes.

'Fuckin' bitch!'

He slapped the back of his hand across her face fast and

341

as she cried out and staggered back, he seized the phone from her grasp and struck her with it hard above the ear.

Eve screamed and sank towards the floor.

'Shane! What the hell you doin'?'

Angel pulled at his arm and he shoved her away.

'She was only shopping us, wasn't she? Lyin' fuckin' bitch!'

Eve whimpered and as he bent down to hit her again she covered her face as best she could with her fleshy arms.

'Shane, don't! Oh, Mum, Mum, Mum.'

Angel dropped into a crouch, putting herself between the older woman and Shane, but he caught hold of her wrist and pulled her away.

'Shane, don't. Please. Not any more.'

He drew back his leg and kicked Eve Branscombe in the side.

'Shane . . .'

'Okay, let's go. We're out of here now.'

'We can't leave her.'

'Cunt. I hope she dies.'

Less than five minutes later they were out of the house and running down the street, Angel having to be half-dragged but going anyway, a rucksack on her back and a bag in each hand, sniffing back tears.

42

'What's got into you?' Shane asked. They were in a lay-by off the Nantwich to Wrexham road, south of Crewe.

'Nothing,' Angel said.

'Yeah? Then what you like that for?'

'Like what?'

'Face like a horse's arse. Not sayin' a thing.'

Angel turned away and he moved to confront her.

'Well?'

'I'm thinking about mum.'

'She's not your fuckin' mum. She never was your fuckin' mum.'

'You know what I mean.'

'She was shoppin' us, right?'

'Shane, you could have killed her.'

'Serve her fuckin' right.'

Angel tipped the remainder of her tea over the ground and walked away, and this time he didn't follow. Traffic, not heavy, trailed past on the other side of a ragged length of hawthorn hedge. The weather was on the turn maybe, clouds darkening high to the west and the temperature falling.

Shane looked at Angel standing head down near the

grass verge, her hair just long enough now to lift in the breeze. Something pulled at his gut and he wanted to go to where she stood, put an arm around her and say it was going to be okay, but instead he stayed where he was.

A car transporter pulled in slowly with six new Skoda Fabias, blue, red and green, shining behind. When the driver jumped down he stared at Angel for a moment and she stared back. Half an hour with him in his cab, Shane thought, and she could earn them fifty quid easy, maybe more. Cash, that's what they needed; what little they had, his mad money aside, was running out.

Angel's idea was go to London, lose themselves there easy, that's what she said. But McKeirnan had always said London was full of losers, blacks and queers, and Shane reckoned he was probably right. Asylum seekers now, Afghans or whatever they were, Africans, Iraqis, something like that, he didn't know. Wales, that's what they should do, hitch into Wales. No one would find them there. It was where he'd always wanted to go.

As if she'd made up her mind about something, Angel turned and came towards him, conjuring up a smile.

'I'm hungry,' she said. 'D'you want anything?'

'No, 'sall right.'

'I'm going to have a burger.'

'I'll have a bite of yours.'

'Says who?' She kissed him on the side of his mouth.

Inside the bun the meat was grey and thin and Angel smothered it with ketchup, mustard too. When Shane bit into it, a splash of red and yellow ran down his chin and when he tried to wipe it away it smeared all over his hand; Angel laughed and said could she have her burger back please and Shane pretended to hurl it at her but then

344

handed it to her, almost graciously, instead. It's going to be all right, Angel thought, it's going to be all right, the two of us: for one whole minute believing it, maybe two. That night, she'd tried once or twice bringing the conversation round to Shane going to the police, giving himself up, but all he had done was scowl and tell her not to be so fucking daft.

'We've got to split up,' Angel said. The burger was finished and they were drinking Coke to swill away the taste. 'Just for a bit. A week or so.'

'No way.' Shane shook his head.

She came close and wound her fingers inside the cuff of his sleeve.

'We've got to. After what's happened. We're too obvious like this. Someone will spot us if we're together, you know they will.'

'They haven't before.'

'That was different. If Mum hadn't talked to the police earlier, she certainly will've by now.' She pulled lightly at his arm. 'Shane, it makes sense, you know it does.'

'How long?' he said after several moments. 'How long'd this be for?'

'Just a week or so, like I say. Then we'll meet up again.'

'You won't, though, will you? You'll bugger off. It's just an excuse to get away.'

'Don't say that.'

'It's fucking true.'

'No. No, it's not. I promise you. Promise. Look, we'll name a place, right? Motorway services, south of Birmingham. The M5. First services you come to, yeah? A week today. Early evening. Six or seven. We'll wait for one another. Then we can go anywhere. Wales, like you wanted. Like you said. Okay? Shane, okay?'

'Okay.' When he looked at her there was sadness in his eyes.

'I'll be there, I promise.' She kissed him hard and stepped away, knowing she had to go now if at all.

The driver of the car transporter was on his way back from his break. 'Want a lift?' he said, seeing Angel now standing alone.

'Yes,' she said. 'Yes, thanks. Hang on, I'll just get my bag.'

Shane watched, then turned away.

◆

Happy to deflect the media from the true focus of their inquiry, the police did nothing to dissuade them from the view that Shane Donald was still the principal suspect in their investigation into Emma Harrison's murder. Public relations set up a press interview with Elder and agreed that he could be interviewed on local television on the clear grounds that nothing was asked which might be prejudicial to any future trial. So Elder graced *Midlands Today*, fielding his one minute and forty seconds of questioning about Donald brusquely if competently and then providing the young feature writer from the *Post* with sufficient material for a half-page, double-column side-bar in which the unsolved disappearance of Susan Blacklock loomed large.

Front-page photographs of Shane and Angel lined up along the newsagents' shelves. A couple of dangerous young villains on the run.

'*21st Century Bonnie and Clyde*' some sub-editor dubbed them, though as far as anyone knew they had yet to rob a bank or brandish a gun. Even the arts pages of the *Independent* got in on the act, publishing stills from movies featuring pairs of runaway fugitives: John Dall and Peggy Cummings in *Gun Crazy*; Farley Granger and Cathy O'Donnell in *They Live By Night*; Martin Sheen and Sissy Spacek as fictional versions of Charles Starkweather and Caril Fulgate in Terrence Malick's *Badlands*.

And all the while the search for Adam Keach was progressing; relatives, friends and associates were being traced and questioned as urgently as possible.

◆

Elder drove the relatively short distance to Crewe and talked to Eve Branscombe, whose injuries, fortunately, were less serious than they had at first appeared. She looked at him out of a round, doughy face and when she spoke of Angel her voice was filled with genuine sadness and concern: a good girl gone astray. When he asked her about Shane Donald, tears brimmed in her eyes but they were tears of anger and fear; describing how he turned on her, she flinched as if his hand were striking her cheek again, his foot driving into her side.

'He killed her, didn't he? That poor girl. Emma, isn't that her name?'

'We don't know, Mrs Branscombe,' Elder said.

'If she hadn't pulled him off me, Angel, he would have killed me too.'

◆

'Where have you been?' Maureen asked, when Elder walked back into the office. 'I've been trying to get you on your mobile.'

'Sorry. It was switched off.'

'Useful.'

'What was it anyway?'

'Angel Ryan.'

'What about her?'

'She's phoned in three times. She wants to meet you.'

'Why me?'

Maureen smiled caustically. 'Something to do with all this publicity you've been getting?'

43

Angel was sitting on a bench in the Broad Marsh bus station in Nottingham, head down, smoking a cigarette. Her blue jeans were stained on one leg with grease or oil and almost threadbare at the knees, grubby trainers on her feet; she wore a thin cotton T-shirt beneath a man's unbuttoned denim shirt, and over that a short rust-coloured corduroy jacket, new enough to have been liberated from somewhere like River Island earlier that day.

As Elder approached her, crossing from the underpass, she looked up.

'Angel Ryan?'

Taking one last drag at her cigarette, she dropped it to the ground. 'Recognised me, then?'

Elder glanced left towards a pair of men sitting hunched over their cans of Strongbow, right to where a harassed woman was doing her best to marshal four small children and stop them running out in front of oncoming buses.

'Not too difficult,' he said, and held out a hand. 'Frank Elder.'

'And you're not with the police?'

'Not exactly. Not any more.'

Despite the fact that it was far from cold, Angel began fastening the buttons on her jacket. Fastening and then unfastening nervously.

'Do you want to walk?' Elder asked.

Angel shrugged.

'Come on, no sense staying here.'

She followed him through the Broad Marsh centre and up the escalator on to Low Pavement, from there along narrow streets that ran between old Victorian factories which were gradually being renovated and remodelled into loft apartments, chichi little shops that seemed to Elder to sell things he neither wanted nor could easily afford.

As they walked Elder chatted about this and that, nothing substantial, seeking to put Angel at her ease. At the corner of Stoney Street and High Pavement, he pointed towards a bench inside St Mary's churchyard.

'Let's sit for a bit.'

Inside the church, someone was practising the organ, scales and then a tune, something Elder thought might well have been Bach.

'You wanted to talk to me?' he said.

'Yeah, I suppose.'

'About Shane?'

Angel glanced up at him and then back down at the ground. 'Yes.'

'Where is he?'

'I don't know.'

'Really?'

'Not where he is right now, no.'

'But you could get in touch with him. If you wanted to.'

'Maybe. Yeah, maybe.'

Angel looked at him again quickly. Old, about her father's age, she supposed. Nice hands. And not rushing her, she liked that. Pretending to be her friend. She'd had social workers who were like that, a few; psychologists too. She wondered if she could trust Elder more than she had them. If she could trust anyone, including herself.

'What if he wanted to give himself up?' Angel asked, her voice quiet, as if she herself didn't want to hear what she'd said.

'Is that what he wants to do?'

'If he did, though,' Angel said, 'what would happen?'

'That depends.'

'This girl, the one in the papers, Emma something, he didn't have nothin' to do with that. I swear.'

Elder nodded, thinking now that it was almost certainly true.

'He'd have to go back to prison, anyway, wouldn't he?' Angel said.

'No way round that, I'm afraid. He's what's called unlawfully at large. His licence would be rescinded and he'd have to serve the remainder of his sentence, that at least. And there'd be new charges, I imagine. The woman in Crewe, Eve was it? Quite possibly his probation officer, too. He'd likely be facing some serious time.'

Angel looked away.

'You've talked about this?' Elder said after several moments. 'You and Shane.'

Angel shook her head. 'Yes. No. No, not really. I mean, I've tried. Tried talking to him, but he won't. He . . . And I'm afraid . . .' She looked at Elder again, still trying to read something in his eyes. 'I'm afraid, if he just carries on . . . if we . . .' She blinked. 'I'm afraid he might get too far out of control, kill someone. Not meaning to, not really, only . . .'

'I understand.'

'Do you?'

'Perhaps. I think so.'

'You were the one, arrested him before.'

Elder nodded.

'He was just a boy,' Angel said.

'A boy who'd helped kill somebody.'

'That was the other one, McKeirnan. Not Shane.'

'The jury didn't agree.'

'And you?'

Elder didn't answer right away. 'At the very least he stood by and let it happen.'

'And for that he has to spend almost half his life inside?'

'It's the law.'

'Fuck the law.'

A Japanese couple glanced round on their way towards the church door. The organist seemed to have finished his impromptu recital or possibly he was just resting.

'Has he ever been aggressive towards you?' Elder asked.

'No. Not really.'

'You're sure?'

'He wouldn't hurt me.'

How many times have I heard that, Elder thought?

'You're not afraid for yourself?' he asked.

Angel shook her head. An ailing lorry went past along the narrow road behind them, flowering black smoke from its exhaust.

'Does he know you're here, talking to me?'

'No.'

'And you really think he'd give himself up? Because if he would, all he has to do is walk into the nearest police station.'

'He wouldn't do that.'

'What then?'

'He'd talk to you.'

'Why me? Like you said, I'm the one who put him away.'

'He trusts you. Least, I think he does. One or two things he's said. That you were a decent bloke. For a copper. Straight. That's what he said.' Slowly, she turned again to face him. 'Is it true?'

'I try to be.'

Elder was already getting to his feet.

'Let's walk a bit more.'

They went down some worn steps at the far end of the churchyard and turned back on to Stoney Street. He was trying to reconcile Angel with the details, sparse as they were, that Maureen had received from social services. He had expected someone with even less confidence, someone who carried the scars of her early life more openly. But the places where Angel had cut herself with razor blades and fragments of shattered mirror glass were mostly healed over now, hidden from sight.

Who, Elder wondered, as he watched Angel cross the street a pace in front of him, was she trying to save most, Shane Donald or herself?

In a café off Stoney Street and High Pavement, Elder drank coffee and watched her while she ate soup and then a bacon-and-tomato roll.

353

'I'm gonna meet him,' Angel said. 'A few days' time. I could phone you, let you know when.'

'You could tell me now.'

'No, later.'

'You don't trust me.'

Angel blinked. 'You'll just talk to him, right? You're not going to grab him or nothing? Because if you do, he'll run. I know.'

'I understand,' Elder said.

'If he doesn't want to go with you, you won't try and stop him?'

'I'm no longer a constable,' Elder said. 'I've no powers of arrest.'

'And there'll be no police, you promise?'

'As long as he wants to talk to me, I'll talk to him alone.'

Elder wrote down his mobile number, went to the counter and paid the bill. On their way out towards the street, he pushed a twenty and two tens down into Angel's hand.

'You will be in touch?' Elder said.

'Yes. I said.'

'And afterwards? I mean, if he does decide to give himself up. What will you do then?'

'I dunno. Go back with the fair, maybe. Della'd always take me in, for sure.'

Elder nodded. 'Try and talk to him again,' he said. 'Work him round.'

They went a short way towards the Broad Marsh together and then he stopped and watched her walk away, hands stuffed into the pockets of her corduroy jacket, a survivor against the odds.

44

He woke with a head like so much wadded cotton wool. At first he thought it had been Katherine, treading round the edges of his dreams, but then he realised it had been Angel. Quickly dressed and feeling the need for space and fresher air, he drove the short distance from Willie Bell's to Wollaton Park and walked down past the house towards the lake. Deer grazed in the adjoining field or stood in twos and threes beneath the trees. If Angel did contact him with Shane Donald's whereabouts, there was no way he could keep them to himself, he understood that. He would have to tell Maureen, at the very least, and once he'd done that everything would be out of his hands.

Elder lengthened his stride; if he could convince them to let him talk to Shane first, there was a chance he might convince him to give himself up. A slim chance, but a chance all the same.

He was rounding the first curve of the lake, where the path opened out to afford an uninterrupted view back towards Wollaton Hall, when his phone began to ring.

'Frank Elder?' The voice was male and what would once have been called well-spoken. Maybe in some places it still was.

'Yes?'

'This is Stephen Bryan. You left your number, asked me to call.'

So much had happened it took Elder a while to connect the name. 'Yes,' he said eventually. 'That's right. A good few days ago.'

'I've been away.'

'It was about Susan Blacklock,' Elder said. 'You were at school with her, I believe. Chesterfield.'

'She hasn't turned up, has she?' With each sentence the regional accent lurking behind the received pronunciation reasserted itself more and more.

'Should she?'

'Depends whose story we're in.'

'Sorry?'

'Downbeat or sentimental. David Lynch or Steven Spielberg. George Eliot, if you like, or Charlotte Brontë.'

'This isn't fiction,' Elder said. 'We don't have a choice.'

There was a laugh at the other end. 'Do you still want to talk? Only if you do I'm afraid the window's fairly small. I'm off to Edinburgh the day after tomorrow.'

'Then how about this afternoon?'

Bryan gave him directions and Elder scribbled them down on the back of his hand.

◆

Clarendon Park was close enough to the centre of the city, the part of Leicester you lived in if you were a teacher near the top of salary scale; better still, a psychotherapist or university lecturer. Victorian villas with stained glass still intact above the doors and Bosch ovens in brushed steel in their remodelled kitchens, Farrow & Ball paint on the interior walls.

Stephen Bryan's house was a part of a terrace of twelve with taller semi-detached villas at either end. From the upper storeys it would be possible to look back through the trees towards the railway station.

'*Stephen Makepiece Bryan*' read the card in black italic script alongside the front door. For someone who must still be only thirty or so, Elder thought, Bryan was doing pretty well for himself.

When he pressed the bell, Elder was treated to a burst of orchestral music, jarring and shrill.

'Apologies,' Bryan said, opening the door almost immediately. 'Bernard Herrmann, the music from *Psycho*. It's meant to scare away gas company cowboys and proselytising Baptists.'

Bryan was wearing blue-black jeans and a thrift-shop fifties print shirt. His feet were bare.

'I assume you're neither of those.'

'Frank Elder. We spoke on the phone.'

Bryan shook his hand and stepped back. 'Come on in.'

Elder followed him into a long and narrow hallway, one side of which was partly blocked by a confusion of cardboard boxes and bulging plastic bags.

'Lodgers,' Bryan explained. 'One lot moving out, another moving in. The bane of my life, in a way, but most months it's the only way to pay the bills. An aunt left me this place and I've been clinging on to it ever since – even if sometimes it does seem I've got half of De Montfort University living in it with me.'

There were posters from the Berlin and Telluride film

festivals and, midway along, a striking black-and-white photograph of someone handsome and young, lit by a spotlight on the opposite wall.

'Beautiful, isn't he?' Bryan said.

'James Dean?'

'Montgomery Clift. *A Place in the Sun.*'

Bryan ushered Elder through the doorway across from the foot of the stairs. The two main ground-floor rooms had been knocked through to make one large space with a square archway at the centre. Rugs on scuffed but polished wooden boards. Shelves, floor to ceiling, were crammed with books, videos and DVDs; the front half was dominated by a large, wide-screen television and separate floor-standing speakers; in the rear an old-fashioned wooden writing desk had been adapted to hold a computer and monitor, a printer on a table alongside. There was a framed painting, vivid with colour, above the tiled mantelpiece, a tall smoked-glass vase of flowers in the fireplace beneath; more flowers on a low table, hedged in by small piles of books.

'I can offer you Yorkshire tea, Nicaraguan coffee or plain water, take your pick.'

Elder shook his head. 'I'm fine, thanks.'

'You won't mind if I make myself some tea?'

'Go ahead.'

Elder sat on a sloping leather armchair and leaned back. Traffic noise was slight and there was very little sound from inside the house itself. Perhaps the last twenty-four hours had taken it out of him more than he'd thought, because he could feel his eyes beginning to close.

Shaking himself, he sat forward and looked at the books on the table: Charles Barr on *Vertigo*, *Wilder on*

Wilder, a couple by Bryan himself: a small, squarish paperback called *Forgotten Stars of the Fifties* and, more weightily, *Shakespeare on Film, Contemporary Interpretations*. The picture on the cover showed a young man in a garish jacket, holding on to a wounded comrade and brandishing a pistol.

'My thesis,' Bryan said, coming back into the room. 'With a few updates and excisions, but it still reads as if untouched by human hand.'

'Film,' Elder said, 'clearly your thing.'

Bryan flopped down on to the settee opposite, almost but not quite spilling his tea. 'Yes. I do a bit of teaching up the road, some criticism – radio mostly, there's a show called *Back Row* – introduce the odd movie at Phoenix Arts. Otherwise, I suppose I'm a bit of a *rentier*, raking in the shekels at the same time as unblocking the toilets and trying to make sure my guests don't annoy the neighbours with Coldplay at two in the morning or smoke anything more serious than cannabis in the common parts.'

'Some would say it sounds a pretty nice life.'

'Most days they'd be right.'

'I've talked to Siobhan Banham and Rob Shriver – it was Rob who gave me your number. Siobham said you and Susan Blacklock were close, that you spent a lot of time talking together.'

Bryan set down his tea. 'I suppose that's true.'

'Can I ask you what you talked about?'

Bryan smiled. 'Aside from contemporary interpretations of Shakespeare, you mean?'

'Aside from that.'

'Mostly, she wanted to talk about her father.'

'She was having problems with him?'

'No, that was Trevor. I don't mean Trevor, I mean her real father.'

Elder felt as if all the air had been suddenly sucked out of him.

'You didn't know?'

'No. I had no idea.'

'Ah.' Bryan drank a mouthful of tea. 'I suppose I knew she kept it pretty quiet, Trevor being her stepfather.'

'You sound as though you knew him?'

'Not really. But he used to pick her up sometimes, after drama club, things like that. Fussed over her, I suppose you'd say. Susan found it . . . well, claustrophobic.'

'But she never treated him as if he weren't her actual father?'

'No, not at all. And I don't think anybody else knew. In fact, I'm sure they didn't.'

'Can I ask how come you did?'

Bryan smiled, remembering. 'It was one of those conversations, in fact. About Shakespeare. We'd been reading *Lear*, doing bits and pieces of improvisation. We were due to see it, in Newcastle . . .'

'The production that was cancelled.'

'Precisely. Anyway, we'd been working in pairs on this scene where one of the daughters turns on her father and tells him if he thinks she's going to look after him in the style he's been accustomed to, he's got another think coming. I'm wildly paraphrasing, of course.'

'Of course.'

'Susan and I were talking about it afterwards and she looked at me, all serious, and said, "I'd never treat my father like that, no matter what he'd done." Well, I'd seen

360

her with Trevor, heard her moan about him often enough, so I must have looked at her a bit gone out and that was when she told me.'

'Go on.'

'Her mother got pregnant with her when she was just sixteen. She'd been seeing this man, older than her by quite a bit he must have been. Met him in the record shop where he worked. Chatted her up, asked her out. Nobody knew, big secret, then wham – secret no longer. At least, not the pregnancy part. According to Susan, her father didn't want to know. Did his best to persuade her mum to have an abortion and when she wouldn't, he washed his hands of her. Refused to speak to her, have anything to do with the baby after it was born.'

'And Susan knew all this?'

'Apparently.'

'And still she felt something for him? Even after he'd deserted her and her mother and everything.'

'Yes. I think so. She'd have forgiven him, no matter what. If she could. But I don't think she'd ever seen him, not knowingly. She certainly didn't know where he was, I'm sure of that, where he lived. I got the impression she'd tried asking her mother about it once and her mother had thrown a fit. So I think she probably spent quite a lot of time thinking about him instead, day-dreaming, I suppose. You know, what she'd say to him if he suddenly materialised one day out of the blue.'

'And, as far as you know, she never talked to any of the others, any of her other friends about this?'

'No, I'm sure she didn't. And she made me promise not to mention it to a soul.'

'And you've been true to your word.'

'Until now.'

Bryan picked up his tea but didn't drink it.

'Is it important?' he asked.

'Now I don't honestly know,' Elder said. 'But to Susan Blacklock it was.'

As Elder was leaving, a white van was drawing up outside to take away the departing lodger's things.

'If you do find out anything,' Bryan said, 'about Susan, I'd appreciate it if you'd let me know.'

'I will,' Elder said as the two men shook hands. 'And I'll listen out for you on – what was it? – *Back Row*?'

'*Back Row*, *Front Row*, all the same.'

Bryan raised a hand as Elder got into his car and then pitched in to help clear the mess from his hall.

45

'Why didn't you tell me?'

Helen Blacklock, eyes bleary from sleep, struggled to focus on Elder's face looming above her in the doorway. She was wearing the lime-green uniform she wore at the shop on the quay.

'I'm sorry, I must have dropped off after work. What did you say?'

'I said, why didn't you tell me?'

'What?'

'The truth.'

It was relatively early, eight thirty at best, a late summer evening with, as yet, no taint of autumn. Whitby Abbey, as Elder topped the gradient of Blue Bank, had stood out clear and precise against the sea.

Ice had all but melted in the glass Helen had filled with tonic and a splash of gin; the butts of two cigarettes were stubbed out in the ashtray; a magazine lay open and upside down on the floor where it had slid from her hands.

'I'm going to have another drink.'

'Go ahead.'

'D'you want one?'

'No,' Elder said a little too sharply, and then, 'Yes. Yes, all right then. I will.'

'Gin? I don't think I've got anything else.'

'Gin's fine.'

The room seemed smaller than in his memory, but then he realised he was comparing it to the spaciousness of Stephen Bryan's house in Leicester.

'Ice and lemon?' Helen called from the kitchen.

'Please.'

'Both?'

'Both.'

The hand with which she passed him the glass was less than steady and her eyes held his for no more than moments before angling away. She waited for him to sit down and then did the same, opposite and just beyond arm's reach should either of them have felt and acted out the need.

'When you say the truth,' Helen said, 'you mean about Dave?'

'I don't know his name.'

'Susan's father.'

'Yes.'

'David Ulney.'

'You never mentioned him.'

'No.'

'Let everyone believe Trevor was Susan's father.'

Helen nodded, still avoiding his eyes.

'The police, me, everyone.'

'Yes.'

'But not Susan herself?'

'I tried.'

'But she knew.'

Helen looked at him then. 'She found a photograph. She was nine, rising ten. Rooting through my things one day, you know the way kids do. Why I'd clung on to it, God alone knows. Dave Ulney in his brothel creepers and his Edwardian suit, velvet collar, drape jacket, the whole Teddy boy bit.' She paused to light a cigarette. 'Susan asked who it was and before you know it there I was telling her.'

'Everything?'

'That he'd gone off and left me, deserted her. Never given either of us a penny. Not that I'd asked. Yes, I told her that, why shouldn't I? And then I tore the damned thing up into little pieces in front of her eyes and threw them in the bin.'

Helen drew hard on her cigarette, holding down the smoke, then releasing it slowly. 'God, I fancied him. Fancied him rotten.' Her laughter was raw and self-deprecating. 'I was sixteen. What did I know about anything? I didn't even know enough to keep my legs together.'

'You knew enough to keep the baby; you made a choice.'

'I was afraid, terrified. Of having an abortion, I mean. And besides, my parents, it was what they wanted, when they knew. "We'll stick by you," they said. "Good riddance to the likes of him." My mum came with me up to school to see the head teacher, the doctor, everything. She was brilliant. She's in a home now, Scarborough, one of those big old hotels on the North Cliff. When my dad died, she fell apart.' For several moments she was silent, thinking her own thoughts. 'I'm sorry, where was I?'

'Having Susan.'

'Yes. I was lucky. It was a doddle, like shelling peas. And then, when she was no more than six months old, there was Trevor, so gobsmacked, bless him, that he practically worshipped the ground I walked on. For a time, anyway. Or was that Susan? Now I'm not so sure. Anyhow, he was prepared to take me on, complete with a little baby, ready-made family, I suppose, and I thought, if I'm to be honest, well, I'll not likely get a better offer. So we got married, just a small registry office job, his folk and mine, no fuss. If anyone asks, he said, tell them the baby's mine. And so I did. It didn't seem too much to ask, after all.'

Elder reached for his glass. Helen seemed to have used a more than liberal amount of gin and he was glad.

'How did Susan act when you told her?'

'How d'you think? Knocked her sideways, poor love. At first she went all quiet, you know, dead quiet. Thoughtful. And then she began to barrage me with questions, on and on, until eventually she twigged I was never going to answer them, and after that she stopped.'

'And do you know if she ever talked about it with Trevor? Asked him?'

'No, I don't think so. He'd have said. Had to.'

'Does that surprise you?'

Helen didn't answer right away. Somewhere a clock was striking nine. 'Now I think about it, yes, I suppose it does. They used to row enough once she was into her teens, heaven knows. Trevor was over-protective sometimes, interfering. He didn't mean to be, meant it all for the best but . . . It was as if he had to try harder, prove to himself he was being a good father, doing what he thought was his duty. She could have blurted it out then, in the middle of one of their set-tos, just to get back at him, you know, in anger, but no, I don't think she ever did.'

'And her father, Dave I mean, did she ever have any contact with him?'

'No, not ever.'

'You're sure?'

'I'd have known, wouldn't I?'

◆

They walked around the near side of the harbour, out to the West Pier. There was the usual smattering of fishermen, a few courting couples snuggling on the wooden benches, men in topcoats and flat caps walking small dogs. The lights from Sandsend just over a mile away were small and steady along the edges of the tide. Helen had changed into a pair of grey cord trousers and a bottle-green hooded sweatshirt; Elder had pulled an old anorak from the boot of the car. Anyone seeing them might have thought they were old friends, little more.

'If I'd told you right off, about Dave,' Helen said, 'it wouldn't have made any difference, would it? To finding Susan. I mean, How could it?'

'I don't know. You're probably right, but I don't know. I mean, we'd have been interested, certainly, followed it up along with everything else . . .'

'And when it didn't lead anywhere?'

Elder didn't answer. A little way along the pier they paused to watch a boat heading out of the harbour, night fishing, lights shining strongly.

When Helen turned to walk on, Elder stayed put

where he was. 'Dave Ulney,' he said, 'what happened to him?'

'How should I know?'

'He just disappeared?'

'As good as. Buggered off to the ends of the earth, first chance he got.'

Elder looked at her questioningly.

'New Zealand. He sent me a card – one – out of the blue after two years. Karori, wherever that is. *'Settled here now. Hope you're well. Dave.'* He didn't even mention Susan, the rotten bastard. He never as much as asked after his own child.' There were tears in her eyes. 'I set light to it there and then.'

'Susan didn't see it? She didn't know?'

'She was two years old.'

'But you didn't tell her about it later? After she'd found the photograph?'

'Why would I do that? It was hard enough for her as it was.'

There was anger still, resentment mixed up with the tears.

'You've never heard from him since? Heard anything about him?'

'Not a word.'

They walked on out to the end of the second, smaller pier and stood there gazing at the lights of a container ship creeping, snail-like, along the horizon. There was wind enough now for the waves to strike the underpinnings with force, water spraying up into their faces.

'I wondered if I'd see you again,' Helen said.

Elder kissed her and she took his hand and slid it up beneath her sweatshirt and held it against her breast. At home, he undressed her slowly, kissing the roll and curve of her body, before turning on to his back so that she could undress him, looking down at him in the half-light, his shirt first and then his trousers. She made a slight gasp as she lowered herself on to him, and then it was slow and knowing, her nipple in his mouth and a tightening shudder of her body his final, all too sudden, undoing.

'I'm sorry,' he said, as she rolled off him.

'That's okay, pet,' she said, smiling. 'You rest, get your strength back.'

But both were sleeping when the sound of the phone awoke them, Elder uncertain for that moment where he was and not immediately recognising the sound of his mobile. Joanne's voice was distant and uneven. 'Frank, it's Kate. She's not come home. I'm worried sick.'

Elder lifted his watch from the bedside table, Helen's alarmed eyes following him. It was half past one.

'Have you called the police?'

'No. I wasn't sure what to do.'

'Phone them now. I'm a couple of hours' drive away. Maybe a little more. I'll be there as soon as I can.'

Helen was standing, naked, by the bedroom door. 'I'll make some coffee while you're getting dressed. A Thermos for the car.'

'Okay, thanks.' He was dialling Maureen Prior's number as he reached for his shirt.

46

Elder drove too fast, coming close to losing control at a curve on the narrow road between Pickering and Malton, then just catching himself drifting asleep, his eyes closing momentarily on the ouside lane of the M18 at between eighty and ninety, all that he could urge out of his ageing Ford. The touch of his outer wheels against the road's edge was enough to jar him awake before he drifted into the central reservation, and at the first service station he came to after switching motorways, he splashed cold water in his face and drank the remainder of the coffee Helen had made for him.

'She'll be all right, Frank. Don't worry.'

The irony of his own words, almost, coming back at him.

The fact that his mind was speeding, skidding from one scenario to another, proved a kind of blessing and prevented him from lingering over whatever images his imagination might have delivered. Imagination and experience.

There was a single police car outside Joanne's house, another, a blue Vauxhall that he recognised as Maureen's, parked close behind it. A uniformed officer opened the front door and made Elder identify himself as he tried to push past. Joanne was standing in the centre of the vast living-room, adrift in space. When she saw Elder she ran towards him, stopped, and, as he reached out his arms, tumbled against him, the tears that she had choked back earlier falling without let or hindrance. Eyes closed, he pressed his face against her hair, her fingers gripping him tightly, her face pressed damp against his chest.

Embarrassed, the young WPC who had been talking to Joanne, going over the notes she had made earlier, looked away. Standing near the spiral staircase, Maureen Prior waited for Elder to raise his head and then exchanged a quick glance with him, a brief sideways shake of her head.

Elder held Joanne, allowing her to cry.

'I'll make coffee, Frank,' Maureen said.

The constable followed her in search of the kitchen, leaving Elder and Joanne alone and faintly reflected in a wall of glass, the garden dark behind.

'Oh, Frank . . .'

Elder led her carefully towards the long settee and, prising free her hands, gently lowered her down.

'Tell me,' he said. 'When you're ready, tell me what happened.'

Joanne felt for a tissue and wiped her eyes, blew her nose.

'Kate was . . . she was out at training, the usual, you know . . . Harvey Hadden Stadium . . . she'd finish somewhere around . . . oh, anywhere between eight and nine . . .'

'Surely by then it's dark?' Elder interrupted.

'Well, maybe it was half past eight, I don't know. Besides, it doesn't matter.'

'It might.'

'Frank, please.'

'I'm sorry, carry on.' He gave her hand a squeeze.

'Sometimes she'd come straight home, but not always. Quite often, I think she'd go for a drink or something, just, you know, hanging out.'

'You didn't know where she was, where she was going?'

'For God's sake, Frank, she's sixteen.'

'Exactly.'

'What's that supposed to mean?'

'It means that if she's only sixteen I'd have thought you wanted to know where she was of an evening.'

'Really? Then maybe if you were that concerned you should have stayed around.'

Elder bit his tongue.

'I'm sorry,' Joanne said.

'No, it's okay. Go on.'

'If she did stay out,' Joanne said, 'she was usually in by half past ten, eleven at the latest. Mid-week especially. When she wasn't here by twelve I started ringing round her friends, those I knew. Several of them from the athletics club had seen her at training earlier on, but not since.'

'Since when? Exactly, I mean?'

'Frank, I didn't get a precise time, I was too worried, I . . .'

'It's all right, it's okay. We can check . . .'

'We already have.' Elder turned sharply at the sound of Maureen's voice; he hadn't been aware she'd come back into the room.

'As far as we can tell,' Maureen said, 'Katherine left the changing rooms at the track between eight thirty and a quarter to nine. One of the others offered her a lift, but she turned it down. Said something about catching a bus.' Maureen paused. 'That's the last sighting of her we've traced so far.'

A quarter to nine to half past four: Elder was doing the arithmetic in his head. Not so far short of eight hours since his daughter had gone missing.

'That boy she was seeing . . .' he said to Joanne.

'Gavin?'

'I don't think so.'

Joanne looked back at him, puzzled, as Elder searched for the name.

'Stuart, I think it might have been.'

'I don't know any Stuart.'

'He was in her athletics club; drove an old 2 CV.'

Joanne shook her head.

'It wasn't one of the names we had,' Maureen said. 'No one we've spoken to so far. I'll have it checked.'

As she left the room, the WPC came in with mugs of coffee on a tray.

'You mentioned Gavin,' Elder said, turning back to Joanne. 'Gavin who?'

'Salter. He's a student, at the university.'

'Which one?'

'Not Trent, at least I don't think so. No, the old one, I'm sure.'

'And Katherine's going out with him?'

'She was. I think they had some sort of a bust-up. Just before the end of the summer term.'

'Have you any idea where he lives?'

'Lenton, somewhere. I don't know exactly.'

'Christ!' Elder exclaimed, just under his breath.

Joanne pressed her forehead against the heel of her hand. 'Frank, please don't make it any more difficult than it already is.'

'There's coffee,' the WPC said.

Nobody moved.

'His name's Stuart Reece,' Maureen said, reappearing from the hallway a few minutes later. 'High jumper, apparently. Lives out at Lady Bay. Someone's on their way to talk to him now.'

Elder nodded and gave her the name of Gavin Salter. It was possible but unlikely, Maureen knew, that the phone book might supply a listing. He could be on the electoral roll, although with the migratory habits of most students that was far from a certainty. Most probably they'd have to wait till morning and check Salter's address with the university.

'Jo,' Elder said quietly, 'why don't you go up and lie down? Get some rest.'

'I couldn't sleep,' Joanne said, but she stood up nevertheless, though less than steadily, and walked towards the staircase, Elder beside her.

'Where's Martyn tonight?' he asked.

She looked at him without her expression changing and then turned away and walked slowly out of sight.

◆

Elder and Maureen Prior sat on the curve of concrete steps that went up to the front door. The door itself was on the latch, Joanne restlessly asleep above. The sky was already lightening noticeably towards the east. Both of the uniformed officers had reported back to the central police station, where a separate inquiry team had been set up with Colin Sherbourne, a youngish DI who had recently transferred from Humberside, in charge. Sherbourne had driven out earlier to talk with Elder and assure him that they were doing everything they could.

'It's not that long since he started shaving,' Elder commented when Sherbourne had gone.

'He's a good officer, Frank. Organised. Not the kind to get into a flap easily.'

'He hasn't the experience . . .'

Maureen laid a hand on his arm. 'Frank, we've got a good start. You know that as well as I do.'

'Eight hours, more now . . .'

'Most cases like this, we likely wouldn't have been alerted till morning.'

Elder let out a deep breath, almost a sigh. 'This isn't a separate investigation.'

'Frank . . .'

'Come on, Maureen,' Elder on his feet now. 'Isn't that what you've been thinking ever since I first called you?'

'No.'

'No? You're a bad liar, Maureen. It doesn't come naturally.'

'What I think, Frank, is that, come morning, Katherine'll come walking back home. A little sheepishly, perhaps, but she'll be back. And not so many hours from now.'

'I'd like to think you were right.'

'You know what I think happened? I think she met up with her student – Gavin, is it? – they met up and made up and she spent the night at his place. Sixteen, Frank, likely not the first time, though you'll not thank me for saying so.'

But Elder was shaking his head. 'He's got her, Maureen. Keach. He's taken her, I know it.'

'Frank, you're not being logical. There's a hundred and one explanations more feasible.'

'Are there?'

'You know there are. And besides, why would Keach do such a thing? Just suppose for a moment it had crossed his mind and somehow he got close enough to have the opportunity, why take the risk?'

'Why kidnap Emma Harrison in broad daylight? Carry her body across open country? Why send a postcard advertising what he'd done? To impress McKeirnan, that's why. And what better way to impress him than to take the daughter of the man who was largely responsible for putting him inside?'

Maureen sat staring off into the gathering dawn; there was an electric glow pale behind a scattering of blinds and curtains now, the early barking of one dog answered by another, far off. What Elder was saying was conjecture and little more, but conjecture was pretty much all they still had. Conjecture plus a feeling in Elder's gut, a feeling that in the past Maureen had learned to trust.

Rising, she stood alongside him.

'There's a massive search on for Adam Keach. And it'll intensify now, I promise you that. If he's moving around he can't stay hidden for long. Meantime, let Colin Sherbourne get on with his job. I'll keep a watching brief on both inquiries, Colin'll not mind that. He'll expect it.'

'And I stand around torturing myself? Kicking my heels?'

'Get some rest, Frank. That's the best thing you can do.'

'You're joking, of course.'

'Stay here at the house, Frank. There must be a spare bed, all these rooms. Joanne'll need you when she wakes up.'

'What are you going to do?'

'Me? Catch a couple of hours. I'll call you round seven thirty if you haven't called me first.'

47

Katherine Elder didn't come walking back home, tail between her legs or otherwise.

A search of the area between the athletics stadium and the bus stop yielded nothing: no discarded articles of clothing, no torn-off buttons nor signs of a struggle. It would all be checked again, centimetre by centimetre, inch by inch.

By a little after two that afternoon, officers had traced all of the athletes who had been at training the previous evening and taken statements. Everything confirmed the story they had first been given: once the session was over, Katherine, sports bag on her shoulder, had gone off alone. Those who had thought about it at all had assumed she was setting out to catch the bus home. Of course, it was possible that she'd arranged to meet somebody, but she hadn't mentioned any such arrangement and no one could recall seeing any cars they couldn't identify parked nearby.

'This youth,' Elder had said to Colin Sherbourne earlier. 'Reece. When you talk to him, I want to come along.'

'I don't know, Frank . . .'

'I've met him, spoken with him.'

'Even so.'

Elder had rested a hand, not heavily, on Sherbourne's arm. 'I won't interfere. Embarrass you, lose control. I promise.'

With some reluctance, the DI had agreed.

Stuart Reece was clearly shocked to hear that Katherine was missing and anxious to help. He had been at the track for a good couple of hours that evening, practising his jumping along with some general fitness and speed training; yes, he'd chatted to Katherine, the last time just before she'd gone off to shower and change.

'How did she seem?' Sherbourne asked.

'Normal. The same as usual.'

'She wasn't worried?'

'No.'

'Preoccupied?'

'No.'

'And what did she say she was going to do later on?'

Reece made a loose, shrugging motion. 'She didn't.'

'You're sure?'

'Yes.'

'You have a car, don't you?'

'Yes, an old 2 CV. Why?'

'Did you use it yesterday evening?'

'Yes, I nearly always do. From where I live it takes an age otherwise, one bus into town and then another out, the same performance coming back.'

'You offered Katherine a lift?'

Before answering, Reece glanced towards where Elder was standing, just a few paces back from Colin Sherbourne's shoulder. 'Yes. Yes, I did. I said did she

379

want a lift home and she said no thanks.' Reece shrugged. 'That was it.'

'And did that surprise you?' Sherbourne asked. 'Her saying no.'

Reece reached up a hand to push the hair away from his eyes. 'Not really. I mean, there wasn't any sort of arrangement, you know. Sometimes she came with me and sometimes she didn't.'

'And you've no idea why, on this particular occasion, she said no?'

Reece shook his head. 'No.'

Elder took a pace forward. 'You like her, Stuart, don't you?' he said.

'Yes, of course. Katherine's great, always good fun. Everyone . . .'

'No, I mean, you like her. Really like her.'

Reece's feet performed an odd little dance. 'Well, yes, you know, like I say, she's . . . Yes, yes, I do.'

'The first time I saw you, the two of you together, you were kissing her.'

Reece flushed. 'That didn't mean anything, it was just . . .'

'Just a bit of fun?'

The redness around Reece's neck and along his cheeks deepened and spread.

'Because it looked more than that to me.'

Reece had to will his gangly body to be still.

'You know what Katherine said to me, Stuart? What she implied? After you'd driven away. That you wanted the relationship to be serious. Is that right?'

Reece was staring at the ground. 'Yes, I suppose so.'

'And how did my daughter feel about that?'

'She didn't want to know.'

'I'm sorry, speak up.'

'She didn't want to know,' Reece almost shouted.

'And how did that make you feel?'

'How d'you think?'

'Pretty lousy. Small. Rejected.'

Reece twisted his head from side to side and breathed deeply through his mouth. 'I'm not stupid. I can see what you're trying to suggest. That I got all screwed up because Katherine turned me down, didn't fancy me, wasn't interested. So screwed up about it that I . . . I don't know, did something, lost my temper, hurt her.' He stopped and steadied himself, looking at Elder directly. 'Look, I like her, you're right. More than she likes me. But that kind of thing happens all the time. There's scores of girls around. At school, athletics, everywhere. And when I get to university there'll be more. I'd've liked to have had a relationship with your daughter, I still would. But the fact that I haven't hasn't made me go crazy. What I told you about last night's the truth. I drove home alone and I was in the house by nine or nine fifteen and if you ask my parents they'll back me up. Okay?'

Elder held the youth's gaze for several seconds and then nodded.

'Thanks for your time,' Colin Sherbourne said. 'We'll speak with your parents in due course. All right, Frank?'

Elder nodded again.

'Katherine, Mr Elder,' Stuart Reece said, 'I hope you find her. I hope she's okay.'

◆

Tracking down Gavin Salter proved less straightforward. The university confirmed that he was a second-year student reading law and provided two addresses, one for term-time, one his parents' home.

The house he shared with six other students in Lenton was just off the main road, a three-storey building with paint flaking away from around the windows and dustbins out front which were overflowing. Four of the students were still around, but Salter wasn't one of them.

Later that morning, two officers from the Hampshire force drew up outside Salter's parents' house in Stockbridge. His mother was just returning from church and met them in the drive; Gavin's younger brother was washing down the Land Rover and Gavin himself was still in bed. 'Sorry,' he said blearily, fastening the belt of his dressing-gown. 'Bit of a night last night, I'm afraid.'

They sat at a round table in the drawing-room; having politely refused the offer of coffee, the officers watched Salter dissolve two Alka-Seltzers in a glass of water, then drink it down.

'Katherine Elder,' the senior of the two men began. 'When did you last see her?'

Salter's answers were cautious, careful: his training in law, perhaps, coming to the fore. He and Katherine had had a bust-up in early June, before the end of term. He'd wanted her to go away with him to France – take Eurostar and then the TGV to somewhere like Avignon – and first off Katherine had said her mother would never let her, but then confessed she didn't really want to go away with him anyway. Salter admitted to saying something rather unpleasant, accusing her of being a silly little schoolgirl

382

who didn't have a mind of her own and it had all got rather heated and nasty.

'How nasty?'

'Well, you know, a certain amount of shouting and bad language.'

'You hit her?'

'Good God, no.'

'The heat of the moment, you're sure?'

'Listen, it's not the way I was brought up. To strike women.'

'So how did you leave it? After this row?'

'We didn't. Kate went storming off, slamming doors – we were at the house in Lenton – and that was that, pretty much.'

'She was angry, upset?'

'I suppose so.'

'And you?'

'I think I was annoyed with myself for losing my temper as much as anything. I mean, Kate and I, we'd had a good time for a couple of terms and France would have been fun, but you know, it had just about run its course. So all for the best, in a way.'

'And did you see her again after that?'

'Not really. Once or twice, perhaps, in passing. Nottingham's not really such a big place, after all.'

'When was this? These one or two occasions?'

'It must have been the same month, June. I've been down here since the end of term.'

'And how much contact have you had with Katherine since you came down?'

'None. None at all.'

'Phone calls, letters? Text messages, emails?'

'As I said, none at all.'

A few minutes later, the two officers were back in their car and heading towards Winchester.

'What d'you think?' the first one said.

'Of him? He's an arrogant little prick who'll be a barrister before you or I get to inspector and he'll earn more in a month than we'll take home after tax in a year, but I believe him, if that's what you mean. I don't think he's involved at all.'

'Shame.'

'Yeah.'

◆

An hour, more or less, after Hampshire police had reported back on their interview with Gavin Salter, Elder took two calls on his mobile. The first was from Helen Blacklock, who had tried several times earlier, enquiring in a concerned voice if there were any news, asking Elder how he was holding up; the second was from Maureen Prior, there'd been what seemed a reliable sighting of Adam Keach in Cleethorpes, some twenty or so miles up the coast from where Emma Harrison's body had been found.

Elder's blood seemed to clot in his veins; the upper part of his left leg felt suddenly numb and he rubbed at it hard to get the circulation moving again. If Keach had taken Katherine within an hour of her leaving training, he could have easily have reached the coast with her by nightfall.

Colin Sherbourne had officers talking to the bus company, checking the times they would have passed along that route, talking to drivers and showing them photographs: do you remember seeing this girl?

What else was there to do? What could he do himself?

◆

As Elder pulled up outside the house, he checked his watch. While the day seemed to be lasting interminably, time was racing away. Alerted by the sound of his car, Joanne met him, anxious, at the door; from the expression on Elder's face she knew there was neither good news nor yet the worst.

She held him quickly and then stepped back.

'Martyn's inside. He just got back twenty minutes ago.'

Martyn Miles was out on the patio, vodka tonic in hand; he was wearing a pale lavender shirt and olive-green moleskin trousers and he removed his dark glasses when Joanne led Elder through from the living-room towards him.

'Frank, I'm sorry,' Martyn said. 'You must be worried sick. Is there any news?'

'No, not really.'

'She's not a stupid girl, she wouldn't have just gone off without telling someone.'

'No.'

'She had her mobile, she'd have phoned.'

'Her phone's switched off,' Joanne said. 'It has been since I first tried last night.'

'Isn't there some way you can trace it anyway?' Martyn asked.

'Not without a signal, no.'

'There must be something can be done.'

'The police are checking with all of Katherine's friends, anyone who might have seen her or spoken to her in the last few days, anyone who knew her well.'

'That student she was seeing . . .' Martyn began.

'Gavin Salter. Down in Hampshire with his parents. Last night he was out getting drunk at someone's twenty-first, witnesses galore.'

'What about a search?'

'The area around Harvey Hadden's was checked over once first thing; there's a fingertip search going on now to see if there's any clue as to what might have happened. There'll be posters up all over the city by the end of the day, the railway station, everywhere. Bulletins on the local news, TV and radio.'

'And that's it? We sit and wait?'

'Until there's a break, it's difficult to know what else to do.'

'There must be something?' Flinging his arm wide, Martyn caught Joanne's arm with his hand and the glass went flying from his hand.

'Fuck it!'

'Are you okay?' Elder asked Joanne.

'I'm fine. But you could ask Martyn what all the sudden histrionics are about.'

Crouching down to pick up the pieces of glass, Martyn looked up at her. 'Meaning what, exactly?'

'Meaning the first thing you did when you walked in and I started telling you Katherine was missing was to ask me to calm down and get you a drink.'

'It was what I needed. And you were so agitated you weren't making any sense.'

'Now Frank's here you're making out you're really worried. As if you really cared.'

'Of course I care.'

'Do you?'

He stood abruptly, his face close to hers. 'Fuck you, Joanne.'

'Nice, Martyn,' she said, and turned aside.

Martyn let the glass he'd been collecting fall from his hands.

'Where were you last night, Martyn?' Elder asked.

'What possible business is it of yours?'

'Just asking, that's all.'

'Am I a suspect or something?'

'Everyone close to Katherine will be being asked the same questions.'

'But not by you.'

'Martyn was down in London on business, weren't you, Martyn? Staying at the Waldorf Meridien. Except that you weren't at the Waldorf because when I phoned there after twelve when Kate hadn't come home, they said they'd no record of you.'

'The night clerk on the desk made a mistake.'

'They'd had a reservation, but it had been cancelled.'

'All right, sweetheart,' Martyn said, 'I was with a woman in her flat in Notting Hill and we were up all night, the best part of it, fucking one another silly. There, now are you satisfied?'

His voice was exultant and loud and directed straight at Joanne's face.

She swung her open hand to slap him and he caught her wrist.

'Let her go,' Elder said.

Martyn relinquished his grip and stepped towards the door. 'Look at you,' he said with a sneer. 'You sorry pair. You deserve each other.'

Fist clenched, Elder started towards him but Joanne stepped in the way. 'Don't, Frank.'

Martyn laughed and took his time sauntering across the living-room floor; moments later they heard the front door slam.

'How long has it been like this?' Elder asked.

Joanne looked at him. 'How long hasn't it?'

48

Elder woke just short of five and was keying in Maureen's number on his mobile before his feet touched the floor. If Keach had Katherine and he were following the same pattern as before, he would have had somewhere secluded picked out in advance, no more than an hour's drive away.

Maureen answered on the fourth ring.

'The girl McKeirnan released,' Elder said. 'Michelle Guest. She was held north of Retford. And the car that was used in Emma Harrison's abduction was stolen from Retford station car park.'

'Frank, stop,' Maureen said. 'We've already made the connection. There'll be a search team on the ground at first light. A police helicopter. Dogs, everything.'

'Why the hell didn't you tell me?'

'I'm telling you now.'

Elder held his breath.

'Come in to the station,' Maureen said. 'We can go over things together on the map.'

There was a pause and then Maureen said, 'Frank – are you holding up all right?'

'I'll see you in an hour,' Elder said and broke the connection.

The Ordnance Survey map was detailed and clear on screen: farms, roads, electricity transmission lines, field boundaries, streams, public rights of way. Sunrise was at twelve minutes past five and on the ground the search was due to commence at six thirty; the police helicopter, equipped with thermal imaging equipment, would make its first pass some twenty minutes later. Elder and Maureen would be on site by a little after seven.

'Michelle Guest was held here,' Maureen said, 'is that right?' She was pointing to a spot on the old Roman road that linked North Wheatley and Clayworth.

'Yes,' Elder said. 'McKeirnan parked the caravan at this point where the road meets up with the Chesterfield Canal. Held her the best part of two days, then pushed her out here, just short of Bole Fields.'

Maureen nodded. 'The plan is to use North Wheatley as a centre point and spread out in an arc from there.'

'And if we find nothing?'

'Unless there's something else concrete to go on, we enlarge the area of the search.' She leaned back in her chair. 'Meantime Colin Sherbourne's running a check on all vehicles stolen in the Retford area.'

'The sighting of Keach in Cleethorpes?'

'We're still checking it, of course. But it looks less likely all the time.'

◆

As they headed north-east out of the city, the roads were mostly clear; Elder's driver mumbled a few quiet words of sympathy and thereafter the journey passed in silence. The search was well under way by the time Elder arrived and he waited, watched and walked the edges of fields, all the while shutting certain images out from his mind. Almost succeeding.

By early afternoon, dispirited and close to exhaustion, Elder signalled that he was ready to call it a day. Just short of the Ollerton roundabout, a call to the car turned them back again. The thermal imaging scan in the helicopter had pinpointed something in a field near Oswald Beck, close to the power lines. Headlights and siren full on, they travelled back at speeds close to a hundred and ten. Alongside the driver, Elder breathed loudly, open-mouthed, sweat gathering in the palms of his hands.

A track just wide enough for farm vehicles to drive along led south and then west. Officers in coveralls were converging on a corner of the field. Blood racing, Elder ran between them, feet sliding on dry earth. Close by the hedgerow, near the broken chassis of an abandoned farm trailer, lay several sheets of heavy black plastic, humped at the point where they came closest to the hedge itself. Elder watched as gloved hands eased back a sheet at a time. Beneath and rotting into the ground lay the decomposing body of a dead sheep.

Elder held his face in his hands and wept.

◆

Back in the city, Elder checked in with Colin Sherbourne. Of fourteen vehicles reported as stolen in the Retford area, all but three – an almost new Ford Fiesta, a Mini Cooper and a Fiat van – had been traced.

The media, having feasted already on Shane and Angel, thought Christmas had come round again early. *DAUGHTER OF SPECIAL POLICE INVESTIGATOR MISSING. EX-SUPER COP'S KATE KIDNAPPED. COPYCAT KILLER ON THE LOOSE.* Files were ransacked for stories about Elder's more sensational cases. A photograph of Katherine crossing the finishing line at Harvey Hadden Stadium was sold and syndicated widely. Reporters laid siege to Joanne's house, begging her fruitlessly for an interview, sneaking shots through the upstairs windows of Martyn and herself in the bedroom, clearly arguing; Joanne alone in the garden, distraught. When Martyn Miles left the house that morning he had to push his way between half a dozen reporters and almost got into an altercation with a freelance photographer, threatening to take his camera and smash it on the ground. Returning, forty minutes later, with three large bunches of flowers, he was captured on video mouthing 'Fuck off the lot of you' before turning the key in the front door.

Reporters or not, Elder needed to talk to Joanne.

He hurried through the small posse of cameramen head down.

Joanne was sitting at a stained-wood table in the dining-room, albums open, photographs of Katherine scattered everywhere: Katherine on her own, squinting against the sun as she stared up into the camera on the beach at St Ives; Katherine nestled back against her father's upper arm, red faced and three days old; the three of them, mother, father, daughter, seated on a bench in a West London park, the camera set to remote.

'Is that what you should be doing?' Elder asked.

'Look at her here,' Joanne said as if she hadn't heard him. 'That bike – her fourth birthday, remember?'

He remembered everything and nothing; as if she were already slipping from his grasp.

'I'm sorry, Frank,' Martyn said, coming hushed into the room. 'Yesterday. I was being an arsehole.'

'What's changed?' Joanne said, without looking round.

Martyn went away and left them alone.

Joanne's skin was bleached of colour, close to translucent, her eyes unnaturally large. Her fingers were never still. Despite his better judgement, Elder sat with her and looked at the photographs. When his head had slumped forward and Joanne realised his eyes had closed, she nudged him awake and led him upstairs to the guest room, pulled off his shoes and closed the blinds. He fell asleep before she had left the room and slept for six hours straight.

When Joanne shook him gently she had his mobile phone in her hand.

'This was in your coat downstairs. There's a call. Someone named Helen?'

She withdrew and left him to it, and Elder talked with Helen Blacklock for some minutes, a halting awkward conversation, both aware of the minefields through which they were treading.

At a decent interval Joanne returned with soup and toast.

'I'm not an invalid, you know,' Elder said. 'You don't have to wait on me.'

'It's something to do.'

He thanked her and she sat with him, talking sporadically, while he ate.

'You don't think there's any news?' she asked.

Elder shook his head. 'Maureen would have phoned.'

Later he surprised himself by sleeping again, finally waking a little after three and going barefooted downstairs. The house was silent save for those small unattributable noises all houses, even new ones, make in the stillness of night. He made tea in the kitchen and sat leafing through back issues of Joanne's magazines, *Vogue* and *Vanity Fair*. Picking up a paperback by Anita Shreve Joanne had been reading, he carried it into the living-room and read several chapters before casting it aside. On his feet, he switched out the light and stood close against the glassed wall, staring out. He was still standing there when Joanne came down the spiral stairs in a long pink robe that swished silkily as she crossed the floor.

When she stood by him, Elder could feel the warmth of her arm against his side.

'Helen,' Joanne said after a while, 'who is she?'

'A friend.'

'And that's all?'

When Elder didn't answer, she threaded her fingers through his.

Their breathing was loud in the room.

He kissed her and she kissed him back and at first he thought it was going to be all right, but when, after a few moments, they broke apart and she said something about kissing a ghost, Elder thought it sounded like a line from the book he'd just been reading and stepped away. He kissed her on the top of her head and went back upstairs to get his coat and shoes. At the door he held her hand and tried not to look into her eyes.

◆

At seven that morning, when the mail van arrived at Gartree prison, the officer on duty, who had been alerted, picked out the card addressed to Alan McKeirnan. The view across Whitby harbour was due north-west, showing the whalebone and the statue of Captain Cook clear near the cliff edge, the sands winding into the distance along the Upgang shore.

49

A police motor cyclist sped the postcard from Gartree to
Bernard Young's office in the Nottinghamshire Major
Crime Unit. The handwriting was recognisably the same
as before. '*Alan – Come on in. The water's fine!*' Safe
inside its plastic envelope, the card was passed from hand
to hand: Young to Gerry Clarke to Maureen Prior to
Colin Sherbourne to Elder himself and then back to the
detective superintendent.

'I'm sorry, Frank,' Young said.

Elder looked at him but made no reply.

'I've been in touch with the Yorkshire force, we'll
have full co-operation. By this afternoon there'll be fifty
or more officers on the ground and twice as many
volunteers. There are dogs, search trained, a lifeboat crew
and a team of divers standing by.'

'Divers?' echoed Clarke.

'The water's fine,' Young quoted back at him.

'You think he means it literally, then?'

'I think it's a chance we can't ignore.'

It was Maureen who said what they were all
thinking. 'As far as we know, when he sent the card
from Mablethorpe Emma Harrison was already dead.'

She was careful not to catch Elder's eye.

'We don't know this is the same,' Young said. 'We must assume it's not. Pray to God we're right.'

The words as much for his sake, Elder knew, as because the superintendent thought they were true. Like the others, he knew Katherine could be already dead. Chances were she was. He forced himself to continue listening nevertheless. His daughter was in the hands of a murderer and they were still sitting there, more than a hundred miles away, the morning sun slanting across the room strongly enough for the motes of dust to shine brightly in its light.

'Frank,' Bernard Young said eventually. 'Your thoughts?'

Elder leaned forward. 'McKeirnan and Donald always denied any involvement in Susan Blacklock's disappearance. Keach might have chosen the location because he wants to show he can go one better. So the spot where Susan Blacklock was last seen – out by Saltwick Nab – that's where I think we should concentrate the search.'

The superintendent nodded. Clarke and Sherbourne were already on their feet.

'We'll find her, Frank,' Young said. He was about to add, don't worry, but stopped himself in time.

Elder was midway across the car park when his mobile rang.

Dread and anticipation all but trembled it from his hands.

'Hello.' The voice was a young woman's, faint and distant.

'Hello, who is this? Kate. Kate, is that you?'

'It's Angel.'

'Who?'

'Angel.'

The skin along the backs of his arms was taut and cold.

'Yes, of course.'

'The meeting place, with Shane . . .'

'Yes?'

'It's the M5. The first services south of Birmingham. We'll be in the cafeteria.'

'What time?'

'Half six, seven. This evening.'

Elder said nothing, shook his head. All around him car doors were opening, being closed, engines switched into life.

'Is that okay?' Angel said, her voice uncertain, anxious.

'Six-thirty today. Yes, that's fine.'

'You'll be there?'

'Yes.'

The line went dead. Maureen was standing alongside a dark blue saloon, waiting. There was no way he could handle this himself now, not any part of it. 'Maureen,' he said, approaching. 'Shane Donald, I've got a location.'

'Good,' she said. 'We'll sort it on the way.'

◆

A centre of operations had been set up in one of the Whitby secondary schools, with Rob Loake the senior officer in charge. Immediately he sought Elder out and, gripping him by the arm, conveyed both anger and concern, brusque but genuine. At a quickly convened meeting, he introduced Elder and Maureen Prior to the local team and priorities were agreed. The majority of the other officers clearly found Elder's presence unsettling and, quick words of sympathy aside, avoided talking to him as much as they could.

From the police helicopter, Elder gazed down at the slabs and pinnacles of black rock edging into the tide round Saltwick Bay; and as they circled again, he could see below them the lines of slow-moving figures inching across the fields behind the holiday park, just as they had fourteen years before.

By dusk, each and every caravan in the park would have been inspected, the farm buildings between the coast and the road checked over two square miles.

Nothing would be found.

'Tomorrow, Frank,' Maureen said. 'We'll find her tomorrow.'

Elder nodded and turned away, his hurt mirrored in her eyes.

◆

Meanwhile, across the county, the West Midland force were responding to the request to pick up Shane Donald. Two teams of four officers were deployed, after descriptions of Donald and Angel Ryan had been relayed over the internet.

The plan was simple. Matt Jolley and Andy Firebrace would approach the pair of them in the cafeteria, with Rose Pearson hanging back by the entrance, Malcolm Meade at the foot of the stairs. The second, back-up team were in their vehicle outside.

Shane and Angel were sitting towards the far side of the smoking area, with a view down over the motorway.

Angel was flicking her disposable lighter at a roll-up, Shane half-turned away from her, glaring into space.

Andy Firebrace got to within twenty metres before he was noticed.

Suddenly Shane was looking directly forward, staring at him, and Firebrace, instead of continuing, stopped and raised a hand, fingers spread.

Scraping back his chair, Shane picked out Matt Jolley to Fairbrace's right.

'You bitch!' he yelled at Angel. 'You fuckin' bitch!'

'No, Shane!'

With a crash of crockery, Shane upended the table and began to run, dummying in one direction and then another. Firebrace, trying to turn, became entangled with a woman carrying a small child. Jolley collided with a table and lost his footing.

Ashen-faced, Angel stood with one arm outstretched, as if to claw him back.

Rose Pearson moved to intercept him and Shane kicked her hard below the knee and caught her with his elbow high on the cheek.

'Police! Clear the way, police!'

Andy Firebrace's voice pursued Shane downstairs, where Malcolm Meade had already lost him amidst a coachload of senior citizens on their way back from the Trossachs and desperate in their search for the toilets and a decent cup of tea.

Two sets of glass doors led out into the car park and when Firebrace pushed his way through there were perhaps two dozen people within sight, none of them Shane Donald.

'Where the fuck's back-up?' he called to no one in particular.

400

Rose Pearson was close to his shoulder now, holding her cheek and talking into her mobile phone.

Matt Jolley was running off right between the lines of parked cars and, yes, there was Donald, some thirty or forty metres ahead of him and almost level with the petrol pumps.

Firebrace set off in pursuit, shouting Shane's name as loud as he could.

The police vehicle, unmarked, came fast now but late along the slip-road behind the garage, braked hard to avoid swiping a Ford Mondeo side on, and skidded to a halt, officers jumping clear.

Shane, running along the perimeter, swerved and sprinted back the other way. Matt Jolley was slowing now as Firebrace called Shane's name and Shane, in response, vaulted onto the hard shoulder at the second attempt.

The driver of an eight-wheeler carrying metal casings south to Bristol saw Shane in the corner of his eye and, guessing his intention, struggled to pull across into the middle lane.

Firebrace's tackle caught Shane below the waist and sent him spinning but safe across rough tarmac. Before he could struggle or kick out, Fairbrace had his arms pushed up tight behind his back and was just reaching for his cuffs when Matt Jolley seized Shane by the hair and yanked his head right back.

'You're one lucky bastard, you know that? If it'd been me, I'd've let you take your chances with the traffic.'

Firebrace slipped the handcuffs into place and locked them tight.

401

At about the same time that Shane Donald was being arrested, Don Guiseley met Elder outside the temporary heaquarters at the school. 'I couldn't be more sorry, Frank.' He took Elder's hand in both of his. 'Esme sends her love. She's thinking of you, your daughter too. Praying is what she said.'

They walked along the harbour and across the bridge to the Board Inn where Guiseley bought them both pints and they sat at the same table where they'd sat before.

'It's a bastard, Frank.'

'Yes.'

'This Keach, what d'you know about him?'

'Not a great deal. Oh, background and such, we know that. Pretty much as you'd expect. Shitty childhood and the rest.'

'Bit like the other lad, then. Donald.'

'Keach is more naturally violent, I'd say. All but killed someone in prison for no more than a chance remark. Brighter, too. High IQ. Took courses when he was inside, GCSEs and the like. But, yes, both loners by all accounts.'

'And both,' Guiseley said, 'thinking the sun shines out of McKeirnan's arse.'

'Yes.' Elder took a swallow of his beer.

'Some well-meaning bunch of paper shufflers,' Guiseley said, 'reckoned it was safe to let him back out.'

'Can't keep them locked up for ever, Don. Not everyone.'

'No?' Guiseley worked tobacco down into the bowl of his pipe. 'Keach and his like, my way of thinking, any doubt, you should make an exception.'

They sat there a while longer, lingering over their pints, but, despite Guiseley's efforts, conversation was sporadic at best. When he left, an hour later, Elder walked around both sides of the harbour, then back inland to Helen's house, a light still showing through the curtains, Helen inside ironing, the radio playing. Elder had phoned earlier, said he would come and see her if he could, depending, and she'd told him she understood.

Now she held him and for only the second time since Katherine had gone missing he cried and she cried with him, the pair of them standing, arms wound about each other, sniffing back tears.

'Oh, Frank . . .'

'I know.'

Both knew too much: there was nothing they could say.

After a while, Helen offered Elder a drink and he shook his head.

'Will you stay?'

'I'd best not. You'd not thank me, like this. I've a room in town.'

'If you change your mind . . .'

'Yes. Thanks.'

When he walked back along the harbour, hands in pockets, there was a chill in the air that had not been there before and more stars than usual showed in the sky. Katherine, he kept repeating to himself, over and over. Katherine.

50

Elder woke at five, hair matted, his pillow beyond damp. The last vestiges of the dream clung to him, a blurry, rancid after-image that cleared only when he lowered his face towards the tap and splashed water, cold, up into his face.

When he sat back on the edge of the bed, his body was still faintly shaking, his feet and legs close to numb.

Some little while later, when he stepped outside, the gloom of early morning had been compounded by a sea fret, waves of mist rolling in off the sea and reducing everything to an amorphous grey. From the head of the road overlooking the east cliff, the light at the pier end was only dimly visible, the horizon unseen.

◆

Not far short of six, a runner, far enough inland for the air to be relatively clear, recognised the van from the pictures that had been shown on the previous night's news: a small Fiat, white with grey trim and a broken wing mirror on the near side. It was standing on the verge of the broad track that twisted down from the village of

Aislaby towards the junction of two roads, one of which bridged the River Esk.

He peered through the windows and, seeing nothing, continued on his way downhill, telephoning the police from a call-box a few hundred metres along the main road.

The duty officer had not long settled down to his desk, mug of tea close by his right hand, when the call came through.

Elder had walked into the communications room moments before, Rob Loake and Maureen there already, standing before the large area map on the wall. Loake chewing his way through the last of a bacon roll.

'Sir,' the officer said, stepping towards them. 'Ma'am. Seems like we've found the van.'

'Where?'

The officer pointed to the spot, just a few miles inland. 'There, sir. Just short of Sleights.'

'What the fuck's it doing there?'

They arrived within minutes, Loake smoking as he drove, headlights on, window down.

The van was parked at an angle, facing uphill; as they approached, birds rose clamorously from the tall trees above them and flew, black, into the still grey sky.

Elder, throat dry, stopped short of the van as Loake tried the handle with the forefinger and thumb of his gloved hand. It was unlocked. He pulled the rear doors open and stepped back, motioning Elder forward. It was damp underfoot.

A single mattress, old and soiled, lay across the floor, edged upwards where it butted up against the front seats. Mattress aside, the interior was bare; there were no discarded items of clothing, no obvious clues, no – Elder held his breath – evident signs of blood.

Elder turned towards Maureen and shook his head.

Other vehicles could be heard arriving on the road below. Briefly, Maureen touched Elder's arm. Loake had moved a few paces off and was talking into his mobile phone. Soon, the track would be cordoned off at both ends and Scene of Crime would set to work on the van; the inhabitants of several large houses, set back behind high walls along the track, would be woken with questions and the focus of the search would shift. The immediate area first, then spreading out along the course of the river, west towards Grosmont and the moor, east to where the estuary opened out into the sea.

Come on in. The water's fine!

Elder walked a short way up the track and looked back down across the rough grass of open fields towards the river bottom. The map, he remembered, showed the Esk meandering through a series of curves and bends, passing between pasture, woodland and high moor, farm buildings dotted in between.

Was that where Katherine was, somewhere there?

When he walked back down, officers in protective clothing were nearing the van.

◆

By mid-morning they had found nothing. The interior of the van had been wiped clean; no hair or fragments of clothing seemed to have been left behind, no prints. The mattress had been wrapped in plastic and removed for further forensic examination. Statements from residents in the area had established that the lane had been empty as late as one thirty; one elderly woman recalled the sound of a vehicle breaking her sleep at close to four. Two hours before the runner had made his discovery: two hours for Keach to move Katherine how far? And how? Could she still be forced to walk or would she have to be carried? Dragged?

The terrain was difficult in places, uneven and overgrown, thick with trees. Going east, back along the river towards the estuary, sudden patches of mist still made visibility limited.

Dispirited, Elder headed back to the town on foot, following both river and railway line to Ruswarp and from there a footpath that brought him close to the centre.

The young officer who had taken the call that morning was standing outside the communications room, finishing a cigarette. Seeing Elder, he stubbed it out and went back inside. Aside from two civilian clerks, one seated at the computer, the other at the phones, they had the place to themselves.

'Couple on lunch,' the officer said, feeling the need to explain. 'Everyone else, you know, out searching.'

Elder nodded: he knew well enough.

He sat on a stiff-backed school chair at the side of the room, listening to the soft clicking of the computer keyboard, while three pairs of eyes avoided his as best they could.

The sound of the telephone made them jump.

The clerk listened briefly and turned, the receiver in her hand. 'Mr Elder. It's for you.'

They've found her, Elder thought, and the blood drained from his face. It was impossible to move.

'Should I take a message?' the woman said.

'No.' With difficulty, he got to his feet.

'Frank Elder.'

'Everyone busy, I hope. Chasing shadows.' It was a voice, a man's voice he didn't recognise.

'Who is this?'

He laughed and then Elder knew who it was. 'I'd've sent a card from Port Mulgrave, only there weren't any.'

And the connection was broken.

'Port Mulgrave,' Elder said. 'Where is it?'

'Up the coast. By Staithes.'

'Show me. Show me on the map.'

The officer pointed to a small indentation in the coast, north of Runswick Bay and close to the main A174 road.

'What's there?'

'Just a few houses. Not a lot more.'

Elder nodded and moved towards the door. 'I think that was him, Keach, on the phone. Tell your boss. Port Mulgrave. Tell Maureen.'

The Ford was in the corner of the car park and it took him two attempts to engage reverse. He could feel the blood pumping back into his veins, a pulse alive at the side of his head. Far too fast into the roundabout that would take him across the back of town and out towards the coast road, he forced himself to slow down, but on the straight stretch past the golf course he pushed the accelerator to the floor. The slow gradient twisting up from Sandsend into Lythe seemed to take an age. The smell of his sweat filled the car. Runswick Bay. Hinderwell. The road to Port Mulgrave turned off just before a church. A pub and then a telephone box some little way along. The phone from which Keach had made his call?

If it had been Keach and not a hoax.

If he had not lied.

Elder drove on to where the road stopped, petered out into a footpath leading off across ploughed fields. The last of the mist had cleared and in its place dark cloud was bulking to the west. Slowly he reversed back, then turned. On the coast side of the road a deep saucer of land had been scooped out or fallen away and it lay there thick with bracken and patched with mud, criss-crossed by broken tracks. Beyond that the tide had rolled back to reveal slabs of grey-black rock and, pushing out above a mesh of sand and shale, the remains of two short piers that seemed to be crumbling into the sea. Huddled close by them, fast in against the cliff, was a ramshackle collection of huts.

Cautious, Elder began to make his way down.

Gulls careened raucously overhead.

Ten metres from the bottom, a flurry of small stones spun out from under his foot and he slithered, balance gone, his left ankle turning painfully beneath him as he fell.

For several moments he stayed crouched down, massaging his ankle, listening. Gulls aside, there was nothing but the shuffling fall and rise of water and his own jagged breath.

Backed up against the cliff, the huts leaned precariously against each other like an ill-assorted deck of cards. Raw planks and sheets of treated timber, patched and covered here and there with heavy plastic and tarpaulin, held with nails and rope. The walls of some were painted weathered reds and blues but most were bare. A jerry-built tin chimney poking from the roof of one; a rusted hasp hanging down from the door of another, the hinges having given way when the padlock held.

A fire had been lit on the beach close by, its embers faintly warm.

Slowly, Elder eased the door back, waited for his eyes to adjust, and stepped inside.

There were more ashes, soft shades of grey close against the corners. Drawings, crude and simplistic, fading on the walls. His ankle felt better now, no more than a twinge of pain when it took his weight.

Standing there, shadowed, quite still, he heard, or thought he heard, a sound from beyond the wall where two broad lengths of wood seemed to have been levered slightly apart. He leaned his weight against one and it gave a couple of centimetres, then refused to budge. Again, the slightest scuffling sound and now a rank smell, feral and damp. He pushed again with no response.

Stepping back, he raised his right foot and drove the sole of his shoe fast and hard against the wood.

It gave and the cats leapt past him, hissing, a mass of moving fur, and as he stumbled back, one jumped at his face, its claws scratching deep into his cheek.

When he touched the side of his face, his fingers came away smeared with blood.

I know this, Elder thought: I know where I am. Like the pulse of an engine, his brain was beginning to misfire and throb.

Ducking his head, he stepped through the space he had made.

An old cupboard stood close, a nest of ageing newspapers on top. Through gaps in the roof, light spilled, weak, across the floor. The bed was where it should be, pushed up against the furthest wall. So much else was right but wrong.

Elder walked slowly forward.

The blanket was not grey but the colour of weeviled flour. The air was thick with the salt-sweet stink of rotting fish and drying blood.

Elder stood by the bed, staring at the shape that lay covered and curled inwards, fearing what he would find. Steeling himself, he gripped the blanket's edge and slowly pulled it back.

Katherine lay turned in upon herself, naked, blood blisters on her arms and legs, bruises discolouring her shoulders and her back.

Elder's heart stopped.

Face close to hers he could hear the rattle of her breath.

'Katherine,' he said softly. 'Kate, it's me.'

When he touched her gently she whimpered and pulled her knees still closer to her chest. Her eyes flickered and then closed.

'Kate.'

He bent his head to kiss her hair. 'You'll be all right. I'll get help.'

Straightening, Elder had half-turned before he was aware of someone else.

The iron bar swung for his head and at the last moment he threw up an arm and blocked its path. Pain jarred deep and keen from his elbow to his wrist, so severe he was sure the bone was broken.

Adam Keach wore a black T-shirt, work boots and black jeans; the muscles of his arms well-defined. His

411

hair was thick and dark, his eyes, even in that dull space, bright blue. A smile scarred his face.

'Beautiful, isn't she?' he said. 'At least she was.' And he laughed. 'Sleeping Beauty. That what you were thinking? Waking her with a kiss?'

Elder moved fast, reaching for the bar, but not fast enough.

Keach swayed back, lifted both arms high, then brought them down. This time he struck Elder across the top of his left shoulder and forced him to his knees.

'Not bad for an old man.'

Keach kicked him in the chest and Elder fell back; a second kick, the toe of the boot hard against the breast-bone and Elder's head jerked forward, choking.

Keach side-swiped him and pushed him flat, kneeling over him with the bar tight across his neck, knees holding it down leaving his hands free. Vomit caught in Elder's throat.

The knife that Keach drew from the sheath at his back had a slender, slightly curving blade. A skinning knife, Elder thought.

'Quite a catch,' Keach said. 'You here. You and her.' He laughed again and when Elder tried to raise himself from the floor he increased the pressure with his knees and rested the knife above the bridge of Elder's nose.

'Alan'd like that. The one who locked him up, put him inside. And of course he'll read about it now, everyone will. How I fucked the daughter half to death and then finished the pair of them, side by side. Famous, eh? Fuckin' famous!'

The tip of the blade slid beneath the skin and pushed against the bone.

Elder roared and rocked backwards, grabbing the underside of the bar with both hands. Blood flooded one of his eyes.

Pushing the bar up, he rolled sideways, swinging his elbow full force into Keach's face even as Keach's knee drove down into his side.

Adrenaline brought Elder to his feet first.

The knife on the floor between them.

Keach cursing, tasting blood.

From outside, unmistakable, the sound of a helicopter approaching, police sirens.

As Keach glanced down, reaching for the knife, Elder aimed a kick between his legs which Keach partly parried, turning now, the knife forgotten, heading for the open door.

The helicopter hovered low overhead, the updraft from its blades tugging at Keach's hair and clothes. From inside its cabin, an armed officer in dark overalls aimed a semi-automatic rifle at his chest.

'Jesus!' Keach exclaimed. 'Jesus fucking Christ!' His words all but lost. And he started to laugh.

Officers, Loake amongst them, were scrambling down the bank.

Staunching the flow of blood from his head with his sleeve, Elder stood outside the hut and watched as Keach, still laughing, raised his hands above his head.

'Crazy, that's what they'll say,' Keach was shouting above the noise. 'Stark raving, got to be. Unfit to plead.'

Rob Loake punched him in the face and when he fell, pulled his arms up high behind his back and cuffed him and still Keach laughed.

Elder turned away, Maureen hurrying to his side.

413

'Katherine . . . ?'

'She's alive.'

'Thank God!'

He winced when she touched his arm. The ambulance had arrived on the road above, paramedics with stretchers running.

'Frank, you've lost a lot of blood.'

'I'll be fine.'

As they stood over Katherine, Elder swayed and Maureen steadied him.

'Kate,' he said. 'It's going to be okay. I promise.'

He kissed her then, but she didn't wake, not till they were in the ambulance and he was sitting beside her, holding her hand.

'Daddy,' she said, opening her eyes. 'Dad.' Then closed her eyes again while Elder cried.

51

They took them, Elder and Katherine, to Leeds Infirmary. Keach, under tight guard, was taken to York. Maureen informed Joanne the first moment she had and Martyn drove her north.

Katherine lay pale beneath white covers, amidst the quiet humming of machinery and muted light, a nurse watchful at her side.

Joanne found Elder in a side room of A & E, a temporary dressing taped to the front of his head.

'Don't worry,' Elder said. 'She's okay.'

Joanne looked at him, incredulous, anger firing the dark shadows around her eyes. 'Okay, Frank? Is that what you call okay?'

'You know what I mean. She's . . .'

'I know what you mean. You saved her. She's alive. She's alive and you're some great hero, your picture all over the papers, all over the screen every time you turn on the bloody TV.'

'Joanne . . .'

'And what happened to her, Frank? You know what. It's your fault.'

'That's not . . .'

'Why do you think he went for her, Frank? Why Katherine?'

Elder turned his face away.

'You nearly killed her, Frank. You. Not him. Because you had to get involved, you couldn't let things be. You always knew better than anybody else, that's why.'

'Joanne . . .'

'And you know what, Frank, you'll get over this. You'll come to terms, find a way. But Katherine, she never will.'

Elder remained there, not moving, long after the door had closed and the sound of Joanne's footsteps had faded to silence along the corridor, her words reverberating loud inside his head.

◆

They kept Elder in overnight: despite careful work by the doctor on duty, his forehead would always bear a scar some seven centimetres long. The longer of the two bones in the forearm was chipped but not broken and he was given a sling and paracetamol for the pain.

Katherine would stay for ten days in intensive care, after which she would be transferred to the Queen's Medical Centre in Nottingham and begin a course of physiotherapy before being allowed home. She was young and fit and given time her body would mend; even her internal injuries would heal. As for the rest . . .

When Elder came to see her she found it difficult to look him in the eye: whether, like her mother, this was because she held him to blame, or because, in some way, she was embarrassed by his knowledge of what had happened to her, he was never sure.

He couldn't ask; she couldn't say.

When they talked, if they talked at all, they stuck to safer things – though for Katherine, who had been snatched off the street and put through days of purgatory and hell, what could be safe again?

'What's happened to him?' Katherine asked one day.

'Who?' Elder asked, though of course he knew.

Both he and Joanne had tried to keep the papers from her, but this was an open ward.

'He's in Rampton.'

'The mental hospital?'

'Secure, yes.'

'They're saying he's insane.'

'He'll be given tests, to see if he's fit to plead.'

'To stand trial, you mean?'

'Yes.'

'And if he's not?'

'They'll keep him there, I suppose. Rampton. Broadmoor.'

'He'll get off.'

'Not exactly.'

'That other poor girl he killed.'

Elder sought and held her hand. He knew all too well what it would be like for her if Keach were brought to trial; one way or another she would have to give evidence, face cross-examination, he did this and then he did that.

'When are you going back to Cornwall?' Katherine asked.

'Not yet.'

'But you will go?'

'I expect so.'

Katherine smiled. 'What about this girlfriend of yours?'

'What girlfriend's this?'

'Mum told me about her.'

'Past fifty,' Elder said, 'there's got to be a better word.'

'Lover,' Katherine suggested. 'Floozy. Bit of stuff.'

'Helen,' Elder said. 'Her name's Helen.'

'And is it serious?'

'I don't know.'

Elder and Helen had spent a day in Sheffield, another in York, anonymous places and convenient, easy enough to pass the time in each other's company, drink coffee, eat lunch, take in the sights. Sometimes she took his arm, less frequently he held her hand. Neither broached what had come between them: the daughter he had found and saved had been his own, not hers.

'You can't still be reading that book,' Katherine said, looking at the thick and curling copy of *David Copperfield*.

'I've had other things on my mind.'

'Like me.'

'Like you. Plus I keep forgetting what's happened and having to go back.'

'Why don't you just give it up? Find something shorter?'

'I hate doing that once I've started. Besides, I want to know what happened.'

'Who did it.'

'Not exactly.'

'I should hate him, shouldn't I?'

'I don't know. Probably. No one'd blame you if you did.'

'Do you?'

'Hate him?'

418

'Mm.'

'Oh, yes. With every bone of my body,' Elder said.

'Even the injured one?'

'Especially that.'

As she smiled, tears flooded her eyes.

◆

At first, Katherine had refused to see the psychotherapist at all. Then, when she did, she would deny her flashbacks and her dreams and say, when pushed, that she remembered nothing, nothing: she had shut it out.

'Why do you want to make me think about it?' she all but screamed. 'Why make me go through it all again?'

At home, she spent much of her time in her room. A few friends visited, brought flowers, selections of chocolates from Thornton's, boxed and tied with ribbon, magazines. But conversation was awkward, what to ask, what to avoid, and after a while they came less often. Katherine didn't seem to mind. Martyn bought her a new television and a DVD player for her room and she watched movies endlessly, back to back. *Spider-Man*. The new *Star Wars*. Anything with Johnny Depp. Ethan Hawke.

One evening Elder sat with her and watched *Hamlet*, a modern version set in New York, Ethan Hawke as the young prince feigning madness, a schoolgirl Ophelia driven to take her own life by circumstances she could not control.

Knowing what happened, he found it compulsive nonetheless, sitting in a chair alongside Katherine's bed, his eyes drawn to her almost as much as the screen, the action played out in images reflected on her face.

419

As the denouement approached, Joanne quietly opened the door, looked in, and quietly went away.

Some half an hour later, order restored and Katherine sleeping, Elder rose and just went downstairs; Joanne was in the kitchen, mixing a gin and tonic.

'You want one, Frank?'

'No, thanks.'

'You're being careful, aren't you?'

'I hope so.'

He watched her as she sliced a lemon and forked one segment into a tall glass.

'This Helen woman,' Joanne said, 'she still just a friend?'

'She's a friend, yes.'

'A friend you fuck, Frank?'

'Aren't they the best kind?' he might have said, smiling, trying for some lightness of tone, or, more caustically, 'You'd know more about that than me.' Instead he said none of these things.

'Cat got your tongue, Frank?'

'It's time,' he said, 'I was leaving.'

Joanne tasted her drink, allowing it to linger a moment on the back of her tongue. 'I'm sorry about what I said. That first day at the hospital. I was upset.'

'I know. And it's all right.'

'Even so.' She touched his arm, his hand. 'We should be friends, Frank. Especially now.'

'We are.'

She kissed him close alongside the mouth and he could smell the gin, this glass not her first.

'He's leaving me, Frank. Just as soon as Katherine's over the worst. Leaving me just like I left you.'

'I'm sorry.'

'Are you? I'd have thought you might be pleased.'

'No.'

'No more than I deserve.' She laughed. 'He's running off to London for some model with no hips and no tits and a mouth like the London drain.'

Elder took a pace away.

'Generous though. Letting me stay here in the house as long as I want. Half the proceeds when it goes up for sale.'

'I'd better go,' Elder said.

'Why don't you stay?'

'No.'

'We were a family,' Joanne said, as he reached the door.

'Yes,' Elder said. 'I remember.'

With barely a hesitation he carried on through, closing the door at his back.

◆

It was one of those strange and sudden days when the beginnings of winter seem to fall away and everything is blue and clear. Sunlight sparkled off the water of the canal and made the brickwork glow. The new Nottingham magistrates court building, glass and steel, shone like a palace in a fairy tale. Adam Keach had already been formally charged and remanded into custody. Some time in the next few weeks, after exhaustive tests, two out of three psychiatrists would find him fit to plead, the date of his trial in the Crown Court still some months in the future.

421

Before that, however, it was Shane Donald's turn to stand before the magistrate, scrawny in grey, face pale, a plaster over his eye from some incident or other, forever picking at the shredded skin raw around his nails. He had seen Angel when he was led into the court and refused to look in her direction since. His licence already revoked, he was remanded on one charge of robbery and one of assault occasioning actual bodily harm. Aside from confirming his name and that he understood the charges, there was little more for him to say.

Angel stood as he was taken down and his name came faint from her lips but if he heard or cared Shane gave no sign. Watching, Elder wanted to go to her and apologise, explain, tell her that it would all turn out for the best, but he thought one betrayal was enough.

52

The Air Malaysia flight left Heathrow Airport, terminal three, at ten-thirty in the evening; at five-thirty the following evening it touched down in Kuala Lumpur and took off again two hours later, finally arriving in Auckland at eleven-fifteen the next morning.

Plenty of time, between surprisingly tasty meals and gobbets of God-awful films, to finish *David Copperfield*. Established as a successful writer and, after an overlong and ill-judged marriage, together with a good woman, Dickens's hero finally enjoyed his quiet triumph. His happiness. Yet Elder couldn't help but wonder if a man whose reading of character had been so woefully wrong and whose choices had been so palpably foolish, could be said to deserve happiness at all.

He wondered about himself.

He set the book aside but found his attention being pulled back to chapter thirty-one, 'A Greater Loss', and the letter young Emily wrote when she fled with her lover, her seducer – '*When you, who love me so much better than I have ever deserved, even when my mind was innocent, see this, I shall be far away.*'

The letter Susan Blacklock perhaps wrote but never sent.

At Auckland, Elder checked his baggage, such as it was, through customs, showed his passport to the officer at immigration.

'Business or pleasure?'

Elder wasn't sure: he suspected the truth might be neither.

Karori, Helen Blacklock had told him, when he'd asked if she knew where Susan's father was living. Wherever that is. It was a suburb of Wellington, Elder had discovered, west of the city. The likelihood that Ulney was still at the same address was not great, but tracking people down was one of the things Elder was trained to do.

The road from the airport soon gave way to narrow streets that rose through a series of sharp twists and turns as they skirted the centre of the city. The taxi let him down beside a small parade of shops, a garage, banks, a library. Elder checked the map he had bought to get his bearings.

The wooden exteriors of the houses were mostly painted white or cream beneath terracotta tiles, with patches of lawn shielded by shrubs and small trees from the wind. The people he spoke to were friendly, not over-suspicious, happy to talk. David Ulney had moved on but not far, exchanged one address in Karori for another, before moving out of the city altogether.

The man sat in front of a partly demolished garage, chipping mortar from one of a haphazard pile of bricks, white dust thick on his shirt and arms and streaked across his face and hair. 'Paekakariki they moved to. Less than an hour's drive up Highway 1. Or you could take the train. We used to have an address for them but not any more. You'll not find it difficult to find them, though. I doubt there's more than a hundred or so places all told and most of them holiday homes. Not too many live there all year round.'

Elder thanked him. 'If you do see him,' the man said, 'ask him why he built this garage the wrong side of the house, the daft bugger, blocking out the light.'

◆

He was woken by rain slashing against the window. The clock at his bedside read 4:27. He pummelled his pillow a little, pulled up the covers and closed his eyes. When they next opened it was 9:23 and the rain had ceased. A quick shower, coffee and toast and he was on his way to the railway station. By the time the train drew into Paekakariki, most of the clouds had dispersed leaving sun and blue sky.

As the train pulled away, the crossing gates swung high and traffic coming off the highway, two dusty trucks and a shiny black four-by-four, rolled along the broad road that led from the rail tracks towards the beach.

Elder asked a woman clearing tables outside a small café if she knew where the Ulneys lived.

Balancing plates and cups, she shook her head. 'Ask Michael over at the book store. He knows everybody.'

Michael O'Leary was a bearded man with long grey hair, wearing a black T-shirt with the words '*Which Way?*' in white across his chest.

Elder introduced himself and held out his hand.

'Ulney,' O'Leary said in response to Elder's question. 'Yes, I might.'

'I'm a friend of the family,' Elder said. 'Lost touch, you know how it can be.'

'And you're visiting?'

'That's right.'

O'Leary took his time, no call to rush. 'You'll find them along the coast road, the Parade. The far corner of Ocean Drive. Small place set back. The woman there, she stops by once in a while, likes to read.'

'That'd be Susan,' Elder said.

The bookseller nodded. 'Susan Ulney, that's right.'

By the door, Elder noticed, amongst a stack of paperbacks, several by Katherine Mansfield, slightly dog-eared and well-thumbed. *D. H. Lawrence, you know, he lived there with Frieda, his wife. One of the cottages. Katherine Mansfield, too, for a while.* His landlady's words when he first rented the house in Cornwall. The one he chose, more or less at random, had a faded picture on the front, a woman seated at a mirror, muted blues and greys. *Bliss and Other Stories.* Six New Zealand dollars.

When he left the shop Michael O'Leary was singing contentedly to himself, something slow and old by the Rolling Stones.

Pocketing the book, Elder followed the road up a slight incline and around to the sea. On one side a mismatch of beach houses stretched as far as the eye could see; along the other ran a promenade, tapering into the distance above a narrowing strip of sand. Black-and-white birds with red legs and long red beaks jittered along the tideline. A handful of children ran, shrieking, in and out of the slow, rolling waves.

The house was small and single-storeyed, raised up on

426

stilts at the front and reached by wooden steps which climbed through a garden that was largely overgrown, small yellow and white flowers growing wild.

At the right, a broad, three-paned window looked out towards the beach; alongside, shaded, a deep porch ran back beneath the roof. The white boards were cracked and weathered and in need of fresh paint; the blue-green guttering sagged and lacked attention.

As Elder watched a woman came out through the door alongside the porch and shook crumbs from the cutting board in her hands. A check shirt, loose over a pale T-shirt, hung outside her blue jeans. Her fair hair had darkened and her figure had thickened but Elder was certain she was the same person who had stood on the cliff path near Saltwick Nab, that Tuesday fourteen years before, buffeted a little by the wind.

She paused for several seconds, staring out over his head, her gaze fastened on something beyond where he stood. And then she turned and was lost to sight.

Blood pulsing faster than it should, Elder pushed open the small gate and walked towards the steps.

'Yes?' She opened the door almost immediately in response to Elder's knock.

Matched against the photographs he had seen, her mouth seemed to have shrunk a little, become turned in; lines of tiredness lightly etched her face and the lustre had gone from her eyes. Life had made her older than her thirty years.

'Susan?'

'Yes.'

'Susan Blacklock?'

For a moment he thought she might run, jump back

inside and bolt the door; all the times she had imagined this happening, her one nightmare, her recurring dream.

Close her eyes and he would disappear: open them and he would be gone.

He was still there.

'Who are you?' she said, her voice pitched low.

'Frank Elder. I was one of the detectives looking into your disappearance.'

'Oh, God!'

Mouth open, the air punched through her and as she swayed forward Elder reached out towards her, but she steadied herself, one hand against the frame of the door.

'How did you . . . No, no, I mean . . . I mean why? Why after all this time?'

'I wanted to be certain.'

'And you came all this way?'

'Yes.'

Tears welled in her eyes and she turned her head aside. Behind her, on the kitchen table, Elder could see a Thermos, slices of freshly buttered bread, the crusts of some removed, cheese and thin slices of ham.

Susan fished a tissue from her jeans pocket and wiped it across her face, blew her nose, apologised.

Elder shook his head.

'You know then,' Susan said, 'what happened?'

'I think so, yes.'

She nodded, sniffed and took half a pace back inside. 'We usually go for a walk about this time. Take sandwiches, a flask. For lunch.' Even after all that time, the more she spoke the more clearly the East Midlands accent showed through. 'If you'd like to wait, we'll not be long.'

Minutes later, rucksack on her back and wearing a fleece against the wind, Susan manoeuvred the wheelchair through the door.

Dave Ulney no longer cut a dash, a ladies' man with kiss-curl quiff, suede shoes and full drape suit. His head lolled to one side, face pale and gaunt, hair sparse and white, his eyes a distant watery blue. Inside his carefully buttoned clothes, blanket wrapped around his legs, his body was shrivelled and old. Sixty-five, Elder thought, seventy at best, he could be a dozen more.

'Dad,' Susan said, 'this is the man I told you about. From England.'

The eyes flickered a little; the hand that rested on the blanket, fingers knotted, lifted and was still.

'He's going to walk with us. So we can talk.'

Saliva dribbled colourless from one corner of her father's mouth and, practised, she dabbed it away.

'Okay, Dad?'

She reversed the wheelchair on the porch and backed towards the steps. When Elder offered to help she shook her head.

'It's all right. I'm used to it now.'

◆

There were a few more clouds, coming in high from the west but not yet threatening. Despite the sun, the chill in the wind was real and Elder was glad to slip his hands into his pockets as they walked. No need to ask questions, he knew she would talk now, in her own time.

On the beach a small, terrier-like dog raced after a ball.

429

'When I found out,' Susan said, 'you know, who my real dad was . . .' She paused and started again. 'Kids, you're always thinking: your parents, they're not your real parents, they can't be, like in fairy stories or *Superman*, and then when . . . when it happens . . . when I found that picture of my dad, that photo . . . I was like, this is all wrong, it isn't me. And Mum, she wouldn't talk about it, tell me anything, where he was or where he'd gone and I suppose I made up this person, this version of who he was. How he'd be different from Trevor, my stepfather, not always getting on at me, and he'd do exciting things, we'd do them together, him and me, and then one day he got in touch with me . . . Dave . . . my real dad. He gave this note to one of the girls in my school. I was fifteen. Just fifteen. Said he'd meet me. And he did. He was waiting . . . he was so . . . he was so . . .'

She stopped and turned away, head down, letting the tears fall, and Elder stood there, awkward, to one side, not knowing what to do or say.

Eventually, she wiped her face and tucked the blanket tighter round her father's legs, pushing on into the wind.

'You met your father,' Elder prompted.

'Yes. We went to this café, he said he didn't have long – Mum'd have killed me if she'd known – he talked to me about where he lived, wonderful he made it seem, the other side of the world. There was this photo booth round the corner, he said he wanted a picture of me to carry with him. And then he said he'd come back for me. He promised. Our secret, he said, our secret. And he did. That summer we were in Whitby. Here, he said, I've got the tickets, yours and mine. A passport, everything. It's all arranged. I didn't know what to do. I thought: I can't

430

just go. But no, now, he said. You must come now. Or not at all. Don't tell your mum. Don't tell a soul.'

She looked at Elder for a moment, then away.

'I know I should have written, left a note, phoned, something. Mum, what she must have been going through. But when I read about all the fuss – it was in the papers, even here – I just couldn't. I don't know if I was embarrassed or ashamed, but the longer I left it, the more impossible it became. And Dad said that was how she'd treated him all those years, as if he was dead. She'll get over it, he said.'

Lightly, she touched his arm. 'She hasn't, has she?'

'Not really, no.'

Elder was thinking about Helen, her marriage falling apart, the pilgrimages she made to lay flowers at what was never quite a grave.

'We usually go just as far as the park,' Susan said, pointing ahead. 'There's a place we can be out of the wind and have our lunch. There's usually a sandwich going spare.'

'Thanks.'

'Better you than the gulls.' In mock anger, she shook her fist towards them as they wheeled over their heads. 'Varmints. Scavenging varmints.' She smiled and when she did her whole face changed. 'A book I had when I was a kid. They were always stealing the lighthouse keeper's lunch. That's what he called them, varmints.'

Still smiling a little, she unscrewed the top of the Thermos and Elder held the cup while she poured.

She helped her father first, tilting back his head a little and catching the liquid that ran back from his mouth with a paper towel.

They sat beside the wheelchair, eating their sandwiches, staring out to sea.

'When I first came it was fine. I finished school, got on really well. And Dad was great, like a friend, a pal. The other girls, they were all jealous: I wish I had a dad like yours. Then after college I got this job with a children's theatre company, doing a bit of everything. It was great. The sort of thing I'd always wanted. We used to go off sometimes, little tours. It was when we were down in Christchurch Dad had his first stroke. He was in hospital when I got back. Not too serious, the doctor said. He'd have to be careful, you know, but most of the use of his limbs had come back. And he could talk, there wasn't anything wrong with his mind, he . . .'

She set down the cup and for a moment closed her eyes.

'He couldn't really work, not any more, but that didn't matter, we managed. And then three years ago he had another massive stroke. After that he needed someone to look after him all the time and it was easier for me just to pack up work. He can't . . . he can't really do anything for himself. Not now.'

Reaching across, she squeezed her father's hand.

'It would have made more sense if we'd stayed in Karori where we were, but he'd always loved it out here. It was one of the first places he brought me when I first arrived. There weren't so many houses back then. It was wild. When I'm dead, he'd say, this is where I want my ashes scattered, here along the beach.'

Standing, she threw the remains of a sandwich down towards one of the gulls and watched the others swarm and call around it.

432

'We ought to be setting off back, I don't want Dad to catch a chill.'

Outside the house they shook hands.

'You won't mind if I don't ask you in?'

Elder shook his head.

'Will you see my mother when you get back?'

'I expect so, yes.'

'Tell her I'm sorry.'

'Yes.'

'Tell her she should have told the truth.'

Elder thought he might not tell her that.

'If things change,' he said, 'do you think you might come back to England?'

'No. I don't think so.'

'Okay.' Elder turned and, hands in pockets, set off back the way he'd come. With any luck he wouldn't have to wait too long for a train. He was trying to imagine what Susan Blacklock's life was like now, knowing without fully understanding why she'd come, why she'd stayed. He saw her patiently unfastening her father's clothes and easing them past his feet and hands, beginning to sponge his sallow skin . . .

In the event one train was cancelled, another delayed. Back outside the café, he opened the book of stories, half a mind to pass it on to Katherine when he was home. She and the writer, namesakes after all. But the stories were too depressing, he realised, too many lives left unfulfilled. He would buy her something at the airport instead. When he got up to go he left the book beside his empty cup.

53

On the seventh day of Christmas and still on remand, Shane Donald gouged a piece out of his arm with a rusted edge of razor blade. After a visit to the hospital and two sessions with the prison psychologist, he was transferred to the secure wing under Rule 43. Vulnerable prisoners like himself.

In Association, free to mill around under the officers' eyes before being locked down, one of the prisoners pushed a scrap of paper into Donald's hand and walked on.

The writing was scribbled and fast.

'Merry Christmas, sweetheart! I'll make sure to give your love to Alan next time he calls. Though what he saw in you fuck knows!'

The paper nearly slipped between Donald's fingers. He read the note again and then once more.

It didn't take him long to pick out Adam Keach through the slow back and forth of other prisoners, alone near the far wall, mocking smile on his face.

Donald shivered, screwed up the piece of paper tight and put it in his mouth, chewed it up and spat it out.

'You all right, son?' one of the officers said.

Donald nodded and moved on.

When he looked again, Keach smiled and blew him a kiss.

◆

Winter became spring. This time Katherine took the train, no argument, and Elder met her at the station in Penzance, driving back across the peninsula by the narrowest of lanes. The following day she felt strong enough to walk along the coast path into St Ives and then back across the fields. If everything went according to plan, she would start some light training when she returned to Nottingham.

That evening Elder suggested dinner in the pub where they had eaten before, but Katherine had wanted to cook. She had shopped in St. Ives for that purpose. Happily, Elder opened a bottle of wine while the kitchen filled with the sweet, sharp smell of onions and garlic softening in the pan, music playing from the radio in another room. Elder laid the table and they sat down to pasta with spinach and blue cheese, some good bread, a salad of cos lettuce and rocket and small tomatoes.

Katherine watched her father take one mouthful, winding the spaghetti on to his fork with care, and then a second.

'Well?'

'Well what?'

'You know damn well.'

'It's lovely.' Laughing. 'Really tasty.'

'You're sure?'

'Sure.'

They had agreed not to talk about what had happened and, in truth, Elder was relieved. I can do all that with my shrink, Katherine had said, it's what she's paid for after all. Since Christmas the sessions had been pulled back to once a week.

Katherine collected up the plates. 'Is it warm enough to sit outside?'

'Just.'

There was a violet light in the sky, the last vestiges of sun leaking into the far edge of sea. They sat with collars up, glasses of wine in their hands.

'Can I ask you something?' Katherine said.

'Ask away.' He thought it would be about her mother, but he was wrong.

'That woman you were seeing, Helen – you don't see her any more.'

'No.'

'Why not?'

The taste of wine was ripe in his mouth, blackcurranty. He had driven up to Whitby almost as soon as he'd arrived back in England. Promises to keep and at last that promise could be fulfilled. Helen's daughter, he had found her. Wasn't that what he'd sworn to do?

Sitting there in that small, cluttered room, he had watched Helen's face as he described what he had found, skin tightening over bone. Watched her expression as she unfolded the sheet of paper on which he had written Susan's address. What had he expected? Tears of joy? Relief? Instead she had stared at the floor and whatever she had felt she had clutched it to herself.

When, later, he had tried to hold her, she had pulled back from his touch.

Her daughter's desertion building a wall between them, brick by brick.

'I don't know,' he said now. 'One of those things.'

Katherine nodded. 'A shame. That time she came to the hospital, I thought she was nice.'

Helen still walked out from time to time, Elder knew, along the cliff path to Saltwick Nab and left flowers at the spot where Susan had disappeared. As if she had not been found; as if she'd died. He didn't know if she had written to her daughter, if she ever would.

'The trial,' Katherine began.

'There's still a chance it might not come to that.'

'What do you mean?'

'He could still plead guilty.'

'Why would he do that?'

'A lighter sentence. If he pleads not guilty and the verdict goes against him, the judge will come down hard.'

'And do you think that's what he'll do?'

'I should think that's what his brief will be telling him to do.'

Katherine fiddled with a strand of hair. 'If he doesn't, though; if I do have to give evidence, promise me you won't be there. In court.'

'Kate . . .'

'Promise me.'

'All right.'

That night, Elder was awoken by the sound of his daughter's screams and when he pushed open the door to her room, she was sitting up in bed, the covers strewn around her, sweat like beads of marble on her cheeks and brow. Her eyes were closed tight as if something sharp was slicing deep into her skull.

437

'Katie . . . Kate . . .'

When she opened her eyes she saw nothing: blinded by the memory of the pain.

'Katherine . . .'

Carefully, Elder took hold of both her hands and spoke her name again and then she saw him and let herself fall back against the pillows. He fetched a towel and wiped her face and sat with her a while longer, not speaking, then when he thought it was all right to do so, went downstairs and made tea while she changed her clothes, sweat pants and a clean T-shirt.

'How long have you been having them?' Elder asked. 'The dreams.'

'Ever since it happened. Since you found me.'

The same moment, Elder thought, that my dream was broken. Disappeared.

'How often?' he asked.

She looked back at him with a wan smile. 'Often enough.'

He poured more tea into her cup, added milk and sugar, stirred.

'Those huts,' Katherine said, 'on the beach – were there cats?'

'Yes. A few. Wild, I suppose.'

'I wasn't sure if they were real or part, you know, of the dream.'

'No, they were real enough.'

'You remember when I was a kid I always wanted one, a kitten?'

'I remember.'

'I must have driven you and Mum crazy.'

'Your mother was allergic.'

438

'I thought that was just to you.'

'Very funny.'

Katherine laughed, then shook her head. 'She's miserable, you know.'

'She'll get over it. Find someone else, I'd not be surprised.'

'You think so.'

'I don't see why not.'

'Or Martyn will come crawling back.'

'Probably.'

'You don't care, do you?'

'I don't want her to be unhappy.'

'I think,' Katherine said, 'I'll go back up to bed.'

'Okay. I'll just rinse these cups.'

Near the top of the stairs, Katherine stopped and called back down. 'These dreams, they will go, won't they? I mean, with time.'

'Yes.' He looked up at her from below. 'Yes, I'm sure they will.'

'Yours did, after all.'

'Yes, mine did.'

She smiled. 'Good-night, Dad.'

'Good-night, love. Sleep well.'

'You too.'

He waited till he heard the door click before going back into the kitchen. There was an almost new bottle of Jameson's in the cupboard and he poured generously into a glass. It was not so far short of four by the clock. Outside it was still dark and he had to stand there for some while before he could make out the edge of stone wall, the shapes of cattle in the field. If he stood there long enough it would begin to get light.

Acknowledgements

Everyone needs a helping hand and in the writing of this novel I've gratefully grasped more than a few.

My special thanks are due to my agent, Sarah Lutyens, and to Andy McKillop, Susan Sandon and Justine Taylor at Random House (UK); to Detective Superintendent Peter Coles (retired) and Caroline Smith, Senior Development Co-ordinator for UK Athletics; to Michael O'Leary, proprietor of the Pukapuka Bookshop in Paekakariki and other friends in New Zealand; to Sarah Boiling and, most especially, to my friend and adviser, Graham Nicholls.

Ash and Bone

Detective Sergeant Maddy Birch will never see thirty again. Nor forty. A lifetime on the force and all she has to show for it is a few hundred pounds in the bank and a mortgaged flat in Highgate Borders. When the take down of a violent criminal goes badly wrong leaving both the target and a young constable dead, something doesn't feel right to Maddy. And her uneasiness is only compounded when she starts to believe someone is following her home.

In Cornwall retired Detective Inspector Elder's solitary life is disturbed by a phone call from his estranged wife Joanne. Seventeen-year-old Katherine is running wild. Elder's fears for his daughter are underscored by remorse and guilt for it was his involvement that led directly to the abduction and rape that has so unbalanced Katherine's' life.

Maddy and Elder have a connection. A brief, clumsy encounter sixteen years earlier. Just a quick grope and a cuddle, leading to nothing, but leaving a trace of lingering regret.

In *Ash and Bone* the unsettled, unhappy Elder is once again persuaded out of retirement. A cold, cold case has a devastating present day impact with sinister implications for the crime squad itself. Elder's investigation takes place against the backdrop of his increasing concern for his daughter and he must battle his own demons before he can uncover the truth.

Read on for an exclusive extract . . .

1

Maddy Birch would never see thirty again. Nor forty either. Stepping back from the mirror, she scowled at the wrinkles that were beginning to show at the edges of her mouth and the corners of her eyes; the grey infiltrating her otherwise dark brown, almost chestnut hair. Next birthday she would be forty-four. Forty-four and a detective sergeant attached to SO7, Serious and Organised Crime. A few hundred in the bank and a mortgaged flat in the part of Upper Holloway that North London estate agents got away with calling Highgate Borders. Not a lot to show for half a lifetime on the force. Wrinkles aside.

Slipping a scarlet band from her pocket, she pulled her hair sharply back and twisted the band into place. Taking a step away, she glanced quickly down at her boots and the front of her jeans, secured the velcro straps of her bullet-proof vest, gave the pony tail a final tug and walked back into the main room.

To accommodate all the personnel involved, the briefing had been held in the hall of an abandoned school, Detective Superintendent George Mallory, in charge of the operation, addressing the troops from the small stage on which head teachers since Victorian times had, each autumn, admonished generations of small children to plough the fields and scatter. The fields, that would be, of Green Lanes and Finsbury Park.

Climbing frames, worn and filmed with grey dust, were still attached to the walls. New flip charts, freshly marked in bright colours, stood at either side of a now blank screen. Officers from the tactical firearms unit, SO19, stood in clusters of three or four, heads down, or sat at trestle tables, mostly silent, with Maddy's new colleagues from Serious Crime. She had been with her particular unit three weeks and two days.

Moving alongside Maddy, Paul Draper gestured towards the watch on his wrist. Ten minutes shy of half-five. 'Waiting. Worst bloody time.'

Maddy nodded.

Draper was a young DC who'd moved down from Manchester a month before, a wife and kid and still not twenty five; he and Maddy had reported for duty at Hendon on the same day.

'Why the hell can't we get on with it?'

Maddy nodded again.

The hall was thick with the smell of sweat and after-shave and the oil that clung to recently cleaned 9mm Brownings, Glock semi-automatic pistols, Heckler and Koch MP5 carbines. Though she'd taken the firearms training course at Lippetts Hill, Maddy herself, like roughly half the officers present, was unarmed.

'All this for one bloke,' Draper said.

This time Maddy didn't even bother to nod. She could sense the fear coming off Draper's body, read it in his eyes.

From his position near the door, the superintendent cast an eye across the hall then spoke to Maurice Repton, his DCI.

Repton smiled and checked his watch. 'All right, gentlemen,' he said. 'And ladies. Let's nail the bastard.'

Outside, the light was just beginning to clear.

Maddy found herself sitting across from Draper inside the transit, their knees almost touching. To her right sat an officer from SO19, ginger moustache curling round his reddish mouth; whenever she looked away, Maddy could feel his eyes following her. When the van went too fast over a speed bump and he jolted against her, his hand, for an instant, rested on her thigh. 'Sorry,' he said and grinned.

Maddy stared straight ahead and for several minutes closed her eyes, willing the image of their target to reappear as it had on the screen. James William Grant. Born, Hainault, Essex, October twentieth, 1952. Not so far then, Maddy thought, off his fifty-second birthday. Birthdays were on her mind.

Armed robbery, money laundering, drug dealing, extortion, conspiracy to murder, more than a dozen arrests and only one conviction: Grant had been a target for years. Phone taps, surveillance, the meticulous unravelling of his financial dealings, here and abroad. The closer they got, the more likely it was that Grant would catch wind and flee somewhere the extradition laws rendered him virtually untouchable.

'It's time we took this one down,' Mallory had said at the end of his briefing. 'Way past time.'

Five years before, an associate of Grant's, ambitious

enough to try and freelance some Colombian cocaine conveniently mislaid between Amsterdam and the Sussex coast, had been shot dead at the traffic lights midway along Pentonville Road, smack in the middle of the London rush hour. After a trial lasting seven weeks and costing three quarters of a million pounds, one of Grant's lieutenants had eventually been convicted of the killing, while Grant himself had slipped away scott free.

'What d'you think?' Paul Draper asked, leaning forward. 'You think he'll be there? Grant?'

Maddy shrugged her head.

'He fuckin' better be,' the Firearms officer said, touching the barrel of his carbine much as earlier he had touched Maddy's leg. 'Feather in our fuckin' cap, landing a bastard like him.' He grinned. 'All I hope is he don't bottle out and give it up, come walking out with his hands behind his fuckin' head.'

As the transit veered left off Liverpool Road, someone towards the rear of the van started humming tunelessly; heads turned sharply in his direction and he ceased as abruptly as he'd begun. Sweat gathered in the palms of Maddy's hands.

'There pretty soon,' Draper said to nobody in particular. 'Got to be.'

Conscious that the man next to her was staring more openly, Maddy turned to face him. 'What?' she said. 'What?'

The man looked away.

Once, after a successful operation in Lincoln, her old patch, a good result, she and this officer who'd been eyeing her all evening had ended up with a quick grope and cuddle in a doorway. His hand on her breast. What in

446

God's name had made her think about that now?

'We're getting close,' the driver said over his shoulder.

One side of York Way was derelict, half-hidden behind blackened walls and wire fencing; on the other, old warehouses and small factories were in the process of being converted into loft apartments. Underground parking, twenty-four hour portering, fifteen-year-old prostitutes with festering sores down their legs and arms a convenient ten minute stroll away.

From the front the building seemed little changed, a high-arched wooden door held fast with double padlock and chain, its paint work blistered and chipped. Small windows whose cobwebbed glass was barred across. Maddy knew from the briefing the guts of the place had already been torn out and restoration was well in hand. A light showed dimly behind one of the windows on the upper floor.

Either side of her, armed officers in black overalls, the single word *Police* picked out in white at the front of their vests, were moving silently into position.

No sweat in her palms now and her throat was dry.

'You bastard!' Laughing.

'What?'

'You know.'

'No. What?'

Wary, Vicki walked over to where Grant was stretched out on the bed, cotton sheet folded back below his waist. For a man of his years, she thought, and not for the first time, he was in good shape. Trim. Lithe. He worked out. And when he'd grabbed her just now, fingers tightening about her wrist, it had been like being locked into a vice.

'C'mere a minute,' he said. 'Come on.' A smile snaking across his face. 'Not gonna do anythin' am I? So soon after the last time. My age.'

She knew he was lying, of course, but complied. Vicki standing there in a tight white t-shirt and silver thong, the t-shirt finishing well above the platinum ring in her navel. What else was it about but this?

When she'd first met him, a month or so before, it had been at the Motor Show, Birmingham. Vicki not wearing a whole lot more than she was now, truth be told, a couple of hundred quid a day to draw attention to the virtues of a 3.2 litre direct injection diesel engine, climate control and all-leather interior.

He'd practically bought the vehicle out from under her and later screwed her on the back seat in a lay-by off the A6. 'Christen the upholstery,' he'd said with a wink, tucking a couple of fifty pound notes down inside her dress. She'd balled them up and thrown them back in his face. He'd paid more attention to her after that.

'I've got this place in London,' he'd said. 'Why don't you come and stay for a bit.'

'A bit of what?'

The first time he'd seen her naked it had stopped him in his tracks: he'd had more beautiful women before but none with buttocks so round and tight and high.

'Jesus!' he'd said.

'What?'

'You've got a gorgeous arse.'

She'd laughed. 'Just don't think you're getting any of it, that's all.'

'We'll see about that,' he'd said.

Fingers resting lightly just below her hips, he'd planted

a careful kiss in the small of her back. 'Who was it?' he'd said, hands sliding down. 'Pushed in his thumb and pulled out a plum? Little Jack Horner? Little Tommy Tucker?'

After that he took her face down on the polished wood floor, bruises on her knees and breasts that smelled of linseed oil.

'Will, don't,' she said now, shaking herself free. 'Not now. I have to go and pee.'

'What's wrong with here?' Pointing at his chest.

'Over you, you mean?'

'Why not? Wouldn't be the first time.'

'You're disgusting.'

'You don't know the half of it.' He reached for her but she skipped away.

'Don't be long,' he said, leaning back against the pillows and watching her as she walked towards the door.

There was access from a courtyard at the rear, stairs leading past three balconies to the upper floor. The loft apartment where Grant lived was entered through double doors, a single emergency exit leading to a fire escape at the furthest end.

Draper close behind her, Maddy turned a corner into the courtyard and flattened herself against the wall. Weapons angled upwards, armed officers were in position at the corners of the square, others scurrying towards the first and second balconies, and she waited for the signal to proceed. When it came, moments later, she sprinted for the stairs.

The walls were exposed brick, furnishings tasteful and sparse. Shifting his position, Grant poured himself

449

another glass of wine. Dusty was still in the CD player and he clicked the remote.

'Why do you listen to that old stuff?' Vicki asked from the far end of the room.

'Greatest white soul singer ever was,' Grant said.

'History,' Vicki replied.

Grant grinned. 'Like me you mean?'

'If you like.'

One knee on the bed, she ran her fingers up through the greying hairs on his chest and, reaching up, he kissed her on the mouth.

At the head of the stairs, Maddy waited, catching her breath, Draper on the landing below. The outer door to Grant's apartment was in clear sight. Mallory appeared level with Draper and then went on past. There was armament everywhere.

'After a little glory?' the superintendent whispered in Maddy's ear.

'No, sir.'

He smiled and there were mint and garlic on his breath. 'Second fiddle this time, Birch. Sweeping up the odds and ends.'

'Yes, sir.'

'You and your pal Draper. Down a floor. Just in case.'

Mallory moved on towards the door, Repton at his back, two officers wielding sledgehammers in their wake.

Volume high, the interior of the loft pulsated with sound: french horn, strings, piano, and then the voice. Unmistakable.

Vicki reached down and touched Grant's face, straddling him. Arching his back, eyes closed, Grant found her nipples with his finger tips.

Dusty swooped and soared and swooped again.

At the first crash, Grant swung Vicki on to her side and sprang clear, one hand clawing at a pair of chinos alongside the bed, the other reaching past Vicki's head.

The outer door splintered inwards off its hinges.

Fear flooded Vicki's face and she began to scream.

The pistol was tight in Grant's grasp as he turned away.

From the landing below, Maddy heard music, shouts, feet moving fast across bare boards, the slamming of doors.

'What the fuck?' Draper said.

'Move,' Maddy said, pushing him aside. 'Now.'

Positioned on the balcony opposite, one of the police marksmen had Grant in his sights for several seconds, a clear shot through plate glass as he raced down the emergency stairs, but without the order to fire the moment passed and Grant was lost to sight.

'In here,' Maddy said, kicking open the door and ducking low.

Draper followed, swerving left.

Maddy could feel the blood jolting through her veins, her heart pumping fast against her ribs. The room they were in ran the length of the building, iron supports strategically placed floor to ceiling. Some of the floor boards had been removed prior to being replaced. Building materials were stacked against the back wall, work begun and then abandoned. Low level light seeped through windows smeared with grease and dust.

Maddy reached for the switch to her left with no result.

Voices from the stairs, urgent and loud, descending; more shouts, muffled, from the courtyard outside.

'Come on,' Draper said. 'Let's go.'

Maddy was almost through the door when she stopped, alerted by the smallest of sounds. She swung back into the room as Grant eased open the door at the far end and stepped through. Bare-chested, barefoot, pistol held down at his side.

Maddy's voice wedged, immovable, in her throat.

'Police,' Draper shouted. 'Put your weapon on the ground now.'

She would wonder afterwards if Grant had truly smiled as he raised his gun and fired.

Draper collapsed back through the doorway, clutching his neck. Instinctively, Maddy turned towards him and, as she did so, Grant ran forward, jumping through a gap in the boards to the floor below. With barely a moment's hesitation she raced after him; when she braced herself, legs hanging through a gap a metre wide, the boards on either side gave way and she was down.

Grant had landed badly, twisting his ankle, and was scrabbling, crab-like, across the floor, seeking the pistol that had been jarred from his grasp. A 9mm Beretta, hard up against the wall. As he pushed himself up and hopped towards it, Maddy launched herself at him, one hand seizing his ankle and bringing him down. Flailing, his hand struck the squared-off butt of the pistol and sent it spinning beyond reach.

'Bitch!'

He kicked out at her and she stumbled back.

'Fucking bitch!'

Grant was on his feet and moving towards her. No smiling now.

Maddy heard movement behind and then the sound of a weapon being discharged close to her ear. Once and then once again. As she watched, Grant skidded backwards then crumpled to his knees, his face all but disappeared in a welter of blood.

'Text book,' Mallory said softly. 'Head and heart.'

Maddy's skin was cold; her body shook.

'You or him, of course. Didn't give me any choice.'

Vomit caught in the back of Maddy's throat. Her eyes fastened on Grant's pistol, still some metres away across the floor.

The superintendent bent low towards the body. 'Ambulance, I dare say. Not that it'll do a scrap of good. He's bleeding out.'

When he stood up, a second weapon, a .22 Derringer, was close by Grant's inturned leg, small enough to hide inside a fist. Now you see it, now you don't. No matter how many times Maddy would run it through in her mind, she would never be sure.

'Trouser pocket,' Mallory was saying conversationally. 'Small of the back.' He shrugged. 'There'll be an enquiry, routine.' His hand on her shoulder was light, almost no pressure at all. 'You'll be a good witness, I know.'

Armed officers were standing at both doors, weapons angled towards the ground.

Lonely Hearts

John Harvey

'Harvey reminds me of Graham Greene – a stylist who tells you everything you need to know while keeping the prose clean and simple'
Elmore Leonard

Shirley Peters is dead. Murdered. Her body is found twelve hours later in her own home. Just one of the many sordid domestic crimes hitting the city.

Tony Macliesch, her rejected boyfriend, is the obvious prime suspect and he's just been picked off the Aberdeen train and put straight into custody.

But then another woman is sexually abused and throttled to death. And suddenly there seems to be one too many connections between these seemingly unrelated crimes.

Because Detective Inspector Resnick is sure that the two murders are the work of one sadistic killer – two lonely hearts broken by one maniac. And it's up to Resnick to put the record straight – and put the bastard where he belongs.

'Crime fiction that . . . gets at something deeper – the sometimes rancid, always pungent smell of real life'
Booklist

arrow books